SOME TIME
TILL
KNOWING

A NOVEL

BRUCE EHLENBECK

Ehlenbeck, Bruce

Some Time Till Knowing/ Bruce Ehlenbeck/ June 2012 U.S. edition

ISBN-13: 978-1-475-22724-6

ISBN-10: 1-475-22724-8

1. Self-Discovery-Fiction 2. Boulder, Colorado-Fiction

3. St. Louis, Missouri-Fiction 4. Relationships-Fiction

5. Women's empowerment in early 1970's America-Fiction

Acknowledgements

For more than 30 years, my wife, Nancy, has encouraged and supported me on my creative path. I've drawn inspiration from her strength and her love. This book is its expression.

Several family members and close friends were readers of early versions of this story. Their input helped me to make improvements in its telling. In particular, I'm indebted to Jim Dunn for his patient review and thoughtful consideration throughout the final months of the writing process.

Also, my editor, Paulette Kinnes, provided the professional eye and earnest critique that the book required. In the end, the pace and power of the story were enhanced by the quality of her editing.

I thank Tim Schuetz for the excellent photograph of the Flat Irons that became the basis for the book's cover. In addition, I recognize Olivia Dombach for her expert design of the cover.

Dedication

To Sam and Toots; for life, for love, for learning

Part One

Once, somewhere
From all time released
A true place
Somehow is revealed

Chapter 1

Mark and Johnny accompanied Luke to the St. Louis airport, only a short car trip from their family's suburban home. His brothers expressed disappointment that he would not be staying through the New Year's celebrations. Johnny planned a party with some of his college friends, while Mark would be sharing a midnight toast with family and friends, including Ted, Luke's closest friend during his high school years.

"So maybe there's a party to go to out there in Colorado?" Mark suggested.

As Luke walked along the concourse, he perused the overhead signs that specified the flight numbers and destinations. "Not that I'm aware of, but staying here doesn't make much sense either. Elizabeth has to work at the hospital tonight, so there wouldn't be anybody for me to kiss at midnight, except for maybe Johnny here."

He bumped Johnny who strode on his left, bounced off him and nudged Mark with his other shoulder. His laugh rang out through the concourse and his brothers joined in.

Johnny responded. "I guess there's a lot of crazy stuff going on in Boulder though."

"Maybe, but I'm not really looking for it, especially since Bake and Jerrod left. Besides we did enough partying over the last few days. Christmas Day was really great with Matt coming home. I may just ease into the New Year."

When they reached Luke's departure gate, he brought them to a halt and released his brothers from their escort duties. "You guys don't have to hang around. I know you've got places to go, people waiting on you. Listen, Mark, I'm serious about making it to an Oakwood game. I definitely want to see you play at least one more time in your college career, especially since you guys are winning."

"That'd be good. All the guys would like that." Mark confirmed.

"And Johnny, I know we've been giving you some grief lately but don't let our kidding around get to you. You've gotten so damn big, a verbal jab or two is all your ol' brothers dare to try anymore. Anyway, you guys take care tonight."

Johnny placed a hand on Luke's shoulder. "You know, Mom and a lot of us don't like it, you being so far from home and all. Just make sure you're taking care, too."

"I will. Don't worry." Luke reassured his younger brothers. "We're going to make this New Year a happy one."

———

Luke approached the house and the entrance to his apartment. With his suitcase in one hand, he slipped past the line of parked cars that extended the length of the driveway. The hike from the Boulder bus station warmed him, and white puffs of his breath pulsed before him, visible in the light cast by the globe above the side porch.

Luke heard a rhythmic sound resonating from the house, and two people climbed the porch steps. When they pulled the screen door open, a knock on the frame of the main door carried to Luke's ears as well.

The brighter lights from the kitchen then flooded the doorway as Luke's landlady, Julia Karsten, leaned forward to hold the screen door wider and allow the couple to enter. A faint Happy New Year exchange floated on the night air, and Luke nodded. He grinned, too, as though the smile that Julia beamed was directed at him instead of the arriving party guests.

When the door latched and the light dimmed, Luke's visage darkened, too. He made his way to the outside stairway that led down to his apartment and paused to search the shadows and check the steepness of the first step. He had spent the previous week in St. Louis celebrating Christmas with his family. There, he found a way to re-enact a few of the best parties of his young life with his friends, his brothers and sister. Without hesitation, he had moved within his family's home, amidst the neighborhoods and throughout the city.

In the familiar places where Elizabeth and he had embraced, he had eased into the deep comfort of their loving relationship, like slipping naked under a pile of down-filled blankets after a months' long sojourn in rugged mountain camps. A warm glow had enfolded them. The yearning lingered, although he had traveled a long distance from her on this night, the last night of 1971.

He had removed himself physically from her and from his family and long-time friends. He had rented a basement apartment on the north side of Boulder, Colorado, eight hundred miles of separation.

Julia's family lived above him. Julia and her daughter, Terry, and a third yet-to-be-born person comprised a family as different from his family as Boulder was different from St. Louis.

With his foot suspended in midair, a sudden flood of light distracted his attention, and he stumbled on the first step of the concrete stairs. He caught himself with his free hand grabbing the pipe railing.

"Hey, be careful, there!" Julia's voice rang overhead.

Luke squinted into the light, while Julia walked toward the end of the porch. "Wasn't paying attention," he admitted.

Julia explained. "I thought I saw you coming up the driveway before. You should've called. Frank or somebody would have come to get you."

"I didn't want to bother anybody. Looks like you've got a big party going on. Terry's happy about that, I bet."

"She was hoping you would make it home in time to join us."

"Actually, I've been thinking that I might just relax and let this New Year take care of itself."

"Well, okay, but it'll probably be noisy. If you change your mind, you know your way. Just be careful on the stairs." She chuckled and retreated to the door.

As Luke entered his apartment, he switched on the overhead light in the front room and made his way to the bedroom where he dropped his suitcase on the bed. He went to the bathroom wash basin and splashed water on his face. After an extra few moments rubbing his eyes with the towel, his solitary reflection in the mirror bounced back a little fuzzy. Above him, he heard the low buzz of human conversation and the faint melody of music.

A louder voice blared, "Let's spend the night together."

A spontaneous smile brushed across his reflection. That rock 'n roll lyric was the title of one of Johnny's favorite Rolling Stones songs. He recognized the voice that blasted it too.

Clay Williams stood two inches taller than Luke, over six foot four, a broader and bigger man. His physical size, thick crop of black hair and fierce brown eyes combined to make him stand out in any crowd. His penetrating voice and brash demeanor forced the spotlight to focus on him. He had achieved a level of local acclaim as a Boulder High School multi-sport star and a CU football player. His athletic achievements fed his ego from an early age.

When they had first met, Luke did not associate Clay with Julia. Their meeting had occurred by chance in the autumn of that year on a basketball court at the CU field house during Sunday afternoon pick-up games. Even with his size advantage Luke bested him in that arena. Luke's basketball skills were not as accomplished as his younger brother's, still he could outplay someone of Clay's ability. When the game moved off of the basketball court and into the party room, Clay could easily outmaneuver, outshine Luke.

While Luke unpacked his suitcase, another voice joined the chorus after the second verse. He assigned that vocal to a friend, a teammate in those pick-up games, Frank Morton. Frank's close cropped hair style led some to believe he was ex-military, but that was not the case. Luke attributed it to Frank's nostalgia for the early 60's and that more clean-cut time.

Frank usually guarded Clay during the basketball games. They banged down low under the basket where Frank's advantage in weight and width offset Clay's height advantage.

Tonight Luke envisioned them leaning on one another again as the lyrics became a chant, *Na-na, na-na, na-na….na….Yeah!* Over and over those two big guys led the cheers, and the party built its own crescendo.

Thanks to his mother, most of Luke's clothes went straight from his suitcase into his closet or a dresser drawer, laundered and pressed. At the bottom of his suitcase, he found the book his mother had given him as a Christmas present, a Ken Kesey novel, *Sometimes a Great Notion.* Luke carried it into the front room and settled into the single easy chair that occupied a space next to an oval table supporting a reading lamp.

A sofa spanned the opposite wall. Above the sofa, two movie posters, *Butch Cassidy and the Sundance Kid* and *Easy Rider,* flanked a wood cut print that portrayed the image of a man drowning in a deep sea made of scores of the word, *words*, printed in black and screened in green.

The movie posters he had inherited from Jerrod, a close college friend, and the print he had purchased himself. Luke's eyes fell there in the middle. *Words* floated on the wall, repeated over and over again, splashing in waves of black and green ink.

Luke wrote letters, his own words, and he sent them to Elizabeth, to his family, and his friends. He had first practiced letter writing while attending Oakwood College, a liberal arts school located in eastern Kansas, a small college where he had had an opportunity to play varsity sports as well.

He wrote with greater frequency after he moved to Boulder. Jerrod and Bake, another of his college friends, and he had lived together for the summer months in a townhouse on the east end of town. When his friends moved back to the Midwest at the end of August, Luke had found this apartment.

He arranged his only decorations on one wall. Intuition placed them there. When he sat in the easy chair, they usually came into clear view. But tonight they appeared hazy, and his thoughts, too, began to drift in an ocean like mist. He had traveled a long way to sit in that chair but found little comfort.

Questions bobbed on the waves of his thinking. He sat alone in the place where he had written many of his recent letters. He wrote the truth as clearly as he could.

Na Na Na Naah, Na Na Na Naah, Hey, Hey...ey. Go...od Bye. The music rumbled down from the party above.

A multitude of male voices sang the crowd pleaser recorded by the band called Steam. He laughed while tears filled his eyes. In the final hours of the year he mixed melancholy and sarcastic schmaltz with wonder about the coming year and about living on his own.

———

A knock at his door pulled Luke from the chair, and he dabbed the corner of his eyes with the end of his shirt sleeve.

"Hello there." Luke motioned for Terry to enter. "Enjoying your party?"

"Yeah, but it's not really my party. Mom and Mr. Williams, they invited everybody. I wanted to invite you, but I didn't know you were here yet."

"Just got here a little while ago." Luke shrugged as Terry entered.

Luke noticed her dress and her sandy-blonde hair styled with what he assumed was hair spray, grown up touches for an eight year old. Terry had always been quick to correct him, insisting she was eight going on nine.

Terry cut short a compliment that Luke formulated. "All the men are singing the songs."

"I know I can hear them."

"When they're too loud, Mom tells them to be quiet."

"She doesn't like it when it gets too loud. I remember that from our other parties."

Terry sighed as she delivered her remarks in a tone like that of a teacher helping a slow learner. "Those weren't parties. Remember? They were just eating supper and watching a movie on TV."

"And you never put on a dress or styled your hair for those times, either."

"Mom helped me. I like real parties."

"Me too. But I don't know whether I'm in the mood for a real party tonight."

"Mr. Morton, he asked about you, and Mom said you were here but you weren't coming. Then I said I would come and get you. Mr. Morton said to tell you it's New Year's Eve. He said to get a beer from the fridge, but I didn't do that."

"You probably don't even like beer." Luke chuckled.

"Not for me, silly, for you to have." Terry frowned then smiled when Luke acted like he just figured it out.

"Oh I see, that makes sense."

"So, then let's go. It's New Year's Eve!" She insisted and motioned to the door.

"You're right about that. And since you put it that way, maybe I should."

"You should. Mom said so too."

"Well, that settles it. But I tell you what. You go ahead. I'm going to put on a different shirt, one for going to a real party."

"See, I told ya."

"I'll be up in a little bit."

Luke decided to wash his face, soap and warm water this time. Before putting on one of the shirts his mother had laundered, he sprayed deodorant under his armpits. He traded his sneakers for a pair of leather loafers. At a final stop in front of the bathroom mirror, he wet his comb to complete the preparations. The light brown strands of his hair needed a little water to keep them in place.

Above his hazel eyes the line that his hair traced across his forehead revealed more of his scalp, and he shook his head at the subtle proof that another year had passed. When the first verse from Crosby, Stills, Nash, and Young's *Suite: Judy Blue Eyes* drifted overhead, he laughed aloud. He voiced the words. *It's getting to the point where I'm no fun anymore.*

Luke bounced up the stairs and entered the side door that led to Julia's kitchen. He fortified himself with a long drink of the beer that he had taken from the refrigerator, and then entered the front room. He estimated thirty people crowded the space. Nearly all of them stood, engaged in small conversational groups.

Frank occupied a spot near the shelving that held the stereo amplifier and turn table. Several album jackets and a few 45 records were scattered on the shelves next to the equipment.

"Fat man, put on some more Stones next!" A demand sounded above the music, and Luke found its source.

A circle of guests shuffled in reverse while Clay laughed as though his rude request was a joke. He stood next to Julia, and he draped one arm over the back of Julia's shoulders. His large frame leaned in her direction, and he tilted a drink glass to his mouth.

At that moment Julia stepped away from Clay, repulsed by his yelling. She poked him in the ribs as a discipline. Her green eyes flashed disappointment in Clay's direction, but even her stern demeanor did not diminish her radiance.

She used a large barrette adorned with emerald-colored stones to pull her shoulder-length blonde hair away from her face. Hints of the green color swirled in the multi-colored blouse that she wore tucked into a black skirt. The wide, black, patent-leather belt clasped around her middle hid a small paunch.

Her smile sent a wave of calm over the nearby group, and they moved in unison toward her. In the process, one of them bumped Clay's arm, and liquid from the glass he had just lowered from his lips splashed across his forearm and onto the carpet.

Like the others he had just witnessed, Luke took one step toward Julia but stopped as her words summarized Clay's actions. "Clay, you big slob!"

And Clay's plea reverberated, just loud enough for most of those in the room to hear. "Come on honey, take it easy on me."

Luke slid in Frank's direction instead.

"You need a hand with the music?" Luke drew close to his friend.

"Hey, Luke!" Frank greeted. "Yeah, the crowd's gettin' testy."

"Just the big guy, he's a little loud." Luke commented.

Then Terry stepped between the two men and spoke up. "Somebody said he's ob-not-shush."

"Obnoxious, yeah. Loud and obnoxious, that's our friend." Frank ushered Luke toward the stereo.

They sorted through the albums and raised their voices a few decibels as the last song of the current selection rang from the speakers that flanked them. Terry took a spot between them again and concentrated her efforts fingering through the records on the lower shelf.

"So, what's been happenin'? Haven't seen you around much lately," Frank inquired.

"Just got back, went home for Christmas."

"St Louie, right?" Frank nodded feeling his guess was correct.

Frank had gotten to know Luke, mostly from teaming with him during the Sunday afternoon basketball games.

"Right." Luke responded.

"How's the family?"

"Good. Real good."

"That's good. But I mean before, too. What've you been doin'?" Frank couldn't remember the last time he saw Luke.

"I put in a lot of hours at the store. I managed to get time off over the Thanksgiving weekend because a friend was in town.

After that, I worked every day right up till I left a couple of days before Christmas. It's the biggest time of the year for the store."

"Yeah, people buy books as Christmas gifts, don't they?"

"I got two books for Christmas. They're over under the tree." Terry offered to show them.

Luke finalized his selection and gave the album to Frank. He agreed to accompany Terry to see all her Christmas gifts after he made one detour.

"But I'm going to get another beer first, okay?" Without looking, Luke strode in the direction of the kitchen.

"Hey, watch it, slick!" Clay balanced his drink at arm's length. "Can't you see I got a drink, here?"

"I can see now." Luke stepped backwards and bumped Frank.

Frank sensed a renewal of the competition between his two friends, even though this was Julia's home and not a basketball court.

Luke explained to Clay. "Frank put on some more music. I'm going to grab a beer. Looks like you got a fresh drink, already."

"Yeah, I'm good." Clay took a gulp from his glass.

He extended both arms. The one with the drink spread across Luke's shoulders, the other snatched Frank's upper arm.

Clay crunched some ice and repeated in a menacing tone.

"I'm good, but Fat Man, he's really missin' you. His team sucks without you. Ain't that right, Fat Man?"

Clay released Frank's arm and lifted his arm from Luke's shoulder, spilling a little of his drink on Luke's shirt in the process.

Frank moved closer to Clay. "Sure missed that sweet jump shot of his."

"That's what it is. Hey, everybody, this is Luke!" Clay wheeled in a half circle away from Luke, while pointing back at him. "He's

Julia's renter and owner of the sweetest jump shot in town, out-side of CU's varsity squad, of course."

Clay laughed and raised his glass toward Luke. A few of the others nearby copied Clay's gesture.

Clay swallowed the contents of his glass before he turned to face Luke again. "So, thought you were out of town or somethin'?"

"Yeah, I just got back a little earlier."

"Yeah, well, Julia's glad. She likes you. So does Terry. Tell me, what does that mean when a little girl likes you, huh? A little girl likin' a grown man. That's a kinda' queer, don't you think?"

"I think it's probably more that she's not afraid of me. She's comfortable being around me. Some people are easier to be around, especially for kids."

"What's that supposed to mean?" Clay poked Luke on the arm.

"Just that some people are a little scary to be around." Luke trained his eyes squarely on Clay.

"You're damn right I'm scary. I know you don't want to mess with me, do ya'?" Clay glared at Luke.

"I thought we were talking about little kids?"

"We were. And skinny guys, they're all punks." Clay's cheeks reddened.

"No, actually kids are just kids. Punks, they come in all siz-es." Luke maintained a surface coolness.

Frank attempted to distract Clay. "Yeah, some might even call me a punk."

"No, you're definitely Fat Man." Clay shot a glance toward Frank, and then came back to Luke like he was turning around a bend in the road. "So where'd you go on your trip, Little Luke?" Clay realized the humor in this impromptu nickname. "Little

Luke, Little Luke from the Real McCoys, that's it! You're Little Luke to me. Little Luke meet Fat Man. Ain't that cool?"

Clay roared and others grinned or chuckled, but only at the sight of Clay swaying side to side with laughter.

"Coo...ol!" Frank and Luke squeezed out the sarcasm in unison.

Clay attempted to control the conversation. "So, you going to tell me where ya' went, or not?"

"Back home for Christmas." Luke shrugged.

"Oh, well now, ain't that nice?" Clay slipped in his own sarcasm. "How're mommy and daddy?"

"Mom's good. My dad...." Luke hesitated. "Actually he's passed away."

"Yeah, my old man's dead too. Liver quit on him, the sorry S-O-B. Ya' know what I say though. To hell with the old man, he never did anything for me anyway. Yours was probably the same."

"Actually no, my dad was a good guy."

"That figures. Julia says you're a nice guy. Good guys fathering nice guys. Ain't that sweet?"

Clay turned the volume of his voice a notch louder. "Luke's so sweet. Terry thinks so, and all the little kids. But, you know what I say. I say, screw the good guys and the nice guys!"

As Clay finished his harangue, Luke braced himself. Frank wedged his sizable frame between the two of them. Another man, a mutual friend, stepped forward too.

"Darrell," Frank called to the other man.

Darrell gripped Clay's forearm and pulled him backwards.

"Let's get you another scotch, big guy." Darrell tugged harder, and Frank steered Clay with the weight of his shoulder leaning into Clay's chest.

Finally, Clay gave in with a suddenly civilized request. "I'll need some ice and a splash of water too, okay?"

"You bet, man. Coming right up," Darrell responded.

Clay felt a strong nudge from Frank. "Whatt'll you have, Fat Man?"

"I'm coming with you. I'll get a beer." Frank pushed Clay toward the kitchen.

The party rolled on, punctuated by rock 'n roll music and toasts to the good times from the year gone by. More and more Clay became the central figure in the room. He engaged the party with entertaining stories in which he and some of the other guests played various roles. He clearly knew many of them, and they appreciated his renditions of their interactions.

Clay slopped some of his drink occasionally, and Luke suspected he slopped some of the stories too. Luke gradually moved toward the fringes of the party circle. On his way to the kitchen for a last beer, he spied Terry curled on the sofa.

He detoured from the beer and approached Julia instead with a suggestion that he carry Terry up to her room and put her to bed. With Terry in his arms, Luke passed Julia in the front hall. She whispered a comment about the repeated trips to the bathroom necessitated by her pregnancy, and Luke only grinned in response.

As Luke climbed the first steps, Frank placed a 45 record on the turntable. When the first notes of Marvin Gaye's *How Sweet It Is* played, many of the people in the room started to dance. Those same notes triggered Luke's memory of past St. Louis parties where that song had been a favorite too.

Terry hadn't awakened when he lifted her from the couch, and she only stirred briefly as he laid her on the bed. Luke used a quilt from the nearby rocking chair to cover her.

Her bedside lamp had been switched to its lowest level, and in its dim light Luke could see Terry's deep and regular breathing. He decided to sit in the rocking chair for a few minutes to make certain that she stayed sound asleep. He crossed his arms and rocked back and forth. After a brief time his head bobbed forward, and with his chin resting on his chest, he followed Terry into a peaceful sleep.

———

Luke awoke and jumped to his feet. He swayed and caught himself with a step to the side. Unsure of where he was and the source of the noise that startled him, he rubbed his eyes, and searched the surroundings.

Terry's room, upstairs in Julia's house, he remembered putting Terry to bed, and he confirmed that she still slept. He stepped quietly into the hall and hustled down the back stairway that led to the dining room and through it into the kitchen.

Julia was bending to pick up the stainless steel pan that had been used to pop the popcorn for the night's festivities. The lid for the pan had come to rest near Clay's feet. His half-successful kick at the lid sent it clanging toward Julia, and the momentum of his effort forced him to tilt against the counter.

Julia shouted, "Clay, will you settle down? You're going to wake the whole neighborhood."

"Yeah, man. Cool it!" Luke demanded.

Clay's eyes flashed for a moment in Luke's direction then darted to the side.

He struggled to orient himself. "Hey, Little Luke, whatta... where've you been?"

"Never mind me. What the hell are you doing?"

"What's it to ya'?" Clay tried to add an edge of confrontation but slurred his words instead.

Luke took the offensive."It's nothing to me except that you're making a mess of the place and an ass of yourself!"

Clay stood more upright. "Hey, fuck you! It's my woman's place and I can do whatever I want."

He then took an unsteady step toward Luke and challenged him verbally. "What the fuck're you doin' here, anyway?"

Luke held his position. "I live here, you asshole. And it's way past time for you to get out of here. You're as fucked up as anybody I've ever seen."

Julia banged the lid and the pan on the stove top, signaling her demands.

She confronted the two men. "Clay, will you please just go! Luke, you can cool it, too."

Clay then pivoted toward Julia.

His assertion smacked of high school, a retort pulled from a ridiculous part of his half-conscious mind. "Hey girlie, you can just blow me! Then maybe I'll consider leavin'."

Julia almost spat the words. "You're disgusting!"

She reached for the lid, an unconscious move as if she would need to defend herself.

Luke marched forward and raised a clenched fist. "I ought to..."

"Ought to what?" Clay shouted as he whirled and unleashed a roundhouse swing in Luke's direction.

Luke ducked and the force of Clay's missed punch, combined with the slipperiness of the oily linoleum floor, swept Clay off of his feet. He fell backwards, hit Julia with a glancing blow from his thigh and his hip, and sprawled against the bottom of the stove. Julia tumbled to her side.

Clay squirmed, and when his arm slipped out from under his upper body, the back of his head hit the oven door and he slumped all the way to the floor. Luke rushed to Julia and helped her to her feet.

"Are you alright?" Luke couldn't believe what had just happened. "The big dumb ass!" he blurted out as he put his arm around Julia's waist.

"I'm okay, I think." Julia gathered herself and her thoughts together.

Just then the kitchen door banged open. Frank and Darrell flew inside and a blast of cold air followed them. Everyone, except Clay, froze upright, stopped for a surprised second.

Frank broke the silence. "Shit! Luke? Julia, Clay, what the hell?"

"Frank," Julia pleaded. "Once and for all, will you and Darrell get Clay out of here?"

Clay groaned at the sound of his name but remained sprawled on the floor.

"Now! Before somebody really gets hurt." Julia's plea became a command.

"Okay, sure." Frank agreed and stepped forward with a final question. "You okay?"

"I'm...." Julia uttered one word.

"I'll make sure she's okay. You and Darrell just get him outta' here." Luke nodded toward Clay.

"Sure, sure. We can do that. We just had trouble getting the car started, but it's right outside now. So we'll take care of him." Frank's words trailed to a mumble, as he motioned to Darrell and grabbed one of Clay's arms.

Darrell took the other side. They tugged simultaneously, and Clay re-gained his feet. The threesome sidestepped through the door. Luke followed them and quickly pulled the screen door closed and then slammed the main door tight.

He turned to Julia and caught her eye but not a hint of brightness until he made a suggestion. "Why don't you go sit down and relax? I'll finish cleaning up in here."

"Yeah, okay," she agreed.

When he accomplished the job for which he had volunteered and judged it completed to his satisfaction, he checked the front room. He switched off the kitchen light on his way.

Julia sat at the end of the sofa, two blankets and two pillows stacked on the floor near her feet. He proceeded slowly and silently, and she didn't notice him at first. She held her head in her hands, rubbing her temples with her fingertips.

When she opened her eyes, she smiled at Luke. "Come sit with me for a minute."

He took a seat on the opposite end of the sofa, and she acknowledged him with an expression of gratitude. "Thanks for cleaning up. I guess this New Year's came in with the proverbial bang."

"Amen to that," Luke conceded and then explained. "I fell asleep in that rocking chair in Terry's room. When I heard the bang, I came running."

"Oh, so that's where...I looked for you at midnight. I just thought you had snuck down to your apartment." Julia stared past Luke toward the kitchen.

Luke didn't try to make eye contact but spoke with assurance. "No, I was upstairs. Fell asleep for some reason. I guess things were quiet enough until that pan fell and..."

"Yeah, Happy New Year." Julia raised her hand in a mock toast.

"Quite the celebration." Luke sensed that the night had tired Julia.

"Not that you would know."

"Sorry I didn't hang in there with you."

"It was mostly Clay's show," Julia admitted.

"I could see that coming. Frank was spinning the records, though. And people were having a good time. Hey, think I should check on Terry, now?" Luke offered additional help.

"No, she's okay. I looked in on her when I went up for the blankets and pillows."

"Good. Then I think I'll head down to my place."

"No wait." Julia leaned forward and picked up the stack of bedding, holding it on her lap. "I've got a favor to ask. Don't think I'm weird."

Her green eyes pulled a quick response from Luke. "I don't think you're weird, but your guy, he's a different story."

Julia placed the stack of bedding on the sofa cushion between them, as she rose to her feet. "I'm too tired to tell you that story now. Maybe some time...Here, you get a blanket but you have to sit there. I didn't know you could sleep sitting up."

The bottom of Julia's blouse hung loose over the top of her skirt, and she no longer wore the belt that she had worn earlier.

Luke thought she had started to relax, but he wasn't sure that he could.

"I can't usually. Tonight, things have been a little different." Luke couldn't offer a better explanation, nor did he fully comprehend all the differences.

Julia picked up one of the blankets and unfolded it to full length. She stretched it over him, covering his legs, pulling it up to his chest, and tucking it under his arms and against the end arm of the sofa.

"There that should keep you warm." She surveyed Luke and then fluffed two pillows against the opposite end arm of the sofa.

She spread the other blanket the length of the sofa and slipped out of her shoes. She switched off the lamp at her end and made her way under the blanket. She lay on her back and lifted her legs in one motion, dropping her feet in Luke's lap while simultaneously wrapping them in the blanket.

Luke followed Julia's lead and switched off the lamp at his end of the sofa. Both of his hands fell onto her feet. Warmth enveloped him, and he relaxed into it. He massaged her feet, and her toes curled and uncurled beneath the blanket.

She breathed deeply and yawned. "Thanks again, Luke, Happy New Year."

"Happy New Year," he whispered.

He rested his head on the top of the cushion, shifted his legs away from the sofa, and closed his eyes. Bright images from the past hours rose before him, and he relived those moments, along with scenes from the recent days and nights. He opened his eyes when he felt Julia stirring.

Her voice carried lazily into the darkness. "I don't usually... these days I can't really sleep through the night. So when I wake up I'll let you have my spot and I'll go upstairs."

"Okay. Yeah, let's just sleep." Luke settled deeper into the cushion of the sofa.

"Okay, good night," Julia whispered so softly Luke did not actually hear her.

He responded anyway. "Good Night."

Some time passed and his breathing rose and fell and rose again, high into the New Year's night. Before a dream of the coming year opened to him, a convergence of pathways, and all the persons who had traveled them, burst like bright colored photographs before him, flashing at hyper-speed from deep within the cosmic consciousness.

Chapter 2

Like many metropolitan regions throughout America in the 1950's and 1960's, the suburban areas of St. Louis emerged from grassy farmlands and wooded acres. Communities exploded by the hundreds, and families expanded by the thousands until over one million people populated St. Louis. The Aurmann family played their part in the emergence.

In the summer of 1951, Jacob and Margaret Aurmann found a house on the western side of St. Louis County, and it became their home, home for their family of four boys. The brothers ranged in age from 3 years to 5 months. Matthew was the oldest, then Luke. Each of them named after the gospels favored by their parents. When two more boys were born in successive years, they were given the names of the remaining gospels, Mark and then John.

They grew from boyhood to near manhood in that home, a perfect place to raise a family their mother often said. They flourished there, in the middle of America, in the middle millions of families that lived in suburban communities.

Luke followed a path, shared by his brothers. Their passion, and the inspiration of his father and mother, and eventually the compassion of his younger sister, influenced him. His friends, classmates and teachers, little league, sandlot, and high school teammates and coaches, their approval encouraged him. He experienced his young life moving right down the middle, safe and satisfied in the midst of the common place.

Throughout that time Luke prepared, a diligent student, a watchful soul, a patient practitioner of the principles he learned from his parents and his elders, the value of hard work and earnest study. He played at making the leap or taking the lead, but he remained there, right there, in the right place, in the middle of everyone and everything.

Even when Mark had made it, had jumped and fell short, but scrambled up the mud embankment and stood on the other side yelling at him, too, Luke still wavered. He swayed from one foot to the other, as the kids on the other side called his name. Matthew warned him. The young boys game that they played meant they had to escape the bad guys. He had to jump or the bad guys would capture him. He had to jump soon, because they needed to hurry to their hideout in the woods.

Once more Mathew yelled, "Come on, Luke!"

"Yeah, you gotta come now!" Someone else pleaded.

"Come on!" The cheers repeated.

"You can make it, Luke!" Mark encouraged.

Luke measured the distance across the ditch in his mind, empty space in between the bank upon which he stood and the place where his friends and brothers called to him, calling upon him to do what they knew, what he knew, he could do. Sweat poured down his face, flowing from the external heat of a St. Louis summer day and the internal heat brought on by tension and embarrassment.

Finally, Matthew turned to go, and the other kids followed him. When Mark was the last to leave, Luke dropped his head to avoid the disappointment showing on Mark's face. Then a rustling in the trees behind Luke caused him to lean in the direction of the unexpected noise. He took a few unconscious steps in that direction. He pivoted as Mark disappeared from view.

With a quick step, then two, and three more long strides, Luke hurled himself at a full run. He planted his lead foot at the edge and flew over the ditch, hit, and rolled forward on the other side. He popped to his feet and ran to catch up with Mark, passed him, and signaled to everybody that someone was coming. He hustled ahead and led the gang to their hideout.

***

During that same period of time, on the far western edge of the Great Plains, Boulder Colorado evolved in a different way. In the early 1950's the Denver Boulder Turnpike opened, a highway connecting the capital city of Denver with the town where the University of Colorado was located. Unlike the highways and boulevards that encouraged the free flow of traffic between the city of St. Louis and its suburbs, this highway was a toll road. Travelers and commuters paid a price to complete the trip.

Broad swaths of wild, grassy hills and wide expanses of mountain vistas stretched out along the Denver Boulder Turnpike. In the fifties and sixties, when the St. Louis suburbs filled such spaces, a traveler could pull off the turnpike at the Boulder overlook and find the lights of residential and commercial development still concentrated in relatively small pockets.

In the latter 1950's, the paving of the canyon highway that served as the route to the mountain town of Nederland was completed. Also, a four lane highway, known as the Diagonal Highway, was built between Boulder and the neighboring town of Longmont. Even as these connections emerged, Boulder held firmly to its separateness.

————

Early in the winter of 1944, Darren Williams completed his training at Fort Carson in Colorado Springs. He had enlisted in the Army and wanted to fight in World War II. One night, while awaiting his final orders, likely an assignment to the Pacific Theater, he received an urgent telephone call from Boulder Community Hospital. The train trip and bus ride back to Boulder, his home town, took the entire night. By dawn his son, Clay, had been born, but his wife, Gloria, had died from the hemorrhaging, a complication of their son's birth.

The doctors were able to stop the bleeding that occurred when Darren punched through the glass frame that protected a photograph of the Flat Irons Mountains. The photograph hung in the hall of the hospital just outside the nursery. Darren shattered the glass with a straight overhand right. Pain from a deeper source caused the tears that filled his eyes.

He didn't feel the treatment and the stitches administered to the back of the hand that had thrown the punch. He resisted the feelings, too, when he held his newborn son for the first time. He extended his arms away from his body and supported his son with his hands only. No part of his heart was connected.

Darren demanded that Clay stay in the hospital until after his wife's burial and wake. The nurses agreed to take care of the baby, although hospital policy did not allow for it. The little house they owned on 18th Street near Boulder High School served as the location for the wake. Darren's younger sister, Marsha, and their friends handled the arrangements. On the day of the wake, Darren wore his uniform for the final time. A young man ready to fight, he fought an unexpected battle from that day until the day of his own death.

Darren drank beer until the last guest bid him good-bye and good luck. A cold wind raced in the door when he held it open for his sister while she carried out the leftover food. After their embrace and her tail lights disappeared up the street, he switched off the lights and sat in the darkness. He drank straight whiskey from the bottle.

The next day he brought his son home from the hospital. Marsha helped Darren and his baby get settled. Darren secured a discharge from the Army and went back to work in the Monarch Coal Mines. Marsha cared for Clay during the day and often prepared dinner for Darren's return home after work.

Some years passed and Marsha married and had a child of her own, a daughter she named Karen. Slowly Marsha pulled back from her brother's life and concentrated on her own family. On occasions when she would visit, she experienced a coldness building inside her brother's home.

She referenced that chill when she commented to her husband. "It's no place to raise a family."

Darren dug in, a coal miner's instinctive reaction. He routinely fortified himself with a beer and a whiskey chaser, all the while teaching his son as best he could to fight for some warmth of his own.

———

On Friday night Darren cashed his paycheck at the grocery store, and then stopped by the house to pick up his son. This mid-November evening had darkened early, the sun pulled behind a thick cloud cover above the foothills to the west. An all-too- familiar chill filled the space between the back of Clay's neck and the collar of his jacket as he ran to his dad's truck. He leapt on the running board, swung the door open and jumped onto the bench seat. At eight years old he had the physical abilities of an eleven-year-old.

"We got to get you into sports of some kind. You're a good runner." His dad said as Clay settled into the seat.

"Yeah, I wanna' play." Clay got excited.

Darren drove them to Larry's Lounge for the fish fry special. Usually after dinner, Clay played the pinball machine until his dad ran out of nickels. Darren took a place at a nearby bar stool and discussed business, jobs, hard earned money, or the lack of it, with Larry. Darren did most of the talking, preaching between swigs of beer and punctuating important points with the smack of a shot glass on the hardwood bar.

"Hey Larr, one more time!" Darren shouted as he swung around on the bar stool to comply with Clay's request for another nickel. "Boy, you're lucky I'm thirsty tonight. You get one more nickel, and I get one more round."

The force of his father's big hand into Clay's chest with that last nickel caused Clay to stumble backwards. The back of his leg knocked against the stool of a neighboring patron, and Clay lost his balance and fell on his rump.

"Don't just sit there, boy. Get up!" His dad coached, "Ya' gotta' learn to stay on your feet if you wanna' play sports."

Clay sprung to his feet without a word and hustled back to the pinball machine.

Later that night at home, Clay and his dad watched the Friday Night Fights on TV. Darren recounted how he had been a good amateur boxer when he was younger. Like many other Friday nights, he demonstrated some punches for Clay.

"Yeah, the straight right hand, that was my best punch. Straight to the other guy's jaw...that'd send him backwards. Sometimes even knock him out. Here, let me show ya'."

His dad threw two lazy left jabs, and then came straight at Clay's chest with a quick right hand. His dad's fist stopped before it met Clay's chest, but Clay flinched and retreated, stepping back from the possible contact. His leg caught the edge of the coffee table that occupied the space in front of the sofa. Clay fell backwards.

"Damn boy, I didn't even touch ya'! Guess we'll have to try a sport other than boxing."

Clay scrambled to his feet and straightened his jeans.

"As long as you're up, grab your old man another beer." His dad commanded.

Clay rushed to the kitchen and back.

"You're pretty fast though," his dad chuckled. "That should come in handy."

"That's the last one." Clay shrugged.

"Okay, we'll get some more tomorrow and maybe some root beers or somethin' for you."

Clay liked going to the store with his dad, better than with his Aunt Marsha. "Yeah, I'd like some more of those, for sure."

His dad dozed before he finished that last beer. The fight ended, when the tall guy won the bout by a knockout. The announcer said a straight overhand right caught his opponent by surprise. Clay never doubted his dad's knowledge of the sport of boxing. He held onto that one connection with a small boy's grasp, held on as long as he could.

When Clay switched off the TV, his dad inexplicably awakened, as though the silence alarmed him.

His abrupt command startled Clay. "Hey, boy, you better go on to bed."

Clay pulled the covers higher, but the chill of the night air still caused him to shiver. As a young boy, he struggled against the cold, pushed back as hard as he could. When he grew tall, strong, and muscular, his heart hardened. He buried the cold deep inside, an ice of separation.

———

Jacob Aurmann played baseball as a young man, and he encouraged his sons to participate in sports. Throughout the summer months when they were boys, Luke and his brothers practiced baseball in their backyard and in the field adjacent to the neighborhood school. Each season, Luke played on the same Little League baseball team.

Like most young boys, he dreamed of being a star player, and although he was a solid defensive first baseman, he was only an average hitter and seldom attained the highest levels of achievement on the baseball diamond. During a makeup game on the Fourth of July, the summer after fifth grade, an opportunity for a stand-out performance availed itself.

In the bottom half of the last inning, Luke's team held a one run lead. Ricky, the team's starting pitcher and best hitter, had already contributed in his usual star-like way by hitting the double that scored the go-ahead run.

When Luke's team took the field, Ricky caused the first batter to pop out. Luke fielded the ball in foul territory very near the fence, a tricky play that he handled easily. With one out secured, Luke, his teammates, his coach and all the fans, his father included, anticipated an easy victory. Ricky might even end the game with two strikeouts, since the next two batters were the weakest hitters on the opposing team. Ricky's fastball routinely overpowered the poorer players, but, unexpectedly, Ricky walked both batters.

At that point, the coach called on Luke to relieve Ricky. Luke had not pitched in an official game since the second grade, but the team's regular relief pitcher was not available because of a family vacation.

When Luke joined Ricky and the coach as they huddled near the pitching mound, the coach shared his reasoning. "Luke, I remember you pitched a few seasons ago. Bobby's gone and Ricky's lost his stuff. You gotta' take over. Just try to throw strikes."

Ricky patted Luke's back with his glove before he took his newly assigned position at first base. From his spot at the end of the dugout, the coach clapped to show his support. Restless murmurings cascaded among the fans of both teams, and even Luke's teammates chattered uneasily as he made the allotted warm-up pitches.

Only Luke's father voiced a distinctive cheer. "Come on Luke, you can do it. Show 'em your stuff!"

After his last warm-up pitch, Luke settled his nerves by scraping the hard, rubber slab of the pitcher's mound with the bottom of his right shoe. Each time he pawed the ground, he recalled the almost daily experience of throwing batting practice to his brothers.

His coach called an instruction. "Just keep it low. Make him hit it on the ground."

And his father yelled as though he was coaching too. "Throw strikes! Make a hitter out of him."

Luke moved with purpose and set a pace that his sinewy muscles remembered from the backyard routines. He delivered a strike, and the batter blinked as it crossed home plate. On the next pitch, Luke made a hitter out of his opponent. Ricky fielded the sharp ground ball bouncing along the first base line and made the out unassisted. The base runners advanced to second and third.

"Out at first, two outs." The umpire summarized.

Luke's coach pointed at him. "Okay, good job! Two away, let's get the big one."

Luke's pitching motion looped and whirled with arms and legs in synchronized rhythm, and the next batter flinched as the first pitch sailed over home plate.

When the umpire called the strike, Luke's father cheered. "Perfect! Peaches!"

Luke threw a second consecutive strike, and a cacophony of cheers rolled through the stands. As the voices diminished, the opposing hitter tapped the plate with his bat and stared at Luke, signaling his determination to hit the next pitch no matter what Luke threw.

Luke pulled off his cap and wiped his forehead with his jersey sleeve. When he replaced the cap, he adjusted the bill, hiding his eyes in the shadow. In that moment he decided to vary his pitching motion and hide the ball from the hitter's view for as long as possible.

Instead of kicking his left leg directly toward home plate, he looped it across his body. Simultaneously, his right arm angled toward the ground so that the ball was hidden behind his leg. An instant later, the ball came into the batter's view, but it appeared like it had been shot from the ground. The funny angle confused the hitter. He chopped wildly with his bat making an off-balance lunge at the ball and missed it entirely.

"Strike three. Batter's out! That's the game." The umpire proclaimed the end.

The crowd roared in celebration. Luke's teammates rushed to the pitching mound to congratulate him. With Luke in the middle they formed a circle near first base to cheer their opponents and Luke's performance.

Luke's coach singled him out. "Luke, that last pitch was really something!"

"Yeah, that was neat. You're somethin' else!" Ricky slapped Luke on the back.

As Luke's father strode toward the team dugout, the coach repeated his congratulations. "Mr. Aurmann, your boy surprised us all today. That was some pitching!"

"We just give 'em all we got. Don't we, Luke?" Jacob replied, as he extended an arm toward his son. Luke circled underneath his father's arm. Jacob kept him there while escorting him to the family car.

"That's one we won't soon forget. We're goin' to enjoy those fireworks tonight!" His father grinned as he opened the passenger door for this son, star of the day.

———

Darren Williams hollered, "Come on boy, get up! You're okay. That was nothin'! Look at the other guys."

"First down," the referee shouted and waved his arms while he blew his whistle. "Time out!"

Clay rolled to his side where he could breathe more easily. Although in eighth grade and a year younger than most of his teammates, Clay was one of the biggest boys on his Junior High team. With better than average speed, his coach regularly called plays with him as the ball carrier.

His coach believed in the running game. "Just get me three or four yards each time, Clay. That's all we need to keep gettin' first downs, and keep movin' the ball. More often than not, we'll come out on top."

Moving the ball on the ground during this game proved to be a difficult strategy. The opponents included twin brothers, nearly as big and as fast as Clay. Like him they played defense and offense. Two star players versus one became the thrust of the contest, and late in the fourth quarter the scoreboard showed twelve to six, a comparative two to one margin in favor of the twin's team.

Clay had run the ball up the middle on this play for the third straight time. The twins anticipated Clay's move, and, just as he pushed through the initial wall of defenders, the twins collapsed on him and sandwiched him with a simultaneous hit, one from each side.

Their shoulder pads struck Clay and squeezed the air out of his lungs, but in the instant that they hit him, their helmets crashed into one another as well. The twins stumbled backwards and fell to the ground while Clay fell forward in a heap.

As Clay took a breath, his coach and his father flanked him on either side, both men down on one knee.

"You okay, Clay? Can ya' get up?" His coach was concerned.

"Come on, boy, you're all right!" His father almost scolded him.

On all fours, Clay removed his helmet. His body responded favorably, except for a tender section on the lower right side of this torso. When he rose to his feet, his coach and his father each grabbed an arm.

"There ya' go," his father stated. "I knew you were okay."

Still unsteady, Clay stumbled forward when his father released his arm and slapped him on the back. Clay brushed against the opposing team's coach, who was standing guard over the twins.

Both of them still lay on the ground with a pair of adults kneeling close by and attending to them. As one adult eased the helmet off of the closest twin, the twin's eyes blinked rapidly, each eyeball focused at an odd angle.

"He okay?" Clay groaned.

"Hope so," the coach answered with an uncertain tone.

Clay's father helped him toward the sideline, while two of his teammates trotted by, each holding a stretcher. They used them to carry the twins off the field. The twins had knocked each other out of the game. They bruised Clay, stunned him, but after missing two plays, he went back into the game.

Without the twins to stop him, Clay dominated. The next time he broke through the middle of the line he stiff-armed his way past the second wave of tacklers, picked up speed, and ran over the opposing safety. He dropped to one knee when he reached the end zone, a forty-three yard touchdown run. He caught his breath and heard his father's voice above his teammates and the other fans.

"There ya' go! That's the way to bust 'em. Right up the gut! They can't take it."

With Clay leading the defense, his team held their opponents to minimal gains on four consecutive running plays. One of the twins was the opposing team's punter, so their team turned the ball over to Clay's team at a spot only seventeen yards from their goal line. The game clocked ticked into the final minute of play.

"Now we got 'em," Clay's father cheered. "Bust another one up the middle!"

Clay's team did just that, but, as Clay cleared the scrum, an arm swung at the lower part of his legs and caused him to drop. Instead of breaking into the clear, Clay tumbled to the ground at the eight yard line. Before his team could set up and run another play, the horn sounded and the referee blew his whistle to signal the end of the game.

Clay trotted to the sideline, and his father met him with a wild gesture. "They're lucky there's no overtime. They ain't nothin' without those twins!"

"Mr. Williams, our team's not much without your boy either." Another father, Bill Morton, explained as he stepped forward to greet his own son.

Darren responded to the compliment. "Hey Bill, how're you doin'? Tell Frank he did a good job, too."

When Clay bumped his father's arm, his father faced him and punched Clay's shoulder pads. "See I told ya'. Just take it right to 'em every time. Right up the gut. Just like boxing, the straight right hand's a knockout punch!"

Chapter 3

Boulder, May 1962

*B*y the time Clay claimed a starting position on the Boulder High School football team, he stood over six feet four inches tall and weighed nearly 200 pounds. He played defensive end and tight end and started at the center position on the basketball team.

The family of the twins that Clay had played against in Junior High moved to Boulder at the start of their sophomore year in high school. Their father's surveying company provided research for site planning and development of the building that would serve as the new headquarters and laboratory facility of the National Center for Atmospheric Research (NCAR).

With Barry Fisher at quarterback and his twin brother, Gary, at running back and each of them manning a position in the defensive secondary, they teamed with Clay to lead the Boulder

High School football program to winning records and prominence in the state-wide rankings. Personally, Clay achieved recognition as an All State player in his junior and senior years.

Clay's success in high school athletics opened many doors for him throughout Boulder's close-knit community. In particular, he connected with the coaching staff and some of the players at the University of Colorado. His hard-charging style and blue collar upbringing matched well with the athletic elite, but he sometimes found himself relegated to the fringes in certain social circles.

In the spring of 1962, Clay's senior year in high school, NCAR's Director and his staff hosted a reception for local and state officials and university staff and students in the departments of earth sciences, physics and engineering. The reception was to be held in the ballroom of the University Memorial Center.

The ongoing contract that Mr. Fisher's company had with NCAR ensured that Mr. Fisher and his family would be invited to the reception. Mr. Fisher insisted that the twins attend, and the Fisher twins invited Clay to join them.

Strands of lights hung from the ceiling of the ballroom with silver and gold tinsel spun around the cabling to add more sparkle. Clay's winning smile gleamed amidst the surroundings as he approached the twins.

He tightened the knot of his necktie. "They got the place lookin' pretty cool. I guess this is no ordinary prom."

"I told you this would be an uptown affair." Barry steered Clay by grabbing his upper arm.

"But no monkey suits, that's the good part." Gary flanked Clay's other side.

"Dad, you remember, Clay Williams." Barry nodded toward Clay.

"Yes I do. What've you been up to since basketball season ended, son?"

"Not a whole lot, studying mostly."

"Really? Wish I could get my boys to do a little more of that. If you don't mind me asking, how'd you do on your college entrance exam?" Mr. Fisher raised an eyebrow.

"Good enough. At least that's what Coach Davis said. I'm goin' to CU next year on a scholarship, so I talked it over with him. Ya' know he wants some of the good local players to build the team again."

"I couldn't believe that Grandelius guy...actually paying those young men to come to CU. I've never heard of such a thing. It's black mark for the Buffaloes." Mr. Fisher made eye contact with all three young men.

"Well, Coach Davis is a Buff through and through. He said he bleeds black and gold. Some of the guys from the team told me he met with Judge White about getting things back on track." Clay thrust his chin forward.

"You mean, Supreme Court Justice White." Mr. Fisher corrected Clay.

"Yes sir, he's the one."

Mr. Fisher wagged a finger at his sons. "There you go boys. That's something to shoot for. An All American football player and a Supreme Court Justice."

Just then, a lady carrying two beverage glasses extended one of them toward Mr. Fisher. "Phillip, here's your drink. You can quit preaching now. We've been over this a hundred times. The boys know what they need to do. Hello, Clay."

"Mrs. Fisher, hello. Nice evening. Nice party." Clay glanced away.

"Yes, it is, and if you boys don't mind, I need to take Mr. Fisher away from you for a minute. There's someone he's supposed to meet. You know, come to think of it. Let's all go. I think you boys will find this interesting too."

Mrs. Fisher motioned for the three young men and her husband to follow her. Clay assumed a place at the back of the line that they formed. Using his height advantage, he perused the room as it grew more crowded.

Mrs. Fisher led them toward a circle consisting of two adult couples and a girl, a young lady. She wore a white dress splashed with large yellow polka-dots. Her blonde hair reflected the overhead lighting like a full moon glowing near the horizon.

As they drew closer, one of the men from the circle stepped forward. "Aahh, Mary, found him did you? Philip, is your drink to your liking? I believe I remembered correctly."

Mr. Fisher and the man shook hands. "Yes, it's perfect. Thanks Ben."

Then Mr. Fisher turned to the woman standing next to Ben. "Hi Beverly, Ben's behaving himself I hope."

"So far, but the night is young." She responded and laughed a socially acceptable laugh.

"Yes, well, I do know the bartender. He's a personal friend." Ben, a short and rotund man stood as tall as he could.

"Just about every bartender in town is, wouldn't you agree?" Mr. Fisher laughed and sipped his drink, as the others laughed with him.

"Philip, Mary, forgive me. These folks, I don't think you've had the pleasure of meeting. Roger and Christine Billings, this is Philip and Mary Fisher."

After the men shook hands and the ladies exchanged nods of acknowledgement, Ben pointed at the twins. "Oh and their boys, Gary and Barry, the twins, they'll have to introduce themselves. Can't tell them apart, sober or drunk, doesn't matter."

The twins introduced themselves individually to Mr. and Mrs. Billings. Gary stumbled over Barry's foot, as he retreated from the center of the gathering.

Then Mr. Billings gestured toward the young lady."Boys, Mr. and Mrs. Fisher, this is our daughter, Julia."

"Isn't she lovely? That dress is just so cute!" Mrs. Fisher exclaimed as she nudged Barry's shoulder.

"Thank you, ma'am." Julia blushed, and when she leaned away, the overhead light fell on the floor before her.

The beam of light now separated her from the twins and their parents, her parents also. She exchanged a glance with Clay, an as yet unknown part of the gathering. He inched in her direction. Her green eyes glistened and drew him closer.

Ben addressed Julia then. "You might know the twins, football and basketball stars at Boulder High School."

"That's true of course, but their friend here." Mr. Fisher tilted his glass toward Clay. "He's the most accomplished of all. Barry, introduce your friend."

"Sorry. Everybody, this is Clay Williams." Barry nodded toward Clay.

"Yeah, he was all-state two years in a row." Gary stated.

Clay raised his hand. "Hi everybody."

He grinned and exchanged a hand shake with Ben and Mr. Billings.

"Nice to meet you folks." He nodded to the women.

He extended his hand to Julia, and she mirrored his gesture. When their eyes met, Clay's voice hesitated and their fingertips touched.

He blurted, "Julia, it's very nice to meet you."

Julia pulled her arm back abruptly. She stood stone still as though embarrassed.

Mr. Fisher rescued the two young people from the awkwardness. "Clay shared with us earlier. He's been accepted at CU. I expect we'll be seeing more headlines about his exploits on the football field."

"Really, that's great, young man." Mr. Billings raised his glass toward Clay and then his daughter. "Julia's a freshman at CU this year."

Ben cautioned Clay and the twins, adding a splash of sarcasm. "Yes, boys don't be distracted by Julia's good looks. She's ahead of her age group, advanced placement or something like that. Smart and pretty, it's a dangerous combination."

Ben's wife, Beverly, made a more circumspect point. "I think all you men better be watching out. We women aren't going to settle for being housewives much longer. We're tired of picking up after you. Isn't that right Mary, Christine?"

"Oh, I had no idea you had it so hard." Ben hung his head in a mock form of grieving.

Beverly slapped his shoulder. "Stop acting silly and get another round of drinks for our friends, you slacker."

"Ah, yes, Roger, Philip, follow me. Let's leave the ladies to solve all our problems. Another glass of wine, and they may figure a way to fly us to the moon, like the President wants us to."

He motioned to the men and signaled the younger ones, too.

"You too boys, clearly we males don't stand a chance in this company."

The older men walked three abreast and the younger ones followed in step. The twins confirmed Clay's assumption. Ben was really Benjamin Elliott, PhD. Dr. Elliott was one of the lead scientists at NCAR, a very influential person. Their father had gotten to know him throughout the planning and site development process for the Table Mesa laboratory. Dr. Elliot was a heralded scientist but also an astute politician.

"Must be some sort of party man, too." Clay surmised.

"My guess is that he just likes to drink and rub elbows with the big shots." Barry quietly shared his opinion.

"But it wouldn't hurt you guys to suck up to him a little. You're the ones goin' to the School of Mines, trying to be engineers and all. That's why your parents wanted you to be here, ain't it?"

"That was their idea. We just thought it would be a good party." Gary interjected.

"I wouldn't necessarily call it a party." Clay bumped both of his friends.

"There're some pretty girls here, though. Like Julia, we both saw that look in your eyes."

"Let's just see how it goes." Clay hinted at the possibilities.

Each of the older men returned with two drinks, one for their spouses and one for themselves. Of the younger men, only Clay had two drinks. He planned to offer a soft drink to Julia, but she had migrated to a spot a discreet distance from her parents and the other adults, where she was involved in conversation with two young men.

Clay resigned himself to passing the time with the twins. He surveyed the room, and some nervousness crept over him when he witnessed how many of the other party-goers engaged in lively conversation while he and his friends stood in silence.

Unconsciously, Clay alternated taking a sip from each of the glasses he held, first the one in his right hand, then the one in his left. Time slowed and pulled his vision downward. The lower levels of liquid in both glasses unnerved him. He grimaced as he glanced around the immediate area.

Clay's expression caused Barry to chuckle. "Thought you got that extra drink for the good lookin' blonde, but I guess you were just really thirsty."

Gary laughed aloud at Clay's consternation. His outburst caused his father to peer in his direction, and he quickly covered his mouth with one hand.

Clay snapped, his voice hushed yet agitated. "Hey, shut up, you guys. I guess I got a little nervous."

"Yeah well, remind me not to ask you to get a drink for me anytime soon." Barry smirked.

"Don't worry, I'd just tell ya' to get your own damn drink." Clay then motioned to his two friends. "Huddle a little closer."

When they did, he held out his left hand. "You guys each pour a little of your drinks into this one."

"Are you nuts? That's not cool." Gary stepped back.

"Don't worry. I'm goin' to offer it to her, but she probably won't even take it. I just want a chance to talk to her."

"Oh yeah, what if that was my plan?" Barry held back.

"You guys aren't ready for someone like her."

"And you are?"

"Well, we both go to CU."

"No she does, you're still in high school."

"Yeah, but I'll soon be playin' football for the Buffaloes. And you guys, you'll be hittin' the books at the School of Mines. Maybe even sportin' pocket protectors like those queers."

Clay jerked his head in the direction of a group of young men whom he assumed were CU students in one of the science departments. He laughed at his slight and drew attention from several people nearby, including Julia and the two guys, with whom she had been talking. He nodded toward Julia and, in that instant, also recognized one of the guys.

Clay turned to his friends and lowered his voice. "Hey, I think that's Jim Karsten talking with Julia. Remember, he was a senior our sophomore year. He played guard, totally kicked my butt in practice, but he was good to have on our side when game time rolled around."

After checking for himself, Barry reported. "I can't see the faces of either of those guys, but Julia was lookin' over this way."

"See! Come on guys, just top off this glass. I gotta' get over there and see what's happening."

"Yeah, yeah, but you are goin' to owe us. In fact, you already owe us for getting you in here in the first place."

"Sure, I'll owe you guys for the rest of my life." Clay chuckled as his friends tipped the liquid from their glasses to the one he held in his left hand.

As Clay traversed toward Julia, the twins stepped in the direction of the drink station.

"See you guys later." Clay tossed the words toward his friends, but he had no intention of re-joining them.

Chapter 4

Spring, 1962

Jim "Duke" Karsten established a reputation early in life as a horseman and ranch hand. Evelyn Karsten and her husband's father raised him that way. As the town of Boulder expanded into the surrounding valley, the amount of land used for raising cattle dwindled, and as a result, the cowboy skills required for working a ranch diminished in importance.

The Karsten ranch was an exception to the pervasive trend. Jim's grandfather taught him the cowboy way because his father had died serving in the army during World War II. Jim won many rodeo awards as a youngster. He matured into a strong, muscular, and determined young man. His shock of wheat-colored hair and his warm brown eyes fit his easy-going manner.

When he sat in the saddle of his large chestnut gelding and rode the fence lines of the ranch or practiced roping in the corral, his stature was often compared to that of a young John Wayne.

He earned the nickname Duke, but only his closest friends called him that at Boulder High School.

His quick feet and hands, and his ability to use physical leverage established him as one of the anchors of a very good offensive line. He personally compared the blocking techniques to steer wrestling. His coaches did not fully understand his explanations, but he routinely impressed them with the effectiveness of his blocks, even against opponents who were physically bigger than him.

Off the field of play and out of the saddle, Jim studied mathematics and science. Early in his tenure at the University of Colorado, he stopped playing football and focused his efforts on an engineering degree. He helped to pay for his college education by joining the ROTC program. In a further departure from the physical nature of his upbringing, he learned to play the guitar, and he would strum the chords that accompanied many of the traditional western and modern folk songs that he sang.

When his mother died during the winter of his sophomore year of college, a melancholy gentleness became his temperament. He moved out of the dormitory and home to the ranch. He turned inward, and, except for the regular Wednesday afternoon gatherings with a few friends at a coffee house on University Hill, he found expression in solitude and quiet times.

During one of these gatherings on the Hill, Jim had just finished playing the last of three songs in succession when the sound of a modest clapping reached his ears. He recognized Sally, the younger sister of one of his friends, as she approached the group. A second young lady whom he did not know accompanied her.

"Hi, sis." Jim's friend, Arthur, rose from his chair. "Shouldn't you and your friend be studying or something?"

"I could say the same to you," Sally replied. "We're taking a break."

"That's what we're about." Arthur concurred.

Arthur motioned to the two chairs that he positioned on either side of his own place. The introductions ended when Jim met Julia for the first time.

She wore her blonde hair at her shoulders with a flip at the ends. Her eyes projected warmth and sincerity, and she chose the seat between Arthur and Jim.

She commented on the song she had just heard. "I liked your song."

Jim quickly clarified. "Oh that wasn't my song. I mean I didn't write it."

Julia rephrased her comment. "I knew that. But I like the way you made it sound just the same."

"Thanks," he muttered.

Arthur steered the conversation toward refreshments. "How about a coffee or something?"

Sally accepted her brother's offer of a coffee, and Jim asked for an iced tea. Julia followed Jim's lead and decided on an iced tea as well.

In the spring semester of her first year at CU, Julia lacked self-confidence, so she often accepted a role as follower. She had advanced through high school at St. Claire's Academy ahead of schedule and was at least one year younger than many of her classmates. Academically, she continued to be successful, but she wanted to broaden her college experience beyond the classroom. On this beautiful day, the week before spring break, her friend, Sally, led her to Jim.

Over spring break Julia's parents flew to Aspen for a week of spring skiing, and they expected her to join them, as she had many times in the past. She declined for an expressed reason, a term paper for psychology that she needed to research. She stayed in Boulder for one unspoken reason.

Each day she drove to the ranch, and Jim taught her to ride a horse. They went for long afternoon sojourns to the remote parts of the property. In particular, a spot in the cottonwoods along Boulder Creek became a favored place. They spread out a blanket. Julia fed Jim fresh strawberries, orange slices, and cheese and crackers that she brought from home. He sang songs to her, ballads and range songs, some she knew, many she didn't.

Their love blossomed there and grew over the weeks that followed. More gently than he had ever touched anyone, he reached for her purely feminine mystery. She responded to his tenderness and extended toward his forthright masculine firmness. They found comfort in love's new embrace.

In May she invited him to an evening event sponsored by her father's employer, NCAR, a reception celebrating the final transfer of the Table Mesa property as the site of the new facility. Although he had met her parents on one occasion at their lavish in-town home, he only agreed to attend this party when she told him how many of the professors and science students from CU would be attending. She expanded her invitation to include his friend Arthur, who was also a student in the engineering department.

That night at the NCAR party, Julia, Jim and Arthur engaged in a conversation. Jim relaxed when they found a place separated from Julia's parents and her parents' friends.

Clay's straightforward advance into the middle of their small group flustered Julia, and it agitated Jim.

"Here's that soda I promised you." Clay extended his left hand to Julia, and, as a reflex, she took the glass.

"Thanks." She responded.

Clay turned to Jim with a nod. "Duke, I'm surprised to see you here. What've you been up to?"

"Just goin' to school mostly." Jim responded while a snicker of delight emanated from Julia and Arthur.

Clay's gaze fell on Jim's friend. His cheeks jiggled when he laughed, and his eyeglasses bumped along in tempo. He pushed his glasses to the bridge of his nose, when he met Clay's eyes.

Clay questioned him directly. "Hey little man, what's so funny?"

Jim inched closer to Clay. "This is my friend, Arthur. Arthur, this is Clay."

The short man surprised Clay with the firmness of his handshake, but he did not speak.

Jim answered for his friend instead. "Nobody calls me Duke anymore. That was more of a high school thing, if you know what I mean."

Clay pressed the matter directly with Jim. "Oh, I always thought it was neat. Guys said you were like a junior John Wayne. I never saw you, but I guess you can really ride a horse, won a bunch of prizes at rodeos."

"Junior rodeos." Jim corrected Clay, a scowl wrinkling his brow.

"Just the same, this guy's a real live cowboy, not just actin' like one." Clay made eye contact with Julia then Arthur. "Anyway, Arthur, that's somethin' I guess you didn't know about your good friend here."

"You're right about that." Arthur answered and nudged his friend. "Duke, that is cool. I can kinda' see it now. And, hey, wasn't John Wayne some kind of engineer in one his war movies? *The Fighting Seabees*, if I remember correctly and I think I do."

"So, there you go." Clay found support for his point. "You can be an engineer and still be Duke at the same time."

"Like I said before, I've left that stuff behind." Jim steeled his eyes.

Clay's eyes projected the glint of an advantage he felt building. He reached out and not too gently pushed one of Jim's shoulders.

He smiled when he puffed his chest a little. "One other thing about Duke...I mean Jim, he totally kicked my butt on the football field. Of course, that was back in high school too. Anyway, I'm thinkin' it'd be wise to go along with whatever he wants. So how about we just call him Jim. Whatta' ya' say, Arthur?"

"Okay," Arthur replied. "But it's not as much fun."

"Yeah, Jim's not as much fun as he used to be." Clay grinned.

When Jim adjusted his stance and stood squarely in front of Clay, Clay took a half step back. He avoided Jim's eyes and changed the subject.

He directed a comment toward Julia. "So, I guess your dad's an engineer or some kinda' scientist here?"

"No, actually he's a pilot." Julia had lost her smile.

"Oh yeah, then where's the connection?" Clay wavered, a hint of nervousness in his voice.

Arthur stepped forward to help Clay. Clay's charismatic presence pulled him closer, even though he sensed the annoyance that had come over Jim.

Arthur glanced sideways at Jim and smiled at Julia. "NCAR needs pilots. Actually, they need really good pilots here. You see, they gather atmospheric samples, sometimes from very high altitudes. That requires a good pilot. Your dad must be very accomplished, Julia."

Arthur beamed a bigger smile at Julia. Ever since he had first met her at the coffee house, he wanted her to notice him. He quickly came to realize that his hopes were slim, especially when she was so clearly enamored with Jim, the Duke.

"He's certainly good at what he does." Julia agreed. "He likes it better than working for the airlines."

Arthur wanted to hold her attention a while longer and edged a little closer. "So, really he could be a Duke too. You know, *The High and the Mighty*, that's a John Wayne movie, too."

Julia managed an awkward grin. "I don't think so. I mean no one calls him that."

Both Jim and Clay extended an arm toward Arthur.

Jim spoke first. "You really need to forget all this Duke stuff. It's old news."

"Yeah, little man, it's not cool." Clay now sided with Jim.

"Jeez guys, give me a break will you?" Arthur backed away, but Julia found a way to save him.

"Yeah, will you two, take it easy? Clay, you're the one who started this nonsense about Duke. That's so high school, anyway. I think it's time you start thinking about college, don't you?" She poked Clay in the ribs.

"Here take this cola back." She winked when she handed Clay the glass that was still filled to the top, and then she drew closer to Arthur. "Arthur's going to buy me a club soda, aren't you?"

"My pleasure." He extended an arm toward her. "How about a wedge of lime with that, my dear?"

She smiled with the light of enjoyment and elbowed Jim on the way by.

She layered a slice of sarcasm atop her words. "Now I'm thinking Duke's kind of cute. Wished I had known before."

"Me, too." Arthur matched her smile as he took her arm in his.

After two quick steps, she pulled him to a stop, and they turned back like it was a dance step that they had practiced. "Okay, you two big oafs can come too."

The two taller, more handsome young men followed behind. Each realized their chance had been fumbled away. Jim longed to be back at the ranch; Clay wanted a more clearly defined playing field. Instead, Jim bought a bottle of Coors beer for Clay and himself.

They discussed football where they stood, huddling an uncomfortable distance from Julia. She laughed and held a lively conversation with Arthur. Occasionally she lifted a glance toward the two of them, but she gave neither of them an advantage, not for the rest of that night.

Chapter 5

Summary, 1962

*J*ulia enrolled in an elective class for the summer semester. Jim needed to fit in a prerequisite engineering class in order to stay on pace for his degree. Julia frequently walked the pathways of campus, from the library to the Norlin Quad, past Varsity Lake and Macky Auditorium. With so few students compared to a normal semester, it was more like a city park.

She arranged picnic lunches with Jim. He joined her when he could, juggling the demands of his class and work on the ranch. They sat in the shade of the broadleaf trees and ate without tasting the food, only the kisses they exchanged. He stretched out on the blanket and lingered in her presence.

The heat of the summer sun burnished the wild grasses of the Boulder foothills a golden color. At the Karsten ranch the young fields of alfalfa hay required irrigation water much earlier than normal. Jim and Julia's relationship evolved within its own growing season, seeds recently planted bursting forth. Then, a few days after the Fourth of July, Jim's ROTC commitment demanded his departure for training camp at Fort Carson, and a five week separation held them in suspension.

Julia questioned Jim's involvement in the military. Even as he explained his need for financial assistance and how the ROTC scholarship replaced his athletic scholarship, she worried about the long term meaning of his commitment. She could not be persuaded by his assurances that the ceasefire in Korea had been maintained for nine years. An official stalemate, a demilitarized zone guarded by the armies of both sides, had been established along the 38th parallel. He explained that America's biggest enemy was now the Soviet Union, but the fight with them was a Cold War, not the kind of war that required foot soldiers, his kind of Army unit.

Sitting beside him at the drive-in on the night before he left, she cried, and the tears could not be traced to the ending of the movie that they had been watching. She rode home in silence. *Soldier Boy* played on the radio, and tears filled her eyes again. When he parked at the curb in front of her house, she pulled him close with a fierce embrace and brushed his cheek with watery kisses and a whisper of good-bye.

The summer session officially ended the next week. Jim had taken his final exam early. Another two weeks passed before Julia agreed to meet Arthur at the engineering building. Prior to his departure, Jim had made arrangements for his friend to check on Julia from time to time. Although Arthur agreed with the concept, Julia resisted until one particular day.

Arthur enticed her with a description of the model he had completed. It was a project that Jim and he had initiated, not a class assignment but a personal idea of Jim's. Arthur expected her to recognize the purpose of the project. She had ridden with Jim over the section of the ranch where the model would find a real life application.

"See, it's really an upgrade to the current irrigation system. Jim says this section isn't getting nearly enough water." Arthur pointed out how the design would work, and Julia agreed.

"I remember. Those fields are very dry."

"It's been an especially hot summer. That's for sure. In fact, I could really use an iced tea. You want to join me over at the coffee house?"

Julia had forgotten how much she enjoyed talking with Arthur. His unassuming way disarmed her. The fan in the coffee house pulled in a steady breeze from the street. The early afternoon air still held a touch of freshness, and Julia relaxed even more.

Arthur contrasted his desire to serve in the Peace Corps with the military service that Jim's ROTC program would require of him. He expounded upon the reading that he had done about young engineers who were helping in many different parts of the world. The people of these poorer countries needed the kind of help he could provide. He might even be able to use the model Jim and he had developed for an irrigation system in some village in Africa.

Arthur ended with a humble summary. "Jim's got his reasons. He'll probably turn out to be more of a Duke than John Wayne ever thought of being. I know he needed the scholarship money. Plus, he probably told you that his dad died in World War II. Anyway, there are other ways to serve."

When they walked out of the coffee house, the sun's glare caught them off guard as it bounced off the glass of the store front. Arthur bumped Julia and then grabbed her arm to help them both regain their balance. A laugh rang out nearby, but they were blinded to its source.

"Hey there, you two been drinkin' or something?" The question was followed by a slap to Arthur's shoulder.

Arthur recognized that gesture as a typical Clay Williams approach. Earlier that summer, Arthur regularly accompanied Jim on visits to the CU field house. Jim missed the camaraderie and interaction with his former football teammates, and he knew their routine included a daily physical workout.

Arthur and Jim had both been surprised to find Clay Williams participating in those sessions. Clay explained that the football coach wanted him to enroll in a math class for that summer. The coach knew the associate professor for this particular class, and he wanted Clay to get a jump on his studies.

Physically, Clay did not require extra help, but he enjoyed the idea of working out with the team. His capabilities met varsity standards even though he was still not even an official member of the freshmen class. He usually just nodded in Jim's direction but would give Arthur a slap on the shoulder as his typical form of greeting.

"Clay, shouldn't you be in the gym?" Arthur shielded his eyes with one hand, while thrusting the other in a stop sign motion toward Clay.

"Captain gave us the afternoon off. It's too damn hot to work out."

Julia finally knew who she was addressing. "Really? I didn't think anything stopped you superior athlete types."

"Well, actually, I did work my upper body a little before I took off." He inhaled until his t-shirt stretched tight across his chest, and he smiled with broad satisfaction.

Julia's smile became a smirk. "Just relax, big fella. I don't want you to overheat."

"Yeah Clay, cool it!" Arthur reinforced Julia's admonishment.

Clay ignored them. "You two need a ride? My truck's just down the street. Pretty sure it's too hot for walkin'."

Arthur answered for himself. "I'm going back to campus. Maybe Julia would like a ride."

Clay pounced on that idea. "I'm at your service, little lady."

Julia circled away from Clay. "Actually I don't live too far from here. I think..."

"Then it won't be any trouble at all." Clay tilted his head, trying to track Julia's movement.

"Okay, I guess." Julia gave in, but stepped toward Arthur instead of Clay.

She hugged Arthur. "I really enjoyed talking to you and seeing your and Jim's project. I like everything about it. I'm sure he'll be proud that you finished it."

"Thanks, I can't wait till he gets back, so we can work on the real thing."

"Yeah, I can't either. It won't be much longer."

"Yeah, that's good. Well, I better go. Bye for now."

Clay couldn't wait any longer. "Yeah, bye Artie. See ya' around."

Clay then escorted Julia with a gentle touch to her elbow. "My truck's right down here."

Clay needed to solidify his understanding, and the ride to Julia's house provided the opportunity. "So, I haven't seen Jim around. He's been out of town I guess?"

"He has ROTC training for a month this summer and next."

"No kiddin'. I didn't think it was that big a deal."

"Actually, it's a lot bigger deal than that even. He'll have four years of active duty after he graduates."

"Bull! He's crazy. That's screwed up. I'm mean, I guess there's no war. But man, don't volunteer like that. Make them draft you. That's what I'm goin' to do. I got two friends from high school, they already enlisted. I told 'em no way! I'm goin' to college, play some ball, whatever I have to do. I had to take a math class this summer. But even that's better than the army. I'm not ready for that stuff."

Clay lost his breath in the torrent of his words. He slammed on the brakes as he reached the stop sign marking the intersection with Baseline Road. Julia lurched forward but braced herself against the dash with her right arm. Clay realized he had gone too far.

He apologized for his misjudgment. "Sorry, I guess I missed the turn back there."

Tears coursed down Julia's cheeks, and Clay realized that he had gone too far in another way, as well.

He only wanted to confirm the location of her house, and while she dabbed her eyes, he spoke softly. "Look, you shouldn't give any credence to what I say. Jim's a real smart guy. I'm just a punk football player. What the hell do I know? Nothing, really. But I just gotta' ask to be sure. You said you lived on Cascade near 7th. Is that right?"

"Yes, but I can just walk from here." Julia reached for the door handle with her right hand, but Clay moved faster and turned her back with a touch to her left forearm.

"No wait! I'm sorry, really I'm sorry. I shouldn't have spouted off like that. I get carried away sometimes. That's all. But you don't have to worry. I'll get you home, safe and sound. Cascade and 7th, is that right?"

"That's right."

"Okay, just sit tight."

Without checking for traffic, Clay turned onto Baseline Road. The driver of an oncoming convertible sports car had to swerve to miss the nose of Clay's truck. The sports car's horn sounded like a train whistle as the car swung in front of the truck. Clay slammed on his brakes and punched the steering wheel.

"Sorry again. We'll be okay, now. I promise."

Clay proceeded slowly onto Baseline. He used the proper hand signal when he turned right onto 7th street. After a few quiet minutes, the slowest Clay could remember, he eased the truck to the curb at the corner of Cascade. Julia moved deliberately.

As she swung the door open, she called without looking back. "Good-bye Clay!" Then she sprinted across the street and flew through the front door of her house.

Chapter 6

For the second successive afternoon, Clay had parked his truck along the curb at the intersection of Cascade and 7th Street, just like he had on the day that he had driven Elizabeth home. Her front door was framed in his windshield.

The heat of the afternoon sun increased as he waited. Perspiration beaded across his forehead, but on this day he was better prepared. After leaving campus, he had stopped at the five and dime and bought a cold bottle of soda pop. He propped it between his legs, and periodically he lifted the bottle and sipped cola through the straw.

He promised himself that he would wait, at least until he finished his soda, compelled to watch for her, although he was unsure why. Then Julia's mother pushed her way through the door carrying a grocery bag in her arms, appearing to support a heavy load. Julia followed behind and stopped on the top step of the porch. A verbal exchange took place, out of range of his hearing.

Unconsciously, Clay drove his truck forward and turned right onto Cascade. He opened the door of his truck and trotted across the street as Julia's mother made her way to the sidewalk that paralleled the front yard.

"Hello there, Mrs. Billings." Clay addressed Julia's mother and offered to help.

Mrs. Billings squinted in Clay's direction. "Why hello there... uhh..."

Clay stood face to face with her. "Clay Williams, ma'am, we met at the NCAR party a couple of months ago."

"Oh yes, well. Nice to see you again. I don't know." Mrs. Billings shifted the bag in her arms.

Julia had moved to her mother's side. "Hello Clay, I'm surprised to see you."

"Actually I..." Clay paused, unsure how to respond. "Actually I came by to see you, but then I saw your mom, and I thought I better help out."

"What do you mean to see me?" Confusion crossed Julia's face, and a hint of anguish crossed her mother's as she steadied the bag in her arms.

"These are books I'm taking to our neighbor. She lives just down the street. I better go." Julia's mother took a step in that direction.

"No really, let me just put them in the truck, and I'll drive you there. They're too heavy to carry, maybe even for me. Besides it's hot again today, and this way you can visit with your friend for a while."

Julia's mother followed Clay's reasoning as he gently lifted the grocery bag of books from her arms. She started across the street toward his truck.

Clay followed his instincts but came to full awareness after a few strides. He turned to find Julia still on the sidewalk. Her lips appeared to be forming a word, a question perhaps, but he did not wait for her to speak.

"I'll be right back. I'd just like to talk to you." He explained as he placed the bag of books in the bed of the truck.

Julia sat in a swing suspended from the ceiling of the front porch by chains attached to each end. She held the swing in a stationary position with her feet firmly on the floor of the porch. She waited in the shade and occupied the place furthest from the front steps.

When Clay hit the top step, she spoke first. "You know we have another car, and I offered to drive her myself."

"I know. That's what she said. I guess she didn't realize how hot it was today."

"I tried to tell her. She just doesn't believe me half the time."

"That's the way mom's are." Clay pointed at the swing, and Julia nodded to the opposite end.

"Yours, too?" Julia thought she might have something in common with Clay after all.

"Well, actually, my Mom died when I was born."

"Oh, I'm sorry."

"That's okay, but my Dad's the same. He's really hard-headed about things like that."

"Yeah, moms and daughters, dads and sons, there's something in all of that, it's hard to explain."

"I don't even try, anymore." Clay shook his head.

"Maybe that's what I should do."

"Whatta' ya' mean?"

"Maybe I should stop trying to explain myself all the time. It just causes arguments, anyway."

"Yeah, I usually just do what I want." Clay thrust his chin forward.

"I can see that."

"Huh?" Clay searched her eyes for a clearer understanding.

She smiled at his quizzical look before offering more details. "I mean I can imagine you doing whatever you want."

"I just take care of myself, ever since about sixth grade."

"That sounds good to me. On days like this it makes perfect sense. But I don't think you came here to talk to me about my relationship with my mother."

"What? No, that's none of my business." Clay dropped his head.

"It seems like you're making it so."

"No, that's not what I wanted..." Clay mumbled.

"Then why did you come to see me today?"

Clay lifted his eyes but directed his words toward the front yard. "I...I wanted to say...to say I'm sorry for the way I drove, the way I acted the other day."

"I think you already said that."

"Yeah, but I didn't want it to end that way."

"What way?" Julia frowned.

"I didn't want you runnin' away and being mad at me."

"I'm not mad."

Clay relaxed at the sound of Julia's words and drew encouragement from the earnest aspect of her eyes. "Good, then maybe tomorrow, maybe you'd let me make it up to you. I'm really not such a bad guy. I just thought if you want, we could go for a drive in the mountains, get away from the heat, maybe up to Estes Park, or Trail Ridge Road even?"

"Tomorrow, you mean Saturday?"

"Yeah, that's tomorrow, ain't it? Unless I'm really confused, it has been pretty hot."

"No you're right but..." Julia hesitated.

Clay amended his proposal, anxious for Julia to agree. "We don't have to go that far, just up to Nederland would be good."

"No I mean, I can't, not tomorrow. My Dad's flying us to Steamboat Springs, me and Mom."

"Damn!" Clay leaned away but quickly realized he over-reacted. "Sorry. Wow, that's cool. It'll be a lot cooler up there, too."

"I suppose. Anyway, we'll be gone for the weekend."

Clay shifted his weight, and the swing swayed with him. "What about Monday, then? Classes are over. Football's done till two-a-days."

"Two-a-days, what do you mean?"

"Two-a-days, that's when we practice football two times a day. It starts the second week of August. Didn't Jim ever tell ya'?"

"No, he doesn't play football anymore. He's just in ROTC. You know he's coming back soon."

"I know. Artie said that. He said he's supposed to take care of you till Jim gets back. I told him I could help take care of you too."

"Oh yeah, what makes you think I need to be taken care of? Don't you think I can take care of myself?"

"I have no doubt about that. Actually it's your mom, I'm worried about." He chuckled and she laughed aloud.

"Oh you're such a good boy scout, helping all the moms of the world."

"No, I'm no boy scout!"

"I imagine you're not."

"You've got to quit imagining things." Clay grinned.

"Sorry, don't think I can do that."

"Then, can you imagine yourself goin' to Estes Park with me on Monday? I'll have to drive ya'. I don't know how to fly."

"But you're a safe driver." Her inflection turned the statement into a question.

"Really I am." He defended himself.

"Okay then."

"Okay, you'll go?" Clay wanted confirmation.

"Okay, I'll go."

"Great!" Clay bounced to his feet and strutted toward the steps, but, instantly he reversed himself and trotted back to her.

"I'll pick you up at eleven. We'll have lunch along the way." He kissed her on the cheek and then bounded across the porch and down the steps.

He waved without looking. "See you then!"

———

They drove through Boulder Canyon with the sun in their eyes. Julia wore white Bermuda shorts and a sleeveless seersucker blouse checkered in blue and white. She carried a red cotton sweater and wore her hair in a pony tail. Relaxed and bright as the summer day, she rode with the truck window half open.

Clay steered with two hands on the wheel, except when shifting gears up or down depending on the steepness of the grade. He wore blue jeans and his cleanest white t-shirt.

His dark eyes squinted into the sun with the determination to demonstrate his safe driving skills. "Ya' know my dad drives this road everyday heading to the mine."

"No I didn't. I guess it's old hat to him. I still like it though. It feels like the start of an adventure each time, all the curves, the cliffs and white water in the creek. I like it."

"Me too, but I'm not expectin' an adventure today."

"You never know with your driving!" Julia laughed out loud.

Clay laughed too. "Ya' got me there, but I promise to do better today."

Clay chose the Nederland Inn as their lunch stop. Their conversation revolved around the beauty of the nearby lake and the quaintness of the town. Julia allowed herself to enjoy the day, while Clay struggled to make the right impression.

Clay didn't fully agree with Julia's opinion about the friendliness of the people. "But these mountain folks can be a little strange at times."

"How would you know?" Julia challenged Clay as though they played a game.

"Some of them are friends with my Dad, so I've been around them."

"Then how are they strange?" She persisted.

"I don't know, strange looking, I guess." Clay chuckled like his answer was the punch line to a joke.

Julia didn't laugh. "That's ridiculous. I'm not going to let you get away with an answer like that."

Clay coughed as her words caught in his throat. When the waitress placed a plate with a golden brown sandwich and a stack of potato chips in front of each of them, Clay found an escape.

"How about these grilled cheese sandwiches, they look good, don't they?" He sipped from his glass of cola.

"You're right about that." Julia bit into her sandwich and then swallowed. "As for the rest, I don't think you know what you are talking about."

———

As Clay drove the Peak to Peak Highway, the distant panorama of the Continental Divide accompanied them. He cruised along and relaxed into the conversation. His voice inflection followed the road, shifting to climb the hills, braking on the downhill side, and sweeping around the curves. He described his past success in football, how he would succeed at CU, and what that would mean for him. He painted a picture in broad strokes as grand as the scenery pouring through the windows of the truck.

"You seem to have it all figured out." Julia smiled as Clay steered the truck on the winding grade that descended into the town of Estes Park.

"I've been around the game since junior high. I know what I'm capable of."

"It's good to be confident in yourself."

"What about you, I guess you got everything figured out where school is concerned, skipping grades and all?"

"That was more my mom's idea. She thinks I should be a lawyer. Really make a mark."

"Yeah maybe you could be a judge someday, a Supreme Court Justice. Ya' know Byron White was an All-American football player from CU, and now he's on the Supreme Court."

"Maybe you should be the lawyer then."

"Not me. I'm goin' to be in Physical Education. That way I can coach once I'm through playin' ball. As for the rest of school, I've been thinkin' that I might be able to get you to help me."

"Is that right? Kind of presumptuous on your part, don't you think?"

"You mean, am I gettin' ahead of myself? I wasn't goin' to bring it up today, but then, it seemed like the right time since we were talkin' about school and what we're studying."

"Never one to miss an opportunity either." Julia had never met anyone as bold as Clay.

"I just think we should get to know one another better. We could be somethin' together."

"Clay, now you've gone too far. We're taking a ride in the mountains. This is the first time I've even talked to you for longer than two minutes. Let's just change the subject."

"Okay then, you should talk for a while, about your family. Your mom wants you to be a lawyer, your dad's a pilot, what else?"

Julia quickly summarized her family background. Her father grew up in Ohio, near Dayton, a city with a heritage in the aviation industry. He learned to fly as a teenager and served in the Air Force during WWII. He met her mother during the war, and Julia was born in a military hospital in North Carolina, while her dad was overseas.

Two summers ago, her dad had flown her to see the place where she was born, just the two of them. She once thought, and still did from time to time, that she wanted to be a pilot.

She reinforced her point, when she said. "Amelia Earhart was a great American, too, greater than Byron White for sure."

Her dad's job as an airline pilot brought the family to Denver in the early 50's and eventually to Boulder when he took his job with NCAR.

"Yeah, this NCAR is a pretty big deal. I did some checkin' around about it."

"Really, why's that?"

"I just wanted to know more about what's goin' on. I could take you on a hike someday around the Flat Irons. From there we could see the place where they're goin' to build the big new laboratory."

"Wow, Clay, I'm impressed. You really have been done some research."

"I just asked around some, talked to Artie and my aunt. She follows what's goin' on around town. She works in the County Clerk's office. She told me about the site in Table Mesa on the south end of town."

"I'll take your...or your aunt's word for it."

The auto traffic through the town of Estes Park crawled along, and Clay moved aggressively into a parking spot that had opened in front of the ice cream and candy store, his personal favorite. Julia gritted her teeth when two nearby cars honked their horns as Clay maneuvered the truck.

Clay pulled on the emergency brake. "We should get an ice cream cone to celebrate."

Julia laughed while she asked, "You mean because you got us here without getting in a wreck or because you successfully squeezed your truck into this parking space?"

"Well, I was thinkin' because we had a nice talk to get to know each other, but those other things are good, too." He chuckled, and she surprised him with a quick kiss on the cheek.

"I'll take a scoop of orange sherbet!" She beamed.

"Ooh, that's kinda' tart isn't it?"

"Maybe, but it's what I like."

"Then that's what you're goin' to get."

The crowd inside the shop mirrored the crowded streets and sidewalks, and the time that they had to spend acquiring their celebration cones took much of the fun out of consuming them. When they returned to the truck, Clay outlined his plan to drive to Rocky Mountain National Park and at least part of the way up Trail Ridge Road.

Julia embraced his plan at first, but she expressed some hesitation as they entered the broad meadows inside the Fall River entrance to the park. She surveyed a wide expanse of ominous clouds piling on top of the higher peaks of the mountain range that appeared before them.

"It'll be okay. Those are just afternoon rain clouds. It's the time of year when we get some storms."

"I know, but those clouds look pretty dark."

"We'll just go a little ways." Clay reassured Julia.

They followed a long line of cars up Trail Ridge Road. Thousands of people traveled hundreds of miles to make the same drive. Clay begrudgingly accepted his spot in the line, but he bypassed the first few pull out spots, each one stacked with cars and tourists. When he rounded Rainbow Curve, the traffic thinned, and only a few cars had pulled into the scenic overlook parking lot. Julia let him take her hand when she stepped from the truck, but he was forced to drop it as she paused to put on her sweater.

"It's not that cool." Clay remarked and swung an arm around her shoulders.

"I'm not a big tough guy like you."

"Oh, okay." Clay couldn't tell if she was being sarcastic, so he steered her toward the wall that marked the mountain's edge. "I always liked the view from this spot."

A stream glistened as it tumbled along a distant ridgeline miles away from the place where they stood. Directly across from them, a snow field plastered itself to the side of the mountain. The sun's rays could only penetrate the whiteness at the edges. Small rivulets formed on the downhill perimeter, but Clay felt certain that the snow would outlast the summer.

"Whatta' ya' think, will that snow field all melt in the next few weeks?"

"I don't know. What do you think?"

"I think no way." He stepped closer to the wall.

Several chipmunks poked their heads above the rocks and scurried toward the wall looking for some human crumbs, a celebration feast for another perfect summer's day and the wealth of tourist traffic that the day represented.

Contrails crisscrossed the sky overhead, and Clay followed one to the place where it disappeared behind a bank of storm clouds. He ignored the gathering darkness and scanned the mountainside across the road from the parking lot. He remembered a path he had climbed a few times. It provided a higher vantage point where the Fall River was visible.

Julia's presence energized him. "Hey, I got an idea. There's a trail across the road. It leads up to a place where we can see the river and more of the valley below. You've got your sneakers on, and your sweater, whatta' ya' say we try a little climb?"

"I don't know. I haven't done much of that."

"But I have. I've gone up this trail a lot of times." He exaggerated but spoke with certainty.

"Well, I guess." She hesitated but agreed.

Clay took her hand firmly as the trail traversed the mountainside. They both kept their focus on the rocks that formed the steps of their steady upward climb. After several minutes, their breathing became labored and their progress slowed. Eventually, Julia tugged them to a complete stop, and they stood atop an outcropping of rocks that formed a ledge.

Clay took a place close to Julia, and enjoyed the scenery from their new vantage point. He inhaled deeply, and Julia did the same. She leaned toward him, and when her shoulder touched his arm, her eyes glanced upward. Out of a background of deep black, his eyes flashed, and she gasped and ducked her head clutching his shirt sleeve.

In that instant, a jagged bolt of lightning struck behind them, and thunder roared. Clay pulled Julia closer. He wrapped his arms around her with an intensity that matched the ferocity of the lightning bolt. Just as suddenly, he gripped her upper arms in his hands, pushed her away and held her there at arm's length. He hunched his shoulders when another flash burned the air surrounding them.

He yelled, "We've got to get back! We have to go now, go as fast as we can!"

Clay grabbed one of her hands in his. He took a step down the path and soon quickened the pace. Julia screamed as the thunder sounded like the snap of a colossal whip driving them faster. Clay pulled her along, yelling as loud as he could to penetrate the violence of the storm with some reassurance.

"It's okay. Just keep moving!"

Julia heard only the roar of the storm. Fear pushed her from behind, and she pulled against Clay's hold, trying in desperation to maintain her balance. Then tears fell flooding her vision, and she lost her way. Clay clung to her hand, but his support felt more like a struggle to her. Finally, her feet slid out of control, and she hit the rocky ground.

She screamed again when Clay snatched her into his arms. In a blink, he held her tightly to his chest, like a father would hold a small child. He careened then, straight down the mountain, jumping from rock to rock. The rain came in huge drops spattering the rocks, and he dodged them like they were tacklers he was avoiding on a sprint down the middle of a football field.

Julia opened her eyes when Clay hit the pavement of the road and slid to a stop. He dropped her on her feet, and they ran to the truck. The few cars that had been parked there had already left the area. They skidded to the passenger side door. Clay flung it wide, and he lifted her while she half-jumped onto the seat. He slammed her door and circled the back of the truck.

When Clay threw open his door, a bold flash of light struck a ragged halo around his head. The force of the bolt stretched the whites of his eyes to the limits of their sockets, and then his pupils dilated even wider, engulfing the whites in pure blackness. Clay slumped forward then, his upper body dropping across the seat toward Julia.

Julia screamed, "Clay!"

She pulled on his arms and tugged at his belt. He did not respond when she yelled his name again. Then she opened her door, ran around the truck, and pushed against his dead weight with her shoulder leaning into his ass. The rain drenched both of them, and she struggled using all of her strength. Finally, his upper body slid forward, and she folded his legs under the steering wheel and closed his door.

Once she made her way to her side of the truck, she removed her soaked sweater. When she flung it behind the seat, she found a worn Army blanket there. She used it to cover Clay.

She dropped onto the floor of the truck and from her knees pushed on Clay's upper torso in order to turn him against the seat back. She scooted her butt onto the edge of the seat cushion and pinned him in that position. She then took his face in her hands and alternately patted and rubbed his cheeks. Cold to the touch, she trembled and fought against a feeling of desperation. The rain pounded relentlessly, and sobs of surrender surged from within her.

She lifted the blanket and draped it over her own shoulders. She covered Clay's upper body with hers and cuddled under the blanket, her cheek resting against his. She spoke his name repeatedly. She tucked the blanket further behind his back and used her free hand to rhythmically rub his chest. The stroking built some warmth within their blanket cocoon, and she heard him moan. Then he coughed and groaned audibly.

She rose to a sitting position, straddling the edge of the seat again. She re-positioned the blanket, swaddling Clay's upper body tightly. His facial muscles scrunched his eyes and then opened them. He blinked with bewilderment.

Julia explained in a quiet voice. "You took a hard shock, a bolt of lightning struck very close by."

The sound of drizzling rain accompanied Clay's sputtering response. "We didn't beat...the rain. Sorry."

"That just got us a little wet. You had me scared there for a while. I didn't know what to do."

Clay grabbed the top of the blanket. "Found my dad's old blanket."

"Yeah, you were cold. So was I." Julia shivered.

Clay poked an arm out of the blanket and used it to push himself upright.

Julia shifted toward the passenger's door as she asked, "You okay to do that."

"Guess so. I'm doin' it, anyway." He leaned a little but managed to maintain a position in the middle of the seat.

Clay then freed the blanket from underneath and behind him and extended the blanket toward Julia. "Here, let's both cover up with this."

She agreed with a smile, and once she felt tucked in, she closed her eyes. The rain storm settled to a slow pitter patter, and she rested in the warmth and safety of the truck with her head nestled on Clay's shoulder.

Some time passed, and a late afternoon sun returned. Clay slid behind the wheel. When they reached the town of Estes Park, he found a parking spot and told her to remain in the truck. He revealed the purpose of their stop, when he presented her with the sweatshirt and pants that he had purchased in one of the gift shops. The words *Estes Park* were screen-printed across the front of the shirt.

While she perused the things he gave to her, he explained. "Sorry about that...they all say somethin' on the front."

"That's okay, but I don't know why you got me these things. You didn't have to."

"Yeah, I did. Your clothes are soaked. We can go to the gas station, and you can use their bathroom to change."

"You don't have to do that either. You just drive. I can do it sitting right here, once we get through town."

As Clay shifted the truck into a lower gear to pull the hill that led out of town, Julia seized the opportunity to make the quick change.

She issued one command. "You just keep your eyes on the road for two minutes, Mr. Williams."

"Yes, ma'am," he replied with a quick affirmative nod.

When she accomplished the task and had stuffed her blouse and shorts into the shopping bag, she poked Clay. She spread her arms and stuck out her chest.

She sang. "Taah-daa!" And posed. "Pretty stylish, don't you think?"

"What'd you expect? I picked 'em out."

"Yeah, you're some kind of style king. I can see that."

"Wearin' my best jeans and t-shirt, can't you tell?"

"Actually, I did kind of figure that. My outfit was new too."

"Then we broke it in good today."

"Yeah, remind me not to wear any new clothes the next time..." She caught herself and hushed her voice. "I go somewhere with you."

Clay heard what he wanted to hear. "So that means you'll give me another chance? Really it's not my...not my usual way...to mess things up like I did today."

"I don't know Clay. We'll just have to see."

"Maybe I'll just come over and sit on your porch swing until you say okay."

She punched Clay in the arm. "Are you crazy? Don't do that. My parents won't like...Jim's coming home soon."

Clay stared plaintively at the road ahead and drove in silence. When they dropped below Barker Dam, he let the truck coast through the curves of the canyon into Boulder. The sun shone more brightly, as he made the turn from 9th street onto Cascade.

At the curb in front of Julia's house, she made a request. "Pull around the corner. I want to go through the back instead."

"Oh..." Clay just nodded and followed her instructions.

"Right here," Julia stated.

Clay stopped where the driveway sloped down to 7th Street. The garage that stood near the house was flanked by a wooden fence. A large maple tree shaded the entry gate to the backyard. Clay turned off the engine. "I like your garage. We don't have one at my house."

"Yes, thank you." Julia turned toward the garage as though she was seeing it for the first time, her tone more formal.

Clay spoke to the back of her head. "Do you think..." He cleared his throat. "Maybe I could call you?"

Even as she faced him, a dissonant air filled the cabin of the truck. Uncertainty darkened the day's end.

She answered with one word, "Maybe."

"But I don't know your phone number." Clay blurted helplessly.

"Clay..." Julia hesitated but held a steady gaze.

His eyes were clear and intense.

"Clay, you look like yourself again." She was certain of that, but little else. "I don't know, because you're you and I...We'll just have to see. That's all. We'll just have to wait."

Clay touched Julia's arm. "I can wait."

For another moment Julia held his eyes with hers, but when she turned away, Clay grabbed her arm. "Really, I can wait, but you got to know...got to know that I don't always mess things up. Really, I don't."

"It's okay. I know. I just want to..." She lifted his hand from her left arm.

Then she cradled his hand in both of hers. "We'll just have to see." She pulled him close and hugged him, then kissed his cheek and leaned away.

"I'm glad you're okay." She kissed his lips so sincerely that tears sparkled in her green eyes as she turned to go. "Goodbye, Clay."

She swung the door open, closed it without looking and trotted up the driveway.

Unwittingly, Clay had draped Julia in the drabbest of colors. He had purchased the smallest size sweat pants and sweatshirt, but they hung loosely on her body. Even more, she was unrecognizable in gray.

As the gate closed behind her, and the sun dipped below the foothills, he pulled away slowly and drove into the shadows. A shiver crossed his shoulders where his t-shirt still held some dampness from the day.

Chapter 7

Christmas 1962 to Summer 1968

Clay did not see Julia again that summer. In fact, the calendar read four days until Christmas when he next bumped into her. Snowflakes, like gossamer wafers made of the sheerest white cotton, floated past her face and puffed around her feet. She lowered her head while she made her way between the shops on Pearl Street, and Clay jogged across the street to intercept her.

"Oh, sorry." He brushed her side and feigned a stumble.

"Clay, what're you doing?"

"The same as you, I guess. A little Christmas shopping." He gave her a direct answer but hoped for something more. "Let me buy you a cup of coffee or hot chocolate. The diner down the street is probably not too crowded."

He held the door for her, and she waited just inside. He stomped his feet to kick some of the snow off his boots. The sound caught the attention of the lady working behind the counter.

"Okay, if we grab a booth?" Clay asked and the lady nodded her assent.

Clay helped Julia with the one bag that she had been carrying and her coat. He placed them in the booth on the seat next to the wall, and they slid into their seats across from each other.

The waitress took their order, hot chocolate for both. When she retreated behind the counter, Clay made a prediction. "I expect we'll get better service here than we did the last time we were together."

Clay remembered that day and held it close.

Julia's memory was a little different. "Oh, I didn't think the service was so bad, neither was the food. Grilled cheese, wasn't it?"

"Come to think of it, that could've been the high point of the day, or maybe those ice cream cones. Although I checked into it later, sherbet isn't really an ice cream. Anyway, I don't have a clear recollection about the rest of the day, except I remember seeing you in those silly sweats I got for you. I don't know what I was thinkin'."

"It's possible that you really weren't thinking at that point."

"I probably wasn't. Ya' know, I got knocked out a couple of times playin' football. It's a little spooky 'cause afterwards you don't remember things. The guys are tellin' you about stuff that happened and you just kinda' go along with it. Hopefully, you won the game so it was worth it in the end."

Clay paused as the waitress placed a mug of hot cocoa in front of each of them. The steam wafted from his mug. He acknowledged the service. "Thanks."

The waitress smiled as she left the table. Julia smiled at Clay's politeness, but he didn't notice.

He reflected on that day. "Was it worth it in the end? That day, I mean? Getting soaked and everything, I was pretty dumb."

"I don't know about that." Julia raised her mug, blew on the hot liquid, and sipped it.

While looking over the top of the mug, she admitted. "I know you really scared me. I was frantic there for a while."

"Sorry about that."

"It's okay, I was okay. I can take a little rain on me. It's you I was worried about." She took another sip. "You never came to see me after that. I did want to know if you were all right."

Clay sipped from his mug and warmed himself before answering. "The truth is I was scared, too. Scared that I made a fool outta' myself again. I know that's what you thought."

"Clay, you can't know that, can't know what I'm thinking. That's dumb."

"I know. I know. I just kinda' waited, thought I'd wait a little while. Then two-a-days started, then school. I was thinkin' I'd see you on campus sometime. But I never did. Anyway, I checked for a little while."

"What do you mean, you checked? Clay, that sounds freaky. You can't be checking on me."

"No, I mean, mostly I found Artie to see if he'd seen you, or Jim maybe."

"Then I guess you know." Julia peered into the mug of chocolate.

"Know what?" Clay wiggled in his seat.

"Artie didn't tell you? I quit school because..."

Clayed leaned over the table. "Really? You're jokin'! No, I didn't know. Artie stopped sayin' much. He just said that I should talk to Jim, but I didn't know. I was kinda' scared to do that. I didn't know if you had told him about that day. After a little while I stopped trying. I just kept thinking, what will be, will be. Ya' know, like the song?"

"Yes, Clay, I know the song. But, I guess you don't really know the other then, either."

"No, I have to admit that I don't know everything you think I should know."

Julia gulped a little too much hot chocolate. The heat gathered in her throat and caused her to cough.

"Take it easy there, little lady. Even I know you can't drink this stuff too fast." Clay tried for some humor, but his voice betrayed his nervousness. He tested his own cocoa.

Julia's eyes blinked a tear, and she dabbed the corner of each with a paper napkin. She wasted the effort to hide her emotions.

She blurted. "Jim and I got married."

The words shook Clay, and he slopped his hot chocolate. It gathered in a ring around the bottom of his mug when he set it on the table.

"Watch it!" He scolded himself but stared at Julia.

"Here, let me!" Julia pulled a few napkins from the dispenser and slipped them under Clay's mug.

As she lifted his mug, Clay blocked her motion with his own hand. Their hands tangled and the jostling spilled more of his chocolate, over her hand and onto the table. Startled by the liquid's temperature and the quick movements, Julia dropped Clay's mug. It landed upright on its bottom but even more chocolate jumped over its rim.

"Just let me do it." Clay snatched a wad of napkins and jammed them all around his mug. He barked. "I can clean up my own messes."

The waitress called to them from the counter. "You kids need some help?"

"No, I got it." Clay shook his head.

"No thanks." Julia confirmed.

She almost whispered her thoughts to Clay. "I'm sorry. I thought that you had probably heard, but you had no way of knowing."

"No that's okay. It's not your fault. I'm a little slow about...I waited too long." He busied himself with the mess he had made, smearing the wad of napkins in a circle, and pushing his mug and its nest of brown mush to the edge of the table.

Outside, the snow continued to fall. The flakes no longer floated but were driven by winter winds that swept down the canyon. Another day approached its end, and Clay's visage reflected in the diner's window, Clay by himself again.

"We should probably go," he murmured. "It's startin' to pile up out there."

The waitress cleared the table and used a wet cloth to wipe the remnants of the spill. "Yeah, they say we might get nearly a foot out of this storm. You finished, too, miss?"

"Yes ma'am."

"Here's your check. You kids be careful going home."

Clay rose from his place and pulled a few dollar bills and some coins from his pocket. He placed three dimes and two dollar bills on the table atop the ticket.

"That should take care of the lady. It was good service."

"Yes, it was. Thanks." Julia agreed.

Clay helped Julia with her long, woolen coat and suggested that she use the hood. "The wind's pickin' up out there."

"What about you?" Julia wondered aloud.

She brightened with the question and reached inside her shopping bag. "Here, I've got something for you...a scarf. You need more than that little jacket. I got it for my dad, but he's already got plenty of them. You should have it."

She wrapped the charcoal gray scarf around Clay's neck, tied it in the front and threw the ends over his shoulders. "There, that should do you."

Clay responded as he reached for the knot. "Julia, I can't take your dad's gift."

He realized once again that he waited too long, when Julia stopped him. "No, I want you to have it. I know you're a big, strong athlete and everything, but I want it this way. And... hey..."

"But..." Clay tugged at the knot. "It's weird."

Julia grabbed his arm. "Wait a minute! I don't remember anything about you making any big plays in football. What happened with you, in football I mean?"

"I'm just a freshman, remember? Freshman, don't play varsity. Just watch next year."

"Oh, I see. Okay."

"I mean it. Come to a game next year. Jim can bring you. Even married guys like football." He chuckled, warming now.

She responded with a smile. "Okay, we will."

"Then I'll have the chance to give you back this scarf."

"You better not, or I'll have to give that sweatshirt back to you."

"You still have it?"

"Yes I do. But I won't keep it unless you keep the scarf." She liked the banter, liked the feel of it and gave him one more instruction. "Now, give me a hug. I got to go. That ranch road gets slippery when it's like this, especially after dark."

"I could give you a ride."

"No, no, I can drive." She insisted with a laugh. "Besides...."

This time he interrupted her. "Besides, you've probably ridden with me enough."

"I didn't want to say anything. I'm tryin' to be nice."

"I always said that you're way too nice."

She rose to her tiptoes and leaned toward him. He responded by lifting her in his arms. He held onto the joy, a precious gift.

When they separated, she spoke first. "This was nice, too. It was nice to see you again."

He turned her shoulders to usher her outside. He vowed silently to remember his delight in the way this day had ended.

When they stepped onto the sidewalk, she turned to face him. This time he spoke first. "I'll keep lookin' for you from time to time. You take care."

With two long strides, Clay found himself running straight into the wind. He held his head against the swirling snow, squinting in order to see, but the cold could not reach him.

In May of 1963 Julia gave birth to a little girl. Jim and she named her Terry Marie. Jim's grandfather died two months later, and Jim was forced to sell the ranch in order to settle a lien for past-due property taxes and pay the inheritance taxes.

The remaining balance they placed in a savings account for their daughter's college education.

They moved from the ranch house into town. Julia's parents had purchased income property years before, a rental home on the northwest side of Boulder. They offered it to Jim and Julia, a place their daughter and her family could call home.

In the fall, Julia and Jim attended two CU football games. Clay started at linebacker in that first year of Eddie Crowder's coaching tenure, and his potential to be a top tier player was evident to Jim. Jim identified Clay's physical strength, quickness and aggressiveness as his best qualities. They both laughed, when Jim described Clay's in-your-face style of play. They knew Clay used that same approach in off-the-field situations, too.

Jim graduated from CU in May of 1964. His friend, Arthur, received honorary acknowledgement at the commencement. He and his sister, Sally, still Julia's best friend, celebrated with Jim and Julia that evening, while Julia's parents cared for Terry.

Jim and Julia spent the first part of the summer in Boulder, a season that deepened their love and wrapped them in a profound peace. In August, Jim moved his family to Texas, the base of this first assignment as a second lieutenant in the U.S. Army. Over the course of the next three years, they made temporary homes in Texas, North Carolina, California, and eventually back in Colorado.

In each place they sought the comfort and serenity that they had come to know in Boulder. Jim took his training in the waging of war, the schooling of battle, but did not allow that learning to permeate the interior of his home. There, he read stories, played games and guitar, sang funny tunes to his infant daughter, and sang love songs to his wife. He strived for peace, but the war in Vietnam raged all around him.

In mid-summer 1967, Jim's company received its orders to join the fight. On his scheduled departure day, Julia arose early with him. Jim and she had agreed that they would say their good-bye's inside their home. Terry slept and Jim slipped into her room for a quiet kiss. At the door, Julia pressed close to him. No matter how far or how long, her love reached out for him.

Jim wrote letters to her, regularly at first, but when the weeks turned into months, his letters became fewer, the words and their meaning more distant. Near the one-year anniversary of the day he shipped out, Julia received Jim's last letter. He described how he had begun marking the days in his notebook, the days until he would come home.

In the end no letter appeared at all. A captain, a staff officer from a Fort Carson Operations Unit, made a personal visit instead. Julia invited him into their home, and they sat facing one another. Terry was spending the afternoon at a neighbor's playing with a friend, so Julia offered the captain an iced tea.

The captain took a sip before speaking. "Ma'am, your husband..."

"Jim..." Julia interrupted because she sensed what the captain was going to say.

She wanted badly to know that someone remembered his name, remembered him in the way she did.

The captain's voice stated with formality and finality. "Yes, Lieutenant Karsten, fulfilled his service commitment with distinction. He was a fine officer, defending his country, his family, our freedom, our way of life, and he died in the line of duty."

In the strange silence that followed the captain's statement, Julia struggled for an adequate response. Instead, she rose from her chair and the captain stood with her. Without a word, she ushered him out the door.

Soon, she wept openly. Wrapping her arms tightly around her torso, she squeezed the ache from the depths of her person. Her cries had been building over the months since Jim had left. Now that she would never hold him again, she could no longer hold the tears in, either. She dropped to her knees, her eyes flashing, and she yearned for a prayer. She longed to know a God who would answer her. She knew one truth about war now. True peace she could not remember.

At the grave side service, the Army Chaplain used the same types of words in similar combinations and phrases as the captain from Fort Carson. The first round of rifle shots stunned Julia. She flinched as the second and third rounds boomed over Logan Cemetery.

Her daughter cried aloud. "Mommy, make them stop. Daddy's gone."

Julia's father lifted his granddaughter into his arms. He held his hand over one of her ears and pressed her head onto his shoulder to shelter her from the blasts. At the conclusion of the service, Julia hugged her family and each of her friends, Jim's friends. One by one they agreed to leave her there.

"I just want a little time alone, just a little more time." She convinced her parents, too. "I'm okay really. Mom, Dad...I'll come by your house to pick up Terry. Maybe she will take a nap on the way home."

As Julia dropped to her knees near the gravestone, tears mixed with mascara and stained the white slab. She stayed there for some time and recited a litany, out of sequence, a rambling prayer. She remembered everything about Boulder and the way they had come together, the coffee house, the ranch, his guitar, his songs, the campus, their home, the foothills, his laughter, his sincerity, his hope, and his loving way.

She stood to take in a wider view, as though she could see across the plains, across the ocean, and the entire planet. Finally, she blew a good-bye kiss to Jim and whispered, "We should've never left."

At peace, she drove home to Boulder.

Chapter 8

St. Louis, 1966

Luke met Elizabeth in the springtime. They were seventeen, living with their families in Middle America. Safe and sheltered, their only uncertainty was how they would find each other at the Moonlight Ballroom on teen nights.

They danced with each other when the band played a slow song. Luke adjusted his six-foot two-inch frame when he took Elizabeth into his arms. She rested her head on his shoulder, while he tilted his head to touch his cheek to hers.

At times, the movements of their dance caused strands of Luke's light brown hair to fall across his forehead. When the song ended, Elizabeth would use her fingertips to brush the strands into place. The tenderness of her touch compelled Luke to respond, and he squeezed her hand in his, signaling a sweet desire to hold her again.

When they separated he would re-convene with his friend, Ted, and she would find the friends who had accompanied her to the ballroom. For Luke and Elizabeth, teen nights were not date nights, only an implied agreement to meet. Elizabeth saved the slow songs, anticipating that Luke would ask her to dance. He rarely disappointed. What they came to know of one other, they learned one slow dance at a time.

During the fast tempo rock 'n roll songs, Elizabeth often danced with one of her girl friends. In St. Louis, just like other parts of the country, girls danced with girls because guys would not learn the steps, or could not master the rhythms required for the swing dance.

Luke believed that Elizabeth practiced the Imperial, a St. Louis adaptation of the eastern swing, as much as he practiced the moves he used on the basketball court. He hoped that Elizabeth might see him play basketball at some point in the future, and that she would enjoy seeing him perform as much as he enjoyed seeing her dance.

Elizabeth whirled around the floor, and her long, auburn hair accentuated her movements. She tied pastel, satin ribbons in her hair, an uncommon style when most of her friends used barrettes or head bands. The crystal-like clarity of her blue eyes, the pleasing features of her smiling face, and the supple shape of her slender body, attracted Luke like the magnetic force that pulls a young planet into the orbit of a new star.

Elizabeth surprised Luke when she invited him to her school's prom. She attended Mary Magdalene High School, a Catholic, all-girls school, and, according to the school's tradition, each girl invited her escort. Junior prom was their first date, and they danced to all the slow songs, an embrace that deepened throughout the night.

At the end of the night, when he walked her to the front door of her family's home, she stood on the top step of the porch. From his position on the step below, he wrapped his arms around her waist. As they kissed good night, he gently lifted her, and they fell for each other, the subtlety of love's first unfolding.

Throughout the summer of 1966, their relationship evolved. Sometimes they spent the evening at her house, and she played albums on the stereo. They sat on the front porch steps and talked about the new songs that they had heard on the radio. Luke would describe how he practiced for the coming basketball season, his senior year, and perhaps his last opportunity to excel.

Elizabeth recounted stories of the young children and other teenagers that swam at the community pool where she was the lifeguard. The day she saved an eight-year-old boy from drowning she expressed, for the first time, the idea of becoming a nurse. She interpreted that incident as a calling, and her conviction pulled Luke closer.

Frequently, they spent their evenings at a neighborhood park or Forest Park. Even after attending a movie at the Esquire Theater, their favorite movie house, they planned for time afterwards to go to Forest Park.

Forest Park held many attractions, including the world renowned St. Louis Zoo, the city Art Museum, an outdoor theater known as the Muny Opera, many memorials, lakes and picnic areas. Luke and Elizabeth chose the stone wall that traversed the top of the hill overlooking the American Legion Fountain as their preferred destination.

Seated on the wall and watching the colored lights splashing in the fountain waters, they discussed the movies they had seen. They enumerated stories about their families and their close friends. The personalities of the people who were important to them came to life in those stories. The frustrations, the celebrations, the commonplace, and the extraordinary, all were illuminated.

When the school year began and autumn shortened the days, Luke and Elizabeth spoke on the telephone more than in-person, and about more than themselves.

They discussed Venus, the evening and the morning star, often the brightest object in the night sky. Elizabeth explained how the concept made sense, because Venus, being closer to the sun than the Earth, could appear at a point in the sky near the rising or the setting sun. She and her senior classmates had heard a lecture at the St. Louis Planetarium.

Luke quoted a Carl Sandburg poem, a reading assignment for his senior composition class. He remembered one line, *I cried for beautiful things knowing no beautiful things last*. They studied both the science and the art and tried to understand how these ideas might influence their lives.

Elizabeth clipped a picture from the daily newspaper and taped it inside her school locker. The photograph showed Luke, along with two of his high school teammates. The associated article predicted a winning season for their basketball team, even though they competed in a conference comprised of the largest, suburban public schools.

On Christmas Eve they attended Midnight Mass. During the drive to Elizabeth's parish church, Luke shared with her aspects of his beliefs and those of his family's. He explained the commitment he and his brothers had made to their parents, how they attended religion classes once a week. His parents couldn't afford to send them to parochial high school, but they believed that ongoing instruction in Catholic teachings were vital to their children's education.

Based on what he had learned about the doctrines of the Second Vatican Council, Luke expected that even the High Mass liturgy of Christmas services would be presented in the English language. Prayers that Elizabeth and he had learned as children, they learned again. They prayed together for the first time that night and understood at least some of the meanings.

That winter Elizabeth did attend one of Luke's basketball games. The opponent that night was the public school located nearest to Elizabeth's home. Although Luke played well, the team lost. Afterwards, she waited for him in the lobby of the gymnasium, and they spoke briefly. He adhered to the team rules and rode the bus back to his school. She blew a kiss in his direction, as the bus left the parking lot. Her actions became the source of the good-natured joking Luke had to endure during the early portion of the trip.

Basketball season ended when Luke's team lost in the finals of the Regional Tournament. Soon afterwards, spring burst forth, and the dances of a new season lifted them.

They glided through graduation. His potential manifested by excellence in academics and athletics. The fine, lace gown Elizabeth wore for the Mary Magdalene ceremony presaged the evolution of her free and fanciful spirit. They celebrated their release, their elevation to another stage of life.

They felt an excitement, like breaking through the soil and experiencing the sun and rain for the first time, seedlings sprouting from a broad plain but close enough to see each other. They had been taught the gender of pronouns and given the sex of education, but they did not know what to expect, so they expected everything. They shared what was especially theirs to share.

―――――――

The summer of 1967 became known as the Summer of Love. The national media focused their reporting on the Haight-Ashbury neighborhood of San Francisco where a haven of hippies congregated. It was estimated that they numbered as many as 100,000. Psychedelic music provided the background and psychoactive drugs the impetus for their communal lifestyle, the self-proclaimed birthplace of free love.

One evening in July, Luke watched the video clips on the evening news with his father and wondered how to interpret his father's comments. His father verbally admonished the young people for what they were doing, but all the while, he maintained a broad grin on his face.

Luke chuckled as he described the scene to Elizabeth later that night. They sat on the wall above the fountain. A strong breeze carried a watery mist and cooled them.

Luke enjoyed sharing stories about his father. "I know he doesn't like the clothes, definitely not the music. I'm sure he prefers a bottle of beer. But, when Walter Cronkite started talking back and forth with a local reporter about the topic of free love, that's when my dad's face lit up."

Luke concluded with a question. "During the commercial, he told me that there's nothing free about love, except for the giving of it. What do you suppose he meant by that?"

Elizabeth answered by kissing Luke's cheek. "I don't know, except maybe your dad's a philosopher."

Luke bumped her. "You know he's an auto mechanic."

She poked his arm. "That's just what he does during the day. At night he's a philosopher."

"And a lover." Luke blushed as he spoke the words.

"Well, he's got five kids." Elizabeth grinned at Luke's demeanor.

"Four handsome boys and one pretty little girl." Luke played along.

"I don't know about all four boys." Elizabeth hugged Luke and whispered in his ear. "I can only vouch for one."

Luke's cheeks flushed again. He paused in her arms, and then leaned back to respond. Before he could say anything, a flash of lightning struck in his peripheral vision. He ducked his head as though dodging a punch.

"Whoa, what the!" He exclaimed then realized what he had seen.

A clap of thunder reverberated overhead, and another lightning bolt hit the lake situated at the bottom of the hill and across the street from the fountain.

"We gotta' go!" He yelled as he flipped his legs around and hopped off of the wall.

He grabbed Elizabeth's hand, and when a second stanza of thunder rolled like the sound of mallets playing the timpani, he squeezed it tightly.

"As fast as we can," he instructed her. "I forgot to tell you. The weather man predicted severe storms."

Luke walked at such a quick pace Elizabeth had to jog to stay along side of him. He regretted his earlier decision to park near the Art Museum. At the time, he thought they would just sit in the car with windows rolled down and listen to the radio. Elizabeth suggested that they walk, and an unspoken desire brought them to their favorite place.

He led her along a gravel path that was the most direct route to the bottom of the hillside. When they reached the sidewalk that bordered the street, sheets of rain met them. The downpour gathered gale force winds. Luke extended one arm over the back of Elizabeth's shoulders, and they stopped for a moment, as though they would huddle and wait out the storm.

She screeched when lightning scorched the sky with a violent light. He grabbed her hand again.

"We need to run!" He cried out over a giant roar of thunder, and the sky pitched black.

Nearby street lamps popped and turned dark. Luke loped, and Elizabeth ran with him. They sloshed their way toward an intersection. His instincts told him it was just ahead.

A car's headlights slowly turned through that intersection and shone a path through the pouring rain. He hoped the street lights still worked in the section of the park that lay ahead, but when the car's tail lights disappeared, total darkness erased that hope.

They splashed through the intersection and kept moving, although Luke slowed their pace. He knew that Elizabeth swam laps at the pool prior to beginning of her lifeguard duty, but he hadn't envisioned the need to test her physical conditioning, certainly not with this type of obstacle course.

Another set of car lights crept from behind them. As the car passed them, its horn sounded, a belated warning of inclement weather. Its lights made the bend in the street and climbed the hill that they would need to take to the Art Museum's parking lot.

"Not much further." Luke sprayed the words of encouragement, but Elizabeth kept her head down.

He released her hand, and she took it as a signal. She set a slower pace as they climbed the hill. The rain thoroughly drenched them, and Luke acted on a notion brought to the surface by a strange sense of chivalry. He unbuttoned his shirt and looped it over Elizabeth's shoulders as though it were a cloak. She resisted his gesture, but he held it in place with one arm across her back.

When he opened the car door, she gave him his shirt and slid into the car. The force of the rain diminished, but the wind still swirled. Luke dropped into the driver's seat.

One lucky aspect came to his mind as he rolled the window to close the two-inch gap he had left at the top. When they parked in the lot nearest the fountain, they would usually leave the windows wide open. Tonight, they had closed the windows, except for the small gap, which Elizabeth also closed on her side of the car.

Another piece of good fortune came to mind, and he described it to Elizabeth, as he reached into the back seat.

"Yesterday was laundry day, so my mom washed the t-shirt, sweatshirt, and towel I usually take to school when I go to play those pick-up games of basketball that I've told you about."

Luke switched on the dome light of the car and handed Elizabeth a neat stack made of all three items. "You can dry off, and then choose which shirt you want. They're all clean, really."

Elizabeth smiled for the first time. "Remind me to send a thank-you note to your mother."

She pinched her shorts and her blouse. When she did, water oozed between her fingertips. She sighed, and tears mixed with the beads of rain that still covered her face.

She lifted the towel from the stack and pressed her face into it. The covering muffled her cry. "I was really afraid."

"It was kind of scary there for a little bit." Luke dabbed his face with the driest part of this shirt.

"Please...never again." Elizabeth smoothed the ends of her hair with the towel, patted her face again, and handed the towel to Luke.

"I promise." Luke spoke the words as though they were a vow.

He used the towel to dry his face and hair. When he finished, he peered past the towel where Elizabeth unbuttoned her blouse. She draped his clean t-shirt and sweatshirt over the back of the seat. Unconsciously, he did the same with the towel and his wet shirt, and then switched off the dome light. Elizabeth scooted next to Luke. She touched his bare shoulder and stroked his neck.

After she kissed him, her breath warmed his lips with the faintest of phrasings. "I love...your way...love you."

He opened his eyes as if by seeing her he would know for certain what she had said. She wiggled out of her blouse and unhooked her bra. Both fell to the seat, and she pushed them behind her, her eyes trained on him. She sensed tension in her nipples, and he shifted in the seat, stiffening where heat rose from deep inside of him.

An electric charge arced between them, when she brushed the side of his face. He followed the line of her arm and grasped her wet and tangled hair. He pulled her close, and his fingertips plunged into the wildness.

Their two hearts wrapped together then, swallowing the heavens like a virulent thunderstorm. They reveled in their own summer of love.

Chapter 9

Late summer to Christmas, 1967

Early on a Friday morning in late August Luke departed St. Louis. His brother, Mark, dropped him at the downtown bus station. Luke gripped Mark's shoulder as a form of good-bye, and Mark did the same with an expression of good-luck. The bus trip took Luke across the state of Missouri, west, and finally north to Flint, Kansas.

He traveled a road that narrowed as it wound its way, first on the Interstate, then a state highway, and finally a county road. At the end of the line he found himself on the campus of Oakwood College for the second time. He had visited for a weekend during the spring semester of his senior year in high school.

When the Oakwood admissions department offered him a scholarship and arranged a student loan to provide the financial means for his attendance, they made his decision easy. Complimentary statements by the head coach about his basketball skills and how he could contribute to the Oakwood Cardinals' future success clinched it for him. His parents allowed him to make the decision, and he decided on a small college in eastern Kansas where he would study liberal arts and play college basketball.

When he unpacked that first afternoon, he chose again: the lower bunk and the gray metal dresser. Other young men scurried in and out of rooms and the various entrances of the men's dormitory. His roommate's arrival had apparently been delayed, so he arranged his clothes and room accessories according to his own plan. The spiral bound notebooks and a small box of pens and pencils he stacked on top of one of the two look-alike desks, the one nearest the window.

After a final survey of his room, he took the hallway that led to the front entrance. He nodded a hello to a few guys along the way, deciding not to offer a handshake introduction unless the other guy initiated it. He chose a packaged meal, crackers with a layer of peanut butter between each set of two, and a Coke from the vending machine before returning to his room.

With his back propped against the wall and cushioned by a pillow, he scanned a book of modern poetry. It was a gift from Elizabeth, and he reviewed the section devoted to Carl Sandburg to find the poem they had discussed. He read it and others by Sandburg, Robert Frost, and poets whose work was not as familiar.

As the sunlight faded from the room, he changed out of his travel clothes into a t-shirt and sweat pants. He grabbed a towel and walked to the common lavatory located at the back of the building. Florescent lights burned brightly overhead, and Luke blinked several times as he walked to the end wash basin. The tile floor felt cool on his bare feet.

At the basin two spots away from his, another guy, whom he assumed was also a freshman, brushed his teeth. Luke had trouble adjusting the water temperature, eventually causing water to splash out of the basin and onto the front of his pants.

His lavatory neighbor spit toothpaste foam into the basin and turned toward Luke with a broad smile, toothpaste still dripping from the corner of his mouth. He licked his lips before he spoke.

"These faucets are a little touchy." He motioned with his hands, pointing out a wet spot on the front of his shorts. "Maybe we'll get some hints during orientation tomorrow."

Since his neighbor wore only a pair of gym shorts, Luke noticed immediately the large scar across the front of his right shoulder.

Luke gestured toward the scar. "Tough summer?"

"Actually, a tough year, I had the first surgery last fall and it took them a while to figure out that it didn't work, so they cut again about eight weeks ago. At least I'm back to brushing my teeth with my right hand. Should be able to take notes during class too. But no more football, at least that's what the doctors are saying." A knowing smile prefaced his summary. "Guess I won't get the chance to be a star in college after all."

Luke sympathized. "Some say that part's overrated anyway."

"Yeah, I'll just rely on my good looks to get all the girls." He laughed then.

"As long as you keep your shirt on, that scar could scare them away."

"Unless I tell them I got wounded in the war."

"Think that's a good idea? I thought the war wasn't all that popular, especially on college campuses."

"This is Kansas, my friend, not California."

"You have point there."

Luke enjoyed the interaction, so when his wash basin neighbor extended his hand, he mirrored that move.

"I'm Jerrod Holt."

"Luke Aurmann, nice to meet you."

"You a freshman, too?" Jerrod gathered his things.

"My guess is a lot of us that arrived today are." Luke nodded.

"Maybe I'll see you tomorrow."

"Probably, orientation starts at eight-thirty, right?"

"But we get breakfast if we come early." Jerrod reminded Luke.

"You can count on me for that part at least." Luke felt hungry.

"Then I'll see you there." Jerrod's blonde hair fell into his eyes.

The overhead light in Luke's room, also a fluorescent fixture, cast too much light, and Luke made a plan to find a store where he could purchase a desk lamp. A faint breeze drifted through the window screen, carrying the last rays of daylight. He pulled his desk chair close to the window.

He wrote a letter to Elizabeth, the first of countless ones that he would address to her. His feelings rolled across the page, borne by a new ball point pen and careful penmanship. He strived to make his letter perfect. He shared some of his reading from the book of poetry, in particular Robert Frost's *Road Not Taken*. He finished when he underlined the words, *for me it's been you who has made all the difference*. He signed the pages, *Yours Forever*.

———————

Elizabeth walked a path at the neighborhood park on Saturday morning. The sunny, hot day lifted her in its arms, like Luke had done so many times throughout that summer. She remembered picnic places, parks and park people, quiet conversations, tender embraces, heart-racing excitations, and wild expectations. She touched him and he held her, a bloom bursting, fragrant and full. She knew she could not forget.

A black man played guitar boldly. He was propped on the end of a picnic table, and the sunlight flashed in his face. A stranger to her, she imagined him as someone who had driven across the city to find a park bench to his liking. He played a blues melody, and she listened without him knowing. He rocked with the rhythm of his music, and his lyrics told the story of love that he had once known. His song conducted the power of the day, her own love story, a story just beginning.

On Sunday morning she went to church with her family and asked for grace to fill her heart, Luke's too. She started her college career the next day.

On the campus of St. Louis College, she found the nursing department office in the building that housed the biology and natural sciences departments. The speaker at the morning freshman orientation had suggested that each student choose an advisor from the faculty of their intended major area of study. Pamela Fisher, a new faculty member, who was also working on an advanced degree at Washington University, became Elizabeth's advisor. Miss Fisher and Elizabeth arranged to meet that afternoon at 1:30 p.m.

Having completed what she deemed as her first assignment, Elizabeth chose a slower pace and headed toward the campus cafeteria. The walkways were crowded, and the endless stream of unfamiliar faces lulled her into a daydream, an image of Luke and her on a path through Forest Park.

She wondered aloud about him. "It's his first day of classes."

"Oh no! No! Classes don't start until Wednesday. Yes, Wednesday the thirty-first, that's what it says here." A red-haired girl, shorter than she, stepped in front of Elizabeth, poking a piece of paper that she held between them.

Elizabeth stopped. "Well, yes, you're right. I was just thinking... thinking of something...someone else. Yes, Wednesday's right."

The redhead lowered the piece of paper and stepped aside. Elizabeth took a step, but the redhead then grabbed her arm.

"We need to pick out the classes we want to take, from this book." A scowl of determination crossed her face as she thrust a course catalogue toward Elizabeth.

"Maybe, but I think we're supposed to talk to our advisor first."

"You have one?" The redhead's face brightened.

"Yes, Miss Fisher. She's new to the nursing department."

"Me, too." The redhead dropped the book in her excitement. "I mean I'm going to be a nurse. I mean, study to be a nurse. You too?" She picked the book off the pavement.

Elizabeth stepped away from her. "Are you asking if I want to be a nurse?"

"Yeah, what do you think?" The redhead brushed a sleeve over the book's cover.

"I'm pretty sure I do." Elizabeth grinned. "But I'm pretty sure you talk too fast, too."

"That's just my way, but it doesn't mean I can't be a good nurse." The redhead extended her hand. This time it was empty. "I'm Debbie McManus."

Elizabeth shook her hand. "Elizabeth Donahue."

"Good." Debbie skipped forward in her mind. "Now that we know each other, maybe we can study together, for nursing I mean."

"I guess," Elizabeth mumbled, and Debbie raced away before Elizabeth expressed her one concern. "I don't know if we're in the same class."

As it happened, they were enrolled in the same biology class, and they agreed on the first day of classes to be lab partners. In the nursing class that they shared, they made a pact to study together. Although she didn't exhibit a level of excitement that matched Debbie's, Elizabeth walked confidently to the bus stop at the end of the day.

As the bus route crossed the city, Luke crossed her mind. She hoped that he had found a friend like she had found Debbie. In fact, she credited Luke with engendering the circumstances that led to her meeting Debbie on the day of orientation.

That night she wrote a letter to him. She ended it with the words that described her feelings. *I rode the bus today. That's a lot like high school. But today, it felt like flying. You are a part of it.* She signed the page, *As Always, Elizabeth*.

On Christmas Eve, Luke arrived at Elizabeth's house just before 10:00 p.m. He adjusted his tie in the rear view mirror of the family car. As he stepped onto the porch, he unbuttoned his coat and smoothed the front of his v-neck sweater.

Mrs. Donahue greeted him with a Merry Christmas. Elizabeth's younger sister smiled and said hello from the place where she stood near the hallway that led to the back of the house.

"I'll tell Elizabeth, you're here." She left without waiting for an acknowledgement.

Mrs. Donahue offered Luke a soda to drink and a place to sit on the sofa. As she sat next to him, she asked about his family and spoke about her family's plans for a gathering and Christmas dinner. Luke nodded as she reported on Elizabeth's first semester grades and responded briefly when she asked about his.

He explained why he had to leave on Christmas afternoon to return to Oakwood. The holiday basketball tournament would start on the 28th so the team needed to be back for a few days of practice. His biggest regret would be missing his family's dinner, but he was happy that Elizabeth and he could be together for Christmas Eve.

As the time lapsed he grew nervous, so when Elizabeth entered the room, he leapt to his feet.

"Hi, Luke." She almost sighed.

"Hello." He beamed as Elizabeth closed the space between them.

"Sounds like Luke might have done a little better than you with his college classes." Mrs. Donahue summarized.

"That doesn't surprise me. I told you he always does well in school."

"But college is different. And besides he's been so far from home. You know how we moms worry."

"Oh, Mom, we're growing up." Elizabeth pulled her mother toward the hallway.

Her mother twisted to make a final point. "Be sure to give your mother an extra big hug before you leave."

"I will." Luke allowed his voice to carry down the hall.

When Elizabeth returned, she had another suggestion. "You can give me a hug, too."

Then she kissed him and apologized. "Sorry to leave you with mom for so long. Hope it wasn't too weird."

"No, she's a lot like my mom."

"I need to finish wrapping some gifts. Wait for just another minute." Elizabeth motioned for Luke to sit again.

She re-entered the room and placed a stack of gift boxes on the sofa next to him. She skipped to the stereo and chose two Christmas albums to accompany their work.

Luke assisted her with a strategically placed finger where the ribbon needed to be pressed while she tied a bow. After they finished their task, Elizabeth arranged the packages under the Christmas tree.

She held out another elaborately wrapped package that she had retrieved from its spot under the tree. "Merry Christmas."

"Wait!" Luke declared too loudly as he took the package from her, nearly sprinting to the coat tree near the door.

He snatched a small package from the inside pocket of his coat. He extended his hand to her. "Merry Christmas."

They sat next to one another on the sofa to open their gifts. Luke struggled with the ribbon that decorated his gift, so Elizabeth succeeded in opening hers first. She raised the necklace out of the box. Two small stars formed from solid gold hung at the end of the fine gold strand. She let it dangle against her red blouse. Her eyes glistened like the polished gold.

"Luke, it's beautiful!" She kissed his cheek. "Here let me help you."

She stretched the ribbon so it would slip off the end of his gift box.

He nodded. "It looked so pretty, I didn't know what to do."

"Just pull on it, silly. Then tear the paper. That's the fun part." She giggled.

The cream-colored shirt matched the heather colors woven into the burgundy crew neck sweater. She apologized that the color of the sweater was not the red of the Oakwood Cardinals, but she liked the combination anyway.

"I like it, too." Luke agreed.

"Good. You'll be so handsome. You have to promise me that you'll tell those Oakwood girls that you already have a girlfriend."

"Don't worry. I only have eyes for you."

"That's the right thing to say. Now help me with my necklace. It'll be perfect for tonight."

She turned her back to him and held her hair atop her head so that he could see the clasp of the necklace. When he had it fastened, she lifted the round collar of her blouse and slid the necklace under it. The stars twinkled against a red background.

They celebrated the gift exchange with a toast, eggnog with the added kick of Irish whiskey mixed according to Mr. Donahue's family recipe. With their spirits warmed, they left for church. The last verse of *I'll Be Home for Christmas* played on the stereo as Luke closed the door.

He parked the car along the street, a discreet distance from the church. When he switched off the headlights and turned off the engine, a moment of quiet anticipation enveloped both of them. It ended in a passionate kiss. Their long embrace fogged the car windows.

Arm in arm, they entered the church. In the midst of the high mass liturgy, they dreamed. They followed the rites and recited the congregational responses with a modicum of conscious effort.

In the sideways glances, in the candlelight reflecting from their eyes, when they clasped hands and interlaced their fingers, they shared a more intense faith. They formed the outward signs of their most fervent prayers, two young souls at peace, and two young hearts in love.

Chapter 10

Spring, 1968 to Spring, 1970

Luke's letters traced the pattern of his first year of college experience. Elizabeth opened them with an excitement that matched the opening of gifts at Christmas. He usually included a report about progress in his classes. Elizabeth suspected he must copy those portions to his parents. She scanned those paragraphs and focused her attention on the other sections.

Those sections told the tale of his evolving friendships and the exploits he shared with those friends. The names of Jerrod *Jerr* Holt, Charles Baker *Bake* Harrison, and Martin *Marty* Teller found their way to his pages on a regular basis.

Jerrod and he had three classes in common. They taught each other in those classes, and Jerrod introduced Luke to some new kinds of music. Bake played on the basketball team with Luke but was also an outstanding football player and had already proven himself on that field of play. Marty was a math and science wizard and applied some of his magic to the everyday and out-of-the-ordinary situations that involved their band of friends.

Other letters recounted basketball games and the bus trips traveling to other colleges, a few of which required several hours drive time. The overnight stays in motels or boarding houses provided the backdrop for additional adventures. He related specific plays accomplished during the games when he contributed with a key basket, a pass, or a defensive play.

After the conclusion of basketball season, he described how he had allowed his hair to grow longer, but not as long as Jerrod's. Some called Jerrod a hippie. Marty bought bell-bottom blue jeans at a shop in Kansas City on one of their group's expeditions into the city. He started to smoke a pipe, and Luke intimated that Marty's pipe could be used for more than just tobacco.

Marty puffed jokes and chronicled the escapades of the four-man team comprised of Luke, Jerrod, Bake, and himself. When he re-enacted the stories to a wider audience of campus friends, the sound of laughter rolled around the circle, followed closely by a passing of the pipe.

Luke wove his feelings into the pages too. As the days warmed, he reflected on their picnics and described his anticipation of the way the summer Sunday afternoons might unfold for them. He filled the space, the physical distance that separated them, there in the lines of his letters.

Throughout that summer, Elizabeth and he found comfort in the picnic places they chose, shady spots in Forest Park. They relaxed on a blanket and linked hands. In their keen attention to one another, a virtual cocoon developed around them, even sheltering them from the tumultuous events that incited many of their generation.

They didn't feel the heat from the violent race riots that swept across the nation in the summer of 1968. Race riots had ignited in early April, shortly after the assassination of Martin Luther King Jr., and the flames of outrage leapt from city to city. From Washington, D.C. to Los Angeles, from April to August, the fires eventually affected over 100 cities.

Political turmoil also added to the pervasive unrest of that time. Robert Kennedy's assassination in June shocked the psyche of the country and opened wounds, still unhealed, from his brother's, President John Kennedy's, assassination five years earlier.

The military escalation of the war in Vietnam, ordered by then President Johnson, spawned a proportionate growth in the ferocity of the anti-war movement. These forces confronted one another at the end of August in Chicago, the site of the Democratic National Convention. Battlefield scenes were broadcast on the nightly news. Chicago police and the Illinois National Guard pitted against crowds of young demonstrators, protesting the Vietnam War, racial inequality, and the political establishment.

All the while, Luke held Elizabeth in the embers of their consensual fire. They fanned the flames of their feelings for one another and allowed the warmth to spread inside every embrace. After he returned to Oakwood for his sophomore year, Luke wrote in his letter about the intensity of that summer.

Luke's second year at Oakwood College was his brother's first. As a freshman, Mark was required to live in the dormitory. Luke moved into the fraternity house, where he shared a room with Jerrod. The two of them, along with Bake and Marty, had joined the same fraternity in the previous semester. In their second year together, they became fraternal brothers in a myriad of ways.

Mark's matriculation at Oakwood boosted Luke's self-confidence. Having his younger brother close-by allowed a sense of stability and confirmed the natural order of things. The proximity of this older brother helped Mark, too. Where Luke excelled academically, Mark felt he could at least make the grade. Where Luke played college basketball, Mark felt he could play as well, maybe even better.

Luke included information about Mark in the letters he wrote to his parents. He considered it his responsibility, even shared an anecdote with Elizabeth from time to time.

———————

Elizabeth allied with Debbie again for their sophomore year at St. Louis College. They studied together for most of their classes, partnered when a lab assignment was required, and became fast friends in the process.

In deference to their growing friendship, Elizabeth would relent at times and accompany Debbie to a house party or fraternity-sponsored evening on the nearby campus of Washington University. Although her short stature made her easy to miss, Debbie's red hair and curvaceous body caught the attentions of many young men. Unfortunately, her fast-paced speech and demanding manner could also deflect those attentions. Debbie knew Elizabeth's quiet and graceful way would provide the perfect balance for any occasion.

Debbie didn't mind that Elizabeth was more often invited on dates by the men she had just met. She expressed surprise, however, when Elizabeth accepted an invitation from a law school student. Elizabeth allowed Debbie to assign an inflated level of significance to the date. Eventually, she explained that this fellow and she had dated before she met Luke.

Elizabeth admitted her initial curiosity had too quickly lapsed into complete boredom. The focal point of the young man's conversation was his past accomplishments and his future prospects, and Elizabeth's memory flashed to his nearly unbearable conceit, even as a teenager. Debbie joked that perhaps she would have been better able to put him in his place.

———

When a world of new relationships, new places, and progress in their individual educations allowed them any number of ways to turn, Luke and Elizabeth turned to one another. They accepted each other.

Their second year of college ended, and as another summer season opened to them, Forest Park beckoned. Luke sat near Elizabeth, while she lay across their blanket.

Even as he settled close to her, Luke spoke as if from a distance. "I know I don't know a whole lot. With two years of college, I know a little bit maybe, about a few things."

Luke trained his eyes on the horizon. "It's a giant world, even a long drive across Missouri to Oakwood. But, I think it's okay. We don't have to worry, do we? I mean about all the rest. It's okay just to be here, just to be with you."

Elizabeth touched Luke's cheek with her fingertips. When he turned, she pulled him closer and kissed that cheek.

She caressed him and enjoyed weaving her fingers through the longer hair at the back of his head.

He relaxed when she spoke. "Don't worry, Luke. For a while we can just be here together."

When Luke leaned away, he broke the peaceful repose. "My mom worries about everything lately. A few weeks ago, the doctor told Dad to quit his job at the garage. That kind of work is too hard on him. So, we don't have much money, but, Jesus, you can't worry about everything. Dad doesn't seem to be worried."

Luke sat and wrapped his arms around his knees. "I didn't get my old summer job back, so Dad and I are going to work together. He's lined up some jobs, painting houses."

Elizabeth assumed a place beside Luke. "You told me the other night. But do you know how to paint?"

"Not really, but my Dad does. His older brother and he did painting jobs before my Dad and Mom got married. Anyway, it's just exterior work. I'll be climbing the ladder, doing most of the high parts. He'll show me what I need to know. I'll learn some more of that Aurmann touch, this time with a paint brush. That sounds okay, doesn't it?"

"Sounds fine." Elizabeth pulled a thermos from the picnic basket.

"A guy doesn't have to know everything. Tomorrow we start painting...nothing to worry about."

Elizabeth handed a cup of lemonade to Luke. "Let's just enjoy being here together, just you and me." She touched her cup to his. "Another whole summer."

Elizabeth filled Luke's summer with light. She became the center of his galaxy. In an orbit around her, he drew energy from her expanding sun. Until, late that summer, a shadow fell over him, eclipsing even her vibrant light.

The clock on the living room wall struck 11:00 a.m., and Luke read the Sunday Post-Dispatch. An article about the Woodstock Festival caught his attention, and he scanned a photograph, an image of a subset of the thousands of young people who had congregated outside a small New York town for a rock concert. He thought perhaps some of his friends from Oakwood could be hidden in the throng, but even if they had been in the foreground of that picture, they would surely have been obscured by the mud that smeared everyone and everything.

He enjoyed the close-ups of the stage, pictures of Janis Joplin, John Sebastian, The Who, and Santana, just a few of the more than thirty rock performers reportedly scheduled to appear. He lay on the sofa and pointed a fan directly at his face. He felt the heat of the day building already. Another hot and humid summer's day was forecast for St. Louis, but the moisture saturating the air was unlikely to produce any precipitation. If the Woodstock organizers had chosen the Aurmann farm, the weather would have been better.

His mother and sister would be arriving home from Mass, and his younger brothers would awaken soon too. The heat of the day served as a reliable alarm clock on weekend mornings. He and his brothers had made it a habit to attend Mass on Saturday evenings during that summer. The Church had changed the rules regarding weekly attendance, and with Sunday now broadened to include Saturday hours, they could fulfill their obligations without missing any morning sleep time.

He moved in the direction of the downstairs shower. He expected it to be cooler there, and he'd be ready for the day before the family reassembled. He had agreed to accompany his mother on a hospital visit. His father's stay had been extended for a few additional days and he needed to discuss business with his father, anyway.

Luke's father rose from the hospital bed slowly. He swung his legs to one side, and Luke positioned the stand that supported his IV line next to his father's left side. Luke helped him to his feet and escorted him out of the room.

His father maintained a grip on Luke's arm at the bicep, and they took slow, deliberate steps along the vinyl floor of the hallway. Except for a rattling sound from the caster wheels of the IV apparatus, they walked in quiet. His father required exercise, so Luke accompanied him, but the austere surroundings of Veterans Hospital inspired very little conversation. The beige and white background was broken sporadically by a smile or a nod from a person they encountered along the way.

Several years had passed since the doctor's diagnosis of lymphatic leukemia had mandated quarterly treatments for his father. The treatments required an overnight stay in the hospital, but they were effective in slowing the progression of the disease.

During this particular round of treatments, the doctors were administering additional drugs and also trying to uncover the reason for his father's weakening condition.

Throughout that summer, Luke and his father had completed several jobs painting houses for friends and acquaintances. His father handled the trim around the windows and doors, the more detailed, yet less physically demanding work. Luke did all the heavy work, climbing the ladders, the vast majority of the brush strokes, but those that required less craftsmanship. Even given this division of labor, they often had to end their workday by mid-afternoon.

When the doctors decided to keep his father in the hospital for a protracted stay, it surprised Luke. They had just started a large two-story house, and it would likely be their last project for the summer. In two weeks Luke would leave for Oakwood. Mark and he would both be living in the fraternity house. He'd probably be doing some painting at that house too.

Luke reported to his father, as they stepped around the last corner of their second lap. "I've just kept going with the fascia boards, and I'll probably finish the high gables and eaves by Tuesday. By then, you should be back, don't you think?"

"I sure hope so," his father replied.

"Does it hurt?"

"A little." His father kept his head down.

"Why, is it getting worse?"

"I don't think so, but they sure have been pokin' around on me a lot. My heart's not hittin' on all cylinders. They say that's why I'm runnin' out of gas so much. I don't think it's related to my other problems, but it's sure getting me down."

One of the nurses met them as they neared the door of his father's room. "Okay, Mr. Aurmann, that's good for today."

"We did two laps. My son's in great shape, probably could run 200 laps. He plays college basketball, you know."

"He looks like a basketball player, tall and slim." The nurse helped Luke's father into bed and adjusted his pillows.

She turned to Luke's mother. "We're going to have to give your husband his shots now, Mrs. Aurmann."

"What's the reason for all the shots he's getting this time?" Luke's mother was more comfortable questioning the nurses.

"Well, the tests that he's taking are stressful. We want to keep up his strength and also ward off any infections."

"That's good." Luke's mother approached the bed from the side opposite where the nurse prepared to administer the medications. "Jacob, we better be going."

"Ah honey, don't go on my account. It's just a couple of shots."

"Luke's got plans, and Evelyn's invited me over for supper." Luke's mother kissed his father's cheek.

"Sure wish I was going with you. You tell everybody hello for me." Luke's father squeezed his mother's hand.

"I will. You get some rest."

"I'll probably listen to the ball game. Thanks for bringin' your transistor radio, Luke."

"No problem, Dad. I'll take care of things till you get back."

"I know you will, son." His father raised a hand as a farewell to Luke and his mother. "Don't you worry, honey. The doc will probably have good news for us tomorrow."

"I hope so." She smiled her bravest smile for him.

On the drive home, Luke encouraged his mother. "It's only a couple more days. Dad'll be okay. You don't have to worry."

"I know. I know. It was good that you brought your radio. He likes the ball games still."

Luke latched onto one of his father's favorite pastimes. "It doesn't even have to be the Cardinals. I remember those country hard ball games we used to go to when we were kids. He got excited about those games and all our Little League games too. He's been cheering for baseball a long time."

"And for your basketball games, and Mark's. He loves to see you boys play, loves a good game."

"Gotta' give it all you got. Win or lose, that's all that matters." Luke verbalized his father's credo.

He glanced at his mother. She smiled, but a tear that glistened in the corner of her eye portrayed her true feelings.

"Don't worry, Mom." Luke repeated a phrase that he had spoken almost daily throughout that summer.

He could not remember those words ever having entered his family's vernacular in the past. Even when his father was first diagnosed with leukemia, he had rallied the family like they were all involved in an important ball game. If the scoreboard showed them falling behind, there was plenty of time to make up the difference.

He finished with a hug for his daughter. He convinced her that everything would work out when he kissed her on the cheek. He tickled her ribs then, and she giggled while the rest of the family laughed along.

Karlton Jacob Aurmann was raised in farming country southwest of St. Louis and developed a sense of pride in the heritage of the hard-working life style and strong community connections that were typical of a 20th century rural American upbringing. After he married Margaret, they moved to the city and ultimately a suburban community, where they instilled the same values in their four sons and their one daughter.

Early on, Jacob's friendly, outgoing demeanor elicited such a warm response from those whom he touched that they naturally shortened his moniker. By the time he had grown to young adulthood, everyone called him Jake.

He gained the respect of his fellow workers and the owner of the auto repair shop where he was employed. He produced quality service, and his sharp wit, along with his casual, yet sincere approach with customers, made him everyone's friend almost immediately. He found joy in his daily work and rarely took a day for granted. From time to time he assumed the role of family disciplinarian. He punished his children if it was necessary, even spanked his oldest son, Matthew, on the occasions when he judged it an appropriate response for particularly bad behavior.

At those times, or any time that his children grew discouraged or disheartened, he was able to melt those negative feelings with a generous smile or a pat on the shoulder. Jake took every opportunity to congratulate his children on a job well done or acknowledge their help with a particular project.

He often professed his good fortune. His lucky circumstances had even become a regular source of family fun. When he engaged in a game of chance, poker or a dice game, he pursued them with enthusiasm of a beginner, but he was a skilled player just the same. If he won the biggest jackpot, he would tip his hat to the table of players.

He gained their agreement when he admitted. "Fellas, I'm just lucky, I guess."

He claimed, too, that he had been forgiven his own transgressions many times. Whether he obtained forgiveness through prayer, or it was carried by a kiss and a word of apology between himself and his wife, or exchanged via a handshake with a family member or friend, he never withheld forgiveness. No matter the number of times he, or his children, spilled the milk, he did not allow tears to be spilt. He possessed a constant capacity for letting go.

———————

Only two days after Luke had told his father that he would take care of things, Karlton Jacob Aurmann died. A massive coronary stopped his huge heart. The hearts that held him closest, his wife's and his children's, continued to beat in the rhythms that attuned their lives to his. But, they struggled and fought the profound aching. His wider family and friends, even mere acquaintances who survived him, felt their own hearts breaking.

They conveyed the depth of their feelings to Margaret. Her four boys and her only daughter stood with her at the front of the room in the funeral home. Streams of grief washed over them throughout the hours of visitation. Condolences were related in a long line of precious memories. Each person shared what they had come to know about Jake.

Luke escorted Elizabeth to the front of the room. When Elizabeth met Luke's mother, she extended both hands. Luke's mother slipped her hands into Elizabeth's.

"Mrs. Aurmann, my deepest sympathy." Elizabeth gripped tightly. "My family sends their condolences as well. I wish there was something I could do."

"I know. I...we all...love him so much."

When his mother began to cry, Luke looped one arm around her and one around Elizabeth.

A moment of mourning enfolded them, and then Annie touched her mother's arm. "Mom, there's somebody over here..."

"I know, honey." Luke's mother turned.

Luke grabbed Elizabeth's hand, and when they exited the side door, the long shadows of the late evening greeted them, and they retreated to a bench. Luke choked on his words, and he held Elizabeth with all his strength.

"Just let go." Elizabeth urged.

Her own tears flowed along her cheeks and creased the collar and shoulder of Luke's starched white shirt. She pressed into his arms where the hot tension of her feelings mingled with his. On a bench under the wide branches of a tall oak tree in the side yard of the funeral home, they faced each other briefly.

He leaned against the bench then and spoke into the shadows. "There've been a lot of people so far. Some of them even Mom doesn't know."

"I know you always said your Dad had a lot of friends."

"It seems people tend not to forget him. Some of my friends and my brothers' and sister's friends and their parents, there's been a steady stream."

"You should be proud. It probably helps your Mom."

"I don't know. She cries almost every time someone new talks with her. That's been hard for me, hard for all of us."

"It'll be hard for a while."

The shadows swallowed further dialogue, but Elizabeth told Luke that she would be unable to attend the burial service. She forced herself to think beyond that day and asked him to do the same.

With her fingertips smudging a tear, she gently turned his face toward hers. "I know you have to leave for school pretty soon, but you can't go without seeing me first. I want to see you before you leave. Will you promise me that?"

Luke responded to the soothing touch of her hand with only one word. "Sure."

Elizabeth dropped her hand but held his attention. "Promise me." She attempted a smile.

"I promise." Luke bowed his head.

Elizabeth kissed the top of his brow, and when he sat more upright, she smoothed a strand of his hair. They kissed once more before she stood.

"Luke, I'm so, so sorry for...It's so sad and I...I love. I've got to go." She walked quickly toward the front of the building.

Luke lost her words and lost sight of her in a blur of tears. Elizabeth turned the wrong way when she exited the parking lot. After a few blocks, she pulled her car to the side of the street and waited while a cascade of tears washed the sadness from that night.

She switched on the headlights and turned the car around. As she drove past the funeral home, she let go of her sadness. All the way home she prayed that Luke would do the same.

Elizabeth's sun rose ever higher. She could not stop it. She felt the sorrow of Luke's loss and would do anything she could for him, for his family. The professors who taught her, the patients at the hospital who relied on her, she wanted to shine for them.

Even through autumn's falling light and throughout the gray of winter, she shone brightly. All the while Luke kept his distance, did not write to her as often. When he came home from Oakwood College, he did not always call. They re-traced all the familiar pathways, but the differences could not be ignored. Luke's smile came slower, and he lingered longer in the shadows.

Luke was reluctant to admit that he flunked Logic class, one of his courses during the fall semester. He explained that he just stopped attending class. He never fully grasped the language of reasoning.

After Christmas Break, he quit playing basketball at Oakwood College.

He told Mark first. "You're the better player. You and the other guys work well together. You continue to play. You'll be a winner. I'll still be around. I just want to try some other things. Don't feel like spending three hours a day on basketball anymore."

"Maybe you can get your grades back up. That's more important anyway." Mark had noticed his older brother's growing disinterest in playing basketball but hoped that that attitude would not carry over to other aspects of their college life.

"You got the picture. You'll get better at basketball. I'll try to stand out in some way, too."

Luke started over again with the spring semester classes. No logic class on his schedule this time, no good reason held him.

Over Spring Break, he made a trip to Colorado with Jerrod, Bake, and Marty. They stayed with the Thompsons, friends of Jerrod's family, in the basement of their home on the northwest edge of the Denver metropolitan area. Each day they traveled to different sites, new places for Luke, Bake, and Marty, and ones only slightly familiar to Jerrod.

Atop Lookout Mountain and Buffalo Bill's grave, at the Coors Brewery in Golden and the Glory Hole Saloon in Central City, they found reason to celebrate the glorious surroundings. In Rocky Mountain National Park, they drove up Trail Ridge Road to the barrier that marked the road's winter closure. There they found a parking spot and climbed onto an outcropping of rocks. The wind stung their eyes, but they lingered for the view. They caught their breath in the awe inspiring panorama, stunned to silence by the vastness of the experience.

Their return route to Denver took them to Nederland and a saloon where Marty played pool with the locals. Bake stood nearby and cheered his good shots. Marty referenced the laws of physics and mathematics while explaining the angles of his shots. Bake slapped Marty on the back and nodded to the other guys when they proclaimed that Marty was full of bullshit. Luke and Jerrod laughed along with their friends and the mountain men that began to gather at that end of bar.

The celebration continued on Pearl Street in Boulder. Larry's Lounge served Coors, cold bottles from the cooler. Bake requested a little more volume on the jukebox, and Marty played Credence Clearwater Revival, *Down on the Corner*, and Three Dog Night's *Celebrate*. Luke and Jerrod ordered hamburgers and French fries. When they finished the food and the last round of beers, they followed the bartender's directions out of town.

"Take Pearl Street to Broadway, then turn right. Go all the way through town. Broadway becomes the Foothills Highway.

When you hit Golden, you're on the west end of Denver." He traced the route with his fingertip across the top of the bar.

Jerrod nodded his consent. "Yeah, we went up Lookout Mountain a couple of days ago. I can turn off before we get to Golden."

"Guess you know where you're goin' then." The bartender cleaned the bar with a swipe of the cloth he carried over his shoulder.

"Come on, man, admit it! You have no idea where we are." Bake complained from his spot in the passenger's seat.

When the light from the front window of the business that they had passed was no longer visible, Bake berated Jerrod. "I told ya' we should've stopped back at that liquor store to make sure that this road goes back to Denver."

Jerrod kept both hands on the wheel until he used one to point something out for his friends. "See that over there? Those lights, those buildings, that's part of the city. I'm telling you I know where we are."

"Yeah, but do you know where we're going?" Luke infused his question with a sarcastic tone.

"Huh? Let's figure out where we are first." Bake got confused.

"I can dig that." Marty confirmed with a chuckle.

"Will you guys cool it? I got it under control." Jerrod insisted.

The large bank of lights and the complex of buildings drew nearer, but the surrounding area held no sign of familiarity.

"Jerr, this whole thing looks a little weird to me." Marty leaned forward from his place right behind Jerrod. "It's stuck out here in the middle of nowhere. I don't think it's the city."

"See?" Bake's voice rose in volume as the car swung around a wide curve in the road. "What the hell?"

The headlights brought into view a huge white sign lettered in black. Jerrod hit the brakes, and his friends slid forward in their seats. They didn't require the closer proximity because the sign clearly read *Rocky Flats, U.S. Department of Energy.*

Marty recognized the place and spoke excitedly. "This is the place where they manufacture parts for the bomb, the nuclear bomb that is."

Jerrod hit the high-beam switch with his foot. Approximately 200 yards beyond the sign, a gate hinged to the side wall of a small stone building stretched across the road. Two guards marched out of the building and took a position in front of the gate. Silhouetted by the distant lights, they stood with one hand clutching the strap of the rifle slung over their shoulder.

"Doesn't look like we'll get that tour tonight, boys!" Marty shouted and slapped Jerrod on the shoulder.

Bake and Luke burst into laughter when Jerrod flinched at the sound of Marty's voice and the pop of his hand.

"Shit!" Jerrod yelled.

"Let's get the hell outta' here." Bake punched Jerrod's arm.

"Relax, man, I got it." Jerrod swung the car in a u-turn. "We're goin'!"

"We need to backtrack the way we came." Luke offered an idea.

Bake knew what that might mean. "Maybe we can stop at that liquor store and get some directions."

Jerrod tried to maintain his calm, but he grew more frustrated as he retraced their route.

"I think I should've gone straight. Remember, back when I turned left?" Jerrod questioned himself.

"Yeah, we should've gone straight a long time ago. But now we could use another six-pack. That'll make it easier to find our way." Bake maintained.

"All right, we'll stop at the liquor store." Jerrod gave in.

"Now you're talking. Whatta' ya' say, Luke? Think we should just go straight the next chance we get?"

"Straight ahead? I hear that can be a tough road," Luke responded.

"We might need a couple of six-packs." Bake laughed.

"Yeah, I'm beginning to like that Coors." Marty proclaimed.

They did stop at the liquor store. The clerk confirmed that they should stay straight for several miles. When they got to 58th Street, they could turn left.

The next day they returned to Oakwood College. *Straight Ahead* became the rallying cry for the rest of that semester. Mark and the rest of the guys reveled in Marty's account of that minor incident. It was a good story that included great beer. At the conclusion of each telling, Bake led everyone in a cheer, *Straight Ahead*.

Luke had difficulty moving straight ahead. He stopped going to his classes, all of them this time. When he finally made up his mind, nobody cheered.

"Man, you're crazy. You can't quit. You're the smart one. You're the one who's got it together." Mark insisted. "Some of the guys said you were cutting classes. I told them you'd be okay. You knew what you were doing."

Luke shuffled, a little off balance. "Mark...I...Shit! I don't know what I'm doing. You carry on. You'll be okay. I just have to work some things out. I don't think I can do it here anymore."

A dark image flew before Mark's eyes, and he shoved Luke. "Come on, man, you're going to break mom's heart. She's counting on you. There're a lot of us counting on you!"

"That's just it! I don't want anybody counting on me, not now. I'm not sure myself. I need some time, a little time."

"Ah, Luke!" Mark punched Luke's shoulder, but he suffered a stinger, too.

Mark let his brother go. Luke withdrew from Oakwood College that spring. His good friends and his brother stayed. They moved straight ahead, Jerrod, Bake and Marty toward the completion of that semester, and a year later graduation. Mark continued, another year of superior basketball and steady progress toward his degree.

Some moved ahead. One stopped.

Chapter 11

Boulder, Spring 1970

The rain stopped just as Clay stepped off the sidewalk at the front of the hospital. A spring storm had swept rapidly through Boulder, carried by a fierce wind that plummeted from the ridge lines of the surrounding foothills. He used his hand to wipe away the last of the rain droplets from his face. He walked grimly toward his truck, resigned, now, to making his own way.

Aunt Marsha's car turned out of the parking lot onto the street. She had called him twice that evening.

The first time she asked. "Did you stop by to see him today?"

"Yeah, I went by after school, the way I always do. He was sleeping. The nurse said not to bother him." Clay spoke impatiently.

"I just talked to the doctor. He said your dad's taken a turn for the worse. I think you should probably come back over here."

"Oh, they don't know how tough he is. I'll just stay here. One of his favorites is the featured bout tonight."

"What do you mean?" Clay's response annoyed her.

Clay delivered what he believed to be a credible explanation. "George Chuvalo's fighting on TV tonight. Dad really likes him. His nick name's *Boom Boom*. He's got a great right hand. I wanna' see the whole thing. Dad'll get a kick outta' hearing about it tomorrow."

"If there is a tomorrow." His aunt tried to catch him off guard.

Clay didn't hesitate. "I'm sure there'll be. I'll call you then."

Only a few weeks into the New Year, Clay's father had been forced to take sick leave from the mine. The liver disease had weakened him to the point where his presence there was unsafe for him and his fellow workers. He rested, more specifically roamed and wandered around the house, for the remainder of the winter season. In late March he returned to work but only lasted one week.

Nearly three weeks had passed since the morning that Clay had found him lying in the hallway, cold and blue. Clay had not hesitated. He had carried his father in his arms, steadied him with a firm grip while he drove to the hospital, and laid him on the gurney at the entrance of the hospital emergency room. Once again the rest, coupled with a different and more potent kind of medicine, seemed to be helping his father regain his strength.

Earlier in the week, during an afternoon walk through the hospital corridors, Clay reported to his father regarding the scheduled fight for that Friday night.

Clay detected a hint of excitement in his father's voice. "He's one tough Canuck. Remember when I won sixty bucks bettin' on that son-of-a-bitch back in '66. I took you out for a fancy supper after that, didn't I?"

"Yes, you did. We went for a steak at The Broker. I remember thinkin' at the time that you were getting all sentimental on me, that you were taken me out to celebrate my graduation from CU." Clay touched his father's arm, but his father kept his head down.

His father's voice rose with the explanation. "It took that bastard, Carney, six weeks to pay off that bet. I almost had to kick his butt to get my money, he was so damn mad about it. I tried to tell him there was no way Cassius Clay was goin' to knock out Chuvalo. Twenty dollars, he says to me. I'll even give you odds, three to one. He stuck his chest out like he was the one was goin' to fight. I just stepped right up in his face and told him that's a bet I'll take."

"So that's been four years ago. Chuvalo must be gettin' close to the end of his career by now." Clay still held his father's boxing opinions in high regard.

"Oh I don't know. He takes a lot of punches. But he's tough, damn tough. I bet he stays around for a few more years. Just last year he knocked out Jerry Quarry. Anyways, I wouldn't bet against him."

"No sir. I suppose I'm a little smarter than Carney where that's concerned."

"Yeah, I suppose you are." Clay's father nudged his son's arm with that final comment.

Stunned by his aunt's second call that night, Clay's hand shook as he grabbed for his jacket, and the coat tree wobbled as he closed the door. He possessed only an average intelligence, but his instincts rarely failed him, especially in his relationship with his father. After all, he had lived with his father, as a child, through high school, and since his graduation from CU, just the two of them.

His aunt stated so simply, "Your father has died. You've got to come now."

When he returned home, he finished the beer that had warmed on the coffee table in the front room. After that he switched to whiskey, a tall glass and a few ice cubes. At the bottom of the fourth tall glass of whiskey, he slumped to his side and curled on the sofa until morning came with a rap on the front door.

Clay's aunt marched inside, down the hall and back. Clay winced when she proclaimed her assessment. "Jeez, this place is a pig sty!"

"Don't get all mad now. With Dad in the hospital lately, I guess I ain't been cleaning much."

"No guessing about it. You're as big a slob as your father."

"Damn, Aunt Marsha, ain't he your older brother? Can't you give him a break? Especially now, couldn't you give a little respect?"

Aunt Marsha started in the kitchen with the stacks of dishes and cooking utensils. She barked the orders, and Clay grabbed a big trash can from the back porch, using it to collect all the loose debris, cans, bottles and newspapers throughout the house.

She clarified for Clay. "Set aside any mail. I'll look through that. I'm sure you owe some bills. After you get everything picked up, vacuum the carpet in the front room and both bedrooms. You do know how to use a vacuum, don't you?"

Clay didn't answer, just performed his assigned task. As he worked, he remembered the times when he and his dad had done some cleaning. He remembered, too, that his father had hired the neighbor lady to do a more thorough cleaning job, usually once in the spring and maybe in the fall. Guests were infrequent, and almost all special occasions were held at his aunt's house, the holidays in particular.

She always decorated her home with stylish touches. The hardwood floors were waxed and buffed to a glistening shine. Clay held a vision of that house like a photograph in a trendy magazine, and he remembered how cautious he needed to be. When he spilled something, he caught a crack atop his head from his father and a verbal reprimand from his aunt.

After Clay had grown to maturity, his father increasingly felt the brunt of his aunt's tirades, because it was invariably his beer that splashed on the sofa cushions or his glass of whiskey that smashed on the hardwood floor.

"Darren, you've had too much to drink already. Clay, come get your dad before he ruins everything in my house." She would yell, hovering near the mess with her mop. "I might just have to slap him with this mop, if you don't."

"Marsha..." his father would slur. "Ya' better watch...that mop of yours. I...I'm still your...big brother."

"But you always drink too much!" She would poke him with the mop handle.

On more than one occasion, the situation required assistance from Uncle Harold and coaxing from his young cousin, Karen, before Clay could usher his father fully from the premises. At times Clay needed to prop his father against the entrance wall of their house in order to remove his jacket. He remembered just this past Christmas when, in that very position, his father had slipped from his grip. Clay's attempt to grab him had missed, and the force of his hand hitting the wall broke off a chunk of plaster the size of his fist.

By lunchtime they had completed most of the cleaning project. After a quick survey, Aunt Marsha made her final assessment. "Well now, that's a whole lot better. I think it'll be okay to have a few people over after the burial."

Clay showered, while his aunt took inventory of the refrigerator and kitchen pantry. She made a shopping list and instructed Clay to retrieve his father's best suit.

He and his aunt had an appointment with the funeral director. As they exited, she nodded toward the wall. "I have an old macramé hanging that we can put over this hole in the plaster. Have you and your dad been throwing things?"

Clay finally spoke. "Well, no, it was an accident."

"I bet," she huffed. "Luckily, your Uncle Harold and I haven't left anything to accident."

"Whatta' ya' mean?"

"We made arrangements, when your dad first got sick. You were still in college then. Last week we had him sign the papers to let you use his checking account. You do know how to write a check, don't you?"

"Aunt Marsha, I'm not stupid. I graduated from CU. Besides I've got my own account."

"Well, now you have to take care of your dad's account, pay the bills and things like that too."

"Oh."

"Yeah, oh, and by the way, your dad had a will. It says that you inherit his estate, which means his truck, his tools and his other things, and this house and everything in it. Did you know your dad had a will?"

"Not really."

"That's something else your Uncle Harold took care of. And life insurance too. We had your dad take out a policy after your mom died. You were just a baby, and we would have been responsible for you if he would've died too. Anyway, he made it a long time, longer than I ever thought he would, and this house is still in good shape, better than I thought it would be. We can be happy about that, at least."

Clay grinned. "Chuvalo ended up winning last night. That would've made Dad happy."

"Your father was hard to understand. If that would've made him happy, then I'm glad. Mostly I'm glad you can remember him that way."

"He liked boxing. I know that. All the rest I was never sure about."

His father's wake evolved into a grand affair. Clay stationed himself near the front door and personally welcomed many of the guests, accepting their expressions of condolence with sincerity, accepting the role of host to the strange celebration. At one point, he concluded with certainty that his father's house, now his house, had never held so many people.

They gathered in the kitchen and the dining room. The counter and table were arranged buffet-style with the food. Most ate where they stood. Some found a folding chair or a place on the sofa in the front room and rested a plate of food in their laps. They mixed their own drinks and helped themselves to bottles of beer.

His father's peers shared stories from work experiences. A few of them had seen him box.

"He could take a punch...had a jaw as hard as a rock. He'd come straight at the other guy." Mr. Stadler, one of his supervisors at the mine, remembered Darren's boxing style.

"I saw him break a guy's jaw once. He had a powerful right hand. Cracked some ribs too." Joe Carney confirmed his toughness.

When one of the oldest guests joined the small circle of men that gathered around Clay, he lent a different perspective. "Yeah, a lot of that stuff was when your dad was a younger man. I like the more recent times, when you were in high school and college. I know he sure liked watching you play football. Some of us lost our sons when they were way too young, and we always enjoyed hearing about how you were doing with your sports."

"That's right, Willy." Carney concurred. "Clay, I can't tell ya' how many times your dad would replay your games in the lunch room."

"Weren't you goin' to play pro football, too?" Willy asked.

Clay relished the opportunity to do more than nod or smile his response. "Well, sir, you might remember how I had that bad knee injury my last year at CU. That pretty much messed up my chances. I got drafted by the Chargers of the AFL, but I hurt that same knee again in a pre-season game. After the second operation, I thought I was a lot stronger, and I tried out the next year with the Redskins. The coaches there said I wasn't fast enough, but I kept at it anyway. Then two years ago at Broncos training camp, I hurt my other knee. I didn't get another shot after that. It's just as well. I like coaching the high school guys now."

Clay interpreted the slaps on his back as a sign of the group's agreement. He hadn't noticed Frank Morton's arrival, but he took the bottle of beer Frank extended to him.

"Here's to your dad!" Frank toasted, and several drinks were raised to the center of the circle.

"Thanks for coming man." Clay touched his bottle to Frank's.

"Sorry I couldn't be there at the burial. Some of the other guys from school should be here soon too."

"Sounds good." Clay nodded and took a big drink.

As the afternoon progressed, the number of guests diminished, and Clay found a chair in the living room. He relaxed with a whiskey and soda. His aunt insisted that he eat the ham sandwich and the plate of potatoes that she had prepared for him.

He focused on that task and did not see his cousin enter the room with two other women. Karen slipped through the space between the young men who stood near Clay. To gain Clay's attention, she touched his shoulder with one hand. With her other hand, she motioned for the men to step to the side and had the two women come closer.

Karen attempted an introduction. "I think you might know this lady. And this is my..." But Karen could not finish as her cousin rose from his chair and brushed past her.

"Julia, my God. Julia, what are you doin' here?"

"Just came to see an old friend. Hope it was all right."

"All right, it's more than that." Clay turned to his cousin. "Karen, I didn't know you knew…"

Karen interrupted him this time. "I don't silly. This is my friend, Susie. She rents the basement apartment at Julia's house. I went to get Susie, and we were talking to Julia…"

Julia spoke over Karen. "I just wanted you to know how sorry I am about your father's passing."

Clay took Julia by the hand. "Yeah…Yes…thank you."

Clay looped one arm around Karen. "Thank you for bringing her." And then he made eye contact with Susie. "Thank you for coming too."

Frank and Clay arranged additional chairs in a semi-circle, one for each of the ladies. Clay ensured that Julia would have a place next to his, while Karen explained how Julia had made the connections during their three-way conversation that afternoon.

Julia summarized. "Terry, my daughter, and I have really enjoyed having Susie around. And we see Karen pretty often too. Of course, I had no idea she was your cousin until today, but I won't hold that against her."

Susie giggled and poked Karen. "Julia showed us that lovely sweatshirt you bought for her."

Clay nudged Julia's side. "God woman, I thought you woulda' burned that by now."

"No way, I wouldn't do that. The *p in park* has kind of worn away over the years though, so now it reads *Estes Ark*."

"Thinkin' back on it, we could've used an ark up on the mountainside that day. It rained so hard." Clay steered his commentary toward his cousin and her friend. "That's why I got her the sweatshirt. We got soaked in that rain storm. Gray was the only color I could find in a small size."

When Aunt Marsha entered the room, Clay made certain that she and Julia were introduced to each other. Aunt Marsha recruited everyone except Clay and Julia for clean-up duty. She sensed an unfamiliar aura of calm in the corner where Clay and Julia sat, and she allowed time for that feeling to build.

With just the two of them in the room, Clay took the initiative. "I have to say something that I should've said a long time ago. When Jim got killed, I was away at training camp, tryin' to make the Broncos team."

Julia nodded. "I know, Frank told me."

"Yeah, but then, when I finally came back, I should've come to see you. I just...I think...I was scared. Anyway, I'm sorry about Jim. Sorry that I didn't come and see you. Sorry for you and your little girl." He pressed her hands with his and their eyes met in the exchange.

"Thank you, Clay." Julia whispered.

Clay turned away. "Jim was a helluva guy. Too many good men have died in that war. It's a cryin' shame."

"Yes, it's sad." Julia concurred.

When Aunt Marsha next appeared, she wore her coat. Clay hustled to meet her at the door. He whispered his thanks as he hugged her close. It was the kindest moment she could recall ever experiencing in that house, and tears filled her eyes as Clay opened the door.

She raised her voice as she breached the threshold. "I know two girls who have classes tomorrow and probably everybody else has to go to work. Let's not be too late tonight."

After the next round of drinks had been consumed, a longer line of good-byes and well wishes were communicated. In the end Clay hugged his cousin and her friend. Finally, he held Julia in an embrace, and she felt herself lingering inside his arms for too long.

Tears pressed between her eyelids, and she could not blink them back. "I'm so sorry, Clay."

Karen followed Susie onto the porch. She did not hear her cousin's response and did not see his tears. In the shadows of the porch, Clay wiped his eyes with one hand.

When the headlights of Karen's car hit him, he waved but did not know if they waved back. He stopped in the front room to pick up the last round of drink glasses. Everything in the kitchen was in order. He checked his father's room, opened the top drawer of his dresser and scanned his father's closet, as if he was searching for a clue.

When he pulled back the covers on his bed, he realized that his aunt had changed the sheets. He found the empty packaging from new linens in the trash can next to his dresser. On the top of the shelf in his closet, a second package had a note taped to it. *Rotate your sheets every Sunday. I took care of the old ones.*

With an underhand motion, he tossed his dirty clothes into the hamper. The sheets were still cool when he squeezed his large frame between them. He searched for warmth, yearning for that feeling, but dreamed an old dream.

Chapter 12

St. Louis, Spring 1970 to Spring 1971

The seasons cycled one full rotation, and Luke remained in St. Louis. Each month Luke flipped the pages on the kitchen calendar in his family's home. The summer months cultivated the familiar feelings of family and friends. Luke's relationship with Elizabeth intensified as the temperatures rose. Whenever and wherever they met, she encouraged him. Her presence was his comfort and perfect pleasure.

On a few raucous occasions, Luke and his younger brothers, Mark and Johnny, rallied their friends and spiked the fun with a unique blend of sodas and distilled spirits. Within a few days of their departure for their next year of college, Matt, Luke's older brother, came home to announce that he had re-enlisted in the Air Force, an additional two years of military service.

Luke's summer job became a fulltime position, and he punched a time clock at a St. Louis factory. The assembly line work provided a paycheck, and most of what he earned he contributed to the payment of the household bills. He slept alone in the bedroom he had shared with his three brothers for most of his life. He ate suppertime meals with his mother and sister and fell into a routine.

In mid-September, the factory closed for a week to re-tool for a new line of products. Luke invited Elizabeth to accompany him for a weekday afternoon picnic. She consented, but only after contacting her friend, Debbie. Debbie agreed to take copious notes during that day's classes.

Elizabeth delighted Luke even as the afternoon began. Awaiting his arrival, she sat on the front porch, picnic basket and blanket beside her. She started across the lawn before he came around the car.

"Hey, this is a surprise!" Luke hustled to meet her.

"I don't want you to get too used to things always being the same." Elizabeth handed him the basket.

She wore a dress he hadn't seen before, robin's egg blue, four tiny pearl buttons spaced evenly along the arc where the scoop neck met her tanned skin. A pastel blue ribbon was tied in her hair.

"Pretty dress," Luke commented and excused himself. "I just went with a t-shirt, but it's a new one."

"Very stylish." Elizabeth smiled.

As she slid into the car beside him, she explained "I just thought the dress would be as cool as anything else. It's going to get hot again today."

"It's very nice, pretty as a summer day." Luke couldn't stop smiling.

The radio played *In the Summer Time* and other familiar tunes as Luke followed the interstate to a two-lane state highway and finally a county road that led them to a dirt country road. Past fields of maturing corn and a grove of walnut trees, he drove along a route he remembered from the many times his father had driven it.

Multiple times in any given summer, when he was younger, and regularly throughout the year, the Aurmann family visited the family farm. In fact, just that previous summer, Luke and his father made a one-day trip to the farm at the request of one of his uncles. Luke eased the car quietly to the side of the road near the turn-off for a short driveway. He pointed to a white clapboard house, shaded by a tall oak tree. A truck patch garden occupied the side yard. Tall rows of green beans and low, spreading carrot and radish plants appeared ready for the harvest. The barn rose in the background, a brighter red than Luke remembered from his last visit.

"This is the farm where my Dad grew up. His two brothers, my uncles, are probably inside somewhere staying out of the heat. Either that, or they're in town at the local tavern."

Although Luke had said it would be a picnic, Elizabeth thought this might be the destination of their trip. "Should we stop in? Is that why we..."

Luke interrupted her. "No, we don't need to. I just thought that while we were in the area I'd show this to you. I really want to have a picnic, not a visit. I wanted to do something a bit different too. There's a place a few miles from here. If I can remember how to get there, it's nice. A channel of the river passes by it."

Another stretch of dirt road swept a wide arc, and a level spot where the wild grass had been flattened came into view. Luke nodded in confirmation of his thinking. On a Wednesday afternoon, the fishermen or weekend campers would likely not be using the spot.

"The place I'm thinking of is right through those trees."

He pulled the car forward onto the grassy area.

Elizabeth scanned the trees. "I'll take your word for it. The only thing I know is that we're way out in the country."

———

Luke swallowed the cup of lemonade and didn't notice when Elizabeth re-filled it. Instead, he consumed an entire sandwich with just a few unconscious bites and then a handful of potato chips. After finishing the second cup, he rubbed the back of his hand across his mouth.

Although the shallow river meandered slowly on its course some fifteen yards from the edge of their blanket, it captured Luke's attention. He sat near Elizabeth on the picnic blanket but was impervious to her and everything else. Elizabeth waited patiently.

When she noticed his concentration breaking and his eyes finally met hers, she grinned. "Hey there, welcome back."

"Huh, oh sorry." Luke mirrored her grin, his askance.

"That's okay. I guess you had some place else you wanted to go too."

"No, this is the place. I was just...just..."

"I know, just thinking." She filled the spaces for him.

Luke held a silent gaze, and Elizabeth gently laid one hand on his arm. "You do that more and more these days."

"What do you mean?"

"I mean, you're out there somewhere, way out there sometimes."

"No, I'm not." Luke conjured a defense and took her hand in his. "I was just thinking about a time when we went swimming in that river, when I was a kid."

"I see, but you didn't tell me to bring a swimsuit."

"Not today, I wasn't thinking of today."

"Like I said you were way out there, or way back there."

"Okay, yeah, I give in. You got me."

"You're too easy. You give up too quickly." Elizabeth smiled broadly now.

"What can I say? I just fall to pieces when I'm with you. You're just so...so..."

"Beautiful?" Elizabeth leaned forward.

"Well I was thinking wonderful, but beautiful works too."

He kissed her cheek then and whispered. "You got me. You really do."

As he leaned back, she wrapped her arms around his shoulders and pushed him to the blanket. She kissed his lips, an instinctive response to his tender admission.

Her words bubbled to the surface. "You got me, too, you know. I'm glad you didn't have to leave again. I'm happy just being here with you, being close to you now."

She lay beside him then, and he grasped her hand, interlacing his fingers with hers. He rested in the warmth, and before long, his eyes closed and he drifted. His fingers loosened from hers, and a slow river of day dreams carried him away. She traveled with him this time, as far away from St. Louis as they had ever been.

Elizabeth packed the leftover food and trash into the picnic basket. She finished her cup of lemonade. She placed her sandals and Luke's shoes at the bottom of the blanket. She took the ribbon from her hair, placed it in her purse, then took her brush and stroked her long, sun-lightened hair from its part in the middle toward the side and back. Where it fell across her shoulders, she brushed the ends. When she finished, she placed her purse and the picnic basket onto the grass at the top of the blanket.

She stretched out on her belly and propped her head on the tripod she formed with her arms bent at the elbow and her hands braced on either side of her chin. Tiny sections of the corn field popped through the branches of the willow trees that hid their picnic spot from the road. A hint of yellow at the tips of some of the ears signified their maturing. She felt Luke stirring close to her, so close.

When a bead of perspiration tracked across Luke's forehead following his hair line, it dropped onto his ear, and the tickling sensation awakened him. He leaned on one elbow.

With their eyes at the same level, she welcomed him. "Hello again."

"Hi, I might've fallen asleep."

"Just a little while." She wanted to know more. "Did you dream?"

"I think so. You and me this time, we were on a boat, floating down the river."

"Sounds good, when do we leave?"

"Whenever you want." Luke rose to a position where he kneeled beside her. He paused there as though awaiting a signal.

"Maybe after I graduate." Elizabeth turned onto her back.

"We'll definitely do something special to celebrate that achievement." Luke leaned over Elizabeth and placed one hand on each side of her head.

"It's been a dream of mine for a long time, to be a nurse." Elizabeth glanced away.

"I know, and you're going to be perfect at that, perfect in every way."

"Let's just say good at that. I want to be good at it." Her gaze reinforced the sincerity in her words.

"If that's what you want, then good it is. But I bet the people you take care of will feel like it's better than good." "Okay, I like better."

She locked both arms around Luke's neck and pulled him close. He kissed her lips, and a fanciful delight passed between them.

She whispered. "There, that's better."

In the juices of another kiss, she met him with a passion that washed over her entire body. He slid to her side and his hand started a soft pattern across her belly.

He pressed his kisses, and the energy of their tongues excited their passions. Her cotton dress began to gather under his palm. She curled her toes and drew her feet toward her buttocks. The blanket rippled beneath her, and her dress fell toward her belly. Soon his hand was stroking her warm flesh there.

The sensation bewitched him, his hand stroking the smooth brown of the skin over her knee and down her thigh. His hand smoothed the mysterious dryness of her thigh.

She opened her legs and her clear, moist eyes. Then he dove toward her, a stirring of desires in a whirlpool of kisses. It felt like a dream, her soft brown skin and her crystalline eyes, at once moist and dry, as if she were made of liquid and land.

It happened in a faraway place between the trees and the river. A shallow current of movements rushed at the edges before dropping into a deeper channel. There the rhythm slowed until their young hearts drove them with a stronger beat. When the final flood of feelings swept over them, he felt the rush of his senses and pressed his nakedness against hers. She held him tightly then and gasped for a last breath before she allowed herself to drown inside a rapturous embrace.

Then they parted, and Elizabeth pulled one side of the blanket over the lower part of her body. As she did, Luke rolled to the opposite side onto the grass, gathered his jeans and underwear, and pulled them to his waist. In a blink, he scrambled to his feet. A dizzy darkness that he did not recognize caused him to turn and compelled him to move away. He lurched in faulty, stumbling strides toward the river and down the rocky embankment.

When he reached the water's edge, he dropped to his knees. The gravel bit through his jeans as he leaned forward and splashed water on his face from a pool that gathered there. He rubbed his eyes to clear his vision. He rose to his feet and wiped his face with the bottom of his t-shirt.

He squared his underwear and jeans, pulled up his zipper and cinched his belt. His shirt tail hung loose, and he stepped back from the water's edge. When he turned to go, a painful sting in his right foot caused him to flinch. He sat down on a large nearby rock and crossed his right leg over his left knee to examine the foot. The skin had been sliced, and a stripe of blood crossed the front pad of his foot. He sat there with his foot suspended, staring toward the water.

By that time, Elizabeth had made her way down the embankment. She wore her sandals and carried his shoes in one hand with the picnic blanket tucked under her arm. Intent on helping, she tended to Luke's injured foot. Without a word, she dipped a corner of the blanket into the river, and then knelt beside Luke, using the damp end of the blanket to wash away the dirt and grit from the scrape.

While she administered to his foot, she explained. "I heard some splashing and thought you might need the blanket to dry off."

She pressed against his foot with a dry section of the blanket. "It looks like a mean scrape, but I don't think it's deep."

Luke avoided eye contact with Elizabeth. "Yeah, I think I slipped on my way down the bank." He touched her hands where she caressed his foot. "Thanks. That feels good. But how about you? Are you..."

"I'm okay." Elizabeth rose to her feet. "Think you can put on your shoes?"

"Yes, but I thought I might have hurt you when we were..." His tongue tied around his feelings, and he lowered his head to tie his shoelaces.

Her calm breathing assumed the rhythm of the river lapping nearby. "No, I'm okay. But..."

Her words could be measured by the slow moving water. "I think...we probably...should go."

He could only agree because ideas of what to do next, what he should do, would not come into his consciousness. "Okay, let's go."

At the picnic spot, Elizabeth picked up her purse and reached for the basket, but Luke snatched it ahead of her. They stood facing each other for a moment. Luke reached with his free hand and touched Elizabeth gently along her cheek where her hair met the skin, tenderly as he had in the early days of seeing her. When he dropped his hand, she grabbed it.

He spoke to her but his voice sounded miles away. "Elizabeth, I didn't know how...after...or what...but you...are beautiful."

As he spoke those last words, he finally met her eyes. She rose to her tiptoes and kissed him. "Let's go home."

Luke fell into a familiar silence as he steered the car along the dirt road. Elizabeth's feelings overturned any need to speak. She sat near the passenger window, and the rows of the cornfield guided her thoughts.

She envisioned a day when the crop would have grown its tallest, a time of harvest. She sensed the progression of that day and the oncoming flow of the seasons. When Luke checked the traffic at the intersection of the county road, they exchanged a brief smile.

Elizabeth's thoughts soared beyond that time, too, and she wondered for Luke, wondered what he would do, how he would be.

———

Luke had practiced his reasons countless evenings. He mumbled the words as he paced in the backyard of his family's home. He recited them to Elizabeth, eventually to his mother and his family.

By the end of May, Jerrod and Bake would be going to Colorado, probably to Boulder. They wanted to spend the summer living in the mountains, and he would join them. He described his first experiences there, and the feelings he remembered. Elizabeth did not see the spring season ending in that way.

A well of tears filled her eyes. "I'll miss you. That's all. It'll be hard. It's been a whole year. You've been home a whole year. I've been happy, and I thought you were happy too."

"When I'm with you, yes, then I'm happy. The rest, I just don't feel like I'm getting anywhere."

"When you quit school, I knew then that that wasn't going to get you anywhere."

"But I came home. I thought I could see things better. Maybe help Mom a little and be with you. Back then, I believed that school wasn't getting me anywhere, but now home's not the right place for me either. Maybe it's just not the right time, not here, not now."

"Luke, you ass! You can't say those things to me. How do you think they make me feel? Like shit, that's how! You can't just leave like this. After all this time, you just can't."

From her place seated next to Luke, atop the stone wall that ran along the hill overlooking the American Legion Fountain in Forest Park, she projected the anger she felt. Her eyes flashed where pools of moisture reflected the colored lights of the fountain. She shoved him with both hands and then drew her knees up, wrapped her arms around them, and buried her face there.

Luke struggled to explain his leaving, and he missed all of Elizabeth's feelings. "I'm pretty sure Jerrod's only staying for the summer. Bake for sure is. I mean, they're both graduating. They just need the summer."

Elizabeth did not follow the logic and hit him with the full force of her words, her feelings. "I'm graduating too, you know. I want to celebrate that with you too. I want to be happy. I want you to be happy for me."

He lost himself in the blur of her wet stare and fought to find his way. "I am happy for...I'm so proud of you. I'm glad for my friends. I think my family's doing good too. I'm the one who's not making it."

"What's that supposed to mean? You've got only yourself to blame for your situation. Nobody's forcing you, forced you to do anything."

"I know. I know. It's me. I know it's me. I just...just feel like I should try this one thing. Maybe I'll learn..."

Elizabeth knew, too, how Luke could learn best.

She insisted. "You should go back to school, if you really want to learn something."

But Luke's thoughts wandered. He imagined another path. "I want to learn what it's like to be on my own. Learn to live on my own."

Elizabeth wiped her eyes with the back of her hand, her view now clouded by confusion. "Now you're really not making any sense."

Luke gave in to that notion. "I know. I wanted it to make sense, but it probably doesn't. I wish I could say the right things."

When he hesitated again, anger built a barrier, created a distance between them.

Elizabeth lashed out. "It's just crazy! I don't know what you think you will find out there. It's just so... so stupid. I..."

Luke touched her arm, and her words stopped. His fingertips traced a line back and forth on her skin.

He followed that rhythm. "Elizabeth, please don't be mad. I'm not trying to escape, not from you. You are with me everywhere. We don't have to hold onto each other. You'll see. You'll graduate. I bet you get a job at Children's Hospital. You'll be happy. I want to find a place too. Believe me. I can't really say when...it may only be for the summer...I don't know, but I know we'll be together again."

Elizabeth softened and allowed him to take her hand. Luke tracked the tears as they crossed her cheek. Her skin held the blush of spring, no longer pale as winter but not yet tanned from the summer sun. His heart pulsed with a humble beat.

Elizabeth knew the essence of that moment. "It just makes me sad, sad when I want to be happy."

She swung her legs away from Luke, and using her arms to lift, she pivoted 180 degrees so that she sat atop the wall but faced in the opposite direction. Luke mirrored her movements and then hopped down from the wall. When he faced her, he tilted his head towards her. As their foreheads touched, her eyes closed. They paused, as though they were figures sculpted into a memorial.

He whispered. "It's going to be okay. I just need some time."

Chapter 13

Boulder, Spring 1971

*J*ulia held Terry on her lap with a gentle caress where they sat on the sofa in their Boulder home. Julia realized that she would now own this house as a part of the estate she had inherited from her parents. With her daughter's head resting in her bosom, she took comfort where she gave it.

"It's just you and me, now." Julia whispered into the room.

"I know." Terry's words were muffled by her mother's embrace. She lifted her head to ask. "We're still going to live here, aren't we?"

Julia didn't respond immediately.

"I want to." Terry stated her preference with all the boldness she could muster. She hoped her mother would agree.

"Yes, honey, we're going to live here for a long, long time. Probably till you're grown up and don't want to live with your old mom anymore." Julia squeezed her daughter.

"Mom, that's silly. I always want to live with you."

"We'll see. You might change your mind." Julia smiled with a mother's tender knowing.

Terry's face livened, the spark of an idea. "I know I can move downstairs where Susie lives. Then we can still see each other, but I'll live in my own apartment, and I can clean it up whenever I want to."

Julia chuckled then. "Oh, yeah, and who's going to wash your clothes, smartie pants?"

Terry hopped off of her mother's lap. "I guess I'll just go to the laundry place. Susie took me once. They've got big machines there."

Julia laughed aloud. "Well then, I guess you've got it all figured out."

Terry stepped back. "Yeah, but I don't want to do that now. Let's do something else."

Julia rose from the sofa. "Okay, let's get out of these old dresses and put on some jeans. Maybe we'll go to the park for a little while before it gets dark. I'll drive in our new car."

Terry felt an enthusiasm for that idea. "Yeah, I like that. Just you and me."

That night, after Terry had fallen asleep, Julia sat alone on the edge of her bed. An unfamiliar weariness held her there, although it was still early. She turned the program over in her hands, from front to back and to the front again. The photo was the same one that hung in the front hallway of her parents' home and also in her upstairs hall near the photos of Jim and Terry. The words *Dearly Departed* were imprinted on the program above the photo with their names below it.

NCAR provided the resources for the program's professional design and printing. She remembered Jim's funeral service and the simple card with his name and the dates of his birth and death imprinted on it, along with the words, *God Bless America*. She flipped her parents' program to the back side again. The order of service was printed there, and Dr. Elliott's eulogy was highlighted in bold.

Julia's part of the service consisted of her recitation of a prayer for peace, the same prayer she had spoken at her husband's funeral. This time, Terry stood by her side and affirmed her mother's prayer, when she spoke aloud the word *Amen* at its conclusion.

Julia remembered a moment of calmness that she had felt when, from their seats at the front of the room, Clay, Frank, Sally and a few of her neighborhood friends repeated Terry's Amen with a tone of conviction more than reverence. She nodded when an echo of Amen's bounced around the room, and Terry re-stated the affirmation for the final time.

As she walked across the room to her dresser, her thoughts flashed forward then to her parents' home. The NCAR administrative staff had arranged the catering for the wake, which was held at her parents' house. Two poster-sized photos had been placed in the entry way of the house. One depicted her father with Dr. Elliott, other NCAR officials, and some of the local elite at the opening ceremony of the new NCAR lab. The other showed her mother and father toasting with Dr. Elliott at the gala celebration.

Julia had spent much of the afternoon stationed in front of those posters. Everyone extended their sincere condolences. Some commented at the irony of her parents' death in a plane crash. They alluded to the surprising power of the spring rainstorm that had been the undoing of such an experienced pilot.

Toward the end of the affair when many of the guests had departed, her father's lawyer had approached her with a reminder that he had an obligation to fulfill. They needed to meet to review the details of her parents' will. She was now the proud owner of a house in Boulder and would be inheriting a substantial amount of money from the estate and life insurance policies.

Clay had waited in his truck and met Julia and Terry when they came through the backyard gate beside the garage. Julia thought that Clay's demeanor of gentleness and thoughtfulness were somewhat out of character, but she appreciated them just the same. He surprised Terry when he swept her into his arms and carried her to the car. Terry giggled while he placed her in the back seat of the car. Her grandfather's Volvo was now her mother's car.

Clay shared his opinion with Julia. "This is a nice car. They're supposed to be real safe cars, too."

Julia blinked, almost expressionless.

Clay questioned her. "You doin' okay?"

"I'm okay." Julia allowed a faint sigh but hid her face with one hand. "You didn't have to wait."

"I wanted to. It's not the first time I've waited for you outside of this house."

Julia rubbed her forehead. "Wait? What?"

"Nothin.' I'll have to tell you sometime."

"I suppose." Julia took a step toward the car.

"I just wanted to say that I'd be more than glad to take you home or help out in any way you need me to."

"I think we'll be all right by ourselves for now."

"Okay. For now then, that's the way it'll be, but I'll come by in a day or two over at your house to see you, if that's okay?"

"I suppose. I've got to go see my dad's lawyer. There're some papers for me to go over. Maybe you could stay with Terry."

"Be happy to." Clay nodded. "I want to help."

"Thanks. I'll take you up on that."

"You better." He grinned as he stepped closer to her.

Late afternoon shadows gathered in the backyard just beyond the gate.

Clay's voice darkened, too, hushed and humble. "Ya know, I'm...we're all really, really sorry about what happened."

Julia rose to her tiptoes and hooked one hand around Clay's neck. She kissed his cheek. "Thank you. That means a lot to me."

When her foot hit the front of the dresser, it startled her. She placed the program on the top of the dresser, pulled a drawer open, and found a clean night gown. She made a silent pledge that she would continue to do her family's laundry and the other household chores. She smiled as she envisioned teaching her daughter how to do these tasks.

When she had finished changing into her gown and brushing her hair, she lifted the program from the dresser again. A final tear splashed on the word *Peace*, and she opened a drawer and tucked the program under some of her clothes.

Under the bed covers she rolled to her side and pulled Jim's pillow toward her. She wrapped her arms around it and hoped that the rest of the spring season would bring gentle rains and the comfort of warm days and nighttimes as soft as a feather pillow. Finally, she fell into a peaceful sleep.

That same night, on the east side of Boulder, Luke sat at the kitchen table and wrote a letter to Elizabeth. He described the townhouse that he now shared with Jerrod and Bake, how he had won the coin toss and had a room to himself, while the two of them shared the other bedroom. Cat Stevens' song *Wild World* streamed in from the front room. Their landlord, an associate professor at the University of Colorado who would be traveling for the summer in Europe, had sublet his place, fully furnished including his stereo, to the three of them.

He wrote about the feeling of exhilaration that he experienced when he and his friends stood at the overlook near the top of Flagstaff Mountain. In the clear springtime air, the view stretched well to the east of the city limits. They would break into spontaneous laughter, a sign of their excitement. All the while, very few words were exchanged.

He encouraged her to listen for more of the songs from the two albums Jerrod had purchased that afternoon, *Tea for the Tillerman* by Cat Stevens and *After the Gold Rush* by Neil Young. He described to her the area located across Broadway from the CU campus. It was called *The Hill*, and he felt certain they would be spending a lot of time there. *The Hill* boasted a record store with a wide range of music, a bookstore where Jerrod and he had browsed some, and a funky restaurant and bar called, *The Sink*. There was even a club that promoted live music.

Only four days had passed since they had traveled across the plains, and they had found a place at the very foot of the Rocky Mountains. Rock formations known as the Flat Irons stood like sentinels there. Baseline Road marked the 40th parallel and their exit from the Denver Boulder Turnpike. He sensed they had made a good choice.

He secured a job, temporary but a chance for a permanent position. He would be a sales clerk at Pearl Street Bookstore. He related a feeling of satisfaction and confirmed his feelings for her. He signed the letter, *Yours Forever*.

After Luke had folded the pages and stuffed them in an envelope, he joined his friends in the front room. They finished the last of the two six packs of Coors that they had purchased at Baseline Liquor on their way home from *The Hill*. Jerrod used the lift-and-place technique with the arm of the turntable to select a few favorites from his new albums.

From his place in any easy chair, Bake propped his feet on top of one of his suitcases. Luke wondered why that one had still not made it to his room.

Bake assured his friends. "We're really going to like it here."

"Oh yeah, and this music, it's perfect, too." Jerrod placed the stereo needle on the appropriate spot.

The first notes of *I Believe in You* by Neil Young played, and he turned to Luke with a suggestion. "You should put some of these words in your letter. Who knows maybe she'll even start to like you again."

"And if that don't work, I'm sure you guys can come up with some good poems to quote from." Bake liked delivering relationship advice, especially when he could lace it with a little sarcasm.

"Thanks. But I think I'll just stick with my own stuff for now. Really, I just want her to know how I feel, understand what I'm doing here."

"Whoa, buddy, that sounds like a bit too much to me. Women, they don't necessarily see things the way we do. I can tell you that for sure. You might as well not even waste your time on that part." Bake sounded convincing.

When Luke took a long drink from his can of Coors, Jerrod chimed in. "Yeah, just a few simple lines, like the title of this song. Don't you think it gets the feeling across?"

Luke found an answer flowing with the taste of that beer. "Only it might not be the way I feel."

"He's got you there, Jerr. How about one more? I think we got a few in the fridge from yesterday. They're all Pabst though. Can you stand it?"

"Sure, one more sounds good." Jerrod agreed and Luke nodded before he tilted his current one for the last time.

"Hey, I like these songs as much as you do, Jerr, but can't we mix in some rock 'n roll, too?" Bake had an answer for his question as he passed around the beers. "Some *James Gang Rides Again* would be good."

From *Funk #49,* Joe Walsh's guitar licks rang in Luke's ears. Bake cranked the volume higher when he played it a second time. Luke passed by the stereo on his way upstairs to his room. He found a stamp for his letter, and as he sealed the envelope, a line from the song's second verse came shining through, *don't misunderstand me.*

Chapter 14

"Hey, shouldn't you guys be hangin' on the hill?" The stranger pointed at Luke and his friends as they crossed Pearl Street.

They chose to ignore him on this Saturday night, just as they had the previous weekend, when the same weirdly dressed man had occupied the identical spot outside of Larry's Lounge.

Tonight the stranger had a second question. "Boulder's easy to get to, ain't it?"

He stood with his arms wrapped around his upper body, and the oversized army coat he wore hugged him with sleeves that were at least two sizes too big. The green duck cloth bunched at his shoulders and neck. He peered out from the tight fitting hood of a brown sweatshirt, and his mouth held a smirk, fuzzy at the edges from a scruff of whiskers. One leg of his faded jeans was ripped just below the knee. The flap of denim hung limply and revealed a dark gash on his pale skin.

Luke wore a pair of clean jeans, sneakers and a blue and white striped cotton shirt with a button down collar. A fray of denim marked the place where Jerrod's bell-bottomed jeans met the tops of his scuffed sandals, but he wore a clean, green t-shirt with an outline of mountain peaks imprinted across the front. Bake's gray t-shirt had a bleached out spot that formed the shape of a badge near his heart. He wore that shirt proudly and tucked it into a pair of black slacks that were creased in unusual places, like he had just pulled them from his suitcase earlier that evening instead of hanging them up three weeks ago when he had first unpacked the rest of his belongings.

On that warm summer night, the stranger's hooded sweatshirt and especially the oversized coat painted a stark contrast to Luke and his friends in their short-sleeved shirts. Luke smiled as he drew closer to the bohemian.

The stranger spoke again. "The hill's up that way."

When he raised his arm to point, Luke ducked but kept on walking, and the stranger directed his monologue at Bake and Jerrod. "Boulder's hard to find sometimes. Easy to get to, but hard to find."

"That doesn't make any sense." Bake responded as he came along side of the stranger.

"Yeah, I know, but you guys just got here." The stranger grinned in retort.

Luke had just grabbed the door handle but dropped his hand and turned instead to get a full view of the street corner scene. His clean-cut friends bunched near one of the weirdest people he had ever encountered.

"What does that mean?" Jerrod probed.

The stranger ignored Jerrod and Bake.

The stranger's voice rose along his line of sight. "Yeah, what does that mean?" He confronted Luke with his question.

"You're a little freaky. That's what that means." Luke answered and smiled in spite of himself.

"You are, too, my friend." The stranger reflected Luke's smile, but his was less friendly.

Luke laughed and called to his friends. "I think it's time we had a beer, before things really do get freaky."

"Makes sense to me." Bake confirmed the one thing that he knew for certain.

"Jerr, you ready?" Bake asked when he already knew the answer.

"Sounds good to me." Jerrod nudged Bake toward Luke and the door to Larry's Lounge, and then he turned to the stranger. "Maybe we'll see you again sometime."

"Yeah maybe, but I'm kinda' hard to find." A crooked grin came to the stranger's face.

His friends shook their heads in a synchronized pattern as they crossed the threshold. Luke called out the bohemian's mantra. "Yeah, hard to find but easy to get to."

The stranger raised his voice too. "Yeah, that's what I mean."

Bake heard that retort and chuckled. "Fellas, this is where we came in, isn't it?"

When the door closed behind him, Luke called out. "We could use three of your coldest beers, my friend."

During the course of several rounds of beers, Luke and his friends bantered about the uniqueness of their Boulder experiences, including that night's encounter with *Army*. Larry, the Saturday night bartender and owner of Larry's Lounge, had identified the stranger as *Army*, although Larry gave credit to one of his other patrons as the original source of that name.

Larry considered *Army,* and other transients like him, to be examples of the bizarre subculture that had been spreading throughout the country. He expressed a sincere concern for those who lived in such wacky ways, and he assured Luke and his friends that Boulder was a college town at its roots, a straightforward and honest place to live.

Luke and his friends accepted Larry's assessment but added their own perspectives. After just a few weeks of living in Boulder, they opened to a full array of experiences. They expected that they might one day bump into Stephen Stills, perhaps Neal Cassady or one the other Merry Pranksters as they made a cross-country bus trip, or maybe even Hunter Thompson. Jerrod had heard that Thompson often chose Colorado as the site for a retreat from his frantic life style.

If, in the meantime, they crossed *Army's* path instead, then they could accept him and his weirdness. They reserved judgments only for the coldness of the beers at Larry's Lounge or The Sink.

As they finished their latest round in unison, Bake pushed the bottles together at the end of the bar. He placed three one-dollar bills under the grouping and reminded Luke and Jerrod of their intention to sample a few cold ones at the Hideout too. Luke signaled their pending departure with a wave to Larry. Don, the bartender at the Hideout, served draft beer in chilled mugs. When they answered Don's last call for drinks, they used that round to toast to their good fortune. As they made their way along the downtown sidewalks, Luke shared a sentiment, a remembrance from earlier that evening.

He looped his arms around the shoulders of his friends. "I don't know about easy to get to, but it sure is easy to live here in Boulder."

Jerrod had the last word. "It's a Boulder way to be."

Chapter 15

"Shhh!" Julia quieted Clay with a forefinger pressed to her lips.

Clay basked in the revelry of the day, a Fourth of July celebration with him at center stage. He felt the day deserved another cheer and released it just as Julia made her way to the bottom of the front stairs. She hushed him and then slipped into the bathroom before joining him on the sofa.

"I think she's finally asleep, but we can't be too loud." Julia relaxed.

"Think she had a good time today?" Clay squeezed Julia's hand.

"I know she did, especially the fireworks tonight. You're little show was quite the thing. Even the older kids liked it."

"Glad we got the neighbors to join in. That really made it fun." Clay scooted closer to Julia.

He had made all the advance arrangements and recruited the supporting cast. Many of Julia's neighbors had participated in the afternoon barbeque. Each family had brought food. Some brought beer, or soda and lemonade. Julia had baked three apple pies. Frank and Darrell had built a small fire pit in one corner of Julia's backyard and engineered a mechanized spit that allowed them to roast two large pork tenderloins. Their work had begun in the morning. Clay had provided an ice chest filled with beer and the supervisory expertise.

Most of the guests had arrived in the mid-afternoon. Clay had planned for a juggler and magician as the afternoon entertainment. Both were fellow teachers with him at the high school. The early evening meal was a feast that overflowed the six picnic tables he had rented and positioned under the shade of the trees. Julia's pies and the homemade ice cream had provided the classic ending for the meal. Everyone agreed that the local trio Clay hired to perform a concert of sing-along tunes, patriotic songs, folk rock, and ballads had provided a relaxing segue way for the grand finale.

Clay had made the trip to Wyoming with Frank. They had purchased a variety of fireworks items, many of which were not available in the state of Colorado. Clay had organized the display and allied with the property owners whose houses held key positions at the top of the street. There, at the base of the foothills, an undeveloped space, two streets intersected and created a strategic launching area. He had even made sure water hoses were available to douse any charges that misfired.

Bill Carney from the mine lent his expertise to the more complex fireworks. The display built a momentum marked by an early wave of oohs and aahs that then rippled into cheers and whistles at the final aerial bursts of red, white, and blue.

Clay had surprised many of the guests and especially Julia and his cousin, Karen, when he rallied a few of the neighborhood pre-teens and some of his friends to follow him as he slid two large trash cans along the pavement and gathered all the spent devices and fragments scattered on the streets. Several of them hopped into the bed of his pickup and rode down the street to Julia's house. Guests who were still making their way home applauded again as they rode past.

"From food to entertainment, and even clean up, you did a great job. It was a great party. Everything, all day long. Terry was still talking a mile a minute when I took her upstairs. She was so excited." Julia smiled broadly, remembering her daughter's reactions.

"What about you, did you have a good time?" Clay pressed against Julia's side.

"Oh, yes." Her eyes met his, and she giggled when she spoke. "I had no idea you were such a party planner. It was quite the event!"

"I kinda approached it like a big game, just mapped everything out as best I could." He dropped her hand and shrugged.

As he let his guard down, she poked him in the ribs, and then kissed him on the cheek.

Her eyes sparkled with her words of praise. "Terry said the neighborhood kids all think she's cool, and you're the coolest."

"Yeah, but what do you think?"

"I think..." She smiled then and cast her eyes toward the ceiling.

"Come on." Clay encouraged her to say something. "It's all that's important to me."

"What you did today was super. It's the most fun we've had in this house since...since..." A watery gleam filled her eyes. "It's been way too long, since we...since I've had so much fun. It was a great day, and it made me happy, really happy." She kissed him on the lips as a quick punctuation.

She offered to get him one last beer, but he surprised her when he declined. Instead, he hugged her close and kissed her with a passion that had its origin in bolts of lightning and surfaced now in the glare of Fourth of July rockets.

"I'd do anything to make you happy." He swallowed her inside a muscular embrace.

———

Julia awoke in the coolness of pre-dawn and nestled closer to Clay. The delights of the previous day and its culmination in a brilliant fireworks display flashed from her subconscious to her conscious awareness. She wrestled then with the sexual fireworks that had transpired, the crisscross of discourse and intercourse that led from that day to this. The giddy euphoria of their mutual release drove a desire now to hold to the happiness she felt. She pledged a silent intention to have it, even if she would have to let go of all that had gone before.

A family of finches chirped from a place just outside her window. She wanted to rise with them but dosed instead. When the sun rose above the horizon and found its way through the window, she rolled away from Clay and tiptoed out of the room.

Terry sat on the floor in the front room and watched cartoons. Her mother's quick kiss on the cheek surprised her.

"Wow, you're up early, little girl! It seems like we just went to bed." Julia nuzzled Terry's neck.

Terry turned with an explanation. "I was wondering what we were goin' to do today, but you were still sleeping and so was Mr. Williams. So, I just came down to see what was on TV."

The sound of an explosion emanated from the TV. It captured Terry's attention, but she made another comment. "I didn't know Mr. Williams slept here."

Julia backtracked and placed the emphasis on her daughter. "Everybody was really tired last night after the...after the fireworks and everything, remember? When I finally got you to go to bed, you said you were going to sleep extra late?"

"But I missed *Porky Pig*. This is just *The Roadrunner*."

"Oh, I see. So you really did sleep late then." Julia giggled. "Let's eat some breakfast."

As she finished her bowl of Corn Flakes, Terry asked the same question for the third time. "So really Mom, what are we goin' to do today?"

Julia responded as she turned from the sink. "I told you. I want to..."

But Clay strode briskly into the room and boomed a bold idea. "I was thinkin' we'd all go to Elitches!"

"What's Elitches?" Terry was startled by Clay's entrance.

"What's Elitches? Only the funnest place around." Clay clarified as he bent down to explain to Terry face-to-face. "Karen and Susie said they'd go too."

"What? Don't they have to work?" Julia was as surprised as her daughter.

"They're workin' for the city parks department this summer. They said that today is a holiday for them. I talked to them last night about it. So, what do you two girls say?"

"I want to do something fun." Terry proclaimed as she scooted toward the back stairway. "But I have to put on my clothes. Come on, Mom, can you help me pick something out?"

"You two take your time. I've got to change, too. Plus I know we'll have to roust those other girls." Clay called after Terry.

He grabbed Julia's arm when she turned to follow Terry. "Hey there, good morning. You okay?"

"I'm fine. Looks like we're going to Elitches," Julia responded.

"It'll be fun." Clay kissed her on the cheek and whirled toward the kitchen door.

———

The days of that summer played in a fast pace of fun activities. Clay arranged outings in the mountains, even one camping trip. Terry liked sleeping in the tent. Julia added picnics in the park, not just the one near their house, but Scott Carpenter Park too. When they went to the swimming pool, Clay taught Terry how to dive head first into the water. He dove from the highest board sometimes, but Julia insisted that Terry was too young to try that.

Those summer nights pulsed with a unique tempo too. Often times the intense nighttime passion consumed the light-hearted essence of the day. Julia decided to purchase a new bed, new pillows and new linens. On the day they were delivered, she took down the one photo of her parents and those of Jim that had been hanging in the upstairs hallway. She painted the walls a cream color and planned to shop for something new to hang there, perhaps paintings or other works of art.

In the middle of August, Susie moved out of the basement apartment. She accepted a scholarship to pursue a graduate degree at UCLA. Clay tried to convince Julia to lower the rent so that Karen could afford to live there during her final year at CU. He made assumptions about Julia's financial situation, and he described the rental income as superfluous.

Julia reacted with surprising vehemence. "It's none of your business what I charge for rent, or what I do with my own house, now is it?"

"Oh honey, don't go gettin' mad. I just thought..."

"No you didn't!" Julia interrupted him.

She clung to this one idea, an idea from the past, one that she and Jim had discussed many years ago, but she chose not to explain it to Clay. She took the initiative to implement the idea and liked the results when Susie became the renter the previous year.

She felt certain she could replicate the experience. "I already put an ad in the paper, and that's all there is to say about it!"

"Jeez. Don't go gettin' your panties in a twist!"

"Clay, I mean it!"

"Okay! Okay!"

When school started and the high school team lost their first two football games, Clay became increasingly agitated.

Terry noticed the difference. "I guess Mr. Williams doesn't really like school, does he Mom?"

Terry puzzled over the difference between her own feelings and those of Mr. Williams. Julia's disappointment at Clay's increasingly dramatic displays of frustration caused her to question some of her own feelings about Clay.

Julia constructed a simple explanation and spoke it as much for her own benefit as for Terry's. "He's having a hard time with the beginning. Maybe we had too much fun this summer."

Chapter 16

Boulder, Autumn 1971

Warm, September winds parched the long grasses that were the typical vegetation of the foothills region around Boulder. In particular, Luke trampled a path through such grass on a hillside near the house where he had rented a basement apartment. That hillside and the ridgeline that ran above it had escaped the housing developments dotting other parts of the foothills. It thrived as a greenbelt, just a few steps beyond the border of town. Elephant-sized boulders marked a midpoint up the hill and provided a vantage point for Luke.

On Saturday afternoon, sometime after two o'clock, the time that Luke punched the time clock at the downtown bookstore where he worked, he stopped at home to check the mail and quench his thirst. He placed Elizabeth's letter inside the pages of one of his books, and then, free to do as he pleased, he found his way to the one of those boulders. There he lay back and placed the book, *The Complete Works of William Blake*, under his head.

He basked in the fullness of the afternoon and the fiery colors that surrounded him. The September sun burnished the leaves of the deciduous trees, turning them yellow and orange. The aspen trees, in particular, burst into an array of golden hues, their leaves outshining all the others.

After the warmth of the day had relaxed him, he sat up and pulled the letter from its place among the pages of the book. Elizabeth's writing would take precedence over that of any other writer, even Blake's poetry. He set the letter aside when two photographs fell into his lap.

In one picture Elizabeth wore a sun dress striped in red and gold. She stood next to her father. His sun burnt face and the fact that he held a BBQ utensil in one hand led Luke to conclude that the occasion was a picnic, perhaps a celebration on Labor Day. In the other photo Elizabeth wore her nursing uniform. She stood in front of a large brick building.

The letter provided details about both photographs. The first was indeed a Labor Day picnic. The second was taken as a commemoration of her first day working at Children's Hospital. After finishing the letter, Luke raised both pictures toward the blue sky, as if in celebration. Elizabeth's dream had been realized. Another glorious aspect added to the montage of that magnificent day.

———

When he closed his eyes again, a rush of images flew toward him. Elizabeth's auburn hair lightened by the summer sun, satin ribbons fluttering, the allure of her soft blue eyes, and the suppleness of her tan and slender body. When the images paused mysteriously, his mind focused on her magical smile. He extended his hand, as though he could touch her. If only he possessed a wizard's wand, he would make one of his dreams come true.

His eyes opened when he felt the tickling of a breeze and a fine dust brushed across his arm. A scattering of leaves broke away from the trees that lined the streets below. They flew freely, some fluttering, some rocketing, and each finding an individual path to the earth. It seemed that they would touch everything while they were most free.

Amidst the maneuvering of the leaves, Luke allowed his thoughts to whirl through time and space. He remembered how he, along with Jerrod and Bake, had scrambled to the top of the canyon wall one Sunday morning during that previous summer. At the pinnacle of the climb, they built a cairn out of a few slabs of shale and some granite rocks.

The three of them stacked a knee high pyramid of beer cans as a memorial to another weekend in the mountains. At their campsite near Nederland, they celebrated meeting Boulder County's rodeo queen and her entourage. Bake laughed incredulously whenever Jerrod would finish a beer with a flourish and a bow to the queen.

When Bake and Jerrod ended their hike above the waterfall in Boulder Canyon by plunging into a pool of frigid water, Luke found a warm spot in the sunshine where they could dry themselves. No photographs were taken, but the impressions were saved. Luke held them still on this autumn afternoon.

He drew from a wealth of memories and missives mailed from places where he lived, places that still lived within him. Jerrod would work the fields at harvest time. Bake would work the sidelines while coaching the high school football team. Elizabeth administered to the young patients given into her care.

She would join him for the last picnic of the year. Perhaps they would again find that place between the river and the trees, or it could be they would come to know another mystical place.

He might run with the falling leaves, or kick through a forest piled with the colors of the season. He might jump for a shot, instant eye contact with the orange painted rim and the basketball through it. Another two points would propel his team to victory, and a cheer would fill the crowded gymnasium. His father would appear, standing at the end of the bleachers, too excited to take a seat.

His father would shout a cheer. "Give 'em all we got!"

It could have happened long ago, or just recently, when he first met Julia Karsten and her daughter, Terry. Julia held out a hand so Terry would come closer and say hello.

He held out his hand and helped Elizabeth to the top of the wall in Forest Park. He exchanged a handshake when he said good-bye to his brothers and his family and just a few weeks ago when he said good-bye to his friends, fellow Boulderites for the summer.

The warmth of the afternoon lingered, and Luke turned the first pages of his book. His senses had been ripened by the splendor of the day, and he opened fully to the imagery in Blake's poetry. He absorbed the essence of the words like the sun's energy saturating the cells of his skin.

Terry startled him when she called from a spot below the outcropping of boulders. "Hi, up there. Hi!"

Luke trained his eyes on Terry. "Hello there. What brings you up here?"

"Ah, nothing. Just walking. What're you doing?"

"Not much, just reading."

"What?"

"A book of poems. Do you know what they are?" Luke couldn't remember reading poetry when he was a young boy.

"Yeah, they rhyme." Terry stood upright like she was answering a question in school.

"Sometimes. Do you come up here a lot?"

"Just sometimes. Do you know what's over there?" Terry pointed to the left.

"Not really. What?"

"Come on, I'll show you!"

Terry walked around the lower perimeter of the outcropping. She circled in the opposite direction of the path that Luke had taken to his vantage point. He re-traced his path but stopped when he realized that Terry had disappeared. A few barely bent stalks of wild grass marked the route that she had taken. Luke stepped in those same spots, and the grass brushed against the knees of his jeans.

After a few strides he called her name. "Terry? Terry, where are you?"

She did not reply, and he continued in the same direction, crunching his own path in the tall grass but holding a course near the bottom of the boulders. The face of the largest boulder steepened as he made slow progress. He counted four more strides and called out again. When he still received no reply, he made an about-face thinking he would backtrack. As he did, Terry jumped out and grabbed his leg.

"Gothcha!" She shouted.

Terry clutched the bottom of Luke's jeans. "What the heck? Where'd you come from?"

Terry parted the grass and revealed the opening of a small cave in the lower portion of the rock face. "Come on!"

Terry waddled like a duck, while Luke dropped to his knees and made his way on all fours. He blinked to adjust his sight and flinched when he expected to hit his head. Terry seemed to stand upright again, and the blackness turned to dark gray. Luke crawled to her side, turned, and propped his upper body against the back wall of the cave.

"Well." Luke sounded relieved.

"Pretty neat, huh?" Terry's voice held excitement.

"I'd say. How'd you find this place?"

"Some of the kids showed me. I come up here sometimes."

"You like it here, then?"

"I do. Almost everybody forgets about it 'cause the grass gets so high and covers up the hole."

"Kinda dark though." Luke assumed most children didn't like the dark.

"You get used to it. I can see good. And it's quiet. I like to just sit in here and be quiet. You can hear the wind if you're quiet."

"It gets hot in here, I bet."

"I just sit in here for a little while. Now that school is started, it'll get colder pretty soon."

"Probably so. You like school?" Luke realized Terry may not be the same as other children.

"It's okay. I like the kids but not the teachers. I don't like the homework that they give."

At least Terry had this one thing in common with many of the children her age.

Luke probed a little more. "What grade are you in?"

"Third."

"What's your teacher's name?"

"Mrs. Tyson. She's old. Mom says she's a good teacher. My mom works at my school."

"I know, she told me. I've seen you two leaving for school in the morning."

"Mom's a secretary in the office. That's neat, I guess. She's not a teacher, but she knows all the teachers. She likes Mrs. Tyson, and Mr. Williams too."

"Who's he?"

"A gym teacher, but not at my school, where the big kids go. He's got big muscles. He can pick me up real easy. He comes over to eat supper and talk to my mom."

"I see his truck in the drive way sometimes."

"His truck is big too. I just ride in my mom's car. You should, too."

Luke misunderstood. He questioned his ability to interpret the meanings of a third-grader. How could he expect to appreciate Blake's poetry?

He pursued a clearer understanding with the question. "Ride in your mom's car?"

"No, silly, come over for dinner. Why don't you?"

"I don't know. I usually cook something in my apartment."

"I know. Sometimes I don't like the smell."

"I admit I'm not a very good cook."

"My mom is. Mr. Williams says so, anyway."

"What about your dad?"

"I don't know him. He was a soldier. Got killed in a war. What about your mom?"

Luke was out-of-sync again. "What do you mean?"

"Does your mom cook?"

"Oh, yes, she's a good cook. Most moms probably are. She lives in St. Louis."

"That's a long ways from here."

"Yeah, kinda."

"What about your dad?" Terry liked to find out things.

"He died, too."

"In the war?"

"No, he got real sick."

"Did you know him?"

"Oh, yeah, I knew him. He and my mom raised me and my brothers and sister."

"I don't have any brothers or sisters. I guess my mom raises me. I had Gramps and Grandma until they crashed in his airplane. Gramps knew how to fly. Mom says, 'it's just you and me now.' I hope that's the way it stays."

"Well, things don't always stay the same."

"I guess. Can you see now?"

Luke responded on the assumption that Terry was asking about his eyesight. "Yeah, pretty good."

"Okay, I think I better go. It's probably supper time." Terry shuffled toward the opening of the cave.

Luke followed on his hands and knees, and when they emerged into the light, he stood to brush the dust from his jeans.

He blinked to adjust his eyes. "Well, maybe I'll see you here again?"

"I don't know. I usually come alone."

"I know. I mean, I'll probably just come to read. I like it best up there." Luke pointed to the top of the boulders, but Terry didn't see him.

When he turned back, she had already made her way to the main trail.

"See ya," he called out.

A faint good-bye drifted through the tall grasses. Terry trotted along the main trail toward the street. She made her way easily, like she had indeed traveled regularly along that path. White puffs of clouds gathered along the southern horizon. Luke ambled to the top of the outcropping and collected his book and Elizabeth's letter, and then followed the path at his own pace.

He was alone, as he had decided to be. He took a step into the street but stopped when a car came upon him too fast. After he crossed to the sidewalk that led to home, he paused to survey the way he had come.

He smiled at the thought of the small cave, a kid's hideout. Beyond the large group of boulders, a trail zigzagged up the hillside to a path that cut a horizontal line heading south, disappearing around the curve of the hill. Golden highlights spun a border around the clouds now, a further indication that it was supper time.

Long shadows of the early evening greeted him when he opened the door of his basement apartment. He turned on the kitchen light and prepared his meal. He ate at the kitchen table staring through the ground level window into the backyard. Wind gusts swirled there, and twigs that supported a few leaves bounced against the screen. Individual leaves danced there, too.

The smaller leaves were the first to fly. Because of their size, they swirled in many directions. They caught the imagination of many passers-by, as they were unique, the first of their kind. The older, stronger leaves, well-anchored during the growing season, were reluctant to let go. They left later in the season and with less flare. They often went unnoticed, although their movement extended farther. Lifted by broader wings, they flew more freely than those that had gone before.

Luke proceeded to the sink, stopped to deposit the butter in the refrigerator, and cleared the table with one more trip across the small kitchen. He washed, rinsed and stacked the dishes in the draining rack. They would remain there until he needed them for the next day's meal.

When he moved in, Julia had described the set of dishes, silverware, and cooking utensils, and all the furnishing in the apartment as hand-me-downs from her family. Just the same, Luke took extra care with them as they appeared to him to be of good quality. He had even invested in Brillo pads to clean the iron skillet after he had over cooked a steak, creating a blackened crust of beef that he feared was permanently imbedded in the bottom of the pan.

After a few weeks of preparing his food, Luke found the meals blending into a single sensation of smell and taste. The pot pie dinners became indistinguishable from the fried hamburger and potato meals. That night he tried a side dish of Rice-A-Roni for the first time, and he complimented himself on the spicy variety he had achieved.

As he passed from the kitchen into the front room, he switched off the light. He forgot about the dry chicken breast he had eaten and tried to remember what he had read of Blake's poetry that afternoon. He chose the overstuffed chair, which had become his favorite spot. He had developed the habit of retreating into the cushions of such a chair in the large room he had shared with his fellows at the fraternity house during his time at Oakwood College.

He relaxed there, while the final rays of that day's sun bounced off the pale gray of the concrete driveway. A pair of feet in sneakers walked with long strides, quickly into and out of the frame formed by the window. Shortly afterwards, a man's voice boomed a greeting, and a woman's voice echoed a muffled response.

He switched on the lamp and picked up his book. He read the first section of *Jerusalem*, one of Blake's longer poems. Blake conjured a myriad of images as Luke settled into the words.

When the night fell into quiet, he completed the day's routine by brushing his teeth. He re-aligned the bath and hand towels on the rack. He laid Blake's book on the nightstand with the pages open at the start of a new section. As he switched off the lamp, an image of *Jerusalem* floated in the afterglow.

Chapter 17

Luke maintained a business-like gait through the front hallway of the school building. The sign for the administration office identified his destination. When he opened the door, Julia smiled quizzically.

She greeted him. "Hello, what brings you to school?"

"One of your teachers ordered twenty copies of *A Wrinkle in Time*. They just arrived this morning at the store, so I was asked to deliver them. Where's Miss Jackson's classroom?"

"That's okay. You can just leave the box here. I'll make sure she gets them. Lunch period starts in a few minutes. I can have her pick them up then."

"Okay, Mrs. Karsten."

Julia smiled again. "Please Luke, only the students call me Mrs. Karsten. To everyone else I'm just Julia."

"Okay then, Julia, thanks."

Julia stood, and when the casters of her desk chair squeaked, Luke glanced over his shoulder.

Julia asked, "Are you going to lunch?"

"Usually I eat later, around one o'clock." Luke turned to face her.

"I was thinking of grabbing a sandwich now, and I thought you might want to join me."

"Maybe, but I should call the store to see."

"Sure, use my phone."

Julia re-appeared from an office in the back of the room as Luke hung up. "What's the verdict?"

"My boss gave me the okay."

"Okay, let's go." Julia led the way out of the office.

Luke tucked in his shirt as he followed behind her. By the time they made it through the front door, they were walking side by side.

"Where would you like to go?"

Luke had no answer. "You choose. I don't go out very often."

"I've noticed. For a single guy, you sure like to cook."

"I wouldn't say that. It's more of a habit, a necessity."

"You want to take my car?" Julia pointed to the Volvo in a nearby parking spot.

"I've got the truck from the store." Luke gestured to the pick-up truck along the curb.

"Maybe we should both drive. That way each of us can get back to work on time. And let's see. How about Larry's?"

"Larry's? You've eaten there?"

"Sure, lots of times. Larry's has great burgers."

Luke followed Julia around the semi-circle drive. Larry's was only a ten minute drive and was located just a few blocks from the bookstore.

Julia sped through an intersection when the traffic light turned yellow. Luke made the stop. When he reached Larry's, he found a parking spot near Julia's car, but it took two tries to parallel-park the truck along Pearl Street.

When Luke entered, Julia waved from a booth near the back of the restaurant.

As he sat down, Julia asked, "Where've you been?"

"Still haven't figured out an easy way to park the truck." Luke fidgeted with the knife and fork placed atop his napkin.

"I see. You always obey the law too?"

"I guess." Luke shook his head, uncertain of the meaning of the question.

"I ordered us each a burger and fries. Hope that's okay. I don't have a whole lot of time. Larry knows I need to get back."

"Sure," Luke responded, certain that this was the first time a woman had ordered a meal for him.

"So, you know Larry?" Luke slipped his napkin from beneath the flatware.

"Jim, my husband, and I used to come here while we were dating, and after we were married, even though I couldn't legally drink at the time, except for 3.2 beer. Sometimes he and his friends moved the tables and created a little dance floor by the juke box. He sang along with the records. Those were good times for us."

Even in the drab surroundings, Julia's eyes twinkled with the recollections. "It was a lot of fun. What about you, been in here before?"

"Oh, yeah, a few times, but not lately. My friends and I hit this place, The Sink, and the Hideout regularly this summer. Lately, it's no fun drinking alone."

"That's the truth!" Julia raised her glass of water.

"What's the truth?" Larry inquired as he placed the plates on the table.

"It's no fun drinking alone." Julia squared the bun over her hamburger.

"Yeah, but we've always got a bartender on duty." Larry positioned the plates nearer his guests.

Julia swallowed her first French fry and motioned to Luke. "This is Luke. He's renting our basement apartment."

"Good to see you again." Larry nodded to Luke. "Couldn't remember your name, but I know you from before. You and your friends. Guess you know you've got the prettiest landlady in town."

Luke mumbled as he swallowed a bite of hamburger. "I guess."

Larry edged toward Julia but spoke to Luke. "So, haven't seen you in a while."

Luke cleared his throat. "My friends went back to Missouri, so I don't go out much anymore."

"You can just stop by for a visit and a quick beer. Bring Julia with you too. It'll class up the joint."

"Larry, stop with that silliness!" Julia tapped Larry's arm.

After Larry left their table, Julia asked, "So, why'd you decide to stay here when your friends left?"

"It just felt like the right thing to do. Nothing, no real reason. Nothing pulling me back there, except..." Luke's head dropped, and he picked up a few French fries.

Julia intuitively found the words Luke hesitated to speak. "There's somebody special waiting for your return."

"Yeah, but it's okay for now. She's a nurse and works a lot because she's just getting started at the hospital. She understands. We've known each other for a lot of years. And some time...well, you know." Luke shrugged.

Julia had not intended for the conversation to become uncomfortable, so she took a bite of her burger and swallowed before summarizing. "Then I suppose you'll head back yourself someday."

"Probably, some time," Luke responded and diverted the attention to Julia. "What about you? How'd you end up here in Boulder, secretary at Westview School and the prettiest landlady in town?"

Julia jabbed a French fry at Luke. "Don't follow Larry's lead with that stuff about being a landlady. He's a little strange."

Luke's smile returned with his response. "I don't know. I think he probably has that part right. But tell me about Boulder and you."

Julia relaxed. "I've lived here since I was a little girl. My dad was a pilot. Our house was over near Chautauqua Park. My parents passed away though, so I sold their house."

Julia took a drink of water, and when Luke took another bite of his hamburger, she shared some more details. "It happened just a few months ago. They died in a plane crash, if you can believe that. My dad was flying them to Aspen. He'd made that trip so many times before. I even went with them when I was young girl. Anyway, something happened and..."

Julia paused and took a bite from her hamburger. They ate in silence, and Luke's pace quickened. He consumed much of the contents of his plate.

He fumbled a French fry. "My dad died a couple of years ago. He'd been sick, though, not in an accident like your parents. It hurts those left behind, I think."

Luke winced and dabbed at the corners of his mouth with his napkin as though his words had formed an impolite drool.

Julia sensed the awkwardness. She didn't know Luke, but she knew his pain. "The accident was a shock, but it didn't hurt like when my husband died. I remember that time even though it's been three years. I'm glad I kept our house. My parents gave it to us right after we got married. I started renting the basement apartment a couple of years ago. Jim and I always talked about doing that. Terry was only five when Jim died. He had been away in Vietnam for almost a year, too, so I don't think she remembers a lot about her dad. It's kind of crazy, don't you think?"

Luke didn't expect to have to render an opinion, and he stalled by stabbing his last French fry into his plate. "I...I know. I mean, I think that kids...Terry seems to be doing just fine. Your basement apartment is great for me."

Luke punctuated his disjointed statements by swallowing the French fry. Julia rose from her side of the booth and found a five dollar bill in her purse. She dropped it on the table as Luke stepped next to her. When Luke dropped his five dollar bill on top of hers, he faced her and the proximity of her smile caused him to blush.

He hoped the low lighting hid that aspect, and he rushed his words. "This was great too, having the chance to talk and get to know one another."

Chapter 18

Luke ate a late breakfast on Sunday morning. He sat at the kitchen table and re-read the letters that he had written the night before. With his senses trained on the words, he ingested the scrambled eggs and toast without tasting them.

Sundays had become a day for relaxing, hiking, reading or writing. The small piece of distant sky framed by the window was a swath of gray clouds, and the tree in the foreground swayed in a mid-October wind. He ruled out a hike to his usual spot on the hillside. He added a t-shirt under his sweatshirt and put on two pairs of socks with his high-top sneakers.

When a wisp of wind found its way under his sweatshirt, Luke decided to jog. He made his way along the mostly-deserted streets, past the closed store fronts of downtown to the post office where he mailed his letters. He remembered comments that fellow workers at the bookstore had made about open gym on Sunday afternoons at the CU field house, so he ran in the direction of the campus.

Inside the field house a dozen players shot and dribbled basketballs at each end of the main court. Others used the side baskets. Luke grabbed the rebound of one of the missed shots, dribbled along the baseline, pivoted and shot. Swish! The first shot of the day and of the new season fell without touching the rim and popped the net.

As the would-be players warmed up and the temperature in field house rose, one individual suggested a method for determining the teams. The first four players to make a free throw would be the *shirts*, the second four would be the *skins*. The first team to score ten baskets would be the winner. Players who didn't make the first two teams would make up teams to challenge the winners. It was the same in Boulder as it was across the country.

Luke took a spot near the end of the line, and when eight of the first eleven players made their shots, he joined the others who had missed or hadn't gotten a chance to shoot outside the lines that marked the perimeter of the court. With four players on each team, the games were oriented so that they used the side baskets of the field house. This arrangement allowed for full court action while only employing one-half of the field house. Before long, another game began at the other end too.

One of the guys standing on the sidelines motioned toward the action. "What do you think?"

"Looks like a few of these guys have some ability." Luke glanced to the side and then back to the court.

"See the guy in the gold shirt? He played on CU's varsity team a few years ago. Same team as Cliff Meeley." Luke's fellow bystander rolled a basketball from one hand to the other.

Luke remembered that name. "Oh, yeah. Meeley had a solid career here. I think he's playing pro ball now."

The guy next to him handed Luke the basketball. "So, do you want to team up and take on the winners?"

"Sure!" Luke bounced the ball in the space between them.

"I'm Frank."

"Luke." He handed the ball back to his new teammate. Frank stood as tall as Luke but with a wider girth and broader shoulders, the stature of a football player, not necessarily a basketball player. He was a good teammate for the upcoming games. Of their other two teammates, one was a shooter and one a ball handler, so their ad hoc team moved with some symmetry and had some success.

After winning two games they tired, especially Frank. He often stayed on the defensive end of the court, while Luke and his other two teammates went three against four at the offensive end. Their team lost the third game, and Luke was happy for the respite the loss would allow.

When the team that had beaten them earlier added another pair of victories to the afternoon's record, Luke and Frank's team took the court. Luke and Frank developed a pick-and-roll play as the game progressed, and it became a two-on-two contest. Frank set a pick that bumped the man defending Luke, as Luke dribbled past Frank's stationary position near the free throw line. Luke moved with a long-practiced rhythm, and Frank's pick created just enough space. Luke scored repeatedly with his jump shot.

Their team quickly dispatched the opponents, but instead of taking on another team, the team they had just beaten challenged them to a rematch.

Frank answered the challenge on behalf of his teammates. "I guess we can let you go again, if it's okay with the guys waiting in the wings."

Frank shouted to the players on the sidelines. "It probably won't take too long for us to take care of these guys! Is it okay if they go again?"

The guys on the sidelines just waved to Frank. Both teams on the floor took that as an okay. The biggest guy on the opposing team snatched up the ball and fired it at Frank.

"Let's get it on!" He snarled.

With the same broad stature as Frank but taller by more than two inches, Luke guessed that this guy was a football player, too. Frank inbounded the ball to Luke and trotted to the offensive end of the court. The opposing big guy bumped Frank where they stood near the free throw line. The guy guarding Luke met him as he dribbled across the half court line, and a familiar intensity arose inside of Luke.

Instinctively, Luke positioned his defender to execute another pick-and-roll play. This time the outcome startled Luke. As he dribbled toward Frank's pick, the big guy slammed into Frank's back with a forearm. This clearly illegal tactic caused Frank to stumble toward him. Luke stopped with a stutter dribble, but the guy defending him tipped the ball away. The two of them scrambled after the ball, but the other guy had a better line.

As Luke's defender grabbed the ball, the big guy ran toward the other end of the court. Luke was now on the defensive. Before he could gather himself, the guy Luke now guarded tossed a long, looping pass down court to the big guy. He took the pass in stride and laid the ball in the basket as Frank trailed several strides behind. Luke hustled to help out but reached the other end just as the big guy took the ball from where it fell through the bottom of the net.

The big guy wheeled on Frank and jammed the ball in Frank's stomach. "How 'bout that, Fat Man?"

While Frank took the ball out of bounds, Luke fired a retort. "Yeah, how 'bout that foul?"

The big guy fumed as he back-pedaled. "Welcome to CU basketball, skinny man!"

Frank tossed the ball to Luke and muttered. "That's a Clay Williams welcome. Nothin' to do with CU or basketball."

"Looked more like football to me," Luke replied.

"You got it. We were teammates at Boulder High. He was all conference linebacker at CU, till he screwed up his knee. But not basketball, he hasn't played since high school." Frank trotted along side of Luke. "What say we lay low the next couple of times down?"

Luke passed the ball to one of his other teammates as he crossed the half court line. "Yeah, we'll let the game come to us."

Luke and Frank's other teammates produced their own two-on-two successes. Luke managed to pull down a couple of offensive rebounds and scored on the put-back shots. With the game tied eight to eight, Luke's team took up their positions on the defensive end of the court.

Luke exhorted his teammates to play harder. "Let's stop 'em this time."

The ball shuffled from one side of the court to the other, and as he and his teammates moved with the flow, Luke switched with Frank. He now guarded Clay Williams near the basket along the side of the free throw lane.

Clay yelled for the ball immediately. "Inside! Inside! This skinny guy can't stop me!"

Clay planted himself with his feet spread apart and his back to the basket. He jabbed at Luke's chest with his left elbow and extended his right arm toward his teammate. Luke leaned on Clay with his right forearm in Clay's back and his left arm extended above his head toward the man with the ball. Clay and Luke jostled for position, and Luke sought all the leverage he could.

He pushed against Clay with the lower part of his body and his legs, and threw his forearm into Clay's back each time Clay flung his elbow. Clay's size and strength inched both of them back toward the basket.

In the instant that the ball was passed to Clay, while it was still in flight, Luke pushed one more time with all his strength against Clay's massive frame. Still, Clay held his position, and the outcome seemed inevitable. Luke's instincts did not yield.

Upon releasing from that final push, Luke stepped sharply to the side. Clay caught the ball, but with no one pressing against him, he stumbled and had to recover by using a dribble. Clay found himself alone but all the way under the basket.

Clay, a clearly determined athlete, gathered himself and went up for the shot, but his position under the basket forced him to jump out and up. Luke took advantage and jumped with him. Just as Clay released the ball from his hands, Luke tipped it. He grabbed the ball and whirled in one motion to throw a long pass to one of his teammates moving toward his side of the court.

Luke's teammate took the ball on a full-speed dribble toward their basket and scored an uncontested lay-up.

"All right, buddy! How 'bout that, big guy?" Frank cheered as he charged toward Clay.

In response Clay pushed Luke in the back. Luke lunged forward but caught his balance and continued in the direction of their offensive end of the court, even though his teammate had already scored. Luke left Frank and Clay sparring behind him, mostly a verbal joust with some pushing and shoving and a high volume of noise and perspiration.

Clay stationed himself again along side of the lane. Frank took a defensive position similar to that used by Luke, but Frank was better able to hold his ground.

Clay called for the ball all the louder. "Come on, guys! Bring it down. I'll ram it down their throats this time!"

Luke moved closer to the guy he would be guarding. His teammates called him Chris, and he positioned himself near the free throw line. Chris was a decent player, but like the rest of the team, he deferred to Clay at crucial times during the game. Chris's teammate advanced the ball toward Clay.

Clay yelled again. "Come on, man, move it!"

At that command, the guy with the ball fumbled his dribble. He snatched the ball, and when he did, Luke's teammate pressed his defensive position. Chris's teammate pivoted toward him in that instant and telegraphed the pass, allowing Luke to intercept the ball. Within two strides Luke dribbled at full speed toward his basket. He felt Chris gaining on him, and he used a reverse lay-up to avoid Chris's defensive pressure.

Frank applauded as he skipped along the route Luke had taken for the winning basket.

He pivoted at mid-court and yelled at the top of his lungs. "Now that's basketball!"

Clay jumped and swatted the net while he moaned aloud. "Ahhh, fuck you!"

Clay slumped in disgust, while Frank lumbered down-court to Luke.

"What a game! What a finish! We definitely need to celebrate. I'll buy at least one pitcher of beer. What do you say? Let's head over to The Sink." Frank bumped Luke.

"I'm with you. I guess we could cool down there."

They used Frank's car for the short trip, but Luke still perspired profusely as they entered The Sink. Patrons filled the stools at the front bar, so Luke and Frank made their way into the dimly lit back room.

Frank listed the highlights of the afternoon's games as they consumed their first pitcher of beer. They were enjoying a hamburger and fries with their second pitcher when Frank gave some background on his position as Assistant Football Coach at Boulder High School. He explained that the big guy they had played against that afternoon held a similar position.

A smattering of cheers interrupted Frank's dissertation on the history of Boulder High School football. The raucous sounds emanated from the front bar.

"They must be watching the Broncos game." Frank commented and picked up his last mug of beer.

He stood and poured the remainder of the pitcher into Luke's mug and suggested. "Let's join the action."

As Luke and Frank pressed closer to the front bar, the TV announcer re-capped the reason for the boisterous chatter. The voice from the TV described a Floyd Little run and emphasized that one particular block allowed Little to score a touchdown from seventeen yards out. The Broncos took the lead over the Oakland Raiders.

From a position in the second row of patrons, Luke alternated standing on one leg then the other. He kept moving in order to relieve some of the stiffness in his legs. Frank squeezed between two bar stools. He explained to the patrons that occupied those stools that he needed to lean on something in order to avoid falling down, and they slid to the edges of their stools to provide as much space as possible for his wide body.

Brad, the bartender, wanted a more complete explanation. "So what have you been up to, Frank?"

"Just came from the field house. Played half a dozen games of full court four-on-four basketball. We won all but one of 'em too." Frank puffed his chest out.

"Basketball?" Brad knew that that wasn't one of Frank's strengths. "Don't you guys have a few more games left in football season?"

"Yeah, but I needed a workout, and it's too cold for jogging outside. So I decided to try some B-ball at the field house. You know, those pick-up games over there can get pretty brutal."

"Especially with you football guys stomping up and down the court."

"Hey, I can handle myself pretty good, right, Luke? Luke's my new, best friend, on the court especially." Frank pointed toward Luke, and Brad's eyes followed Frank's gesture.

Luke raised his mug of beer and his voice. "You're probably best under the boards, Frank."

Brad confirmed that image of Frank. "Yeah, I can see that. Banging bodies, you'd be good at that."

"I got the soft touch, though. It surprises a lot of guys."

"I bet." Brad chuckled and Luke just shrugged.

Frank emphasized a point that Brad could not refute. "Luke here, he's got the range and the touch, a really sweet jump shot."

"Here's to the shooters!" Brad raised a glass of what appeared to be ice water, and Frank and Luke each tipped their mugs of beer.

"Yeah, cool." An older patron, who sat a few stools away, raised his left arm toward the ceiling. "A round of shooters for everybody at this end of the bar! It looks like the Broncos are goin' to beat the Raiders."

Brad lined up the shot glasses and poured from a bottle of tequila. In minutes, a dozen men had sprinkled salt on the back of their left hands and held a shot glass in their right.

"Go Broncos!" Their impromptu leader cheered.

In unison, everyone licked the salt from their left hands and threw the shots down their throats with their right hands. "Yeehaw!" Someone yelled while the rest of the cheering section grabbed for a slice of lime to ease the sting.

After the game ended and they had finished one last beer, Frank settled the tab with Brad. Luke gave his last ten dollar bill to Frank as they exited. Unconsciously, Luke marched shoulder to shoulder with Frank toward the spot where he had parked the car.

When Luke realized that he was headed in the opposite direction of home, he stopped. "Hey, I should actually be going the other way."

Frank came to a halt as well. "What?"

Luke explained, "I live on the north side of town."

"Oh, I thought you lived on campus."

"Me? No. Why'd you think that?"

"I thought you were a CU student."

"No, I work at the Pearl Street Bookstore."

"That's cool. So where'd you park? I can take you to your car."

"I didn't drive, don't have a car. I just jogged to campus today."

"You're in better shape than I am, but then I could tell that from the way you played today." Frank took a step. "Come on. I'll give you a lift home."

Luke hesitated. "That's okay. I can just walk."

Frank spoke over his shoulder. "Don't be crazy. I rent an old farm house out by Lyons. The north end of town is right on my way."

Luke took a few long strides and caught Frank. Luke signaled Frank when to turn off Broadway. After a few more blocks, Luke pointed to a driveway and asked Frank to park at the place where it met the street.

Frank recognized the house immediately. "Hey, this is Julia Karsten's place."

"Yes it is. I rent the basement apartment. So, you know Julia?"

"Yes. As a matter of fact, the big guy whose shot you blocked today, Clay Williams, he's a friend, though you couldn't tell by the way he acts a lot of times. Anyway, he and Julia date. They've been seeing each other since Julia's folks died. That was a sad time, especially for her. Ya know her husband died in 'Nam a few years ago. She's had her share of heartache, for sure. They had a big party here for the Fourth of July. Clay can throw a good party. Julia, she's the sweetest. Clay's a real lucky guy. You, too, I guess."

"So I hear." Luke extended his hand, and Frank shook it. "Thanks for the games, the drinks and food, and the ride home. I'll contribute more financially to the cause the next time."

Frank grinned. "Hey, don't worry about that. It was more than worth it, just to see the look on Clay's face when you blocked his shot and stole that last pass. Two lay-ups to win the game, it was the coolest thing."

As Luke closed the car door, Frank shouted. "We're a good team. Let's do it again!"

Luke responded with a wave. He glanced at the sky, as he approached the house. It had cleared, and the first few stars of the autumn evening crowned the end of a winning day.

Chapter 19

" $\mathcal{I}$ t's like I said earlier. You're known around town. Each time someone finds out I'm renting an apartment from you, they comment on how lucky I am." Luke placed his dinner plate and a serving bowl on the kitchen counter.

Julia set a short stack of plates into the dishwater and didn't allow Luke to make another trip into the dining room without probing a little further. "Like who for instance?"

"A guy named Frank I've been playing basketball with the last few Sundays, and of course, Larry at the Lounge. I don't know. You're some kind of a celebrity, a local star."

"Who's a star?" Terry entered the kitchen.

"Your mom." Luke chuckled.

Julia lost the grip on the pan she was lifting from the stove. The clanging sound reverberated with her words. "Luke's just being facetious, like exaggerating or kidding around."

"Luke and me kid around sometimes too. Don't we?" Terry suggested off-handedly, and Luke hesitated on his way to the dining room.

"Yeah, I guess." He glanced at Julia.

"Up on Elephant Rocks mostly, Luke likes it up there, and so do I."

Julia frowned as her eyes darted from her daughter to Luke. She settled on Luke.

He expounded rapidly. "I do like to hike up to that group of rocks on the hill at the top of the street. I didn't know they were called Elephant Rocks. But anyway, I've seen Terry there a couple of times."

"Terry..." Julia's voice rose as she glared at her daughter. "I thought we had an agreement about you going off on your own. Besides, you're supposed to ask permission before you go anywhere."

"Yeah, I guess."

"No guessing about it. You ask me before you go off like that."

"But I usually only go when I see Luke goin.'"

"Actually I..." Luke tried to mount a defense.

Julia broke in. "But Luke doesn't know you're going up there."

Luke seized on that point. "She's surprised me more than once."

"That's 'cause I know some hiding spots." Terry stood as tall as she could.

"I don't care what you know, little lady. If I don't know, then there's no one to look out for you."

"Luke would, I think." She glanced in his direction.

"I..." Luke faltered, uncertain of his responsibilities.

Terry spoke over him. "Besides, I know where I'm goin.'"

"That's not the point. I'm your mother. You need to ask me before you go anywhere. I mean it. You understand?"

"Yes, mother." Terry fumed and ran out of the room.

Julia suggested to Luke that he retrieve the bottle of wine from the refrigerator and pour each of them a glass. She pointed to the cabinet where the glasses were stored as she spoke. Luke didn't know what to say so he went about his assigned task, and Julia tended to the dishes.

He formulated the beginnings of an apology. "I...I'm sorry about Terry. I truly didn't know she was following me. I used to hike there pretty regularly when it was warmer. To read mostly."

"Don't apologize. It's not your fault. Terry's a wanderer. I'm sure she doesn't remember, but when she was just a toddler her father took her up there. She probably connects to that place without even realizing it."

Julia explained things in terms that Luke did not fully comprehend, but he felt a connection to that place too. "It's a beautiful spot."

"I know." Julia swished the suds in the sink as though she was searching for something.

Anxious to change the subject, Luke offered. "Is there anything else I can do?"

"Double-check in the dining room."

Luke returned with the butter dish, salt and pepper shakers, and a small vase of flowers. "Any special place for these?"

"Butter anywhere in the fridge. Salt and pepper on the back of the stove, and the flowers, just put them on the kitchen table."

Julia placed another dish in the drying rack, and Luke used the flowers as a way to begin the conversation. "Nice flowers, daisies in early November. Something special you're celebrating?"

"Not really. My guy...My friend, Clay, he brings flowers pretty often."

"That's nice."

"He's been sweet in that way ever since my parents died. All the flowers after the service, that kind of got to him. He said he wanted me to have flowers...flowers that would mean better days, better times. So he usually brings different kinds when he comes over. I'm sure the flower shops in town like him."

"Mr. Williams, I think Terry likes him too."

"I suppose. But how would you?"

"One of the times when she surprised me at the place, Elephant Rocks, she mentioned him coming over for dinner. She said that he likes your cooking, and now I know why. Tonight's dinner was very good. I appreciate the invitation."

"It was actually Terry's idea, but thanks for the compliment." She finished the last of the dishes and lifted her glass of wine from the sink and tilted it toward Luke. "What else has Terry been telling you?"

"Well, let's see. I don't think she likes her teacher."

"That little stinker." Julia feigned a degree of agitation.

Luke reacted too quickly, and a drop of wine spilled from his wine glass. "Hey, you can't let her know I told you that. She may not ever ask me over for dinner again."

Luke grabbed the dish cloth and stooped to wipe the red wine. "Lord knows you won't want me back, since I'm so sloppy."

"Oh, but I might, since you've got the inside scoop on what's going on around town."

"You must have me mixed up with someone else. My beat is pretty small. Remember, I don't venture out much."

"What about your basketball buddies or some of the guys you work with? Boulder can be a fun town."

"I've had my share of fun in Boulder, but lately...I..." Luke stumbled to explain himself, but he brightened as he remembered another piece of information. "I guess you have some parties here."

"Not really." Julia took a long drink of her wine.

Luke elaborated, "I heard that the Fourth of July was a big celebration in the backyard."

"Well, yes, but that was a special occasion. It was Clay's idea really. He loves a good party."

"Yeah, he seems to be a pretty enthusiastic kind of guy."

"What do you mean by that?" Julia wondered how he could know Clay.

"I haven't had the pleasure of partying with him, but on the basketball court, he goes all out. Maybe even gets a little carried away at times."

"That sounds like our Clay. He's a football coach at the high school, and at one time was a star player at CU."

"So I heard." Luke smiled and took a sip of wine.

Julia's puzzlement grew to an irritation. "Wait a minute, mister-my-beat's-pretty-small. You seem to know a lot about my guy."

"Well, Frank's filled me in on some things."

"That would be Frank Morton?"

"I think that's his last name. He told me about your Fourth of July party when he dropped me off a few weeks ago."

"I see..." Julia smiled a knowing smile.

Luke did not recognize the nuance. "But really I don't know Clay. I've just played against him in some of the pick-up games at the field house on Sunday afternoons. Frank and I usually team up. I've gotten to know Frank some."

At that point Julia laughed and extended her glass toward Luke. "So, you're the one." She took the last sip of her wine. "That's too precious."

Luke struggled to see the hilarity but formed a crooked grin. When he extended his free hand palm up, like he was asking for an indulgence, Julia realized he didn't fully understand.

She apologized, "I'm sorry. It's just too cute, too ironic." She outlined the connections for Luke. "The last couple of weeks Clay has been telling me about this skinny guy who's making his team look bad on the basketball court. He mentioned Frank, but it seems Frank never told Clay about who you are. That's interesting."

Julia refilled her wine glass from the bottle she had retrieved from the refrigerator. Luke stood silently, unable to appreciate why he would be a source of amusement for his hostess.

Julia's delight shone clearly on her face. "Ooh, you must be a pretty good basketball player. Clay doesn't like to lose, especially at sports. You've got him frustrated. Wait till I tell him that you're renting the apartment. He'll go nuts."

"They're just pick-up games." Luke tried to minimize the situation.

"Oh, I know. I'm being facetious. He'll be cool about it. But, he'll be a little shocked too. I think it's wonderful." Julia took Luke's arm and led him toward the front room.

Terry reappeared. "What's wonderful?"

"Remember the party we had on the Fourth of July?" Julia dropped Luke's arm and looped hers across Terry's shoulders.

Terry had been fascinated by that day. "That was wonderful!" She still remembered it. "Mr. Williams shot off the fireworks. We had a magician. That was so much fun. Susie still lived here. We liked her."

Luke's shoulders drooped, and Terry noticed his reaction. "Susie lived where you are now. We don't know you as well, but maybe you can come to our next party."

"Whenever that might be." Julia patted the top of Terry's head.

"Whenever will that be, Mom?"

"I don't know. How about tonight? Tonight's a party, isn't it?"

"Not really. It's dinner and I thought TV. The TV book said George Girl is the movie tonight."

"That's *Georgie Girl*. It's about a young woman named Georgie," Julia explained as she switched on the TV.

"Sounds okay, but it's not a party, I don't think." Terry jumped and plopped into a seat on the sofa.

Luke finished his wine and placed the glass on the lamp table near the end of the sofa. "I believe I should make my way downstairs. You two enjoy the movie. Thanks again for everything. It's been fun."

He grabbed his jacket from the back of the sofa.

As Luke put on his jacket, Terry emphasized her point. "Maybe it was fun, but it wasn't a party, not really."

"There're all kinds of parties." Luke touched the top of Terry's head, mimicking Julia's earlier gesture. "And I think we just had one. Good night, Julia. See ya' Terry."

After she heard the kitchen door close, Terry tried for the final word. "Luke's not like Mr. Williams. He doesn't stay very long. Susie would usually stay after dinner, too. Luke's different, but he's nice. Don't you think?"

"Yes, he's nice." Julia hugged her daughter.

The theme song from the movie drew Terry's attention to the TV. Julia's thoughts drifted to CU campus and Elephant Rocks.

"Mom, the people sound funny."

"It's a British accent, honey. They're in England."

"Oh, it's different."

"I know." Julia mused about more than the TV movie.

Chapter 20

"Jerr! Come on in. It's great to see you!" Luke escorted him toward a chair. "Sit down. I'll get us a beer. How was your trip?"

"Think I'll stand. It's still a long drive." Jerrod circled the front room of Luke's apartment.

Jerrod described the sun's slow descent to the western horizon and extolled the reliability of the Plymouth he had inherited from his father. Luke re-created a few of the journeys they had made together in that car, each one an adventure.

Luke brought the conversation back to a more recent time. "So, from your letters it sounds like the harvest season went well. Worked your ass off, I bet!"

"It has been a while since I've had to work that hard. It felt good for the most part. But it's good to have some time off too."

"What about things at Oakwood? You wrote that the old alma mater was doing okay." Luke had enjoyed the stories Jerrod related in his letter about homecoming weekend.

"It was kind of neat going back for Homecoming as an alum for the first time. I got there on Friday night and drank some beers with the guys at the fraternity house. Smoked some dope too. The younger guys get into it a little more. They get it from south of the border now. It's better than the stuff we used to do. Anyway, we had a mellow night."

"What about Mark?"

"Being president of the fraternity, he tried to maintain his cool, didn't party too much. I think some guys are intimidated by him. I told them about Mark puking his guts out the first couple of times he went into Kansas City to party with us. He swore that he wasn't the only one who needed to be taken care of."

"That's the truth." Luke clicked his bottle of beer against Jerrod's, as they stood facing one another. "I know you saw Bake."

"He arrived on Saturday afternoon, just as the game was starting. His team had won a big game against their rivals the night before."

"Yeah he sent me clippings about the game from the local paper. He was psyched, I bet."

"He said he never stopped celebrating, and if you could've seen him, you wouldn't have denied it. He was wild. Everybody rallied for a giant blowout. Marty didn't make it, though. Nobody's heard from him lately."

"Guess you couldn't rally him or anybody else for the trip out here."

"All the guys are working regular jobs. Mark has basketball. So it's just me, buddy." Jerrod took a seat in the one chair in the room, so Luke found a spot on the sofa.

"I see you hung a couple of the posters. You're quite the decorator." Jerrod drank his beer.

"Don't have the flair that some guys have."

"I like your place though." Jerrod swept his arm in arc.

"It agrees with me." Luke concluded with a long drink.

They each finished that first beer, and as they partook of a few more, they cheered the antics of their past, laughed at those exploits, and left open the possibility of their reoccurrence.

Just before it was too late, they drove downtown to a diner for the Day-After-Thanksgiving Special, which was the turkey and dressing that Luke and the other patrons had not finished on Thanksgiving itself. Afterwards, they walked around the corner to Larry's Lounge.

"Remember this place?" Luke opened the door for Jerrod.

"Good burgers and cold beer, I remember. And what about Army, whatever happened to him?"

"He could be stoking the campfires somewhere in the mountains." Luke motioned to a bar stool.

"Let's try not to get that crazy." Jerrod signaled the bartender for two beers.

In the spirit of the holiday, they verbalized thanks for the food, the refreshments, and the friendship. They interspersed a shot of Jack Daniels with the beers that followed. A warm glow beamed from their faces.

Luke thought ahead one day. "Tomorrow we'll head into the foothills near my apartment. There's a new place I want to show you."

"I like the new. Here's to the new." Jerrod lifted his bottle.

"The new and the known." Luke met Jerrod's bottle.

———

Saturday morning became the perfect host. A day of crisp, clear air greeted Luke and Jerrod. After a late breakfast of English muffins and juice, and a brief time for personal clean-up, Luke led Jerrod to Elephant Rocks. Luke wore a jacket over his sweatshirt and a Denver Bears ball cap. Jerrod didn't need the cap, but Luke thought he better wear a jacket.

The hike had them both perspiring by the time they stretched out on one of the large boulders.

Luke wiped his forehead on the back of his jacket sleeve. "Letting a little of the wildness out."

"I can tell I've been back on the flat land the last few months." Jerrod inhaled the cool air and surveyed the scene. "Great spot, though, great view!"

"I've been a regular here. Some of the neighborhood folks like it up here, but most prefer the community park." Luke pointed to a spot in the foreground. "I like a little more elevation."

"I remember that from at least one occasion, the day that we climbed out of Gold Creek Canyon last summer."

"If I recall, that worked out all right." Luke bumped Jerrod.

"Things always seemed to work out in those days."

"It was just a few months ago."

"Seems so far away, though." Jerrod missed the mountains.

"That spot is only a few miles from here. But for now let's check out another place. It's above here."

Jerrod perused the foothills beyond where they had been sitting.

Luke reassured him. "Don't worry, there're no mountains to climb."

"Lead on!" Jerrod gestured to Luke.

The trail above Elephant Rocks steepened, and the footing required negotiating loose slag stones in certain places. The climb challenged their agility and their physical condition. They stopped periodically to replenish their lungs with an intake of fresh air.

When they reached level terrain, Luke paused for the widening view of Boulder valley. After a few minutes of silent repose, they traversed the hillside, striding shoulder to shoulder. Luke passed the sign, but Jerrod stopped to read it.

Jerrod re-phrased the message. "Says here that the trail ends in a steep drop off."

"Maybe it does, but that's not what I want to show you."

"That's good. I likely wouldn't follow you there, anyway."

"Not much farther." Luke took the lead position when the trail narrowed again.

Soon, Luke moved to the inside segment of the trail and stopped. He pointed down the trail to a place several yards away.

"Aren't these trees fantastic?" Luke edged closer to the two tall pines that projected skyward from what appeared to be the naturally hard surface of the Rocky Mountains.

"They're growing right out of the rocks. Far out!" Jerrod's excitement pulled him toward the trees.

"Mountain miracles. They never cease to amaze." Luke nudged Jerrod. "You want to see what those trees are guarding?"

"I assume it's the drop off. Nice of God to put those trees there to mark the spot."

"Somehow, someone's looking out for us." Luke sounded like he was praying.

Jerrod blessed them both. "Amen to that, brother!"

On their return, they slowed only when the footing was unstable. At Elephant Rocks they reveled in the day for a while longer.

Luke posed a practical question. "How about an early dinner?"

"Sounds good to me. I might even be ready for a beer soon." Jerrod realized the hike had carved a hollow in his stomach, but it also cleared his head.

After Larry's Lounge and tasty hamburgers digested with the help of a few beers, they assumed their stations on two barstools at the Hideout. There, Don the bartender kept the beers flowing. The festive mood culminated in a familiar refrain.

Jerrod voiced it. "Ah Boulder, there's no place like it on the planet!"

"I have to agree with that."

"And it seems like it agrees with you."

"That too." Luke settled their tab. "Let's head home."

The following morning Luke arose the earliest of the two. He dressed quietly and slipped on his jacket. He chose the path to the backyard. Another day's sun climbed toward its apex, and he leaned against an end pole of the swing set.

"Hi, what're you doin'?" Terry walked toward him with her inquiry, her hands tucked in her jacket pockets.

"Hey there, not much," Luke responded in a lazy voice.

"Do you see something up there?"

"Just the sun on the hillside. It's pretty, isn't it?"

"I guess, but the flowers are gone and all the leaves are off the trees."

"The sky's so blue and the sun's shining high in the sky. We've got a lot to be thankful for." Luke's words reflected his view.

"That's what Mom said on Thanksgiving Day, especially this year."

"Especially this year, what?" Julia asked as she approached.

"Terry and I were sharing a Thanksgiving thought." Luke replied for both of them.

"It's another beautiful day, isn't it? But I'm surprised you were able to get out and enjoy it." Julia brushed past Luke and gave Terry a starting push on the swing.

"Not sure I know what you mean." Luke feigned surprise at Julia's comment.

Terry gained height as she swung, and Julia came closer to Luke before she spoke. "It was kind of a late night, wasn't it?"

"Were we too loud?" Luke's voice revealed his sincere concern.

"Not really, I just happened to be up."

"So, you were out partying, too?"

"Nothing like that. Just had trouble sleeping."

"I'm thinking we'll all have a little sleep to catch up on. My friend heads back today. We'll get a late breakfast in town, and then he'll be on his way."

"Sounds like a good plan." Jerrod's voice carried from behind Luke.

"Hey, man, thought you'd sleep a while longer."

"Even in a basement room you can't keep out a day as bright as this." Jerrod nodded at his friend and the lady near his side. "Hello, I'm Jerrod."

"I'm sorry." Luke opened his arms as though he would connect his friend and Julia. "Jerrod, this is Julia Karsten and that's her daughter, Terry." Luke pointed to Terry as she slowed the swing.

"Nice to meet you." Jerrod extended his hand toward Julia. "Luke's been a hermit so long that he's forgotten his manners."

"Nice to meet you, Jerrod." Julia smiled.

"Just call me Jerr."

"Okay, well, you two enjoy the rest of your day." Julia took Terry's hand as she came along side. They strolled toward the house, leaving Luke and Jerrod by the swing set.

Jerrod leaned closer to Luke. "She seems nice and nice looking too."

Julia turned at the edge of the lawn and raised her voice with a question. "Do you guys want to eat here instead of going into town?"

When Jerrod nodded in the affirmative, Luke assented but with a qualification. "Yeah, that sounds great. If you're sure?"

"Yes, silly, come on." Julia waved to them.

Jerrod stepped beside Luke. "Yeah, she's real nice."

The kitchen held a delicious aroma as they entered. Luke thought it was a pie baking, or perhaps a cake, but blueberry muffins were the source. Julia lifted the pan of muffins from the oven and covered them with a cloth. She retrieved a package of bacon and carton of eggs from the refrigerator.

At that point, Luke and Jerrod exchanged a glance, and it served as a silent signal between them. They offered to help with the preparations, and Julia provided instructions on the utensils that they should use. She specified the quantities for the bacon and the eggs, making it clear that she would not be partaking of either.

"Breakfast doesn't seem to agree with me lately." Julia explained casually, as she and Terry carried plates and flatware into the dining room.

Soon the four of them sat around the dining room table enjoying a family-style breakfast. Luke scooped a spoonful of scrambled eggs for Terry, and Jerrod and he split the remainder when Julia declined even a small portion.

Luke and Jerrod lavished their compliments regarding the taste of the muffins, as each of them took a third one from the basket.

Julia deflected the compliments with a gracefulness befitting a Sunday morning. "You guys have been celebrating hard, and, Jerrod, you'll need some sustenance before making the long drive home."

Jerrod recounted some of the activities of the last forty-eight hours. Terry expressed disappointment that she didn't get to accompany them when they went to Elephant Rocks. When Jerrod explained Don the bartender's talent of drawing multiple drafts of beer at one time, Terry questioned the need for such a technique.

"Mom, Mr. Williams drinks beer, but not four at a time, and from a bottle, not from a glass."

Julia chuckled before she clarified. "Honey, sometimes at a place like the Hideout, people drink beer out of a glass. Really it's a mug with a handle, like the ones we get at the root beer stand. Anyway, the bartender doesn't give all the beers to one person. He's got a lot of people that want a beer."

"And some people that want a lot of beers." Jerrod poked Luke in the ribs and laughed.

Terry rocked side to side in her chair, but her grin betrayed her confusion.

Luke addressed Terry. "Jerr is just kidding around."

Terry brightened at that notion. "Like you and me do sometimes?"

"That's right. Luke and Jerrod have been having a lot of fun lately. It's good that our friends are happy, don't you think?" Julia addressed her daughter, as she stood.

Terry scooted off her chair. "We can be thankful for that too."

"Amen to that." Jerrod folded his hands as though he had just been blessed by the preacher at a Sunday service.

"And we're thankful for this fine breakfast." Luke blocked Julia's hand as she leaned over to take his plate.

He squeezed her hand as he rose from his place. "This really was nice. Let us take care of clearing the table."

Once the dishes were stacked near the sink, Julia excused Luke and Jerrod. They expressed their gratitude to her and waved good-bye to Terry while she stood at the front of the TV rotating the dial that changed the channels.

Inside Luke's apartment, Jerrod stuffed clothing and other belongings in a duffle bag. "I hate to eat and run, but the highway's calling my name."

"And time's a wastin'." Luke conjured some song lyrics, a country western tune that he didn't fully remember.

After he zipped the bag, Jerrod half-heartedly searched the pockets of his jacket for his keys. "One thing before I go. When Bake and I left, I wasn't so sure it was a good idea for you to stay here. But it looks like you're doing okay. You've got a nice place, a real nice landlady."

"But she didn't seem to be feeling too good today. Wonder what that was all about? Putting on some weight maybe." Luke tried to answer his own question.

Jerrod shook his head. "It could be she's pregnant."

"You think so?"

"Not feeling like she wanted to eat, especially in the morning, putting on weight, they're all signs. My older sister was the same way." Jerrod elaborated but had a question. "Where's the father?"

"I don't know. Her husband was killed in Vietnam a few years ago. She's been seeing a guy, but they're not married."

"Obviously, you don't have to be."

"I know that, but pregnant? Do you think so?"

Jerrod faced his friend directly, uncertainty reflected in his tone. "It's none of my business, but that's what I'd say. It's not something you need to worry about, is it?"

"Me? No, not me," Luke stated with certainty.

"Good." Jerrod allowed himself a calming breath. "I would've had to re-think what I just said about you staying here on your own. But, that's why I worry about you. For a smart guy, you still have a lot of things to learn."

Jerrod slung the duffle bag onto his shoulder. "But this place is probably as good a place as any for doing just that."

"I believe it is." Luke flung the door open and stepped to the side so his friend could exit first.

Jerrod backed out of the driveway, and Luke followed until he yelled. "Take care!"

When Jerrod waved, Luke pivoted toward the house. He paused and closed his eyes. He envisioned the route Jerrod would take on his return trip and re-traced some of his own travels with Jerrod, Bake, his other friends, and his family. He prayed for guidance in Boulder and beyond.

Chapter 21

St. Louis, Christmas 1971

Luke's United Airlines flight landed at St. Louis's Lambert Airport in the late afternoon of December 23rd. His younger brothers, Mark and Johnny, met him there, and his mother met him at the door of their home with a hug and a kiss on the cheek. She prepared supper while Luke visited with his sister and brothers.

Mark discussed arrangements he had made for some friends to stop by the house. A Styrofoam cooler in the kitchen that was loaded with beer and bulging with ice cubes, along with the beer bottles stacked strategically around the Christmas ham and the other food stuffs in the family refrigerator, foretold of a grand party.

After dinner, Luke phoned Elizabeth. He expressed a cheerful Merry Christmas to Elizabeth's mother when she answered the phone.

Elizabeth's home telephone was equipped with an extra long cord. She carried the phone into her room. With curlers still pinned in the hair atop her head, she was glad Luke remembered to call. She reflected on the many times Luke would come home for a visit from college, but she didn't recognize his voice at first. He spoke so rapidly.

She listened as he rattled on about Ted, his best friend from high school, and other friends of his and Mark's who had all been invited to the house. A pre-Christmas celebration had been planned. Mark had to leave on Christmas night. Mark would come back for New Year's, but he wanted to have a party to-night, just the guys. He asked if she remembered how he had had to return to Oakwood during Christmas break for basketball tournaments.

He rushed without allowing her to answer and asked if he could call tomorrow in the afternoon. He wanted them to be together for Christmas Eve, like they had for past Christmases. He wondered if that would be okay. Could he wait until tomorrow to see her?

Luke stopped talking, when Elizabeth's laugh rang in his ear. "Luke? It's okay. You're talking way too fast. Just call tomorrow afternoon. I'll be here."

"Then it's okay?"

"Yes, Luke, it's okay. I'll talk to you tomorrow."

"Okay, talk to you then. Elizabeth?"

"Yes?"

"Elizabeth, I'll talk to you tomorrow."

"Okay, good-bye."

"Bye."

As Luke grabbed a beer from the refrigerator, his mother questioned the outcome of the phone call. "Will you see her tonight?"

"No, tomorrow." Luke used the opener on the kitchen counter to pry the cap from the bottle of beer.

"You're sure?"

"I'll be talking to her tomorrow."

"Will you go to Midnight Mass?"

"I don't know. We'll decide tomorrow."

"Luke, it's been such a long time."

"Only seven months, it's okay. We'll be together for Christmas Eve. We haven't missed one since our senior year in high school."

"Have you got a gift for her?"

"Of course, Mom, I got her a very nice silver chain. I'll show you tomorrow."

"Well, I didn't know if..."

"We've been writing to each other all the time. We'll be okay."

From around the corner came the booming voice and the substantial frame that belonged to Ted. "Hey, got a beer for an old friend?"

"Ted, you son-of-a-gun. Here, I just opened this one. Good to see you, buddy!"

"Good to see you. Looking good, except something. Goddammit, man, you're losing some hair!" Ted leaned closer to Luke. "That's it. You're losing your hair, aren't you?"

"Just got it cut, maybe shorter than usual. Finding a little in the shower."

"A little! I suspect it's more like a handful. Damn man, you're growing old right before my eyes. Mom, your little boy's damn near an old man."

"Yeah, and it's about time that he settles down, don't you think?" Luke's mom stared at the two young men.

Ted answered when he wrapped a long arm around Luke's shoulder. "There's plenty of time for that. I'll look after him tonight."

Ted escorted Luke toward the front room. They moved slowly so that they were able to drink as they walked. They each secured a second bottle of beer, expecting to share with a friend or planning to hold one in reserve.

Many friends rallied to toast the holiday that night. All the beers were eventually consumed in celebration of an especially cherished memory or some ridiculously garnished tinsel as it hung from an unsuspecting ear.

When the final good-nights and Merry Christmases had been exchanged with their guests, Luke relaxed with his brothers in the front room. Johnny chose a Dionne Warwick album, one of Luke's favorites, for the last songs of the night, but Johnny only listened to the first two selections before slipping away to the bedroom. Mark patted Luke's shoulder and suggested that they should get some sleep, too. Luke motioned for Mark to lead the way but sunk into a chair on the way to unplugging the lights of the Christmas tree.

The lilting waltz of *What the World Needs Now* eased him into a dream state until the record needle slid into the center of the album. The soft scratching sound awakened him, and he found his own way to the bedroom.

For Luke and Elizabeth, Christmas Eve had evolved as the zenith of the entire season. Wrapped in the unhurried excitement of the kiss they had anticipated for many months, they lingered for the first moments of the night. Except for *Welcome Home* or *Merry Christmas*, they barely spoke. They communicated with a magical sequence of kisses until they left Elizabeth's house.

They had planned an early dinner at an Italian restaurant in the St. Louis neighborhood known as The Hill, a drive through Forest Park, Midnight Mass at Elizabeth's parish church, and then a return to her house for the earliest of Christmas celebrations. They shared a dream of giving to one another. A joyful spirit encircled them, especially on this night.

At dinner they engaged in a quiet conversation about their families. Elizabeth's mother was unhappy that she had to work on Christmas Day and would miss the dinner when her aunt and uncle, her cousins, and her family would all be together. Luke shared his mother's sadness over Matt, his older brother, missing another Christmas.

Luke expressed his earnest desires. "I'm happy that we can be together. I never want that to change."

Elizabeth sensed his sincerity. "I want the same thing."

In Forest Park Luke chose a parking spot near the Art Museum with a view of nearby buildings outlined in holiday lights. They could not resist the heat of their mutual passion, and the view was rendered meaningless by their steamy embrace.

Elizabeth pressed so close to Luke that only the resonance of his voice distinguished him from her. She yearned for its soothing tone and asked him to tell her more about Boulder.

"But I write to you all the time about Boulder." Luke reminded her.

"I know. You write the best letters. And the other things you've written, they're like poems. I've kept them all, but I want to hear more."

Luke depicted Boulder's unique setting, a positive aura that he felt just by living there. He described the Flat Irons rock formation, the foothills and waterfalls. He learned to appreciate the way the sun shone nearly every day and how it warmed even the coldest days.

He emphasized that point with an example. "Boulder has gotten some snow already, and I know it hasn't snowed here. But the snow doesn't usually stay on the ground for more than a few days. It's actually warmer in that way, warmer than St. Louis, at least so far."

He related how the diversity of people sometimes surprised him. Boulder engendered a mixture of college students, hippies, transients, and mountain folk, as well as typical middle class American families. The bookstore was successful. He liked the people he worked with and many of the store's customers. Pickup games of basketball were the same there. He'd made some friends in that way.

When Luke paused, he unconsciously added significance to what he said. "The attitudes seem different somehow, less judgmental."

"I like the sound of that." Elizabeth sat more upright.

"You'd definitely like it there. Everybody kind of lets you do your own thing. I guess I don't really know anybody there, not like I know you, or Ted, or Jerrod. And with no family, there's no one demanding anything of me. Now that I say that, I realize that that would be true of any new place I'd go, but Boulder has something. I can't describe it, but I like the way it makes me feel."

"I can tell from your letters that you're happy there." Elizabeth kissed his cheek.

Luke grasped her hands in his. The foggy light revealed her eyes had dampened with tears, and he reached with one hand and caught a teardrop with his fingertips where it fell onto her cheek.

He did the same on her other cheek. "Don't be sad. That's not what I want."

"I know." She found a tissue in her purse and gently dabbed the corner of her eyes.

When he asked her to tell him about her work at Children's Hospital, the glum expression disappeared.

"I'm missing Christmas dinner tomorrow. Almost twenty-three years old and it's the first time that's ever happened. But I love my work, love taking care of the children. All the families will appreciate me being there tomorrow. Most of them treat me like family too. You get to know the families as well as the kids. That's another good thing."

"I didn't realize that. I mean, aren't the kids just in the hospital for a few days?"

"Most are, but some have to stay for weeks or longer. If they're really sick, it takes time for the doctors to diagnose exactly what's going on and then how to best treat it."

"So, you get a little attached to them, I bet."

"That definitely happens. Sometimes their condition can be so serious that they'll probably never fully recover. You do the best you can for them, but when they go home, you know you'll see them again. When things get really bad, that's when you have to be the strongest. It's not an easy thing to do."

"Elizabeth, I know you're a strong person, but I don't know how you do what you do. To me, it's incredible."

"The kids are the ones that are courageous. I'm just there to help out when I can. Provide them comfort."

"And I'm sure you do. I'm sure you help a lot. That's the part that makes you so beautiful."

Luke kissed her, and before their warmth could steam the windows, Elizabeth urged Luke to drive them to church. She reminded him of the commitment they had each made to their parents.

On the way across the city, they spoke again of how the time had passed, her in St. Louis, him in Boulder. He had read more books, while she had seen more movies. His experience was more solitary. Jerrod described Luke as a hermit when he visited over Thanksgiving. She, of course, had her family, and Debbie, her good friend. Debbie and Elizabeth went out to night clubs to hear the music and indulge in a drink or two, even accompanied one another to a few parties.

After Luke parked at the curb, a block from the church, Elizabeth clutched his hand tightly. She waited for his eyes to meet hers.

She spoke sincerely. "I worry that you're lonely in Boulder. Don't you feel lonely sometimes?"

He tried not to waver in his response. "I guess, sometimes. But then I pick up my pen. The letters are a way for me to handle what I'm feeling. If you ever stop getting them, then you can really start to worry."

As they made their way through the church foyer, he whispered, "You can pray for me too. I need all the help I can get."

She dipped her fingertips in the holy water and blessed herself. "I do. All this time I never stopped."

The liturgy of the Mass, the Christmas story, and the carols sung by the choir took them to a peaceful place. She held his hand, even through the ritual kneeling, standing and sitting. She held onto him and held her love for him. In spite of the months that had separated them, she loved him still. Later at her home, Luke helped her finish the bows on the gifts meant for members of her family. As they worked quietly at the kitchen table, he complained about the difficulties he had had wrapping the gifts that he had brought home, just wrapping paper, no ribbon or bows.

Elizabeth carried the stack into the front room and placed the presents under the tree. She returned with one gift box, Luke's Christmas present. When she placed it on the table in front of him, Luke stood and handed her a small box. It was wrapped in red paper speckled with silver snowflakes.

Another kiss marked the exchange. Luke received a multi-colored knit hat and pair of leather, fleece-lined gloves. He gave Elizabeth a silver necklace with a crystal pendant.

"Luke, it's beautiful! Thank you." Elizabeth always opened her gift more quickly than Luke. "I hope you like the colors in your hat."

He put on the hat and gloves. "My jacket's solid blue, and there's blue in the hat. The gloves are great. Now I'm ready for the rest of winter. Thank you."

Elizabeth dangled the necklace, and Luke questioned her. "Do you like the crystal? It's rose quartz. The red shows better in the sunlight. I like that it's kind of heart-shaped too. Silver jewelry's big in Boulder. I know it's a little different. I know..."

"Luke, I like it. I like it a lot. Thank you so much." She pulled off his hat and kissed him on the cheek.

"And thank you." He took off his gloves. "These things are perfect."

She led him then into the front room, and they listened to a favorite Johnny Mathis album. He asked her to dance, and they drifted on the melodies. They felt the joy in holding one another, the best of their Christmas exchange. When *The Twelfth of Never* ended, she pulled him toward the front door. Only a few hours remained until her alarm clock would send her off to work.

"Tell all your family Merry Christmas for me." Elizabeth kissed him deeply.

"Tell yours Merry Christmas, too." He held her closer. "I don't want to let you go."

"I feel that way, too, but I have to get some rest. You should too."

"I'll call you tomorrow night."

"That's good, maybe around 10:00. Everybody will be gone by then."

"Ten it is." He released her and put on his coat.

He reached for the door handle, but pivoted as he spoke. "My present, I almost forgot."

He grabbed the gift box below the coat tree. Elizabeth opened the door for him. She shivered as the cold air rushed in. He slid past her but caught a cloud of her warm breath when he kissed her a final time.

On Christmas morning, Luke shuffled along the short hallway toward the kitchen. His mother's voice mingled with a male voice that he didn't recognize as Mark's or Johnny's. When he stepped around the corner, he blinked and stumbled backwards as a pair of arms clothed in military garb lifted him off the kitchen floor.

He re-gained his balance as his older brother spoke. "Hey there, little brother, Merry Christmas!"

"Matt, you wild man, how'd you get here?"

"I'm in the Air Force, you know. We got our ways of getting around."

Matthew described how he had caught a pre-dawn flight into Scott Air Force base and a ride to the Missouri side of the river, then a bus trip out to the west end and an invigorating walk in the morning air through the old neighborhood.

"Wanted to surprise Mom and you guys. How'd I do?"

"Perfect, just perfect," Luke responded.

"Isn't it something else?" Their mother grabbed one of each of her son's hands. "All you boys home for Christmas."

That Christmas day Luke and his family partook of the delights of the holiday, the holy day. A spirit of joy stirred in their home, the echoes of past Christmases. The sounds of celebration bounced from wall to wall all throughout the day and long into the night.

Part Two

Inspired time
When love still presides
In bold hearts
Knowing, there abides

Chapter 22

Boulder, New Year's Day, 1972

On the first morning of the New Year, Terry jostled Luke, but he wasn't yet fully conscious when she asked him to play a game with her. He had his eyesight but few other cognitive faculties.

"Terry?" He licked his lips and swallowed while lifting his head from the pillow. "What are...what? Oh, yeah."

He stammered and then recognized his surroundings, the front room of Julia's house and his fully clothed body lying on her sofa covered with a blanket.

Terry tapped the pillow where his head had been resting. "Mom sleeps here, too, sometimes. I didn't know you did."

"Yeah, no." Luke moved to a seated position. "This is the first time."

"You sound a little funny." Terry pointed at Luke's shirt. "And your shirt is all wrinkled."

"I got tired after the party ended last night. Your mom let me sleep here, but I need to wake up more." Luke yawned and stretched his arms above his head.

"Yeah, because we're going to play a game." Terry pulled on one of his arms.

"I don't know. Maybe I better start with a shower."

"Mom's already taking her shower."

"Then I should go down to my apartment."

"Okay, but then you'll come back, right?" She nodded her head as though she was answering her own question.

After a long shower, Luke dressed in another set of the freshly laundered clothes that he had unpacked the night before. He quietly climbed the steps leading to the kitchen entrance, eased the screen door open, and knocked on the main door.

Julia met him with a pleasant smile. "Hey there, Happy New Year."

"It's starting to shape up that way. Thought I better check on Terry. Make sure I didn't freak her out earlier."

"She's fine. You want some coffee?"

"No thanks, I'm good for now," he answered, although he realized then that he was thirsty. "I might just have a glass of water."

Julia smiled more broadly as she handed him the water. "Let's start over. Are you okay?"

"Yeah, when Terry woke me up, I must've been dreaming. Things were a little, you know, everything and everybody all jumbled together. Anyway, I'm sure I didn't make any sense when I was talking to her."

"She didn't say anything to me. She's playing in the living room. I was going to have some toast. You want something to eat?"

"Well...I..."

"Luke, it's not going to be fancy. I'll put a second piece of bread in the toaster. Terry will eat a scrambled egg, so let me do a couple for you, too."

"Okay, that sounds good."

When Terry joined them for the impromptu breakfast at the kitchen table, they talked briefly about the New Year's Party. Terry compared it to the Fourth of July party, and her opinion was that New Year's didn't measure up.

She presented details to support her point. "I liked the popcorn and the potato chips, but the music was too loud, and there wasn't apple pie, ice cream, or fireworks."

"Honey, it's winter. Ice cream's better in the summer." Julia cleared Terry's plate.

"I know. That's why we should have a party in the summer."

"Sounds like you want to party outside?" Luke took the last bite of his eggs.

"Yeah, that's what I mean."

"And I think you've made an excellent case for a party in the summertime." Luke chuckled and winked at Julia.

"See, Mom. Luke thinks so. Everybody'll have fun, like last summer."

"We'll see." Julia dunked the breakfast dishes in the sink.

"That's what you always say, Mom. But that's okay 'cause it's just the start of the year. Anyway, now we can play one of my new games. Remember Luke, you said after you took a shower."

"Well, yeah, but..." Luke stayed in his chair while Terry scooted toward the front room.

Julia interceded on Luke's behalf. "Terry, Luke just got home last night, remember? Then he came to our party right away. He might have some things to do today."

"Mom, it's New Years Day." Terry faced her mother. "There's no school or work. Ain't that right?"

"Isn't that right?" Julia corrected.

"Yeah, that's what I said." Terry shifted her stare between her mother and Luke.

"Well, I guess. Just one game." Luke relented when Terry mouthed the word, please, as she walked toward him.

"Good." Terry grabbed Luke's hand and pulled him to his feet.

Julia's voice contained an element of discipline within her reminder. "Terry, Luke said one game. After I finish these few dishes, we'll watch the Rose Parade. You can play with your new doll too."

"Yeah, I like all the flowers in the parade." Terry agreed with that idea. "That's another good thing about the summer. All the flowers, huh Luke?"

"Another excellent point," Luke agreed. He turned to Julia as Terry pulled him along. "We'll be in the other room when you're ready to have some real fun."

Luke excused himself when Terry's attention diverted to the telecast of the Rose Parade. At midday Luke made his way to Elephant Rocks. His new hat covered his head, and his new gloves kept his hands warm as he stood to survey Boulder. Out of the north, a cold wind hit his face, the sign of a gathering storm.

He sought comfort to the south, where the Flat Irons maintained their vigil. Luke slipped into a waking dream where flower blossoms danced to the rhythm of a summer breeze, and he walked hand in hand with Elizabeth along a distant garden path.

Then the wind rushed past, a winter's day in Boulder chilled him, and he retreated to home. A snow flurry accompanied him most of the way, and by the time he reached the driveway, the snowflakes had increased in size. Clay's truck was parked alongside of the house. He whisked some of the flakes from the truck's fender as he walked by.

He heated his last pot pie for dinner and afterwards read the first few chapters of *Sometimes a Great Notion*. When his stomach growled, he paused to scratch a grocery list on a page of his notebook. A cheer rang out from the room above him, and he assigned it to Clay and a Big Eight team that he favored in the Orange Bowl game.

When the hum of activities and the television broadcast had fallen silent, Luke slipped on his jacket and stepped outside. At the top of the stairway, Luke estimated that four inches of snow had fallen. The light cast by the globe over the porch revealed a few flakes fluttering to the ground. On his way to bed, he added soup to his list. He fell asleep with thoughts of a warm belly.

Chapter 23

Boulder, end of February, 1972

*E*lizabeth called the Pearl Street Bookstore from a pay phone at the Boulder bus station on Canyon Street. She had orchestrated a grand surprise for Luke's birthday, and it would soon come to fruition.

Luke couldn't remember ever receiving a phone call at the store.

"Hello?" Luke's voice held an inquisitive tone.

"Hello, Luke. Happy Birthday!" Elizabeth exclaimed.

"Elizabeth?"

"Luke, I need you to come get me."

"Come get you? What do you mean?"

"I'm at the bus station in Boulder. I'm here in Colorado."

"You're kidding?"

"No, I'm really here. It's a surprise…for your birthday. Happy Birthday!"

"You're not kidding?"

"No, I'm not. You said sometimes your boss lets you use the delivery truck. Ask him if you can come and get me."

"Yeah, I will. I mean I think I can. At the bus station? I can't believe it. It's only a couple of minutes. I'll clock out. I'll be right there. Elizabeth?"

"Yes."

"I'll be right there."

"I'll be waiting."

Luke rushed through the station door. On this Friday in the mid-afternoon, only a few people milled in the spacious, open lobby. Elizabeth stood in a spot of sunlight that streamed from a high window.

He called her name as he hustled toward her and then lifted her in a whirling embrace. "Now who's the crazy one? This is wild! How'd you get here? You came for my birthday?"

"Yes, silly. I flew into the Denver airport and caught the bus to Boulder. Not bad for a girl from Mary Magdalene High, wouldn't you say?"

"Not bad? It's amazing! I don't know what to say."

Luke grinned and fumbled Elizabeth's cosmetic case when it bumped against her suitcase. "I guess we'll go to my apartment. My boss said we can use the pick-up truck."

On the way, Elizabeth recounted the advanced telephone contacts she had made with Julia and Luke's boss. His boss agreed to allow him to have Saturday off and the use of the pickup if it was needed. Julia even offered to host a dinner for them.

"You're kidding? Elizabeth, you're incredible!"

"Actually Luke, people here seem to like you. It wasn't that big a deal to get them to help me out. After all, it's your birthday."

"When you said in your last letter that you had something special in mind for my birthday, I had no idea. Man, I still can't believe it."

"That's woman, sir. Woman!"

"Oh, yes, my apologies to you and Helen Reddy. *Woman, hear me roar.* Far out!"

As Luke steered the truck into the driveway, he gestured. "Well, here we are."

"Luke, this is nice."

"Now remember, I live in the basement. But you're in luck because I just cleaned the place."

Luke hopped out of the truck and grabbed Elizabeth's suitcase and cosmetic bag. She joined him on his side of the truck.

"Watch your step. It's kind of narrow." Luke cautioned as he led the way.

He escorted Elizabeth on a quick tour of the apartment. She commented on the tidy appearance and the natural light coming through the window in the kitchen and the front room. They allowed just enough brightness to the surroundings.

"I like your place. It suits you." She pointed to the décor on the wall above the sofa. "I didn't realize you had these posters. And what's this print all about?"

"The posters were Jerr's. I inherited them. The print is a woodcut, I think. The artist's son is supposedly a writer. I like the irony of it portraying a man drowning in a sea of words. Maybe it's a family joke."

"You'd think a father would be more supportive."

"Artists can be temperamental." Luke pointed at the easy chair across the room. "Most of the time I sit in this chair when

I'm reading or writing. So, it acts as a reminder not to get too wordy in my letters or other writing."

"But I like your letters just the way they are." She kissed his cheek. "The way you write is perfect for me."

"That's really all that matters to me."

He kissed her passionately, nearly lifting her off the floor.

"This is a dream come true." He coaxed her to sit beside him on the sofa.

Elizabeth snuggled underneath Luke's arm. He enfolded her, and even as she rested, her essence excited him. His heart pounded, titillated at every breath.

He formed the words on his lips, quieter than a whisper. "It's you. In every dream, it's you."

At Elizabeth's insistence, Luke drank a beer while she showered and changed her clothes. He drank a second one during the time it took him to change into a pair of slacks, a shirt, and a sweater. He used a dash of cologne as the final touch.

Elizabeth complimented him on the fragrance as he held the door for her.

"Glad you like it. My favorite girl gave me the cologne."

"Ooh, she's got good taste."

"And good taste in men, too. Don't you think?"

With that, Elizabeth broke the hold that Luke had on her hand and elbowed him through the doorway. "Don't get conceited on me now. Just because I told you that the people here seem to like you."

"Who me?" He chuckled and glanced sideways.

In the process he stumbled on the first step and laughed aloud.

"See." Elizabeth scolded him. "You'd better watch yourself."

"Yes, ma'am, I surely will."

Luke knocked on the side door of the house.

Elizabeth issued one last reminder as they waited. "It's your birthday, but you better be good if you want any presents."

"You know I'll be good. I promise."

"Promise what?" Terry asked as she pulled the door open.

"I promise to be good, so that I get some presents for my birthday," Luke replied and then introduced Elizabeth.

Terry escorted them through the kitchen.

"Clay, dammit!" A curse from a female voice was followed by the sound of slap.

Terry's shoulders dropped as though she were avoiding a blow. Luke squeezed Elizabeth's hand. When they entered the front room, Clay and Julia stood to greet them.

Julia embraced Elizabeth like an old friend. "You look beautiful, just as Luke has described you. Welcome."

"Thank you." Elizabeth averted her eyes as she accepted the compliment and responded with one of her own. "Your house is very nice. Luke really likes living here."

"Thank you. I'm sure he likes it even better now that you are here."

"Yeah, I bet. Some of us were startin' to wonder about Little Luke, but now I see why he wasn't hittin' on any of the local chicks. Luke you devil, she's niiice!" Clay's booming voice rolled over top of the group as he slapped Luke on the shoulder.

Luke winced before he spoke. "Clay Williams. Elizabeth Donahue. Elizabeth this is Clay."

"Nice to meet you, Clay," Elizabeth said.

"Pleasure's all mine, little lady."

"Clay, please behave, will you?" Julia's stern look caused Clay to retreat one step.

"Yeah, Clay, you better behave!" Another male voice came from the kitchen, and then its owner squeezed into the group. "You must be Elizabeth. I'm Frank. Luke and me play basketball. We're usually on the same team, Sundays at the field house. If you'd like, you can come and watch."

"Frank, I'm sure there are other things that Elizabeth and Luke will want to do this weekend." Julia expounded with certainty as she winked at Elizabeth.

"Yeah, Fat Man. She sure as hell don't want to come see you play basketball." Clay's voice held a caustic tone.

"Clay, I mean it. You better settle down." Julia restated her earlier cautionary note.

"Yeah, down big boy." Frank stroked Clay's shoulder.

Julia motioned to Elizabeth. "Let me show you the rest of the house."

Both Luke and Clay accepted Frank's offer of a beer. Clay jostled Luke, and a verbal exchange followed. Their voices carried into the dining room where Julia pointed to the dining room table, already set for the evening's meal.

"I thought that we'd use the good china, since it's a special occasion. It was a wedding gift for my husband and me, Terry's father that is. Luke probably hasn't told you. My husband was killed in Vietnam. Clay and I aren't married. Not sure if I'll get married again. The baby I'm carrying is his. He wants to get married. Says it's the right thing. I'm just not sure I like...love him. I guess I love him in a way, but like him enough to live with him? Or subject Terry to him? Not sure about that at all."

"Sounds like you've thought it through." Elizabeth smiled reassuringly.

"It's obvious that I didn't think it through on at least one occasion. But lately I'm thinking that I've got to keep a little distance between me and Clay. He can be a lot to handle sometimes. It'll be better for all of us. Me, Terry, our new little one, and him, too."

Julia directed Elizabeth toward the back stairway. Elizabeth climbed the narrow passage way ahead of Julia and waited at the top.

Julia came along side of Elizabeth. "I grew up here. I have a lot of friends who can help me through this."

"That's good." Elizabeth walked beside Julia.

"And Luke, he's been a big help too. Terry just adores him. Your guy, he has a pleasant way about him. My Terry, she's such a dreamer. Luke seems to encourage that. Most young men have this get-real attitude, always rushing to get it today. Luke is more patient, I guess. We like that."

"Me too." Elizabeth smiled.

"Listen to me," Julia excused herself, "telling you about your guy. I'm sure you know."

"Well, we do know one another pretty well." Elizabeth glanced away, not as willing to share.

They encountered Terry in her room. Julia gave her instructions regarding a friend who would be a guest for the evening. The two girls would eat their dinner in Terry's room and be able to play afterwards.

As Julia flipped the light switch in the room next to Terry's, she explained. "This will be the nursery. We'll be clearing all this stuff out of here. Luke said he'd paint it for me."

"He and his dad painted together one summer. I'm sure he'll do a good job."

Upon hitting the bottom of the front stairway, they heard what sounded like Frank's voice rumbling through the house. "Sally's got the main dish on the table. Where are you girls?"

Julia provided an explanation to Elizabeth as they crossed the front room. "Sally's one of my best friends. Frank and she date from time to time. She's also Home Ec teacher at the high school, so I asked her to make lasagna and some garlic bread for tonight. I made the salad and baked a cake earlier."

When they entered the dining room, Frank conducted the introductions. Julia outlined the seating arrangements.

She made a step toward the kitchen. "I'll get the salad, and we'll get started."

But Luke announced as he nearly bumped into Julia. "I've got the salad."

"And here's the dressing." Clay chimed in and then reminded Frank that he was responsible for the drinks that would accompany dinner.

"Ah, yes." Frank added a dramatic flair to his offer. "I chose a fine red wine. Would the ladies care for a glass of wine?"

"Knock it off Fat Man! You're scarin' everybody, including" me!" Clay blocked Frank with his shoulder.

After pouring the wine, Frank took his place at the table. Clay raised his glass and toasted a happy birthday to Luke. Luke touched his glass with each person around the table.

"Thanks for everything!" He beamed a broad grin to everyone.

Dinner provided tasty sustenance and pleasant conversation. Even Clay conducted himself with civility. Elizabeth radiated happiness and interjected unknown tidbits of information about Luke. She delighted the group and drew sheepish admissions of their validity from Luke.

Luke chuckled with embarrassment at the off-key singing of the birthday song, and his cheeks reddened at Clay's off-color comment about the birthday spanking Elizabeth would have to administer. The candles stood in five rows of four and one row of three. They were no match for Luke's enthusiastic exhalation.

Afterwards, a game of charades pitted the team of ladies against the gentlemen. Clay appreciated his teammates' clever way of acting out the clues. He drank heartily in celebration of each successful turn. He kept score although no one else felt that it was necessary.

"Just like a set of tennis," Clay said, "first to six, ahead by two."

Frank took best actor honors on the male side, while Clay struggled. He couldn't use his strongest asset, the spoken, or shouted, word. Elizabeth performed well for the females, and overall the female team had better talent. No matter how much the guys cheered or jeered, or how much they fought it, they could not avoid the upset. They found it hard to accept defeat, seven to five.

"Let's face it, guys. You just shouldn't try to match wits with the ladies!" Julia proclaimed as she hugged Sally.

Frank said, "I'll drink to that."

Clay took consolation. "I'll drink, but not to that. Luke, can we get one for you?"

"Thanks, guys, but I think the ladies have fallen behind, and that's working against us."

"You're right, man. Ladies, how about a drink? Wine? Rum and Coke?" Frank motioned as though he was pouring the drinks, still playing the game.

"Yeah, belly up to the bar, girls!" Clay challenged them with a wave of his arm.

Julia reminded the men of her limitation. "Sorry, guys, my belly's not supposed to be pressing against any bar."

"Yeah, and we're supporting Julia and her condition, aren't we Elizabeth?" Sally nudged Elizabeth.

"So true." Elizabeth wrapped one arm around each of her teammates.

"I have noticed that you girls like to stick together." Luke bowed in the direction of the ladies.

With that, the three women started into the chorus of Helen Reddy's popular song. Luke hummed along with them until their brief rendition trailed toward silence.

Luke detected a humorous twist in the lyrics. "That part about being too big to ignore is closer to the truth every day, for some of you anyway."

Julia interrupted Luke's chuckling with a poke to the chest, and Elizabeth caught him in the arm with an elbow. Just then Clay and Frank shuffled into the room.

"Ladies, ladies, please. No fair picking on the birthday boy. And Luke, what did I tell you about being on your best behavior?" Clay admonished them with a dose of sarcasm.

Julia threw everyone off-balance when she barked at Clay. "Oh Clay, put a sock in it!"

"I'd like to put a sock in it." Clay misinterpreted Julia's intent. He danced toward her with his wide hips gyrating.

"No way!" Julia pushed him away, but Clay kept coming.

Clay acted now, a charade he had likely practiced. He reached toward Julia's midsection.

With the audience watching, he delivered his line perfectly. "Oh come on, baby. You know you want to."

Julia slapped his face and spewed her words like venom. "You're disgusting!"

She stormed from the room and up the stairs.

"You bitch. I ought to..."

"Clay, cool it!" Luke shouted to drown out whatever Clay was about to say.

Frank moved into Clay's line of sight. "What say we take this one to go, big guy?"

"Yeah, let's head down to the Hideout. Plenty of women there who would be happy to join us in a drink, you hear that? What the hell did I do anyway? I played your fuckin' game of Charades. I've got your act right here. I'm the best lover around. Just ask any woman in town."

"Yeah, yeah, Clay, here's your coat. Let's see what's happenin' downtown tonight." Frank forced Clay to accept his jacket.

On their way to the kitchen, Frank cocked his head. "Sorry, Sally. Luke, Elizabeth enjoy. Tell Julia that I'm sorry."

Still scuffling with one another, the two big men finally made it out the side door. From the end of the driveway, Clay let out a violent roar. It trailed into the living room with the rumble of Frank's tail pipes as his car sped down the street. Sally addressed Elizabeth. "Well, that's our Clay. No one quite like him. Actually, he can be charming at times. I better go look in on Julia. You can show yourselves out, okay?"

"Yes, we're fine," Luke said.

"Tell Julia thanks for everything." Elizabeth added.

As Luke and Elizabeth relaxed on the sofa in his apartment, their conversation became a review of the players that populated the evening's activity.

Elizabeth relished the positives. "Julia is very sweet, like you've said in your letters. Her daughter is well behaved too."

"Terry really is. It was nice of Sally to bring over someone for Terry to play with. It seems that as long as she has someone to be with, she's happy. Wish the same could be said about the adults."

"Wow, that Clay, I can see where he'd be a handful. One of the first things Julia told me was that she doubted that she and Clay would ever get married. Seems he's proven on many occasions how difficult he can be."

"I wrote you about the New Year's party, didn't I?" Luke had described it as though it were the scene from a movie.

"You did, and I can't imagine what that was like, given tonight's finale. Tonight was just supposed to be a quiet get together."

"With Clay nothing happens quietly, and any evening can become a big event."

Luke had accepted that aspect of Clay's approach to life, but he still could not justify it. "Besides, tonight was kind of a big event, your first trip to Colorado and my birthday."

"But that's about you, not him. It wasn't supposed to be about him."

"He has a way of consuming the spotlight, though. All of life is his stage, or so he thinks."

"He's not much of a silent actor, though, is he?" Elizabeth offered a critique of his part in the game of charades.

"Loves to talk, that's for sure."

"Julia had a lot to say too, about you. She said you help her out. Says you're going to paint the nursery. And that Terry likes you a lot."

"It's probably more that I'm around a lot. I just do what I can. I think I can paint the baby's room. Probably only take a weekend or two. It'll be good for a free meal."

"So, that's the pay off!"

"Well, I get tired of my own cooking."

"And I guess it doesn't always smell too good, either, or so they say." Elizabeth jabbed at Luke as she repeated Terry's comment.

"Once or twice, I've burned something. Most of the time I do okay. I just keep trying to get it right."

"Julia said that you're a patient person."

"Jeez, didn't you girls have anything else to do but talk about me?"

"It was fun hearing what your Colorado friends think about you. Frank says you should be playing college basketball somewhere."

"Ah, he tends to exaggerate."

"Maybe, but there's a lot of truth in that statement and the other things that I heard tonight."

"Maybe, just maybe." Luke clung to doubts about many of these characterizations.

Elizabeth proceeded without reservation. She readied herself in the bathroom, while Luke scurried around the bedroom unsure of how to prepare the bed. As a practical step, he placed a kitchen chair in the corner of the bedroom, using it as a stand for Elizabeth's suitcase.

He tossed his clothes in the basket on the closet floor and switched on the reading lamp and the radio. *Just My Imagination* was playing softly, as he turned off the overhead light.

When Elizabeth entered the room, Luke stumbled at the corner of the bed.

"I...you...Would you like to dance?" Embarrassed as soon as the words left his lips, his cheeks flashed a little red, and *Color My World* came in right on cue.

"Always," she replied.

He took her into his dancer's embrace, and another slow dance began. His cheeks cooled, but the entirety of his body warmed.

"I've always loved dancing with you." She whispered into his ear.

"I love holding you. We just seem to fit together." He kissed her, a tiny wave rocking them gently within an ocean of feelings.

"I love you." She kissed him and sailed smoothly into his waters.

As the song ended, they danced around the corner of the bed. He swung her fully off the floor and cradled her in his arms. He placed her on the bed, lowering her with one knee on the bed to steady himself. She slipped under the covers.

After he switched off the radio and the lamp, they found a rhythm beneath the hot blanket of their love. They stirred their movements into an intoxicating drink of desire. She drank before him and took all that she wanted with a deep release. More bubbled before him until the final quenching climax of his unspoken yearning. They floated from desire into dreams.

———

Elizabeth awoke before Luke, scrambled two eggs, and poured two glasses of juice. They ate in silence, their fingertips intertwined across the corner of the table. Luke suggested a drive up Boulder Canyon.

As Luke closed the door on Elizabeth's side of the truck, Julia came through the door with two grocery bags propped precariously, one in each arm.

"Hey, where're you going with those?" Luke asked although the answer was obvious.

"They're just trash."

"Let me help you." Luke grabbed one in each hand. "Just get the lid off the can."

Elizabeth admired Luke's kindness but posed her question with a chuckle. "You really do help a lot, don't you?"

"Come on, it's no big deal to take out the trash." Luke backed the truck into the street. "Besides, pregnant women aren't supposed to be straining themselves, are they?"

"Well, you've got a point there. But they're not that delicate either, at least not most of them."

"I'll have to take your word for it." Luke shifted the truck into a higher gear. "But I just thought I'd better give a hand. I'd do the same for you, if you ever, you know, if you..."

Luke made the turn onto Canyon Boulevard, confident of the road he traveled but uncertain of the path his words were taking.

Elizabeth touched Luke's hand where it rested on the shifting column. "Luke, I was just having a little fun. Don't worry."

"I'm not...worried." Luke insisted, although the tone of his words revealed some lingering doubts.

As Luke steered along the winding road, he spoke in short spurts. "I shouldn't be worried...that is...should I? I mean, I didn't...we should've...before we...before last night."

"Luke, I used a diaphragm for birth control," Elizabeth said softly, surely.

"Oh." Luke pumped the clutch pedal twice before he was able to shift the truck into a lower gear.

"Luke, it's okay." Elizabeth steadied her voice as the truck climbed a steep grade. "I just thought I better..."

"Yeah, sure. I mean...that's a good thing."

A series of curves ended in a straightaway, and Luke nosed the truck into a spot at a roadside parking lot. He was happy to be on solid ground again and led Elizabeth along a path that dropped from the level of the road to a bridge that crossed the creek.

"This is Boulder Creek." He pointed ahead where the path paralleled the creek. "There's a nice view if we follow the path."

Luke led Elizabeth to higher ground. At one point he helped her complete an extra long stride where the boulders of the hillside created an uneven stairway. A familiar excitement grew as he ushered Elizabeth to the perfect vantage point.

"It's too bad the waterfall is barely trickling. Two more months and it will be roaring." Luke held Elizabeth's hand, and they took a seat on the high side of the trail.

The wide gulch lay serenely below them, only the sound of water trickling over the rocks broke the quiet. At the base of the waterfall, a shallow pool glistened in the morning sun.

Elizabeth rested her head on Luke's shoulder. "I'll just have to come back in a few months."

"You should. It's pretty amazing when the water is higher."

Luke shared other aspects of this part of the canyon, fond memories of the past summer. He described the places above the waterfall where Bake and Jerrod routinely performed a ritual by jumping into the creek. He reiterated their claim that it was the best antidote for the nights when they consumed too many beers or other libations.

"What about you?" Elizabeth remembered similar depictions from Luke's letters and never had the chance to ask him that question.

"Well, only a couple of times. That water's pretty cold, basically melted snow, even at the height of summer. See the snow in the cracks and shady spots?" Luke pointed although the snow banks were obvious. "At higher elevations, there's still a ton of snow. In fact, that's where we should go next."

Luke drove to the top of the canyon and past Barker Dam. He pointed out the town of Nederland, as the highway skirted the town's perimeter. He outlined his idea to stop at Brainard Lake where a panoramic view of the Continental Divide would provide proof of his assertion about the snowmelt that formed the waters of Boulder Creek.

Before the road that led to Brainard Lake intersected the highway, Luke eased the truck onto the shoulder and stopped. He pointed to the valley below. A forest of aspen trees stood barren of leaves, a blanket of snow piled against the bottom of the tree trunks. He described the glorious nature of the yellow and gold leaves in the autumn season, although he knew that his description could not compare to the natural images.

The road that led to Brainard Lake was snow-packed, and the truck fishtailed whenever Luke had to downshift. He feathered the steering wheel, as he guided the truck around the bends in the road and eventually into a parking lot across from the lake.

A broad expanse of mountaintops overflowed the windshield on both sides. The depth of the snow in the parking lot did not allow Luke to reach the sign that provided a diagram of what they were seeing. He convinced Elizabeth to make the hike to the sign. They trudged hand in hand as the snow covered the tops of their boots.

Elizabeth's excitement grew. "Look at all the snow!"

"Imagine the waterfall when all this melts." Luke's voice echoed around the lake.

When they reached the sign, Luke shouted excitedly. "Far out! These are the true Rocky Mountains!"

He gestured from the sign to the mountain panorama. "M'lady, I give you the Continental Divide."

Luke swept his arm in a long arc and bowed at the waist.

"For me?" Elizabeth placed both hands over her heart.

"This day, only for you." Luke lifted her in his arms.

"Okay, but just for today." She kissed him when he lowered her to the snowy ground.

When the day bridged into night, they agreed on another walk. This time their destination was Larry's Lounge for burgers, and then the downtown theater for a movie.

Afterwards, Elizabeth's pace slowed, and Luke realized he may have asked too much of her. "I should have asked before. I hope you don't mind walking. It's how I usually get around."

"No, it's been fine. I've always liked walking with you. I just need to catch my breath." Elizabeth tightened her grip on Luke's hand, and they stopped at an intersection.

"I guess I'll get a car someday." Luke scanned the sidewalk to the point where it disappeared. "Mr. Harris at the bookstore has talked about getting a new delivery truck. Maybe I'll get him to sell me the truck we used today. How about that? Me driving a pickup, then I'd really be a mountain man."

"It probably takes more than that, but the truck seems to do all right. It'd get you around okay."

Luke was content to wait at the intersection for a while longer. "And besides, we can't be walking into the drive-in movie this summer."

"So now I'm here this summer too. And I don't think we've ever gone to the drive-in together."

"It'll be something new that we'll do when we're living here. We'll spend the day in the mountains, picnic in Rocky Mountain National Park instead of Forest Park. We'll time it just right. The drive-in's on the way home. If we don't like the movie, we'll climb in the bed of the pickup, stretch out, and watch the stars instead. How's that sound?"

"Sounds like you've got it all figured out."

"Just dreaming out loud."

Luke deliberately shortened his stride the remainder of the way home while his dream expanded to infinity.

———————

Just before he awoke, Luke dreamed that Elizabeth lay next to him in the pale light of the early morning. When he awoke into the reality of the new Boulder day, his breath warmed her face. Elizabeth opened her eyes with a blink and a sleepy smile, warmer blue eyes than his imagination had ever conjured. She rolled to her side and snuggled toward Luke. He swaddled her in the blankets, and in his arms. He wrapped himself in a living dream.

Later that Sunday they used the store's truck to drive to the University campus. Luke escorted Elizabeth to the library and the field house, the only buildings that he frequented. At the field house they climbed a stairway to the balcony section. Unnoticed, they quietly cheered Frank as he battled Clay on the basketball court. Luke described their play for a few minutes, and they shared a chuckle when one of Clay's shots missed everything.

Of course, they heard Frank's hand slap Clay's arm even from a distance, and the whole gym heard Clay's call. "Foul! Fat man, that's a foul! Goddamn, man!"

"Sometimes it gets a little loud in there." Luke explained, as they exited the field house. "Let's try something quieter."

Luke drove them to the lookout on Flagstaff Mountain. The view spread over Boulder town and onto the plains.

Elizabeth made known her appreciation. "I can see why you like it here. It's breathtaking."

"It's a place to be..." Luke couldn't complete his thought.

"It's beautiful."

"With you here, it's a dream come true." He kissed her then.

Long into that night, they resisted sleep and surrendered to the dream they shared. They fulfilled one another within a cocoon of love. Once more, in Boulder, they came together.

The alarm blared and displayed Monday at 5:30 a.m. Elizabeth's bus would depart Boulder in one hour. Luke held her hand for most of that time. As he parked the truck in the lot behind the store, he still tasted her tears.

Chapter 24

Luke clocked out and grabbed the duffle bag from the stock room.

"See you guys Monday morning." He signaled his co-workers at the book store with a wave of his hand.

It had only been a few days since he had said good-bye to Elizabeth, and now a trip of his own making would take him to Hays, Kansas. He threw the duffle bag onto the back seat of Frank's car, a '68 Chevelle two-door. It landed next to a small Styrofoam cooler. Frank had purchased some refreshments for their trip.

Frank checked on their timing. "How long do ya' think it'll take to get there?"

"Let's see Hays is about..." Luke hesitated. "About a six pack, maybe two."

"I got some quart bottles. Always liked them for a road trip."

"That'll work."

"When's the game start?"

"Jerrod, he's one of my good friends from college, thought at seven."

"That's only five hours. We'll have to hustle to make the tip-off. Sorry I couldn't get away from school any sooner."

"Don't worry about it. We'll surprise my little brother. Maybe sit in the balcony till halftime, then squeeze in behind the bench."

"Sounds like a plan. Your friend, he's comin'?"

"Pretty sure."

"Sounds like a party, maybe."

"Pretty sure of that, too."

Luke passed one of the quart bottles to Frank when they sped by the Boulder overlook, heading east on the Denver-Boulder Turnpike.

He toasted to the start of the weekend. "Let the good times roll."

One pit-stop near the state line, one extra quart for each of them, they arrived about 7:30 on that Friday night in early March. From the foyer of the gymnasium, Luke spotted Jerrod and Bake sitting in the bleachers behind the bench, but his attention quickly diverted to the game.

Oakwood had just rebounded the ball at the opposite end of the court. The outlet pass went to Bailey, their point guard. Mark had already reached half court and took a long pass from Bailey. He dribbled the ball at full stride into Oakwood's offensive end of the court. As he split two defenders near the top of the key, one of them tipped the ball away. Mark pushed through the two of them and snatched the ball. After one more dribble, he slid under the basket for a reverse lay-up, avoiding a block attempt from the bigger of the two defenders.

"Let me guess." Frank slapped Luke's shoulder, as some of the crowd broke into a cheer. "That was your little brother."

"You got it!" Luke elbowed Frank. "Never met a double team that could slow him down."

Luke steered Frank toward a flight of stairs, and they claimed two seats in the balcony, near half court and opposite the team benches. Mark scored two more times in the first half. He hit two running jumpers in the lane off of set plays. As the plays developed, Luke described them to Frank.

"I guess you still remember the offense." Frank commented.

"A little. I used to try defending that particular play during practices. Gets real crowded in there. Perfect for Mark though, he always liked to mix it up."

Oakwood led by five points at half time. Luke and Frank followed some of the balcony crowd to the foyer.

"This is good basketball. Oakwood knows what they're doin'." Frank rendered his opinion with a hint of surprise.

"Well, it's not Big Eight ball. No Wilt Chamberlain, or even Cliff Meeley for that matter, but it's a quality game, especially at tournament time. Coach Ferguson has them playing well."

"Hey, no long hairs allowed in the gym." Luke was compelled to haze his friends. Each of them had allowed their hair to grow long enough to cover their shirt collars.

Jerrod stood his ground. "Haven't you heard? This is America. We're free to go where we want."

Luke and Jerrod shook hands, while Bake bumped Luke's shoulder.

"Jeez man, you need to let that hair of yours grow a little. Out there in Boulder, you probably stick out as much as the two of us do here." Bake looped an arm around Luke like they were forming the beginning of a huddle. "Did you think coach was going to need you to suit up tonight? You missed the first half."

As Luke explained that they had seen part of the game from the balcony, he widened the space between himself and his friends and introduced Frank.

The three exchanged handshakes, and Frank provided some background information. "Luke and me play pick-up basketball together every week. He claimed his brother was better than him. Had to see for myself."

All four of them engaged in a round table discussion about the Oakwood team. Bake delineated the differences in style of play of the Aurmann brothers. Mark's slashing moves had produced for the team tonight. Luke possessed a purer outside shot, and Bake joked that the team might need Luke if their opponent, Pittsburg State, should go to a zone defense in the second half.

Luke steered the conversation in another direction. "Jack Swanson just needs to get his shots to start falling. I guess he's been their leading scorer this season. And he still has great leaping ability."

Frank shared his own insights about Swanson. "Yeah, he got up there on a couple of pick-n-roll plays, once with Luke's brother and once with the other guard. Luke said his name was Bailey."

"Those three guys are the mainstays of the team. You're right about Swanson being top scorer, but Mark's not far off his pace. Bailey has had a few good games too." Jerrod outlined the team's scoring like a sportswriter would.

"Hey, let's get back in there. I want to get to that spot behind the bench where you guys were. Might as well let my little brother know I'm here." Luke led them into the gym, and they marched in single file along the sidelines.

The crowd buzzed with chatter as both teams had already returned to the floor. Oakwood used the basket at the end of the floor opposite the foyer. Mark and his teammates took warm-up shots, except for Jack Swanson, who sat on the bench with a towel over his head. Luke thought to himself that Jack must have seen one of the pros doing that and felt that it would be a cool practice to adopt.

Just in case, Luke cocked his head to the side and called to Bake, who was right behind him. "Swanson's not hurt, is he?"

"Nah, his pride maybe, but that's about all."

As Luke came within a few steps of Swanson, he barked aloud. "Keep your head up, Jack. They'll start falling!"

"Luke, Luke Aurmann! Son of a..." Jack Swanson stood to acknowledge Luke.

"Hey, Jack." Luke slapped Jack on the shoulder as he slipped past.

Bake, Jerrod, and Frank bunched near Jack and then climbed into the bleachers. They rearranged some coats and made a place for each of them to sit, including one for Luke.

Luke increased the length of his strides and closed the distance between himself and Mark, without Mark noticing. Mark took a shot from a spot along the baseline but missed, and one of his teammates passed another ball to him.

As Mark twirled the ball in his hands, Luke used a stern tone to deliver his coaching instruction. "You better keep practicing your outside shot. Bake thinks they may go to a zone in the second half."

"Luke? Goddamn man. What the hell are you?" Mark couldn't complete a thought.

"You didn't think I'd miss the whole season, did you? Besides I told you I'd make a game."

"How'd you?" Mark was still shocked.

"I got a ride from a friend, a fan of basketball. Told him he'd see some good ball. So far you haven't let us down."

"Got it going a little." Mark dribbled the ball between them switching from hand to hand and then casually handed it to Luke.

Luke squeezed it before flipping it back. "You better get in a few more practice shots. We'll wait for you after the game. Good luck."

"Great! Good! I'll look for you then." Mark took one dribble to the side and shot. When it fell through the net, he pivoted toward Luke.

"That's the way. Give 'em all you got." Luke pointed at his brother.

Pittsburg State did come out in a zone defense, and the Oakwood team struggled to score until they changed their offensive alignment. Jack Swanson posted in the middle, while Mark and Bailey took spots on the wings at the outside perimeter.

As the Oakwood team came into the offensive end of the court, Luke would often yell to the players, as much instructing them as he was cheering their effort.

Sometimes he offered loud encouragement to everyone. "You've got to pass the ball, inside then out, down low then out to the top."

Other times, he singled out Mark. "You've got to get your feet set. Be ready to shoot."

As the game evolved, Jack used his jumping ability to score several inside shots. Mark's outside jump shot started to fall, and he finished with 21 points. Jack scored 24, and Oakwood secured a victory that meant that they would advance to the regional championship the following night.

Luke, Bake, Jerrod, and Frank waited at the end of the court where Oakwood's team would be exiting the locker room. Bake suggested that they would be welcome inside the locker room, but Luke declined that notion.

Bake teased his friend. "Yeah, you're right. Plus, I suspect Ferguson doesn't necessarily want to hear any more of your coaching tips."

"Jeez," Frank expressed his own amazement. "You always that way when you're watching a game?"

Jerrod answered Frank's question on Luke's behalf. "Only when his kid brother's playing and especially when it's this team. He knows this team inside out, even though it has been two years since he's been in the locker room with them."

"That's probably right." Luke admitted, and a few of the members of Oakwood's team exited the locker room.

"No probably about it. But right now I'm getting thirsty. Don't you suppose that we should start celebrating this big win?" Bake fidgeted as the once packed gymnasium was now nearly empty.

"They got any saloons in this town?" Frank had never been farther east than Limon, Colorado.

"I suspect Bake knows of a few. He's had some experience in this part of Kansas." Jerrod answered on behalf of his other friend.

"There's one place for sure. It's called The Fort, always great music and plenty of cold beer." Bake's description had the ring of a radio slogan.

Mark and Jack approached Luke and the fanatical cheering section that gathered around him.

Luke raised an arm in a mock toast. "A round or two of cold beers should do the trick. Here's to the Cardinals!"

Luke hugged Mark and saluted Jack. "Great game you guys!"

"Good coaching, too." Jack nodded in Luke's direction. "We heard you every time we came to the bench."

"There were plenty of other times too." Mark jabbed Luke in the ribs.

"Can't help myself, I guess." Luke bounced against Mark's side.

"He's always coachin' our team, too." Frank nudged his way into the conversation.

Luke introduced Frank. "Mark, Jack, this is a friend from Boulder, Frank Morton. He and I play on a rec league team together."

"Get used to it." Mark joked with his brother's friend. "He's been coaching me since I was eleven. Playground, high school game, or college tournament, it doesn't matter where the game is."

"But look how far we've come." Luke raised his arm, this time sweeping it in an arc.

"Yeah, here we are in Hays, Kansas. We've hit the big time." Mark chuckled at the realization.

Bake still wanted to know what was next. "Screw the big time! Let's hit The Fort."

After the cheering section reached a unanimous decision regarding their destination, Luke invited Mark and Jack. "Think you guys can get away?"

Jack answered for both of them. "Not tonight, man. There'll be a bed check."

"Maybe tomorrow night. You guys staying on?" Mark had always enjoyed nights-out with his brother and his brother's friends.

"Definitely. We're looking forward to the championship game. Bake was saying that Doane won handily in the early game." Luke shared a general scouting report about Oakwood's next opponent.

"We'll have practice in the morning and get a game plan together then. We know Doane will be tough, but we'll be ready." Mark spoke confidently.

"Let's meet after your practice. I'll find you then."

Luke, Mark, and the group left the gym together.

On the way through the door, Mark feigned his best parental voice. "You guys stay out of trouble tonight."

"Not a chance." Bake pledged with a sly chuckle.

———

The Fort hosted a band based in Kansas City, Diamond in the Rough. Cold beer combined with solid rock 'n roll music. The vocals were strained, but the rhythm guitar and back beat were strong. The band's repertoire included several favorites.

Almost everyone danced, even Frank and Bake. Luke and Jerrod exchanged a few stories, talking over the music. Mostly, they enjoyed the sounds and sight of their friends bouncing on the floor with two local ladies.

The table expanded to make room for the newly acquainted. As they took their seats, Bake suggested that these two young women were good people to know because they knew the bartender. They insisted that everyone partake of the bartender's favorite, a round of tequila shots.

Bake echoed his earlier premise. "See, I told you. These girls know what they're doing."

"But, do we?" Jerrod asked what he believed to be a relevant question.

"It's just a little tequila." The girl named Jenny assured Jerrod of its innocence but also winked mischievously. "Even though you might prefer some grass."

"I just might." Jerrod nodded.

"Yeah, Buddy!" Bake cheered as he tossed the tequila down his throat and bit into a lime wedge.

"Woo, wee!" Frank wailed as the tequila hit his stomach. "That'll get ya' goin'."

"Whoa!" Luke's intuition told him to slow down.

The band played the first few bars of *The Letter*.

"Can't stop now." Jenny proclaimed and pulled Frank to his feet.

"We're just getting started." Her friend, Mary Ann, said as she hopped up.

"You heard the lady." Bake stood and chugged his beer before dancing away from the table.

Luke expressed his disbelief to Jerrod as this Friday night's festivities took shape. "Last week was quite a bit different."

Luke shared his memories of Elizabeth's visit in Boulder. Jerrod sensed the powerful emotion of that time, as Luke described how he felt. Luke admitted that he had written Elizabeth twice since she had departed just five days earlier. He poured his feelings into those pages.

Jerrod admired Luke's abilities. "You are a man of letters."

Additional rounds of beer accompanied another set of rock songs, while tequila shots were interspersed at opportune times. For Luke and his friends, the night devolved into an alcohol-induced blur, until a new voice penetrated the smoky hall.

A guest vocalist had joined the band. She sang *Different Drum*, her phrasing clear and tantalizing. When her song ended the hall rocked with enthusiastic cheers.

"That's Melinda Baxter." Jenny said. "She's from around here."

"She's real good." Frank offered his assessment.

"Most of the guys think so." Mary Ann elbowed Bake.

"What do you think, guys?" Bake leaned toward the center of the table.

No one responded to Bake because Melinda Baxter silenced the entire gathering with her rendition of *Crazy*. Her melodious voice was as pure as Patsy Cline's.

Luke yelled over the raucous applause to no one in particular. "I like her style."

Crazy was the theme of the rest of the night, at least in the area immediately surrounding the table where Luke and his friends presided. Jenny talked Melinda into joining their group. At first, Melinda was the center of attention, but eventually her celebrity was eclipsed by her more flamboyant and boisterous friends.

Luke and his friends were drawn in the direction of the bawdy ladies, preconditioned as they were by the similar levels of alcoholic intake. Melinda sipped rum and Coke, and she slipped into a backstage role.

When Bake stumbled on the way back from the dance floor and dropped into his chair with a thud, Mary Ann kissed him on the forehead as if in congratulations. Bake smiled a shot-from-tequila grin, and a chorus of laughter celebrated him.

Luke nudged Melinda. "This is crazy with a little different tune than the one you know. But crazy just the same."

On Saturday night the fast action of the basketball game spread a contagious excitement through the packed gymnasium and pulled the fans to their feet repeatedly. Mark, Jack, and the other Oakwood players hit a greater majority of their shots in the second half, and the momentum swung solidly in their favor. Bake led an impromptu Oakwood cheer. *All Night Long* sounded from the section just behind the team's bench.

Oakwood's opponents fell off the pace, and an Oakwood championship was assured. As the last few seconds of the game ticked away, Mark crossed the half court line with his dribble and launched a forty-foot shot. It dropped through the hoop and snapped the net with a swish. The final horn sounded, and a climatic *All Night Long* rang out from the bleachers.

"Let the celebration begin!" Frank bounced down the bleachers and onto the floor.

Bake nudged Luke and described his next move. "Frank and me are going to get a head-start over to the saloon. You and Jerr can bring Mark. Maybe Jack'll come too. Coach'll trust Jerr to get them back to campus tomorrow. It's better if Coach doesn't see me anyway, if you know what I mean."

"You mean that Coach'll know that things are likely to get out of hand if he knows you're a part of the plan." Jerrod restated what he realized was a valid point.

"You guys hold off on that tequila till we get there!" Luke shouted as his friends disappeared into the exiting crowd.

Luke and Jerrod waited near the locker room and recounted some of the game's action, as well as Oakwood's basketball history. Jerrod thought that the last time Oakwood had reached the quarterfinals of the national championship was 1959. Since Jerrod had held the position of Sports Information Director for his last three years at Oakwood, Luke trusted his memory regarding this fact.

When Mark and Jack joined them, Jack confirmed it. "Coach Ferguson said we're the first Oakwood team since '59 to make it this far in the tournament."

"Yeah, Coach is as high as I've ever seen him." Mark beamed with pride.

"He gave you the okay?" Luke asked of Mark and Jack.

"Kind of." Mark glanced over his shoulder at the locker room door.

Jack provided more detail. "We're okay to stay behind. Need to get our own room, though. Unless we can stay with you guys."

"If things work out like they did last night that won't be a problem." Jerrod delineated the previous night's outcome.

Bake and Frank had secured unexpected accommodations with two new, female friends. As a result, in Luke's room and his, one bed was not used. In his estimation the likelihood of a repeat performance was very high.

Mark skipped ahead to the coming days. "Coach'll probably check with our profs on Monday to make sure we're in class. Plus, we'll have practice. Our next opponent will be the winner of the Texas district on Wednesday. Not too far to travel for us. Kansas City Auditorium, it'll be like a home game."

Luke demanded that his brother savor this night. "Hey, not so fast! Let's celebrate tonight's win. Remember?"

"It was a good one, wasn't it?" Mark surveyed the gym.

"And what's with the rainbow at the buzzer?" Luke jabbed Mark.

"Ah, just having a little fun." Mark grinned and slapped Luke's shoulder.

"All night long!" Frank shouted as Mark, Jack, Luke and Jerrod approached the tables he and Bake had arranged at the saloon. "Have a seat, guys. Bake saw you come in and went for some beers. No tequila yet. Coach Luke said we need to hold off till he gives the go-ahead."

"Coaching here in the saloon too, are you?" Mark played along.

"You'll soon find out that Frank's full of shit."

Luke wanted to shift the discussion, and Bake provided the means when he distributed the bottles of beer.

Luke raised his bottle, and everybody followed. "Here's to the Cardinals!"

"Great game, guys!" Jerrod touched his bottle to Mark's and then Jack's.

"Where's the women Jerr was telling us about?" Mark questioned Bake. "Jack was getting all excited. You know these country girls are his thing."

"Don't you worry, Jack. Miss Mary Ann and her wild friend, Jenny, we've talked to them. Told them a couple of basketball stars would be here tonight. They said they'd round up some friends." Bake took a long drink of his beer.

"Round up? Sounds more like livestock than women." Jerrod pointed out the humorous aspect of the way the previous night unfolded.

Bake defended the ladies who had been so gracious to Frank and him. "These girls got class. You should see their place."

"Real blue ribbon stock I'm sure." Jerrod prodded Bake.

Frank cut into the dialogue. "I grew up in Boulder. Don't know about award winners, but I used to go down to the National Western Stock Show just to admire the pretty girls. Nothing wrong with a country girl. Besides, like Bake said, their ranch is real cool."

Frank swallowed the contents of his bottle of beer, as though that was the final word on the subject. When he proposed another round of beers, Luke agreed to accompany him.

"All night long!" Mark stood up. "I'll run the point for you guys."

The band hit the introductory licks to *Proud Mary* as the next round was served. Before the song ended Mary Ann, Jenny, and their friends arrived.

The party rolled then. The band wasn't as polished as the group from the previous night. Wild Prairie hailed from Wichita. A little more country, they complimented the impromptu theme for the night's festivities. Oakwood's victory party spiked with tequila shots at a raucous, small town saloon.

Melinda Baxter performed again. *Leaving on a Jet Plane* and *Sweet Dreams* mixed folk rock and a country ballad.

As she completed her second song, Jerrod spoke over the chatter that circled the table. "You have to like this girl's style."

Luke responded when no one else did. "There's definitely something about her."

With Melinda's third song, *He'd Rather Be in Colorado*, the Oakwood party settled in their chairs.

After the first verse, Mark asked of Luke. "Does she know you?"

"Not really. We talked a little last night."

While the last note still hung above the smoke of the saloon, the crowd broke into applause, and Melinda turned to smile and curtsy toward the Oakwood table. Luke grinned and Frank raised his bottle of beer.

Frank whistled and cheered. "Now that is cool, the ultimate in cool."

The band leader then coaxed another round of applause for Melinda.

Luke spoke over the din. "There's at least one classy country girl."

"Classy's your thing." Mark touched his beer bottle to Luke's.

A Creedence introductory guitar riff elicited a unified movement across the saloon. Even the guys and girls of the Oakwood table moved toward the dance floor. Luke laughed at Mark and

Jack. Neither of them moved as well on the dance floor as they did on the basketball court, but they couldn't be denied the celebration.

Luke found Melinda near the bar. "Thanks for the John Denver song. I like this saloon, but it isn't quite Boulder, Colorado." Luke offered Melinda a rum 'N Coke.'

"I wouldn't know. Never been, but I like that song," Melinda replied.

"We'll have to get you out there sometime then. We can always make room for a beautiful voice like yours. Tulagi's would be a great place for your Colorado debut."

"Tulagi's?"

Luke provided more detail. "It's a small music hall on The Hill, across from CU campus. Though the folk rock or country sound might not work, the crowd would love your voice."

"Think so?"

"Yes, I do believe that is so." Luke touched his beer to her drink glass.

"What's so?" An unknown male voice made the inquiry as a young man approached them.

Melinda shuffled toward the young man. "Luke, this is Jeff, my...my friend."

"Luke, good to meet you." Jeff and Luke exchanged a nod.

Luke explained the comment that Jeff had overheard. "We were just talking about Melinda's last song, *He'd Rather Be in Colorado.* I'm from Boulder and I think Melinda should come to Boulder to sing."

"Think so?" Jeff repeated Melinda's question.

His inquiry contained no curiosity, more of a threatening tone.

Luke was undeterred. "I really do think so."

"Boulder's a long way from Hays." Jeff slipped an arm around Melinda's waist.

"I've always wanted to travel." Melinda stated.

"It's only about six hours drive." Luke minimized the distance of the trip to Boulder.

"Doesn't sound that far." Melinda edged toward Luke.

"A lot farther than Kansas City or Wichita." Jeff contended. "And I'm sure it's a lot different."

"Well, I grew up in Missouri. Only been in Boulder for about a year but I don't think it's that different. You've got some mountain folks and hippie types. But I just let them do their thing, and they treat me the same way."

Jeff finished his beer with a long drink and signaled the close of the conversation when he touched Melinda's elbow and then tapped his wrist watch.

Jeff directed his words to Melinda. "We should get going. I told them we'd be at the party by now."

"Yeah, I know." Melinda's voice wavered, and her soft, brown eyes focused on Luke instead of Jeff.

Luke misread the message in Melinda's eyes. "Hey, I'm sorry. Didn't know you had places to go."

"That's okay." Jeff said and tugged Melinda's arm.

"Well, I don't necessarily have to go, but..." Melinda held her position.

Jeff released Melinda's arm but his voice did not relinquish its hold on her. "You're done singing, aren't you?"

"Yeah, I guess."

"Then, let's go!"

"Okay, I guess." Melinda hesitated, as though she sought a reason to stay.

Luke's response confused her. "It was good hearing your songs and talking to you. Hey, before you go, do me a favor. Wait here, just a second."

Luke slipped past her and returned with a bar napkin and a pencil, which he gave to Melinda. "Write down your name and address. I'll get some information on Tulagi's and send it to you. I'll write you."

"Really?" Melinda's gaze searched Luke's eyes for confirmation.

"My friend Jerr, you met him last night. He says I'm a man of letters." Luke explained as Melinda wrote.

Melinda paused before handing the napkin to Luke.

"Thanks, I will write you." Luke touched Melinda's hand as she released the napkin. "I do like your music. It's classy."

"Thanks." Melinda said.

"Yeah, thanks," Jeff said as he latched onto Melinda's arm, escorting her in the direction of the door.

Luke carefully folded the napkin and tucked it in his wallet. He thumbed the bills that straddled the napkin, assessing the number of beers he could afford to supply to his table of friends. On his way to the bar, Melinda intercepted him and kissed his cheek.

A blush of color crossed her own cheeks as she spoke. "You're nice. Even if you don't write. Thanks."

"I usually do what I say I'm going to do. You'll see. Someday maybe I'll see you in Boulder."

"Maybe, bye." Melinda dashed away.

Six young men circled near the trunk end of two cars in the parking lot of the Hays Roadway Inn. The exhaust fumes from the cars contributed to the murky cloud that wafted in the midst of the group. The previous night's sloppy beers, saloon shots, rock 'n roll songs, lady's perfume and men's perspiration formed a powerful potion in that morning's atmosphere.

Jack Swanson broke the silence. "See you later, Aurnmann."

"Yeah, Jack. Good luck the rest of the way. Don't be afraid to mix things up a little."

"Right, coach."

"You, too, man." Luke grabbed Mark's shoulder. "You guys get past the quarterfinals, and I'll get Frank to drive us to K.C."

"Sounds fine to me." Frank coughed to clear his throat. "You guys play like you did the last couple of nights, and you'll be hard to beat."

"We'll give it a shot." Mark's voice was shaky.

"Give 'em all we got." Luke spoke with more conviction.

"All we got." Mark elbowed his brother.

Shared admiration for the quality play of basketball and amusement at the lack of rhythm on the dance floor ended with a final round of good-byes. The syncopated slamming of the car doors punctuated mutual urgings for a safe trip and a commitment to connect again should the Oakwood Cardinals advance beyond their midweek game in the National Tournament.

Chapter 25

Boulder, End of March 1972

Luke sat on the floor a few feet from the corner of the empty room. He then dipped his paint brush in the small can and lay on his side while reaching past his head. He stroked the pale blue paint along the top line of the baseboard trim.

Two weeks had passed since the long weekend in Kansas City. Oakwood did make it to the national semifinals, and as Luke had promised, he and Frank made the trip to Kansas City. It meant a Friday morning departure and an all day drive to see the game. Oakwood lost a close one to Alabama Baptist College.

Their six-foot, ten-inch center hit a hook shot from the left side of the lane. Oakwood knew he would be the player to take the last shot. Luke and Frank, Jerrod and Bake, the whole crowd knew too.

Oakwood couldn't stop him. They couldn't match his height, couldn't stop him the whole game. His shot hit the backboard and fell through the net as the buzzer sounded. Alabama Baptist won by two points. Oakwood had fought hard to tie the game with ten seconds to go. Jack and Mark double teamed the ball, and Jack tipped it away. Mark snatched the ball as it headed toward the sidelines and flung it toward Bailey. Bailey broke away for an easy basket, but Oakwood had no answer for the big guy, and the game and their season ended that night.

Luke felt the stiffness in his hips as he pursued another commitment he had made to paint the room that would be the nursery for Julia's baby. For two nights, one in the hotel in downtown Kansas City and one at the fraternity house on Oakwood's campus, he had slept on the floor. The thin carpet at the hotel and the thinner blanket at the fraternity house provided minimal comfort to his bony body. Sporadic twinges of pain served as reminders of his weekend in the Midwest.

Within the first few days of his return to Boulder, Luke's head had cleared, and he had settled into a routine. He worked an extra hour each weekday and worked through the afternoon each Saturday. He painted on Sundays, starting with the ceiling and now the walls.

Luke checked on the baby's due date with Julia each Sunday. "They're still saying May 3rd. But I'm ready anytime this little guy wants to come." Julia rubbed her midsection.

"You don't want him to be premature. It's a him?"

"I'm not sure, but I think it will be. That's why you're doing the light blue, but we'll do some other decorating touches just in case my intuition fails me."

"Yeah, me and Mom are going to do some decorating whenever you get done." Terry had made that point the previous Sunday as well.

"I guarantee that my part will be done soon, no later than the middle of April."

Terry explained that they would be using stencils and yellow paint to make stars. The corner of one wall and maybe part of the ceiling would be covered with them. Her mom would employ the ladder to reach the ceiling, but only if she promised to be careful.

Terry had grown impatient with the amount of time that Luke needed to finish the painting. He assured her that the brush work was the most time consuming and solicited her help for the time when he would be using the roller to paint the wider surfaces of the walls.

A snow storm covered the grass in the backyard, a deepening white, while Luke applied the blue paint in a pattern the width of two brush strokes around the perimeter of the window. Then heavy footsteps drew his attention.

Frank bounded into the room. "I came to see if you were still alive, or maybe if you had decided to run off to Hays or Kansas City."

"No, I've just been working, at the store and here too. Those two weekends were enough for me."

"What about some basketball?" Frank tossed Luke a ball.

Luke snatched the ball with one hand. "Can't do it, have to stick with the painting until I finish."

Luke bounced the ball twice and tossed it to Frank. Not long after Frank departed, larger flakes of snow piled white on white, and Luke's pace with the paint brush quickened. He stood in the middle of the room reviewing the quality of his work but was distracted by the whirlwind of snow that blew past the window.

Terry caught him unaware when she entered the room. "Mom's making the soup. She says it'll be good on a day like today. You're supposed to come down for lunch."

"Yeah, that does sound good. The snow's getting deep."

"Maybe they'll call off school if it gets real deep." Terry sounded hopeful.

"Maybe work too." Luke conjured a child's wish too.

"I don't think they call off work, just school." Terry corrected Luke.

"You're probably right." Luke said with a finishing stroke. "Let's try that soup, and after lunch I'll show you how to use the roller."

Luke applied the paint to the roller and demonstrated the technique for Terry. They worked side by side for a short time, until Terry decided that painting wasn't enough fun. Luke completed the walls by mid-afternoon. He projected that he could finish the trim the following Sunday.

While Luke cleaned the brush and roller in the kitchen sink, Julia and Terry surveyed the nursery, assessing Luke's progress. Luke stacked the old blankets he had been using for drop cloths, the ladder and other supplies next to the kitchen door in preparation for carrying them to the garage.

Julia caught him as he was putting on his sweatshirt. "The painting looks perfect. I can't tell you how much I appreciate you doing it."

"Don't mention it." Luke straightened his shirt collar where it bunched under the sweatshirt. "Next week I'll do the trim, and then the room will be ready for some furniture."

"Should we do the stars first?" Terry rested a foot on the lowest step of the ladder and posed there as though she was ready to climb and begin decorating at that moment.

Luke grinned as he responded. "Yes, that would be best. But I thought your mom was going to use the ladder for the high parts. So you probably don't need to practice climbing on it."

"I'm not." Terry backed away from the ladder. "I just wanted to see...I wanted to know when we were going to get to do our part."

"Maybe in two weeks." Julia rested one hand on Terry's shoulder. "We have plenty of time before the baby comes."

"So, is it okay if I take the ladder and other stuff out to the garage?" Luke assumed a positive response and lifted the stack of blankets and supplies.

"Thanks again." Julia held the screen door to allow Luke to exit.

When he returned for the ladder, he suggested to Julia that he shovel the accumulated snow, at least a walking path to the front sidewalk.

Julia had her own suggestion. "Use Jim's old parka. It's hanging on a hook in the back of the garage."

Luke worked along a line from the garage to the house and then toward the stairway that led to his apartment. The weight of the snow made it difficult to throw, so he carried each scoop and dumped it onto the neighbor's side yard.

He made slow progress but finally reached the front sidewalk. The snow still covered the street and continued to fall from the sky. As he dumped the first scoop of snow to widen the path and work back to the house, a set of headlights pierced the lengthening shadows of the late afternoon.

The beams from the headlights fishtailed from one side of the street to the other. A gust of wind whipped the snow into the hood of the parka that Luke wore. The lights now cut a line through the whirling snow, aimed directly at Luke, and they drew ever closer.

The snow gathered force and the lights brightened but did not stop. Luke made his retreat. Dropping the shovel, he took two big strides and then jumped behind the big maple tree that stood in the corner of Julia's front yard.

The left front fender of what now appeared to be a pickup truck struck a glancing blow to the side of the tree opposite where Luke had landed. The truck then came to a final stop with the right rear wheel in the shoveled path of the driveway and the other three wheels firmly entrenched in the snow.

The driver of the truck bumped twice against the door, and the metal of the hinge side of the door creaked. It rubbed the metal of the front fender where the two sections had been smashed together.

Grunting and cussing emanated from inside the truck. "Goddammit, come on!"

A third thrust from the driver's shoulder was accompanied by a roar, and the driver catapulted from the truck, landing face first a few feet from Luke's position.

"Damn! Shit!" The driver pushed up with his arms and shook his head like a dog trying to clear slop from his face. Wiping his eyes with one sleeve, Luke came into view. "Luke, little Luke, what the hell are you doin' out here?"

Clay had made another exciting appearance.

"I might ask you the same thing," Luke responded, as he rose to brush the snow from his clothes. "Are you all right, you crazy son of a bitch?"

Luke extended a helping hand toward Clay, but he slapped at it. Clay scrambled to his feet and kicked the snow in frustration.

"Yeah, I'm okay. Looks like the truck may need a little work though." Clay bent at the waist to survey the damage. "We'll know better in the morning."

"Probably so. I'll shovel again then, anyway, before I go to work."

"I doubt any of us will have to go to work. At least that's what I'm banking on. I'm thinkin' me and the little lady should have a snow-storm party tonight, snuggle on the sofa. That kinda' stuff."

"Could be romantic." Luke picked up the shovel as he shook his head in a form of denial.

"Now you're talkin'." Clay slapped Luke on the shoulder and stomped his feet and dusted the snow from his jacket.

After taking a few steps along the shoveled path, he yelled "Honey, I'm home!"

Just then the light above the kitchen entrance came on, and Julia leaned across the threshold of the door. "Clay is that you? What the hell is going on out there?"

"Oh, just brushed that tree a little with my truck. Damned near hit Luke though. Crazy guy's out playin' in the snow."

"Luke, are you okay?" Julia called. "You boys better come inside now."

"I'm on my way." Clay increased the pace of his walk.

"I'm right behind him." Luke shouted.

Luke shoveled as he followed Clay. He diverted toward the garage and placed the shovel inside the door. Julia opened the door wider, as Clay stomped inside.

She called again to Luke. "Thought you were coming in?"

"I'll just head downstairs." Luke trotted across the path that he had just shoveled.

"You stay warm tonight, Luke!" Julia commanded as she closed the door.

"I'll be fine." Luke's words were lost in the blowing snow.

Chapter 26

St. Louis, Early April 1972

The rain fell along a more vertical plane as the wind subsided, and Debbie parked her car in front of the Clayton Café. Elizabeth and she dashed through the café's front door. They chose a booth at the back of the room, even though only a few patrons remained in the restaurant. They each ordered a Coke and decided to split an order of fries. At 2:00 p.m., the normal lunch hour had passed, but they were excited, not hungry.

Over the course of the previous few weeks, the two of them had spent time together searching for places to rent. On this day, they decided a house that they had seen early in the process was their favorite.

From the café's telephone booth, Debbie called Mr. Canton, their prospective landlord, to confirm that the small house in a nearby neighborhood was still available. Elizabeth and Debbie asked for one consideration from him, a more modern look to the rooms. They suggested that the front room and kitchen should be painted.

When they first met Mr. Canton, he had told them about the recent history of the house. After being his mother's home for nearly twenty years, he had moved his mother into a nursing home. He lived in Clayton as well and had helped with the upkeep of the house until the demands of her everyday care required round-the-clock professional assistance.

Elizabeth and Debbie envisioned new colors on the walls as a way to transform the house into a place with an up-to-date décor, more suited to their younger sense of style. When they agreed to do the painting themselves, the deal was finalized.

Before the sun had set, they were roommates.

At 9:00 a.m. on the next Saturday, Elizabeth and Debbie met at their new house with friends and acquaintances from Children's Hospital. Francine, their supervisor, and her husband, Howard, a handyman by trade, arrived before the others they had recruited.

Francine, a black woman who had achieved managerial status at the hospital, lived her life as though she were continually being tested. In turn, she routinely questioned the younger nurses about patient care. When Elizabeth and Debbie told her of the decision they had made regarding renting an older house in Clayton, and their commitment to paint some of the rooms, her innate skepticism surfaced.

After a brief tour of the house, Francine posed the underlying question. "So, you think this old place can be fixed up, do you?"

Elizabeth allayed Francine's concerns. "Francine, we're just renting the house for one year. We only want to paint the walls in a couple of rooms. That's not too much is it?"

Francine deferred to her husband. "Howard, what do you think?"

Howard agreed with Elizabeth, the task for the day would be to paint the walls in the front room and the kitchen. He brought in the supplies and ladders from his truck and then outlined his work plan to the three ladies.

His only concern was a lack of experienced help. "Francine, I thought you said Lil' Mack was coming."

"Did I hear someone call?" Mack Summers, an orderly from the hospital, strolled into the room right on cue. "Howie, ya' know ya' can't do this kinda job without me. Let me get up on that ladder."

At the sound of Mack's voice, Howard stepped off the ladder. Francine, Debbie and Elizabeth diverted their attention from Howard's instructions to the slender, young black man who entered the room.

"You always miss the set-up," Howard said.

"No, ya' always get started too early." Mack responded. "Though the missus is with ya' today. So I shoulda' known to be early."

"That's right. No lolly-gaggin' is allowed on my shift." Francine stated.

"Now, Miss Francine, Howie and me we'll take care of this job in no time. 'Sides, it's Saturday. A man's got to get some rest on the weekend. Don't you think so, Miss Debbie? " Mack re-routed the conversation to a friendlier source.

"Early or late I'm glad you're here either way." Debbie ushered Mack toward the ladder.

"See, somebody's glad to see me." Mack smiled in Francine's direction.

"Yeah, but somebody don't know you like I do." Francine simply shook her head.

Howard interrupted the superfluous exchange. "Here's what I think. All this talking's not getting any paint on these walls. Mack, get up on that ladder. You know what to do."

"Yes, sir, believe I do." Mack climbed the ladder, paint brush in hand.

"Not sure I do, though." James Conroe's words resonated throughout the room.

A stout black man with a deep voice, James was one of the hospital janitors. Francine had suggested that Elizabeth ask him to help. She knew that James liked Elizabeth. For that matter, everyone at the hospital did.

Francine knew James to be a hard worker, but he didn't like to constantly be told what to do. That put him at odds with her, but whenever Elizabeth needed help, he rarely hesitated. As James peeled off his jacket and rolled up his shirt sleeves, Francine introduced him to her husband.

Howard adjusted everyone's duties. "Mack, let James do the work on the ladder, and you take the baseboard. Francine, you and Miss Debbie stand by for a while and let these guys get ahead of you. After they do the brush work at the top and the bottom of the wall, then you two can use the rollers to fill in. Miss Elizabeth, you come with me to the kitchen."

Howard and Elizabeth made good progress in the kitchen, while the other four worked in the living room. By lunch time things were going well enough that Howard decided the crew should paint the trim of the picture window in the front room and around the door that separated that room from the kitchen. He would handle the kitchen window and the door frame from the side facing the kitchen.

They would use a half gallon of semi-gloss white that Howard had brought with him. It was left over from a job he had completed the previous week. He swiped some of the white paint onto a piece of scrap board and held it up to one of the freshly painted walls.

Both Elizabeth and Debbie liked the way it looked against the light gold of the front room walls, and they thought it worked in the kitchen with the green walls, too. They questioned Howard about payment for the extra paint, and they reached mutual agreement about a beer or two in celebration after the job was completed.

The additional work that Howard outlined slowed progress in both rooms, but the entire job was completed by late afternoon.

When the whole crew gathered in the front room, Debbie acknowledged their work. "We can't tell you how much we appreciate each one of you. Our new house looks so cool."

Elizabeth echoed Debbie's words. "And Howard, you even did our little back porch. You're the coolest, all of you!"

"It's time to celebrate!" Debbie nudged Mack and hugged Francine.

"Now, you're talkin'!" Mack marched toward the door.

"How about Angelina's for some pizza and beer?" Elizabeth made an enthusiastic recommendation. "You know, it's in the

Italian neighborhood on The Hill. That's not too far, and the food's really good."

"Not sure about that part of the city for us folks." James sounded a cautionary note.

Mack returned to the group. "Yeah, how 'bout my uncle's place? It's just a little ways off the highway, north on Grand. They have real good fried chicken and fish and food like that, cold beer and big drinks. It's called Sammy's."

"But how about me and Elizabeth down there?" Debbie expressed her own reservations based on her knowledge of that part of St. Louis.

"It's my uncle's place. Nobody's goin' to try nothin' if you're with me. 'Sides James and Howard will be there, too." Mack nodded toward them. "Right guys?"

"Actually, I been there a few times myself." James smiled reassuringly at Elizabeth and Debbie. "It's like a family place really, not really a night spot. The food's good for sure."

"Okay then, I guess it's Sammy's for some fish 'n chips and a pint or two." Debbie wrapped an arm around Elizabeth's waist.

"Yeah, they give ya' a bag 'a chips when you get a fish sandwich." Mack misinterpreted Debbie's allusion to English style fish and chips.

Debbie stammered when she tried to explain her comment, and Elizabeth interrupted her. "Sammy's sounds perfect. But give me a minute to put on a sweater and some different shoes."

"Yeah, guys, give us girls a chance to freshen up a bit." Debbie raised the index finger of one hand and gestured toward Francine with the other hand. "Francine, you can use the bathroom."

"Don't be taking too long now, you hear?" Howard continued to try to manage the progress of the day's activities.

As the group departed, Debbie and Elizabeth were the last to step onto the front porch. They turned simultaneously to lock the front door. Elizabeth bumped Debbie, and Debbie stumbled to the side. They giggled, and Elizabeth missed with her initial attempt to insert the key into the lock. Debbie laughed louder, when Elizabeth feigned a staggering motion.

"Hey, are you two already fighting? You've only been room-mates for one day." A new male voice carried onto the front porch.

Andy, Debbie's older brother, strolled across the front lawn. A second young man trailed near his right shoulder.

"Already quitting for the day?" Andy's second question sounded more earnest.

Debbie responded to her brother with an air of indignation. "We're quitting because the job's finished. No thanks to you and your friend. Where were you guys eight hours ago?"

The two young men stood on the front lawn, while Debbie and Elizabeth maintained their position on the porch, standing regally two feet higher than the male supplicants.

Andy's wiry, red hair curled tightly against his scalp and wrinkled forehead. His eyes, bloodshot and red at the corners, reinforced his case.

Andy explained how he had missed the volunteer work because his job as a tax accountant demanded his presence at the office. Since early February, he had worked every Saturday. Even though the filing deadline had past, he had used extensions for many of his corporate clients and working on those returns had compromised this day.

He foresaw continued Saturday work. "Sis, I told you I'd try to make it. I said we still had a lot of bullshit work at the office. Besides, I thought you girls would be working long after dark."

"We actually have friends, dependable friends who are good workers and excellent painters." Elizabeth expounded and pointed toward those in the driveway near their vehicles.

Francine waved and pulled Howard toward the front door. Mack and James moved in the same direction.

"Isn't she your supervisor at the hospital?" Andy asked.

Elizabeth answered, "Our supervisor and our friend, the guys are our friends, too."

"I understand just about everyone at Children's is your friend." Andy's friend surprised Elizabeth with his comment.

Andy's friend stood a few inches taller than Andy. His wavy, brown hair was trimmed on the sides, almost military-like. His bright, blue eyes contrasted with Andy's and shone like a mirror image of Elizabeth's. Elizabeth raised an inquisitive eyebrow but did not speak.

Debbie formulated her own demand of the handsome stranger. "How would you know? For that matter, who are you?"

Andy responded to his sister. "Debbie, Elizabeth, this is my friend who happens to be a doctor and who also happened to get called-in to work today, but who checked with me and said he'd still be willing to help out after he finished the urgent surgical procedure he had to perform this afternoon. So, that's who he is and how he knows what he knows."

"But, Andy wait..." Debbie tried to stop her brother.

Andy pushed on. "No really, do you believe me now when I tell you we had things, important things, we had to do today?"

Debbie waved a hand in her brother's direction. "I meant what's his name, stupid?"

Elizabeth giggled then. "This is getting a little weird."

Elizabeth's comment caused a brief silence to fall over the porch, as her friends approached.

Francine clarified one point. "Let me guess. This is the brother you always talk about, huh Debbie?"

Debbie introduced Andy to her friends. She passed her arm over the group and ended by pointing at her brother. Judgment tinged her introduction.

Andy winced under Debbie's stare. "Jeez, sis. You never let..."

Andy's friend grabbed Andy's arm with one hand and extended the other toward Debbie. "Let me introduce myself. I'm Mitch Hanson."

"Hi," Debbie replied with a press of her hand into his. "Doctor Hanson, is it?"

"I'm a resident at Barnes, in surgery, but I'm Mitch to my friends."

"And I guess you already know Elizabeth." Debbie released his hand.

"Not really, but I've seen her at the hospital a few times." Mitch explained as he extended the same hand to Elizabeth.

"It's a pleasure to meet you. I'm..."

Elizabeth interrupted Mitch. "I heard, Mitch to my friends. Is that right?"

Elizabeth's fingertips met Mitch's, but he flinched at her remark. Everyone in the gathering chuckled. Andy slapped Mitch on the back and winked at Elizabeth. He offered to buy a round of beers, and Debbie increased the stakes, when she commanded that her brother would be responsible for more than just one round of drinks.

Sammy's was the family style place Mack had described. The bar stretched across the back of the long, narrow room directly opposite the front door. Mack held the door for his friends, and when the mixed-race paint crew walked in, they were met by stares of consternation from the restaurant's patrons.

Mack was the last of the crew to make his entrance. He enjoyed the attention. "Hey, everybody! You don't have to look thatta' way. These are my friends from the hospital and around. So, jus' go on and relax. Uncle Sammy, can we push them two tables together over there and make a place for everybody? We're goin' eat some supper and do some drinkin' too. These boys say they're buying."

Mack laughed and brushed between Andy and Mitch. An echo of chuckling and smattering of smiles formed a new greeting for the party of painters. Mack socialized with a few people on his way to the table, and then introduced his friends to his Uncle Sammy as everyone took their seat. Uncle Sammy introduced Emma, their waitress for the evening.

After a dinner of deep-fried entrees and two rounds of beers to help the food digest, Mack offered to secure the next round of drinks. When he explained that, if he went direct to the bar, he could take advantage of a family discount, Elizabeth and Debbie switched to rum and Coke. Howard and Francine requested a high ball, and Mitch and Andy a scotch and soda.

James helped Mack carry the drinks to the table. As James distributed the last of the mixed drinks, three bottles of Miller High Life remained on the tray. Mack winked at James and divided the three bottles by placing one in front of James and taking the other two, one in each hand.

Before taking his seat, Mack swallowed one beer in two long gulps. He took the other beer with him when he strolled to the juke box on the other side of the restaurant.

Mack returned to the table, his fingers snapping to the beat of his first selection. The songs from the juke box provided a rhythm to the conversations bouncing around the table of new friends. The last remnants of guardedness fell away. A party tone rose in its place.

The song selections were primarily Motown, and after most of the supper crowd had left, Sammy allowed Mack to raise the volume. James and Mack rearranged some of the tables near the jukebox and cleared the space for an impromptu dance floor. Francine guessed what was on the minds of the younger men.

She called them to the table before the festivities moved in that direction. "You young folks can carry on, but Howard and me need to be getting home. We should get our ticket and pay what we owe so far."

"Yes, ma'am, Missus Butler, we'll get right on that," Mack said with a sideways grin. "I'll get Miss Emma over here straight away."

"Don't you get all sassy with me, young man!" Francine wagged a finger in Mack's direction.

"Ah, Francine, I'm just havin' a little fun. It must be all the High Life talkin'."

"Yeah, I know all about your high life. That's why it's time for us to go." Francine rose from her chair.

Emma arrived with the bill, and Andy perused it. With Mitch's help, he paid out the lion's share and assigned Howard, James, and Mack the difference. Mack included an extra tip for Emma in his share.

After Francine and Howard's departure, Elizabeth and Debbie took a spot near the impromptu dance floor where Mack and Emma had become the center of attention. Dancing was another of Mack's talents, and his St. Louis swing led Emma in rhythmic swirls. The Motown beat converted that side of Sammy's into a hip dance club. Soon, James tapped Elizabeth on the shoulder and motioned for her to join him.

They stole some of the spotlight from Mack and Emma, not because of their style, but as a consequence of their blending of human color. The remainder of the restaurant's patrons, who weren't already watching that part of the room, had now focused their attention there. Andy and Mitch joined Debbie at the fringe. It wasn't unheard of, but it was still a very uncommon scene, a white woman following the lead of a black man on a dance floor.

Debbie laughed at the scene unfolding. Her friend's bright smile and fluid movement contrasted with the faraway look that streamed from her eyes. Elizabeth seldom looked at James, but stayed with his rhythm as he moved her around and around. The song built to a crescendo and two more couples slid onto the floor. Just as the song came to an end, Debbie pulled Andy toward the group.

"Ooh, saved by the bell," Andy said as he slipped his hand out of Debbie's grasp.

A new song started and Debbie grabbed him again. "Not so fast. This is a good song."

"Not so good. You know I'm no dancer." Andy resisted his sister.

Mitch stepped between them.

He asked with feigned gallantry. "May I have this dance?"

"No doubt about it," Andy replied for his sister.

Debbie's face brightened with her own smile, as Mitch and she joined the other couples. The beat expanded, hands clapped, feet stomped, and laughter filled Sammy's to the edges and all along the bar. When the song ended, Mack rallied his new friends.

His eyes flashed at them. "See, I told you all, Sammy's can be a real hangout. I know what's goin' on."

James pulled a handkerchief from his hip pocket and used it to wipe the perspiration from his forehead.

He admitted, "Never been here when it was like this."

Mack used the back of one hand to wipe his forehead. "Yeah, but ya' never been here when I been here either, have ya?"

"You're right 'bout that part too." James beamed at the circle of friends.

Another couple selected songs from the jukebox. This round started at a slower pace with the Temptations, *My Girl*. Emma slipped away, and Mack and James succumbed to the need to quench their own thirst. They stepped in the direction of the bar. Andy motioned to Debbie and the others and scooted to the side making a space for them to join him at the end of the bar, too.

When Elizabeth took a step to follow Debbie, Mitch hooked her arm. "I thought perhaps we could last for one more song. Would you give this guy a chance?"

Elizabeth responded, "Sure."

In their dancer's embrace, Elizabeth glanced into Mitch's eyes and then relaxed inside his arms. Debbie didn't realize that Elizabeth and Mitch had stayed behind until she reached the bar.

Andy motioned to his friend and her friend. "What do you think, sis?"

When she pivoted, her lower jaw dropped in a reflexive response. Her lips tightened then, and she hummed along with the chorus. Softly, slowly, no words came to her consciousness.

Sammy stepped toward her and asked what she wanted to drink.

"Make hers a tall rum and coke and mine a scotch and soda." Andy answered for them both.

After two more drinks at the bar and one more Shake-A-Tail-Feather dance, Mitch suggested to his new friends that the party should move to a different hangout. "This club's a different atmosphere, the lights are lower, and the music's more jazz, less rock. It's not too far from here, though, just down Grand Avenue. It's called The Sweet Spot."

"I knew I'd seen ya' before tonight," Mack proclaimed, "and that's probably where. You like The Sweet Spot, huh? I can see it, that's cool. Ya' like Big Jim on his sax, he's the coolest, they say."

Mack's voice lowered to a murmur. "I better be stayin' here though. They don't like me much at the Sweet Spot these days. Too cool for me maybe. 'Sides, this is more my style. I'm in my groove right here."

"Yeah, folks, I'm thinkin' 'bout grooving, too. You know what I mean." James allowed a suddenly slick smile, as he pointed toward two young women at the juke box.

"That's my man." Mack slapped James' shoulder.

Elizabeth turned to Mitch. "You think we'll be okay?"

Mack spoke on Mitch's behalf. "Oh, they get a nice mix in there, especially on Saturday night. You all will be fine."

"There you have it, assurance from the man himself." Mitch swallowed the last of his drink.

"Well, thank you, my man." Mack motioned everyone closer. "You guys take care of these ladies, ya' hear?"

"Thanks for today and tonight." Elizabeth hugged Mack and James.

Debbie did the same. "You guys are the best, and you're not bad dancers, either."

Everyone laughed, and James Brown counted one-two-three from the jukebox as Debbie, Elizabeth, Andy, and Mitch exited Sammy's.

The two couples entered the Sweet Spot through a short, dimly lit hallway. Once they stepped into the night club, the stage came into view at the very front of the room. There, a quartet of musicians used an unspoken language to agree on their next song. A large black man fronted the group with a saxophone strapped around his neck. He motioned with the countdown, and the song began.

Most of the ladies wore party dresses and high heels. For them it was clearly a night out-on-the-town. Elizabeth took consolation in the fact that she and Debbie had at least changed out of their workday attire. Still, she hesitated to follow Mitch as he led her and Debbie and Andy past the bar to a semicircle-shaped booth on the far side of the room.

Mitch allowed Elizabeth to slide in first, and he took a spot beside her. Debbie circled around from the other side of the booth and Andy assumed the outside spot across from Mitch.

Just as quickly as they had taken their places a waitress stood before them. Mitch ordered for the group, the same drinks they had ended with at Sammy's. Elizabeth recognized *Someone to Watch over Me* as they waited for their drinks.

She relaxed into the booth. "Nice sound. This is a beautiful song."

Mitch touched Elizabeth's arm. "Yeah, it's kind of a standard. Can't think of the name, though."

"It's Nat King Cole, isn't it? *Unforgettable*, I think." Andy made a guess.

Elizabeth spoke with certainty. "No, it's *Someone to Watch over Me*."

"Really?" Andy leaned toward the stage as though he required a better angle. "Yeah, maybe, I don't know though."

Just then Debbie cleared her throat and sang with the sax. "Someone to watch over me."

Elizabeth giggled and poked Debbie to quiet her. Mitch chuckled, and Andy relented.

"Guess *Unforgettable* is not so unforgettable after all." Debbie nudged her brother. "You goof ball, what do you know about music anyway?"

Andy's station as older brother was challenged, and he puffed his chest. "Just as much as you!"

"But apparently not as much as Elizabeth." Debbie gave no ground.

"It was just a lucky guess." Elizabeth diffused the banter as the waitress appeared with their drinks.

When the song ended and the room filled with applause, Mitch raised his glass. "Nice song."

He touched each glass around the table. "Good friends."

He spoke to Elizabeth in a tone only she perceived. "Glad I've had this chance to finally meet you."

Elizabeth smiled, radiant even in the dim light, but made no verbal reply.

The saxophone player introduced the band's next selection, a Count Basie song called *Corner Pocket*. A jazzier, up-tempo tune, this song caused some fingers to tap on tables throughout the club and feet moved with the beat. Andy extended his leg into the aisle, and he kept the beat with his heel going up and down, bouncing his lower leg along with the rhythm.

The waitress worked her way along the aisle, and Andy's knee caught her leg, which caused a sideways step. Her tray of drinks jostled precariously near a patron's head.

As she re-gained her balance, she spoke to Andy. "Careful there, honey, we don't want you gettin' too excited."

"Yeah, honey, calm down, we had no idea you were so into the music." Debbie prodded her brother with sarcasm.

"Well, I like this music better than the jukebox at Sammy's, that's for sure." Andy scooted toward the center of the booth.

"That's cool," Mitch said.

"It's okay," Debbie admitted, "but I like the atmosphere."

"The music is what really makes it cool." Elizabeth punctuated her opinion with a long drink.

The band took a break, and the club lights brightened.

Andy caught the waitress, this time with an empty tray. "Miss, we'll have another round here."

Mitch tipped his glass to get the last few drops of liquid. "As our friend, Mack, would say, now you're talking."

When he tapped his glass on the table to emphasize his point, the foursome laughed in unison. The sound caught the band leader's attention. Big Jim had been working his way from the stage to the bar but diverted toward the table of four along the side wall.

He chuckled as he approached them. "You all sound like your havin' a good time."

He nimbly turned a chair and placed it with its back to the outside edge of the table and straddled it, all in one motion. "What are we celebrating?"

A wide smile emanated from Big Jim's round face. Debbie leaned toward the questioner.

"My friend and I just moved into a new house." Debbie spoke in her typical straightforward fashion.

"That right? Your place near here then?"

"No, it's in Clayton near the west end of the city." Debbie held Big Jim's stare.

"Oh yeah, I hear that's nice."

Debbie carried on as though Big Jim was an old friend whom she had not seen in a long while. "We had some friends come over today to help with the painting. Then we all ate at Sammy's before some of us came here."

"Did you say Sammy's? Now that is nice."

"Mack recommended it. Sammy's his uncle." Debbie lost contact with Big Jim's eyes.

Big Jim craned his head around and laughed. "Not little Mack? He better not be here wit' you. George is the man around here, and he and Lil' Mack ain't gettin' along lately. George calls him Lil' Jack cause he's always trying to drink that Black Jack on the rocks, but it only takes one and he's outta' control. Ya' know what I mean?"

"Yeah, I think I've seen that before myself." Mitch interjected a comment.

Big Jim allowed himself a moment to scan Mitch's face. "You do look a little familiar. I remember most of the white people that come in here."

While Big Jim's words hung between them, an arm came into view and a hip came to rest near Big Jim's shoulder. The waitress served the round of drinks while leaning heavily on Big Jim.

As she finished, she bumped Big Jim. "I didn't know these folks were friends of yours, Jim."

"Actually we're just gettin' to know one another. Fact, just so ya' know, my name's James Kilgore, but everybody calls me Big Jim. 'Cept Lilly here, she just calls me Jim, as you plainly heard."

Big Jim hushed his voice and drew Lilly closer to the table. "Lilly, these folks say their friends of Lil' Mack, though I advised them to keep that on the Q.T. around here."

Big Jim roared with laughter as he pounded the table with his fist. When liquid slurped over the rim of the nearest drink glasses, Lilly punched his shoulder.

Lilly shook her head. "That Lil' Mack thinks he's a big man, but really he's just big trouble."

"Oh but you girls think he's kinda cute, now don't ya'?" Big Jim nudged Lilly and winked at Debbie.

"Depends on the girl, I guess," Debbie replied.

Lilly hit Big Jim again. "That's right, sister. It'd have to be the right kind of girl to take a likin' to that wild man, and that sure ain't me. 'Sides, I'm workin'. I ain't got no time to be messin' with any man, much less that one."

Lilly turned to leave the table, but Big Jim grabbed her arm. "Bring our friends here another round in a little while. It'll be on me, okay?"

Lilly reminded Big Jim of his work as well. "I can do that, but ya' better get back to workin' too."

Big Jim rose and flipped his chair back to its original place across the aisle. "She's right, just like usual. Time for some more music, but you gotta' tell me your names before I go."

Big Jim found each pair of eyes with a nod, and as his gaze formed an arc around the table, each of them responded with their name. Mitch was in the last position.

Big Jim smiled at him. "Mitch, I do believe I've seen you in here before. You come back now, ya' hear."

Then, inexplicably, Big Jim placed one hand near the middle of table and settled his smile on Elizabeth.

"Elizabeth," he said her name with a silky resonance, like it was a measure of blues notes played on his saxophone. "Ya' sure this ain't a special night out? It seems like somethin' special to me, maybe love."

Big Jim shot a glance at Mitch but steadied his gaze on Elizabeth. "Looks like love to me."

Elizabeth responded quickly, "No, it's just friends. Like Debbie said we're celebrating our new house."

"That's right. Maybe it's just me and that Lilly. Sweet Lil I call her 'cause she sure is sweet to me. Anyway, Elizabeth and all, you all should try us again. It's cool. Fact, here's a little somthin' for you ladies and your celebration, but don't tell nobody I gave it to you."

Concurrent with his suggestion, Big Jim slid his hand into his jacket pocket, and with his thumb tucked under the palm, he extended his hand toward Debbie. He placed the hand palm down in front of her, and when he lifted his hand, two marijuana joints were revealed.

"It's cool. They're from my own stash. Enjoy." Big Jim winked at Debbie and Elizabeth.

On his way to the stage he turned abruptly, and with a laugh that matched his stature, he shared a final word. "Tell Lil' Mack to chill!"

"Jesus, Debbie, what are you doing?" Andy eyes widened, as his sister swept the joints into her purse.

"I'm doing like the man suggested, and I'm going to enjoy myself."

"I don't know. It's just not right. In fact it's for sure not legal."

"Oh God, Andy will you just cool it?" Debbie took a drink and crunched an ice cube.

Elizabeth pinched Debbie's forearm as though she were disciplining her friend.

Her words belied her actions. "Our new friend did say that it was cool."

"No, I think he must have meant that we're cool." Debbie laughed, and Elizabeth and Mitch joined her.

"That's right, go on and laugh." Andy complained but couldn't help but laugh, too.

As the last notes of the second song in the set hung over the room, Lilly placed the next round of drinks before the celebrants. Andy toasted Lil' Mack's exuberance and the way events had unfolded at Sammy's. They shared surprise about Elizabeth's dancing ability, and how James showed more enthusiasm as the volume of the music increased.

Elizabeth felt the power of this most recent drink flood her face. "Ooohhh, this is a strong one!"

"Mm, mmm! And your cheeks are starting to turn a little rosy." Mitch winked at Elizabeth.

"That's nothing," Debbie proclaimed, "how about my brother's nose? It's starting to look like Daddy's schnozz after he's had one too many martinis, pulsing red."

She pointed and laughed while nudging Elizabeth with her elbow. Elizabeth spilled some of her drink when her glass was caught by Debbie's bump.

A few drops of liquid squeezed from the corner of Elizabeth's lips as she continued to muffle her laugh and swallow what was left in her mouth. "I see what you mean. It's a little bit like a blinking stoplight, or wait that might just be the lights from the stage."

Elizabeth and Debbie laughed in unison.

"You girls are both hallucinating." Andy defended himself. "And you're getting sloppy, too."

"Now friend, it's just these drinks are a little strong. I don't think they're laced with any hallucinogenic." Mitch used a tone of mock reassurance.

Debbie was insistent. "Oh but I'm serious, brother. Your nose really is getting red."

She couldn't hold in her giggles. "We better get out of here before the rest of the club sees you."

A swell of giggles poured from deep inside her, and Elizabeth caught the contagion, too. The sound filled a void, as the band paused between songs.

Mitch noticed a few nearby patrons glancing at their table. "Ladies, we don't want to cause any distractions. Remember our friend, Lil' Mack, we don't want to get on the bad side of these folks like he did. Besides, this is Big Jim's show."

Elizabeth straightened herself, and Debbie covered her mouth, but it was too late.

Big Jim's voice rang out. "Sounds like my new friends are havin' some fun over there."

He nodded in the general direction of their table and spoke as though he were entertaining a few friends he had invited to dinner. "They're celebratin' somethin'. We got a song that might apply."

The stage lights brightened, and the first few notes of *The Look of Love* resonated from Big Jim's saxophone.

"I don't know where he's getting that idea." Elizabeth related her confusion.

"Well, we told him we were celebrating," Andy explained. "You girls really have lost it."

"No, I mean the look of love." Elizabeth clarified.

"Huh? What do you mean?" Andy questioned.

"I think she means this song. It's called *The Look of Love*, and Big Jim thinks it applies to us." Mitch waved a hand at Andy's blank stare.

"To who?" Andy shook his head.

"To Elizabeth and Mitch, remember?" Debbie sounded incredulous. "Jesus, you're the one who's lost. Come on, guys, we better take my brother home."

"You mean I better take you girls home." Andy spoke louder as the music rose to a crescendo.

"Yeah, yeah, let's get going." Debbie nudged her brother.

Andy moved heavily into the aisle, and within moments the entourage followed his lead through the club, the girls positioned between him and Mitch. They took a more circuitous route toward the door, and when they broke into the clear at the far end of the bar, they turned in unison to put on their jackets.

Big Jim crooned the last lines of the chorus. "Now that I have found you...You've got..." As he sang, he shielded his eyes with one hand and scanned the room.

He stopped when his line of sight aligned with Elizabeth and her group. He pointed in their direction and then reconnected with his sax to play the last few bars of the song. Elizabeth responded with a wave as she stood in the glow of the exit sign.

"The Sweet Spot, huh?" Elizabeth asked, as she slipped past Mitch, while he held the door to the back seat of Andy's car.

"Yeah, did you like it?" Mitch responded with a question, intending to better understand Elizabeth's feelings.

"I did, I really did. Most of the songs were...were sweet."

Debbie heard the last word of that exchange, and it did not resonate with her increasing sense of agitation.

She resigned herself to the front seat next to her brother. "Try to get us home without wrecking."

As Andy steered the car down Grand Avenue and past the highway entrance, he leaned toward the back seat with a question. "I'll drop you off first, okay, Mitch?"

After a lull and a rustling from the back seat Mitch answered, "Yeah, that's cool."

Debbie attempted pleasant conversation with the back seat passengers, but her effort was lost on them.

"So, you live in the south part of the city?" She paused when the street lamps threw a light into the back seat. "Oh, sorry." Her lips closed tightly, dampening her voice to a murmur.

She blinked deliberately but saw for a second time what she did not comprehend at first. Her friend and her brother's friend were wrapped in a deep embrace, a passion play of kisses. Debbie turned to the front.

She mumbled to herself. "Maybe Big Jim was right."

The radio played softly *Anyone Who Ever Loved*.

"What'd you say, sis?"

Debbie jerked her head toward the back seat with her answer. "Big Jim may have been right about those two."

Andy glanced to the side and then into the rear view mirror. He adjusted the mirror as if to confirm what he had seen.

Debbie slapped his hand. "Leave them alone."

In front of his apartment building, Mitch pulled Elizabeth from the car, and they stood on the sidewalk holding hands. They kissed in the midst of a verbal exchange.

When he finally turned and walked to the door, Elizabeth hopped in the car and gave Andy instructions. "We better go."

"Yeah, I'll say we better go." Debbie motioned to her brother.

The drive to their house lapsed in silence, except for a final exchange of good-byes and thanks. The night ended for Andy, but for the two roommates it continued well into the morning hours. The marijuana joints lighted their way, and they talked about love, delights, delusions, and the smoky dreams that now seemed to unfold before them.

Chapter 27

At the deep surge in her stomach, Elizabeth awakened to half consciousness. She rolled to one side and positioned one hand to push her body upward. At the moment she thought she had succeeded, the blanket that she pushed against slipped on the hardwood floor and sent her flailing. She hit the floor with a moan, and the thud brought her surroundings in focus, her new home, her bedroom floor.

After another convulsion, she rolled to her stomach and made her way to her hands and knees. The heat flushed her face and burned her eyeballs, but she found her feet and moved into the hallway. She guided herself with one hand on the wall and dropped again to her hands and knees as she entered the bathroom.

Her skull rattled and her stomach rumbled until she spewed its contents into and around the toilet bowl.

As the sound of her second heave bounced off the porcelain, Debbie burst into the bathroom. "Oh, shit, girl! Take it easy. I'll be right back."

Debbie sprinted to retrieve two wash cloths and a towel from her bedroom. At the bathroom basin, she soaked one cloth in cold water and placed it across the back of Elizabeth's neck. Simultaneously, she flushed the toilet.

"Ugghh..." Elizabeth vomited a third time.

"Damn!" Debbie exclaimed. "Might as well let it all come out."

With the next retch, bile fell from Elizabeth's open mouth, along with one hard word. "Shit!"

She spat and let go of the rim of the bowl with one hand so that she could rub her forehead and temples with her fingertips and thumb.

"Ooohhh..." She groaned with a lurch toward the commode.

Debbie rinsed the wash cloth in cold water again and positioned it as a compress, holding the cold cloth to the fire of Elizabeth's forehead. The next heave was a dry one, and so were the next and the next.

Debbie left the room but came back with a glass. She filled it with water and held it before Elizabeth, who was now more upright but still on her knees.

"Just a little sip or two." Debbie put the glass in Elizabeth's hand. "Rinse your mouth out at least."

Elizabeth sipped and spat twice before swallowing a mouthful of water. It gurgled in her stomach, but the agitation stopped. Debbie took the glass and helped Elizabeth to her feet. Debbie steadied her against the wall and leaned into the bathtub to start the water. "I think a nice hot bath should be next."

Elizabeth slipped out of her pajama top and panties. A thought entered her mind, that, other than her mother, Debbie was the first woman to see her naked. She stepped into the tub using Debbie's arm as a brace.

While the hot water filled the tub, Elizabeth pulled her knees to her chest. Her muscles relaxed as the steamy water covered her hips and her buttocks. Meanwhile, Debbie had left the room and returned with some cleaning supplies. She flushed the toilet to clear as much of the remaining vomit as possible.

Debbie kneeled to wipe the rest. "Just like work, only I thought I'd have the whole weekend off."

Debbie paused to assess her progress and the depth of the bath water. Elizabeth leaned against the back of the tub, the wash cloth draped over her face and most of her body immersed in the soothing water. Debbie cranked the faucet off and pulled the shower curtain closed. Elizabeth murmured a thank-you, as Debbie completed the cleaning task.

"Damn, I don't think I've ever been that sick." Elizabeth hoarse voice trembled as she entered the kitchen.

She slumped at the table in yesterday's work jeans and a sweatshirt. Debbie placed a piece of toast in front of her, and it sufficed as her entire breakfast. While she ate she re-constructed the events of the previous night.

"So, I feel like hell, but considering everything, I deserve to be." Elizabeth swallowed the last bite of toast.

"You mean all the alcohol, smoking those joints or the make-out session with a total stranger?" Debbie responded with a dose of sarcasm. "You know we talked about all this last night, and you said you weren't going to feel bad about it."

Elizabeth winced at the memory. "I was drunk or high or seeing things, feeling things I had never felt before. Of course I didn't feel bad then."

Debbie struggled to sound sympathetic. "But now the retching has your attention. Literally in your gut, you're thinking that maybe we had it wrong last night. They say that the marijuana can make you see things in a different way."

Elizabeth rubbed her forehead where the heat smoldered. Debbie swallowed the last of a cup of coffee. "You know, I'm feeling a little pukey myself, and like I said last night, that last drink at The Sweet Spot was pretty strong. I think Big Jim was behind that."

A fuzziness cloaked Elizabeth eyes, just as it did her thinking. "I remember you saying that. But I still don't know what you mean."

Debbie cradled the toaster against her stomach, as though it would comfort her. "Your're kidding? I just think he was trying to stir up some action. I mean with the heavy dose of alcohol and sliding those joints our way. Between you and Mitch, or maybe between you and him, maybe that's what was going on."

Debbie opened two cabinets in search of the spot from which she had taken the toaster. Only after neither cabinet provided an obvious place did she remember that she had taken it from the box setting on the counter. She made a mental note to sort through all the things in that box.

Elizabeth's head hung over her plate, as though the crumbs of toast could be read like runes cast by a Druid priestess. Debbie drew Elizabeth's attention when she touched her shoulder.

"Don't you see?" Debbie expounded, "It's starting to make sense to me. Jesus, Elizabeth, that big, black son...he was smooth, though, I've got to give him that. Even those sweet songs he was playing, he had his eyes on you. Little did he know that he set Mitch up perfectly. *The Look of Love,* bullshit! That was the look of a dirty, old man."

"He's not that old, do you think?" Elizabeth clung to one minor aspect.

"Too old for you, that's for sure. Besides, that's not the point. That was not cool, not cool at all. Now you're feeling like shit, and I'm not feeling too good myself."

"But his music was cool." Elizabeth desired the coolness because her face was still on fire.

"Yeah, it was, but he's a professional, and it's probably a means to an end."

"Jeez, Debbie, that's pretty cynical!"

"Well, damn, we need to grow up. We're out on our own now, and we can't let these guys, these men, take advantage of us, no matter how cool they are."

"Okay, okay." Elizabeth gave in. "Didn't you make that point last night too? So, let's not make a big deal out of it, some drinks, some kissing, and a couple of joints."

Debbie shivered as a reaction to her own recollection of the previous night. "Yeah, well, I'm going to take a shower."

In her lingering confusion about her purpose for the day, Elizabeth followed Debbie out of the kitchen. As they reached the hall, a knock came at the front door.

Debbie opened it to discover Mitch. Her jaw dropped, and she stepped to the side, swinging the door wider. Elizabeth brushed her fingers through her thick hair.

Mitch spoke as he entered. "Hi, I thought I'd stop by to make sure you girls were doing okay. Things got a little wild last night."

"It definitely did for some of us," Debbie stated. "You two can work it out if you want to. I'm on my way to the shower."

Debbie pushed the door closed behind Mitch and brushed past the two of them. Elizabeth pushed her hair away from her face. A blush of embarrassment spread across her cheeks.

She offered an explanation. "Debbie's feeling a little down today. My day hasn't started too good, either. We think it was that last drink."

Mitch agreed. "Yeah, it was kind of strong. It definitely got things, well it made me, it seemed like I was a little out of control. Anyway, I wanted to make sure. I mean, I wanted to say that I hope...I mean..."

Elizabeth made an unsteady stride toward Mitch. He stiffened to keep from swaying.

He stopped stuttering. "I'm not feeling very steady myself today."

Elizabeth sensed his uncertainty, and she realized that neither of them held an advantage. "I'm starting to feel a little better."

She stroked the back of her head, unsure of how her hair looked.

She was certain of one thing. "Thanks for stopping by."

"I thought if you want to, I'd buy you breakfast or lunch or something."

"Thanks, but food doesn't hold much appeal for me right now. My stomach's a little sensitive."

"They say that a Bloody Mary is the best thing for the morning after."

"Not sure that's for me, either. I need to get ready to go home. I have some plans with my family this afternoon."

"Oh, do they live near here?"

"On the north side of the city. That's where I grew up."

"That's nice."

"Yeah, they'll be anxious to hear about my first day on my own." Elizabeth saw how this day might unfold.

Mitch winced as he envisioned Elizabeth discussing events with her parents.

Elizabeth responded to Mitch's discomfort. "Don't worry, there are certain things that don't need to be revealed."

He relaxed and projected beyond the day. "I'd like to see you again. Can I call you?"

"Don't have a phone yet."

"Maybe at the hospital, then?"

"Maybe. I owe the hospital a bunch of hours to make up for the last two weekends. I'm scheduled to work the surgical floor. I'll probably ask for extra shifts, need to make some extra money."

"At the hospital then, I'll look for you there."

"Okay. That'll be okay." She repeated herself because his eyes urged her to linger a while.

Mitch was not as tall as Luke, so Elizabeth faced him more directly. Luke's eyes were a mixture of green and blue, Mitch's were distinctly blue. A jumble of memories were released, the music and dancing, the surge of kisses, and the tangled embraces. Luke and Mitch scrambled together.

More straightforward than Luke, Mitch spoke. "I have to see you again."

"Okay." Elizabeth managed only a one-word agreement.

Then, in an awkward shuffle, she ushered him out of the door. She latched it with the weight of her shoulder forcing it closed and then banged her head against the hardwood.

Her brain buzzed as she found the bottle of shampoo and a towel in her bedroom and waited at the kitchen sink for the water to warm. After washing her hair and changing her clothes, her outlook cleared.

At her bedroom door, Debbie offered. "If you need the bathroom mirror to finish up, I'm done in there."

"Thanks."

Debbie followed Elizabeth to the bathroom. "So, what did Mitch want?"

"He wanted to buy us breakfast or lunch. I think he wanted to say he was sorry for..."

"For being totally uncool? So, what'd you say?"

"I told him it was okay."

"What was okay?"

"Everything, that everything's okay."

"Really?" A rush of agitation sharpened Debbie's tone.

"Don't get upset. He was very sweet. I don't think he's the type to take advantage."

"Maybe, but I bet he asked you out again, didn't he?"

"Yeah, but I didn't agree to a date."

"Good!" Debbie hoped Elizabeth understood the situation in the same way that she did.

"He said he'd try to find me at the hospital one day this week."

"What does that mean?"

"Well, I told him I'd be working a lot this week and next, and he said he'd call me at the hospital so we could talk. I guess when I'm on a break."

"That doesn't sound right." Debbie was suspicious.

"He just wants to get to know me."

"No kidding!" Debbie's sarcasm built to a shout.

"I think he likes me." Elizabeth smiled in the mirror.

Elizabeth exited the bathroom with Debbie on her heels.

Debbie's suspicion reverted to derision. "You think he likes you, do you? Jesus, girl, this ain't high school!"

"Will you quit it?" Elizabeth snatched her jacket from its spot on the floor.

The two of them marched side by side down the hallway. Elizabeth allowed Debbie to take the lead, and when Debbie turned at the door, Elizabeth surprised her with a hug.

"It's okay. Everything's going to be okay." Elizabeth smiled the first smile of the day for her roommate and friend. "I've got to take the car home. To my parent's house, I mean. I'm planning to sleep there tonight. Tomorrow morning my dad's going to load an old dresser in his truck and follow me to the furniture store where the guys will help him load my new bed. Then he's going to follow me here, and we're going to set up my room. So, you see, everything is going to be okay."

"Well, that part sounds good."

"Then I'll see you at the hospital tomorrow afternoon."

———

By mid-morning, the furniture and the bed were arranged the way Elizabeth wanted them.

Her father gathered his tools. "You okay with the way this is set up?"

"It's fine. Besides, like I said before, you and mom can come over for dinner on my next day off. We can switch things around then, if we want to."

Elizabeth motioned her father toward the hallway. "By then, we'll have some furniture in the living room too. Debbie's cousin has some that we're inheriting. I'll cook some spaghetti or some other kind of pasta."

"Whatta ya' mean other pasta, not spaghetti?"

"Daddy, come on, there are other kinds of noodles, you know."

"Yeah, but, your mother always makes spaghetti."

"I know. I know. That's why I was thinking of doing something different."

"I know you like that I-talian food you're always getting when you go out, but I like my meat and potatoes, nothing fancy."

"I know, Daddy. I know. Then spaghetti it will be. Hope that's not too fancy."

"I already said I like the spaghetti your mother makes."

"I'll try to do as good as mom."

"That's fine with me. One more thing before I skedaddle. I couldn't help but hear you in the hall bathroom this morning. You sick or somethin'?"

"No, I don't think so. My stomach's been a little queasy since Saturday night. It's probably just that fancy food we ate for our celebration dinner." Her voice lingered over the food reference.

"I thought you said you went to some diner on Grand. That doesn't sound so fancy to me."

"We did, and I was just trying to be a little sarcastic."

"Don't know about sarcastic, but I know when someone's sick. Your Aunt Barbara, she had an ulcer that caused her to vomit a lot. Hope you don't have one of those. You're too young for that. But you kids are always goin' and goin' like sixty."

"Now, Daddy, don't you worry about us kids. It's just a little hangover. We celebrated too much maybe. But hey, it's my first house, my first time on my own."

"That's got me nervous, too, even if you're not."

"You should be happy, not nervous. Maybe even proud, because your daughter's got a good job and her own place to live."

Elizabeth took her father's hand. "Now let's get you on your way. Besides, if you don't get out of here and let me get ready for work, I'm going to be late. Got rent to pay, you know."

"You want me to wait? I can drop you off on my way."

"No, I want you to go. I'll take the bus, just like I plan to do every other day. "

"Aren't you gettin' tired of takin' the bus? Don't you think it'd been better if you would've used some of your hard earned money to buy a car instead of using it for rent?"

"No, I'll get a car some day. The bus works fine for getting me to work. And for now, Debbie doesn't mind driving when we go out. It's going to work out well, because now she doesn't have anywhere near as far to take me when it's time to go home. You see, we live in the same house instead of across the city from each other."

Elizabeth chuckled as she caught her own joke, although her father did not smile.

He persisted along his own path of thinking even as she coaxed him through the door. "That's another thing. I'm not so sure your mother and me like you living way over here on the other side of the city."

"But, it's a lot closer to work and to my best friend. And that's just the way it is!"

At the door she hugged him and kissed his cheek.

With no hint of sarcasm or doubt, she expressed her feelings. "Thanks for all your help today. I love you and Mom. Everything's going to be okay. Now give me a smile and let me know that you're okay, too."

"I'm fine. I'm fine. You're welcome." He winked and an unfamiliar tone accompanied his parting words. "And I hope that that spaghetti's as good as your mother's."

"Did I detect a little sarcasm there, Mr. Donahue?"

"Maybe, and maybe your old dad still knows a thing or two." He waved his hand without looking back.

———

Several days into her new life on her own and one afternoon at the hospital over a Coke in the cafeteria, Elizabeth met Mitch. She shared some details about her life in the North County and how she and Debbie had met at college. She recalled her desire to be a nurse and her hope to soothe at least some of the pain of the children whose care had been entrusted to her.

He shared an observation with her. "I knew that part of you. I saw it from afar many months before I met you the other night. It is an aspect of your beauty."

She interrupted his embarrassing conclusion with her own investigatory question. "So, how is it that a hot-shot surgeon from Barnes would be considering giving up the excitement of the operating room for a boring practice in family medicine?

"Where'd you hear that?"

"I've been doing some of my own homework."

"Oh, yeah. Well, your homework is a little incomplete. It's not family medicine. What I want to do is go to Mexico or South America and help some of the people there. Children, adults, the elderly, the whole spectrum. Besides, who says I'm a hot-shot surgeon?"

"Just about everybody I've talked to. Or was that hot-dog surgeon?" She laughed out loud.

"Ooh, a funny and beautiful woman, quite the combination."

"Will you quit with the beautiful stuff?"

"Will you quit with the surgeon stuff?"

"Okay." She gave in.

"Okay." He raised his cup of Coke, and she raised hers to his.

They exchanged a smile. He saw beauty in that too but did not verbalize it.

She didn't want the conversation to end there. "Why Mexico or South America?"

"I grew up in New Jersey, outside New York City. I got my undergrad at Rutgers, my medical degree from Wash U., and my internship and residency in surgery here at Barnes. After getting to this point, I'm realizing that I don't really care about any of it anymore. I don't think I'm making the difference I want to make."

"Mitch, really? Everybody says you are an outstanding surgeon. You've saved many lives already, and you're just getting started."

"That might be, but I'm not feeling it. Not like you. I've seen you, and I've seen the kids you're taking care of. I've seen how they respond to you."

"I don't know how you can say that, how you can know that."

"Okay, here's the whole story."

Mitch told her about his cousins and his aunt and uncle, who lived in the St. Louis area. His older cousin had a child, a son by the name of Billy. Little Billy was three years old and had been sick for most of the last year. He had been in and out of the hospital, Children's Hospital, from August through late November. At that point in time, Mitch's cousin, William Redmond, moved his family to Prescott Arizona on the advice of Billy's doctors, who reasoned that the drier climate would be easier on Billy. His lung disease was made more insidious by the humidity and smog in St. Louis.

He went on to describe how his aunt and uncle missed their grandson, but according to them, the only person in St. Louis that Little Billy missed was Nurse Elizabeth at Children's.

Mitch's eyes sparkled with his revelation. "Though you clearly did not remember me, I surely remembered you the moment we officially met the other night. I had come to the hospital last year on several occasions to visit Billy. You and I passed each other in the hall from time to time. I had to clear out of the room whenever it was time for you to stop by. He liked his one-on-one time with you. Do you remember Billy Redmond?"

"Yes, I do, but I remember his parents, too. William and Doris Redmond, I remember them being around a lot of the time. Billy and I had very little one-on-one time, just briefly after visiting hours and before he fell asleep."

"Outside of normal visiting hours, that's when I stopped by most often. I used some of my free time, during my shifts at Barnes. When you were on duty, Billy was happier, able to rest a little easier. I saw you a lot, but I know you don't remember me. That's okay. Walking in those corridors, I was just another doctor to you. But you remember Billy, and Billy sure remembers you. That's what I want from my medical career, someone to remember me."

"But it's different for you doctors. You don't have the time, don't have the..." Elizabeth lost her point in his blue eyes. "I don't know how to explain it, but it's different for you as a doctor."

"Thanks for giving me a break. And you're right for the most part it is different, but I'm beginning to think that it shouldn't be. Hell, I'd give anything for Billy to remember me, or for that matter, even for Nurse Elizabeth to remember me." He averted his eyes as though the words had induced a throb of pain.

"I'm sorry. I really don't, not from then." Elizabeth stroked his arm.

He laughed then. "I know. I know, and can't you see that it's killing me?"

She only smiled. "I think you'll live."

"Yeah, but will I be happy?"

"You could be."

"Yes, I would be, if you would just go out with me. Tomorrow night, I already checked the schedule, and I know you have the night off, so what do you say?"

"I say you're crazy, but I also think you're cute."

"Cute's not memorable, but it's a start. So are you saying yes?"

"Yes, but you know that Debbie's going to say that I'm the crazy one now."

"Why's that?"

"No doctors, don't date the doctors. Let them buy you drinks but no dating, no relationships. It's nothing but heartache. That's what she says."

"What do you say?"

"I say that I can make up my own mind. Anyway, who knows? You may be worth getting to know. Months from now I may even remember you."

"That's what I'm living for." He rose from his chair and kissed her on the cheek. "See you tomorrow night about eight."

The next night Mitch took Elizabeth to The Sweet Spot. The Thursday crowd was sparse, and they sat at a table close to the stage. Elizabeth accepted the joint that Big Jim passed to her. She shared it with Mitch at his apartment, and in the darkness of the first hours of another day, she shared the passionate kisses that they had known on the night that they first met. She fell into a trance of mellow hallucination and rested in his arms for long stretches of the time.

At her insistent good-bye, he walked her to the door, where she allowed him only a single kiss. She slept soundly in her new bed, comfortable in the house that had become her home but awakened to the painfully regular discomfort in her stomach.

She had not been eating in large quantities recently, so the regular practice of cleaning her own vomit was easier. She pondered the sick routine as she stepped under the shower. A question formed in the bubbles of the shampoo that she lathered on her head.

"What's the matter with me?" Her words drowned in the pouring water.

No answer flowed there, but as she wrapped her head in a towel, she made a decision to see a doctor soon.

———————

As Dr. Susan Patterson entered the room, Elizabeth sat straighter and dropped the pamphlet that she had been reading onto the doctor's desk. The doctor scanned the pages of test results, and briefly met Elizabeth's eyes, a concerned glance.

Elizabeth stood. "Sorry doctor, I should not have been looking at the materials on your desk."

The doctor replied, "Oh, that's not a problem. Besides, like I've said before, you can just call me Susan. Have a seat again."

After Elizabeth did so, the doctor scooted her chair close to Elizabeth. She settled a hand on Elizabeth's knee, a gesture intended as a comfort, but her eyes still registered concern.

The doctor's rapid-fire questions jolted Elizabeth. "Elizabeth, how long has it been since your last period? Are you late?"

Elizabeth recoiled, confused by the questions and the calculations involved in the answers. "I might be late, a few days, maybe more."

"Have you had a period since you returned from your trip to Boulder to see your boyfriend?"

"No. But I've been thinking that I would start any day now."

"Elizabeth, you said that you've been vomiting in the morning."

"But, I've been drinking a little more than I'm used to."

"And you've been smoking marijuana?"

"Yes, for the first time ever. I guess it would show up in the blood test, huh? I don't think it's helping my stomach any, either."

"Elizabeth, it's not the alcohol or the marijuana. You're pregnant."

"But, Susan, how can that be? I used the diaphragm while I was with Luke. I'm sure I did."

"Apparently it didn't work."

"I don't understand. I followed your instructions perfectly. I took extra time in the bathroom and made sure everything was okay."

"Sometimes these things just happen, no matter how we protect ourselves."

"No, it just doesn't make any sense. I couldn't have even been ovulating by then. It was only a few days after my period. I know how to count during my cycle. I know that much."

"Elizabeth, you haven't had another period, have you?"

"I told you. I'm expecting to start any day now. I could start any minute."

But her tears started instead, and they flowed with a stream of consciousness. "I just moved into my new house. Debbie and I are roommates now. And Mitch, we just met. And Luke, I'm figuring that out. I remember him asking afterwards. He was worried. I told him that everything was going to be okay. And my mom and dad are coming over for dinner tonight. Spaghetti, nothing fancy, we're celebrating because I'm on my own now. I told my dad everything's going to be okay. And it is. Or it was."

Dr. Susan passed some tissues to Elizabeth. "Elizabeth, everything is going to be okay, but you have to think about this. You should talk to somebody. How about Luke? Can you call him?"

"No. I don't know. I have to think about that."

"Debbie, she might be a good one to talk to about this. You two are close."

"But she might get a little too excited. I need to think about this on my own."

"I'm going to schedule an appointment for you. Five days from now. You think about it, and we'll talk some more. How does that sound?"

"Okay. I need to look at the schedule at work."

"You just tell your supervisor that you need an hour or so. I'm sure she'll be able to arrange that."

"Yeah, thanks. I'll see you then."

"Elizabeth, I'll have my assistant call you at work tomorrow to confirm."

"That's a good idea."

"You take care of yourself and call me if you have any questions before then. You hear."

"I better get going." Elizabeth took a few more tissues as she rose.

Dr. Susan walked Elizabeth to the office door. "Call if you need me."

Elizabeth waited at the elevator doors, but when they opened for her, she retreated into a restroom at the end of the hallway. Inside a stall, she bent to one knee and cried into the hands that covered her face. She groaned and cursed between the sobs.

Soon the vomit filled her mouth. She regurgitated fear not food. She spat a torrent of tears, liquid made not of acidic bile, only angry denial.

She lamented in low, guttural tones. "No! No!"

On the street she walked with her head down, lost in her thoughts. She found herself entering a church that she did not know, on a street she did not remember. St. Anthony, Patron Saint of the lost, she must have taken a wrong turn somewhere.

Too early, or too late, she did not know, but wandered inside the church and found a pew. She knelt and prayed to find her way. She sought a place of peace in her mind, a time of forgiveness in her heart, and grace for her soul.

Chapter 28

Boulder, May 1st, 1972

It began early Wednesday in the half-light of dawn, accompanied by a half-memory of a time some nine years previous. Julia felt the warm liquid between her legs, flipped the sheet back, and swung her legs off the bed onto the floor. The cool hardwood beneath her feet alerted her senses, and then a surge of pain hunched her at the waist. She gripped the mattress and panted to bring relief.

Under the quick breaths she encouraged herself. "Let's get moving."

She called Sally, and they implemented the plan that they had been discussing for several weeks. Julia waited at the kitchen window. Shortly after Sally pulled into the driveway, Luke charged through the kitchen door. Julia couldn't stop his outburst.

Luke's voice boomed her name. "Julia!"

"Luke, shssst! I'm right here. Don't wake Terry. Just help get me to the car."

"Oh, sure. Here, take my arm."

Luke escorted Julia and gently helped her into the front seat of Sally's car.

Julia grabbed Luke's hand. "Oh, shit, I forgot my bag. Luke, you have to get it."

"I'm on my way," Luke declared.

"Quietly, though," Julia called after him.

Luke set the suitcase on the back seat of the car. Julia listed the components of the plan that involved Luke. As he had agreed, he would be staying home with Terry, allowing Terry to sleep until she awakened naturally. Julia didn't want Terry to go to school on this day, so Luke would need to call the school to excuse her.

Luke confirmed his understanding. "I've got it. I need to call the store, then I'll call Terry's school."

"Sally will call you when..." Julia's voice trailed to a low groan.

Sally squeezed Julia's hand. "Luke, close the door. You take care of things here. I'll call you later."

Later that morning, when Terry awoke and they were eating breakfast, Luke explained what had transpired earlier. Terry didn't seem too concerned. She just wanted to make sure that Luke had called her school. She finished her breakfast and dressed very quickly. She wanted Sally to call and said so several times. Luke tried to slow her down.

"Let's check out what's on TV. We'll just have to be patient and wait to hear from Sally or maybe your mom will call." Luke held only a remote idea of what would transpire on this day.

The phone rang as Luke flipped the second of two grilled cheese sandwiches in the skillet. He lowered the flame under the sandwiches and lifted the receiver of the phone that hung on the kitchen wall.

Sally instructed him. "Have Terry get on the phone in Julia's room."

"Wait a minute." Luke turned off the burner on the stove and walked to the bottom of the back stairway where he called to Terry.

When he picked up the kitchen extension, he heard Sally speaking to Terry.

Her voice combined the sounds of relief and excitement. "Well, Terry, as of about an hour ago, you have a little brother. Your mom and the baby are doing fine. She said that it was definitely faster this time than when she had you. She had to work pretty hard, though. I got to watch while they cleaned, measured, and weighed the baby. Then your mom finally got to hold him for a while. He looks so cute. You just wait and see."

"And his name," Luke inquired.

"Daniel," Sally responded.

"Yeah, Daniel, that's what Mom said before." Terry's voice hinted at her excitement. "So, can I talk to my mom now?"

"Well, they've taken her back to her regular room, and the baby will be going to the nursery soon. They both have to rest for a while. Maybe she can call you later. Clay is with her now, but he'll have to leave her alone, too, so she can sleep. It's a lot of hard work, giving birth."

"Yeah." Luke reinforced Sally's point. "Terry, we'll let your Mom rest for a while. Sally can tell her to call after she wakes up. You and I will have our sandwiches."

After lunch and clean-up, Luke and Terry hiked to Elephant Rocks. The soft, spring earth smelled of renewal as they made their way in silence to Luke's usual perch.

Luke pointed out the top of the hospital building. "Hope your little brother is having a nice nap."

The early afternoon sun warmed the stone slab.

Terry sat beside Luke. "And Mom too. When do you think they'll be coming home?"

"I'm not sure, maybe tomorrow. Your mom and I never discussed what would happen afterwards. Let's remember to ask her when we talk later on."

After a few moments of silence, Luke related a story based on memories from his boyhood. "I remember when my little sister was born. I was only four and half at the time. My mom stayed in the hospital for a few days, and my grandma took care of me and my brothers. It was the middle of summer, and my dad and my uncles were working to finish a new bedroom they were adding onto our house. Maybe that's why mom stayed in the hospital those extra days, but grandma said, 'your mom needs to rest up before she comes home to this house full'. When you're little you don't think about it, but with my three brothers, and then my sister and me, and my mom, dad, and grandma, we had eight people in our house. It got a little bigger with the extra bedroom, but looking back on it, I'm sure it was a real house full."

Terry pointed at a flock of blackbirds taking flight below them.

She appeared to be counting them and then provided a census of her own. "We have three now. Plus, when you're there and Mr. Williams, that makes five."

"That's pretty many." Luke remembered the point of his story. "One afternoon, just before my dad went to get my mom and bring her and my little sister home, he asked my big brother and me to wait in the living room because he had a job for us. I thought it would be something important, but it turned out to just be the laundry. Dad came in from the backyard with a basket overflowing with clothes. In those days when it was warm enough outside, all the laundry got hung on a clothes line in the backyard."

Terry interrupted Luke with a question. "What do you mean by that?"

"We didn't have a clothes dryer in those days, so the laundry was hung on a line in the backyard to dry. There were three or four ropes or wires stretched between two poles with a cross bar at the top. See the telephone poles down there along the street?"

Several blackbirds landed on the telephone lines. Terry nodded.

"Clothes lines were like that, only shorter of course. Everybody had them in their backyards. That's the way you did it most of the time, and in the winter when it was too cold, you hung the laundry in the basement. Now we just use the dryer."

Terry squirmed, and Luke brought his story to a conclusion. "Anyway, I remember standing across from my dad and holding one end of the sheet, while he showed me how to fold it. 'It's easiest as a two man job,' he said, 'so, you and your brother may have to do this and help your mom and grandma out.' I know it was the first time I had seen my dad doing the laundry, so I thought that if he was willing to help out, then I should too. My dad raised his voice to make sure that my older brother and I both understood. 'You hear, Matt, I'm expecting you and Luke to be helpin' out around here for the rest of the summer. Your mom and grandma are goin' to need some help with this house full of little ones.'"

"Well, I already do help at our house, like clean my room and stuff like that." Terry stood to emphasize her point.

"I know, and I've seen you help clear the dishes from the table after dinner sometimes, but maybe there will be other things you can do too."

"But, I'll have to have mom show me how to fold the sheets. Besides, your dad said it's a two man job, so two girls could do it just as good too." Terry stomped one foot.

Luke chuckled as he stood. "Oh, I have no doubt about that, and your mom would agree completely. Let's head back home, so we don't miss your mom's call. Besides, maybe there's some things we can do at your house this afternoon."

———

Two days passed before Terry saw her baby brother. Daniel took on a yellowish color the night of his birth, and the doctors decided to keep him in the hospital to treat the jaundice. His mother stayed with him and re-learned the art of breast feeding. When Terry arrived home from school on Friday afternoon, her mother and brother were waiting for her.

Danny rested in a cradle-like seat. The seat was made of molded plastic and cushioned with a vinyl pad, which was covered with a blue quilted material. Julia had swaddled Danny in a blanket. His eyes were scrunched closed.

"He's littler than I thought." Terry touched the top of Daniel's head. "I like this thing he's in. It looks cozy."

"It's called a pumpkin seat. It's good for the day time when I want him to be with us."

"I like his name. Daniel sounds neat."

"We can call him Danny too."

"Do you think he likes his room?"

"I'm not sure. I laid him down for a nap as soon as we got home, but he just cried. I carried him around, and he finally fell asleep, so I put him in his seat. Since then, I've been looking for something to do, like maybe some cleaning."

"But the house is so clean that you couldn't find anything to do, huh?" Terry squared her shoulders.

"Yes, everything's very nice."

Terry rushed into an explanation. "The first day me and Luke did some cleaning and straightening up. Then yesterday after school Sally and me cleaned some more and did the laundry. We even did your room. We folded the sheets together. Luke said it was a two man job, and Sally said that sounded like a good idea. Then we made sure everything was just right in Danny's room. I think he'll get used to it, don't you? It's only his first day home."

"I'm sure he will. And little Miss, I thank you, and Danny thanks you for all your hard work."

Terry remembered Luke's story and shared its conclusion. "Luke said, 'you gotta' help out with this house full of little ones!'"

Julia laughed, and Terry grinned but didn't fully comprehend the source of the humor. "Luke says some funny things, doesn't he?"

Julia felt a tug at her mid-section. "He can get a little carried away. We don't exactly have a house full of little ones. Just one little one, Danny here."

"I think he meant his house when he was little. I think he helped his mom too."

"Yes, I'm sure he did. We're going to have to do something nice for him and for Sally too. Maybe a present."

"I can help you pick something out." Terry stroked the top of Danny's head, and his eyes opened.

Danny whimpered, and Julia lifted Danny into her arms. "We'll go out real soon. But now I'm going to feed your little brother, and then I'm sure he'll want to sleep."

———————

"You can thank Clay for the barbeque," Julia stated.

Luke turned to Clay with a gesture of appreciation and amazement. "I wouldn't have picked cooking as one of your talents. Good job, the chops taste great!"

"Don't act so surprised. I keep tellin' ya' I got a lot of talents. You've only seen me on the basketball floor."

Luke couldn't resist another memory. "Well, there was that time I saw you on the kitchen floor too. Quite impressive!"

Frank, Julia and Sally laughed with Luke. Terry smiled quizzically and Daniel rocked in his mother's arms.

Clay managed to snicker with his retort. "If I recall correctly, you were down there with me."

"Actually, that was me down there with you." Julia interjected.

Luke shared his recollections of how that night had ended. "The only reason I got down on the floor was to clean up the mess you made."

"That's beside the point. I'm tellin' ya' I know my way around the kitchen. If Julia would let me, I'd be the regular cook around here. Honey, how 'bout we make arrangements to have me be the full time cook?"

"Let's just start with you being the full time barbeque cook?"

"I guess that's a start. The summer's coming on fast, and there'll be lots of chances for us to do some grillin'. The hot times are comin' honey, I can feel it. How 'bout you?"

"If you mean the weather, I can feel that for sure. Or maybe it's this baby that I'm holding."

Sally offered to hold Danny, and as Julia passed the baby to her, Luke cleared plates and serving dishes from the dining room table. Terry followed Luke's lead, and Frank took the opportunity to retrieve a round of beers.

Julia heard the scrape of leftovers sliding off of plates and water running in the sink as Frank swung the kitchen door open.

Julia wiped her mouth with a napkin. "Luke, what are you and Terry doing in there? Why don't you wait, and I'll help with that?"

"We're just tidying up a little," Luke responded.

"Yeah, Mom, Luke says we need to soak the bean pot, and we're covering the slaw with the plastic stuff like you do."

"Okay, sweetie, but then you two come back into the dining room. We have something else to do, remember?"

"Oh, yeah." Terry closed the refrigerator. "I almost forgot."

Terry followed Luke into the dining room, and Julia sent her to find Sally. Julia finished the last bite of her pork chop.

She winked at Clay. "That really was tasty. Thanks for barbequing. You're such a darling when you wear your BBQ apron."

"You hear that, Frank? Some day somebody might call you darling too."

"Yeah, if only I could barbeque like you." Frank added a touch of sarcasm to his comment, as though he was slathering it on a grill full of chops.

When Sally returned, three gift boxes adorned the center of the table. Julia presented one of them to Sally, and they switched the baby for the gift. Julia then gave one box to Luke.

"Danny and I wanted to say thanks for all the help that you have given us during the last couple of weeks." Julia then slid the third box across to Terry. "And here's one for you, Little Miss."

"Mom, I didn't know I was..."

"Well, I can still surprise you sometimes, can't I, even though you are getting to be such a big girl?"

"Yeah, I guess, but what kind of surprise?"

"Open it up and see, silly girl!"

Terry went to work on her present, but Sally was already holding hers.

"Wow!" Frank exclaimed, "That's beautiful."

Sally held a silk blouse, pearly white with a pastel swirl of pink and purple color across the front and at the tips of the collar. "Oh, Julia, it's lovely! Thank you so much, but you didn't have to do this. It might be too nice for me to wear."

"We'll just have to get Frank here to take you out for a nice dinner, say, at the Broker. How about it, Frank?"

"Well..." Frank hesitated.

Clay couldn't resist the opportunity. "Oh man, you got a free meal tonight, but the next one's goin' to cost ya,' buddy!"

"Clay, be nice." Julia encouraged a more lighthearted approach.

"Oh, yeah, but this could be your chance to be a darling too." Clay resurrected an earlier idea.

"Don't you know I've always wanted to follow in your foot-steps?" Frank punched Clay's arm and then turned to Sally. "Madame, I would be honored to be your escort. Name the time, name the place."

Sally smiled, glanced downward, and lifted her hand toward Frank. He gently kissed her hand.

They acted a scene from a Victorian play. "Madame, you are the fairest maiden in the land."

"Sir, such flattery may be your undoing."

Clay dropped the curtain on the scene. "Hey, man, I'm get-tin' a little excited. Either you two quit it, or take it to the other room."

Terry exclaimed, "I guess I am the big sister now, huh?"

"You sure are." Julia lifted her glass of water in celebration.

Sally chimed in. "What a cute shirt! Stand up. Let us all see."

Terry draped the T-shirt in front of her. It was tie died, bright with color, and in an arch over the breast pocket the words *Big Sister* were imprinted with black ink.

"That's perfect." Sally concluded and turned to Luke. "You have to share, too, Luke."

Luke showed a large photograph. Framed in oak with a light blue mat, the photo captured Elephant Rocks surrounded in a sea of golden grass and a background of Boulder foothills bathed in the pinks of a fast approaching sunset.

"It's beautiful, don't you think?" Luke passed the photograph to Frank, and he passed it around the table.

When it came to Terry, she added an insight. "It's your favor-ite place! Mom and me found it in a store downtown."

"We thought you might like it." Julia concurred.

"It's perfect, but like Sally said, you really didn't have to."

"Maybe, but we wanted to, so we did."

Expressions of gratitude and delight accented the dessert course, chocolate chip ice cream. Danny's persistent cry ended the celebration dinner prematurely. Julia excused herself and insisted that Clay accompany her to Danny's room where she would feed him and put him to bed.

Sally coaxed Frank to leave with her, an opportunity to discuss a future night-out. Luke and Terry retired to the front room, and when the TV programs disappointed, Terry challenged Luke to a game of Chutes & Ladders.

Just as Terry was making the slide toward the finish line of their second game, Clay and Julia entered the room.

"Hey, big guy, here's the game for you. Terry's the champion. She's beat me twice now. Maybe you can take the belt away from her."

"Me? No, these kids definitely are getting the better of me."

Luke chuckled as he rose to his knees. "Not sure I know what you mean."

Julia helped with the explanation. "Oh, Danny's still fussing a little, and his father can't seem to handle it."

"No, it's not that. He just isn't listenin' to me."

Julia jabbed Clay's arm. "Listening to you? You act like he's one of your football players. He's two and half weeks old."

"You know what I mean. No matter what I do, he just keeps on cryin' till you come in. I guess he's just a Momma's boy."

"You're incredible! You really don't get it." Julia allowed the exasperation to ring in her voice.

"Now, don't you start in on me again!"

"Somebody needs to straighten you out. It's not always about you."

Luke stood in front of Clay. "At this point any baby's going to be more attached to the mother. It's only natural. Besides, I suspect that this won't be the last time the kids get the better of you. That's the natural progression of things."

"I don't know about that, either. But I do know that right now I could use a cold beer. I'm thinkin' Larry's is the place to get one. How 'bout you, Luke, you thirsty? Betcha' we find Fat Man there."

"Not tonight, man. You take care and if you see Frank, tell him I'm counting on him for a good game tomorrow at the field house."

After Clay left, Julia turned to Luke. "You don't have to stay here. We ladies can take care of ourselves."

"Oh, I've no doubt about that. I was actually thinking that I have a letter to finish writing. Then I'll hit the rack. Have to stay one step ahead of the kids you know. This time I'm talking about those college guys Frank and I play basketball with on Sundays. It's their last weekend in town. Finals next week, then they'll be heading home for the summer."

"Hey, I've been meaning to ask you, how's Elizabeth doing? She's so sweet."

"To be honest, I'm not sure. She hasn't sent a letter in the last few weeks. I didn't tell you, but last month she moved into her own place with a girl friend. They're sharing a house in Clayton. It's a nice part of St. Louis. She's probably too busy partying with her friends."

"I doubt that. It's more likely that she's still working overtime to pay for that trip she made out here to see you." Julia provided an explanation that simultaneously defended the integrity of her gender. "I was thinking you could ask her what to do with our fussy, little guy."

"I guess I could, so I better get to it. You two enjoy the rest of your evening. Thanks for dinner and the gift, and the games. You're too kind. See ya' Terry. Give Danny Boy a hug for me. There you go. Try that Irish tune with him, *Oh Danny Boy*."

Luke hummed the tune to *Danny Boy* on his way through the kitchen and out of the door.

Terry switched both game pieces to the starting point of the board. "Luke is nice isn't he?"

"Yes, he is, very nice."

When the sound of three short taps carried through the floor, Julia smiled. "Sounds like he's hanging up that photograph. Guess he really did like it after all. I just hope he's doing all right."

As Julia verbalized her concern for Luke, a bewitching aura surrounded her. Her forehead furrowed, and she listened for another indication of his well being.

Terry broke the spell. "I think Luke's a lot better at basketball than he is at Chutes & Ladders."

When Terry caught her mother's eye, she asked, "How about you and me playing a game?"

"Okay, but I'm not going to let you win like Luke always does." Julia dropped to the floor and gave her daughter a hug.

Terry wiggled free and proclaimed with righteousness. "I'm the champion fair and square!"

Chapter 29

St. Louis, mid May 1972

"You can't be serious! Damn, Elizabeth, there has got to be another way. Just has to be!" Debbie gripped Elizabeth's hand. Shocked, excited, so certain, so confused, Debbie squeezed tighter. "You're crazy if you think I'll let you...How long have you known? That's what the pukin' has been about. I should have guessed. I should have picked up on it. Is it Mitch? No, it hasn't been long enough. Luke, have you told him? Have you told him what you're planning to do? Dr. Anderson, you better talk to her about this."

Elizabeth yanked her hand from Debbie's grasp and moved to the end of the sofa. She answered Debbie's questions, hollow recitations she had been keeping to herself.

Her feelings flowed to the surface. "Debbie, I'm scared, really scared. It's not right, not right, I know. But I'm not ready. I can't be a mother. I'm not a mother. I'm not married. I'm not anything. I'm just pregnant. I'm pregnant, and now what? I'm going to have an abortion. I think...I just don't know anymore."

Tears flooded her face, and Debbie moved to Elizabeth's side. She pressed her cheek against Elizabeth's shoulder, and her own cheeks dampened. She breathed in her judgments, and her thoughts tossed her back to the time when Elizabeth and she first met, in and out of the years since then, a myriad of images.

Elizabeth had always been the stable one, organized and prepared. She was steady and kind, caring and loving. She knew how to have fun. She knew when to be serious. She was everything you would want in a friend, a lover, a nurse, a roommate. People were attracted to her, adults and children. She was attractive. Her eyes were clear, except recently, and Debbie scolded herself for missing that aspect.

Elizabeth saw things the way they were. Even as she accepted them for what they were, she tried to make things better, for me, for her patients, for everybody.

"I don't know how to make this better, to make you feel better." Debbie's admission was a whispered confession.

Debbie straightened, and then an uncontrolled litany spewed from her. "I know that an abortion's not legal, not right. It's against our religion. Hell, birth control is against our religion. I thought you used a diaphragm. What happened? How could this have happened to you? To me maybe, but not to you! Who else knows about this? Have you told your mom? I can't imagine. You can't even get an abortion, can you? What? Do you have to go over to the east side?"

Elizabeth's head rattled as though the vehemence of Debbie's words shook her entire body.

Sobs accompanied Elizabeth's response. "I've seen Dr. Anderson twice. She said, 'sometimes these things happen.'"

"That's what she said about why the diaphragm didn't work." Debbie massaged her thighs, pressing so hard it hurt.

Acknowledgment again that the diaphragm had not worked forced a crimson color to Elizabeth's cheeks. "That's what she said. She gave me some prenatal vitamins on my second visit. I couldn't ask her about what to do. It didn't feel right to me. I was talking to Mitch..."

Debbie needed a target for her growing frustration. "Mitch? You told him! That son of a bitch, he's the one. He told you about the abortion. That's a doctor for you, think they're God. He's not God, Goddammit! You don't have to listen to him. You don't even have to see him anymore."

Elizabeth stopped Debbie when she clenched Debbie's arm in a vice grip. "Debbie, I asked him about abortions. He only remembered some things from medical school. If he ends up going to South America, he may have to learn about them. He may have to do them down there. It could be a necessity to save a young girl's life."

"But South America and St. Louis...I may not know my geography very well, but I know they're worlds apart. You and some poor, ignorant girl? There's a big difference."

Elizabeth stroked Debbie's arm, as her desperation surfaced. "I know. I know all of that. And I can't stop thinking about it. There's so much shit to think about. But I don't want to think about it anymore. I've been racking my brain trying to think of what to do, who to talk to. I've tried over and over again to write it down in a letter to Luke. He's probably wondering about me because I haven't written him. I can't write to him about this. I need to see him, right now. He's supposed to be here. But, how's that going to happen? How's he supposed to know?"

Debbie latched onto the notion that Luke could intervene somehow. "Just call him or his landlady like you did before your trip. She will let him call back on her phone. You just need to tell him that he needs to come home to you."

Elizabeth imagined Luke in Boulder. "Colorado's his home now. That's what I think."

"I thought he said that he'd be coming back to you someday."

"That was a year ago. Things are changing. Things have changed."

Debbie agreed with Elizabeth's statement. "That part is the truest thing you've said so far. Anyway, without Luke, that leaves me and Mitch, since you've told him. What's he going to do, anyway?"

Elizabeth related the initial steps. "He said that he'd do some research, talk to other doctors, but not here. He knows doctors on the East Coast where he's from."

"Where's he from?"

"Near New York"

"At least he's smart enough not to talk to anybody around here."

"Debbie, he's plenty smart. You know some people say that he's brilliant."

"And good looking. And believe me, he knows it."

"Debbie, you've got to give him a break. Besides, he's coming over soon to talk some more. And I want you to be here, okay? I want you to hear what he has to say. But I need you to try to stay calm, no matter what comes up. I need you to help me think about this."

"Maybe we should just pray about it." Debbie wanted to stop the whirlwind.

"That's the first time I've heard you say that, since the Anatomy final our junior year." Elizabeth formed a smile inside the puffy redness.

"Well, I was desperate then, or at least that's what I thought. I should have saved those prayers for something really important, like this."

When a knock came at the door, it startled both of them. Debbie was the first to rise. "That would be doctor good-looking."

Elizabeth admonished her. "Debbie, please try to be nice. None of this is his fault."

"I'll be nice, but he better not be coming around here with wild-ass ideas."

Elizabeth welcomed Mitch, but when she offered him a place on the sofa, he excused himself to the kitchen. He positioned a kitchen chair directly in front of Elizabeth.

He gently held her hand in his. "Even though we only met a little while ago, and you may think I'm crazy for what I'm about to say, I want you to hear me out."

He shifted in his seat, and Debbie lurched forward in that moment. "Mitch, there's enough craziness already without you adding to it."

"I know, I know." Mitch blocked out Debbie's words and remained steadfast in his attention to Elizabeth. "I care deeply for you. Elizabeth, I love you, and if you want to have your baby, I want to marry you. We can just elope, and that will be that. You can have your baby. I'll love your baby as my own."

Mitch dropped to one knee and pressed Elizabeth's hand in both of his. "I love you now. I'll love you forever. Elizabeth, will you marry me?"

Elizabeth burst into tears. She wrapped her arms around Mitch's shoulders. She heaved, and Mitch's question rode on a tide made of her sobs.

Debbie sucked air into her lungs and held it there. A vacuum enveloped all three of them until Elizabeth lifted her head.

She wiped her tears with a shirt sleeve. "Mitch, I have so many emotions right now. I feel what you feel, but I can't...I won't marry you. Because of those feelings, because of how mixed up I am. That's too far out there, way too far."

Debbie was compelled to strengthen Elizabeth's response. "Mitch, are you nuts? I thought you were coming here to help Elizabeth. This doesn't help. It's crazy. I thought you were going to look into ways to end the pregnancy."

He turned to Debbie before he spoke. "I know and I did. I did. But I just wanted Elizabeth to know how I felt."

"Mitch, it's not about you. It's about Elizabeth. She's the one who is pregnant. It's her decision to make."

"I know and I'm totally committed to her. I'll do whatever you want, Elizabeth."

Mitch and Debbie's eyes trained on Elizabeth, and she only wanted one thing. "I want to know what you found out about terminating my pregnancy, about an abortion. Is it even an option?"

Mitch's answer was straightforward, gentle but matter-of-fact. "Yes, you have options."

He described two clinics located in the New York City area. Each was staffed by doctors, nurses, and counselors. He related background information on New York's laws and the legalization of abortion there.

A non-surgical procedure is employed for pregnancies in the first trimester. Safe and simple, the doctor would use a soft tube like a vacuum inserted in the uterus. It would require local anesthesia but would only take about twenty minutes. Someone on staff would explain everything beforehand. The clinics accept patients from all over the country.

Mitch summarized by saying. "If they need a referral, I'll act as your doctor. We can make an appointment as soon as you want. It makes sense to me. They say it gives women a better chance, a choice. I guess it's not any easier, but at least they have a choice. You have a choice, Elizabeth. I'll help you in any way you want."

Elizabeth breathed in all of the information. "At least I have a choice. That makes me feel better. But New York? Isn't there some place closer? I don't see how I can make that work."

"I only talked to doctors there, people I know, and people whom I could ask questions of without having to get into explanations. People I trust, too. I didn't ask about other places. I don't know if there are other clinics, but I do have an idea about how this can work, if it's what you want to do?"

"I don't know if it's what I want to do until I know everything. I need to know how it could work before I can even say that it's the way that I want it to work. Ugghh! I'm going in circles again. My mind is going in circles."

"Just hang on. Here's how it can work."

Mitch outlined the way he saw it happening. He explained that his hometown of Somerville, New Jersey was approximately an hour from New York. He offered to travel with her and assured her that they could stay at his family's home. He would accompany her to the clinic. He reiterated that, in the first trimester, the procedure could be done in one day.

He paused for a relaxing breath. "I think it's the best way. The people I've talked to say it's the best available. It's professional. These clinics know what they're doing. That's how it could work, but, like you said, you have to decide. I promise I'll do whatever you want."

With those last words, his eyes met Elizabeth's. He held steady until she looked toward Debbie, then he looked in that direction, too.

"I'm going to get a glass of water. I need something...a minute." Debbie rushed to the kitchen.

Mitch took a place on the sofa close to Elizabeth.

"I'll be damned!" Debbie mumbled as the tap water filled the glass.

She leaned against the kitchen counter and sipped from the glass, staring over the rim into the backyard. A new growth of green from the trees and the grass met her stare.

"Can you believe this?" she asked for something beyond what she could see.

As Debbie burst into the room, Elizabeth broke from Mitch's embrace. Debbie marched toward Mitch, and he reacted defensively to her quickness. When he stood, she latched onto his arm.

She spoke calmly as she steered him to the door. "Mitch, we really appreciate all your...your help. We need some time to talk about this, just Elizabeth and me."

He couldn't stop her momentum, and his good-bye was caught in the latch of the door.

Debbie returned with a plan and an opinion simultaneously forming in her mind. "Mitch is crazy about you, but he could also be just plain crazy. All this while I thought he was so cool. Can't see that now. He's just a little too weird, or conceited maybe. Thinks he can just come in here and solve everything. Thinks that getting married is going to solve everything. At least you knew better than that. Even in your state, you knew to step back from that."

Elizabeth fought the weight of all the words and lifted her eyes and hands toward the heavens.

Debbie's proposed a final question. "How crazy can you get?"

Elizabeth exhaled with a whoosh of exasperation. "I know! I know! Crazy!"

As she took a seat next to Elizabeth, Debbie responded. "I'm not talking about you. I was talking about Mitch."

"Yes, but I'm talking about me! I've been living with this for too long. I'm tired of thinking, tired of sitting here and wondering. It's time to just do something. Can't I just do something?"

Debbie answered with her plan. "Yes, you can! We can. We can just go to New York ourselves. No Mitch, no men, just you and me. I've got my TWA Travel Card. I can get us the plane tickets. We'll call work and tell Francine we need three days off. We'll go together. If New York is the best place to go to get this done, then that's where we'll go. I'll get the name and address of the clinic from Doctor Cool, but no doctors, just you and me, just the women. We're the ones who have to do it. It's our decision to make. Guess that's the way it's always been. I think it's the way it's going to have to be."

Elizabeth hugged Debbie, her bewilderment transformed into strength.

Chapter 30

St. Louis, Mid May 1972

People jammed two to three deep around the conveyors in the baggage claim area on the lower level of the terminal at Lambert Air Field. Like many modern airports, the space was designed linearly, stretching half the length of a football field. For a Thursday night it was crowded, but even at that, Luke spied his two younger brothers immediately upon entering the area.

He weaved through the crowd and closed the distance between them before Johnny or Mark saw him. "Hey, you two! Thanks for coming."

On the ride home, Luke congratulated Mark on his graduation from Oakwood, and on the fact that he had been hired by a large St. Louis company as a customer service representative. Johnny claimed Mark's position sounded more professional than it really was. Mark insisted that it wasn't a career move, just an interim step until he could secure a position as a high school teacher and coach.

Johnny asked for Luke's support when their mother expressed her concerns over the fact that he had not yet found a summer job. Luke agreed to help him in that way but joked with Johnny that he would be on his own if she challenged him about yard work that had not been completed.

Luke remembered well the start of the summer season in St. Louis. Especially since their father's death, their mother had been a task master. Loving and kind, she consistently provided a hot meal at the end of the workday, but she was insistent that her sons would work. She upheld a high standard of performance, an aspect of their father's legacy.

Johnny described a new band playing on the weekends at a club in the Soulard district of St. Louis, a blues group led by a guitarist. Willy Black impressed Johnny with the intensity of his sound, and he urged Luke to make an effort to hear for himself.

Luke could not make that kind of commitment. "There's only one thing that I need to do this weekend. I need to see Elizabeth."

"Mom said that's why you were coming home. What's happening with Elizabeth?" Johnny asked.

Before Luke could respond, Mark added a comment. "You two have been writing letters to one another since you left for freshman year at Oakwood. Now that's just stopped. It doesn't sound right."

"Exactly, so I figured I better come in person. I want to make sure she's all right."

After Debbie unlocked the door she swung it wide so that her brother could make it across the threshold, one suitcase in each hand. "Watch out for the mail on the floor. Just put those in the hall."

Andy did as he was told. Except for such brief instructions and short verbal exchanges, it had been a quiet ride between the airport and Debbie and Elizabeth's house.

He attempted to persuade both of them once more. "You sure you girls wouldn't like me to get something for you to eat. I could grab some hamburgers easily enough. And..."

Debbie stopped him. "It's okay, Andy. We're okay. We'll take it from here. Elizabeth just needs to rest. I'll call you tomorrow after we're settled."

Debbie stooped to retrieve the mail and handed it to Elizabeth.

"Thanks for coming to get us." Elizabeth pointed to Andy with the envelopes she held.

"You're welcome." Andy replied, "Talk to you tomorrow, Sis."

After closing the door, Debbie announced. "I need to use the bathroom, unless you need it first."

Elizabeth scanned the mail and saw a letter with familiar handwriting on it. "No I'm okay. You go ahead."

As Debbie entered the front room, Elizabeth nearly shouted. "Shit! He's coming here tonight. Tonight! He may be here any minute. He was probably at the airport when we were. Shit, I'm glad he didn't see me there. How would I have explained that? Damn, what am I going to tell him, anyway? I look like shit. I feel like shit. I might as well be..."

"Calm down! What, who are you talking about?"

"Luke, it's in his letter. He's in St. Louis, arrived about the same time we did. Said he hopes everything's all right. He's coming home to see me."

"Damn! You got to be kidding. Does he even know where our house is?"

"He knows the address, and he grew up here. I'm sure he can find it."

"I guess, but he'll probably call. I'll just tell him that you're working."

"He won't necessarily call. Besides, if he thinks I'm at the hospital, he could just as easily go there to find me."

"Damn it, Elizabeth, I wished you would've written to tell him something, just made something up."

"I know, I know. I've made a mess of everything, and now... now I've got to talk to him."

"No, not necessarily tonight. When he comes I'll just tell him you're sick, and he should come back tomorrow. Maybe around lunch, that'll give you time to sleep in, rest up a little and get ready."

———

The noon crowd of cars filled the spaces at Steak 'N Shake, and the carhops rushed the food orders to and from the kitchen. Luke commented on the level of activity and the fact that Boulder didn't have a burger place like Steak 'N Shake.

He did most of the talking as they ate their hamburgers. He shared how Boulder wasn't yet as green as St. Louis, trees had much smaller leaves, and many of the spring flowers had not yet bloomed. He reviewed the current status of his family members: Mark's graduation, jobs that Mark and Johnny were pursuing, Matt getting his discharge from the Air Force in early June, Annie's work at Famous Barr, and his mother's health.

His litany echoed inside the car as he drove along the boulevard that formed one of the borders of Forest Park. At the traffic lights, he alternated his view of the signals and a vigil of Elizabeth. He glimpsed a faint smile when he related the story of how Johnny had been shirking the yard work and Johnny's offer to pay him to come home and take care of those chores.

Otherwise, Elizabeth's pallid expression caused an increasing uneasiness for Luke. Her terse replies to his questions often ended with comments that spurred more of his ramblings. He was certain that he had relayed most of this information in recent letters, but he couldn't stop his monologue.

When he turned into Forest Park and onto the drive that led to the American Legion Fountain, he fell silent. Neil Young's *Heart of Gold* played on the radio.

When they converged at the front of the car, Luke took Elizabeth's hand. "Hi there, I've missed you. You must really have been sick. You don't seem to be yourself. We could've just stayed at your house."

"I know. I'm okay really. How is it you used to say that? 'I've just been thinking.'"

"Oh, so you're turning the tables on me? I guess that's fair. What have you been thinking about?"

"You and me," she answered.

"And it's been making you sick?" An uneasy chuckle followed his question.

"No, don't be stupid. That has nothing to do with it." She blurted out reflexively but then blushed with the irony of her choice of words.

He edged closer to her as they sat on the wall above the fountain, his hand in hers. He arched his back and breathed the warm, moist air. Except for the intermittent rattle of cars passing on the street below, they were surrounded by a peaceful silence.

"This is how I remembered it, except I was hoping that the fountain would be working. I wonder why it hasn't been cleaned, yet. Do you get a chance to come here often?"

"Not really. Besides, it wouldn't be the same without you." Finally a smile he recognized, one similar to the one he remembered from his dreams.

"I understand that. For a few days after you were in Boulder, I didn't like coming home. It wasn't the same without you there."

"The bus goes right by Forest Park on the way to the hospital. I watch from the window, but I think it's better for me not to stop, just go on to work."

"I guess it's been busy at work for you."

"Pretty busy. Since Debbie and I moved into the house, we've both been working a lot."

"Have to pay that rent. I know what you mean. But you have a nice house. I like what I've seen."

"It's been perfect for us."

No safe topics presented themselves, and Luke couldn't summon the courage to ask Elizabeth why she hadn't written to him. An uneasy silence formed a barrier between them, until Elizabeth determined a way to break through it.

She verbalized her impromptu idea. "Luke, there's a lot that we should talk about, but I don't want to do it now. I think

Debbie told you that I have to work tonight. We should be getting back so I can get ready, but I want you to come over to the house tomorrow night, not too early. I have to cover the afternoon part of a day shift for one of my friends, so I won't be home till around six. Debbie has to work the night shift, so we can have the house to ourselves. I'll fix some dinner. You come over around seven, and we'll have lots of time. Can you do that?"

"Sure, but you don't have to cook."

"It's okay. I'll make something simple."

"Whatever you do, it'll be fine."

———

Luke couldn't remember The Blues like that, was sure he had never heard them in person before, not like that. The saxophone, bass, and the percussion established the vibe, but Johnny was oh, so right about the guitar. There, in the stage lights, the hunkering shoulders, the strain of the brow, the sheer force of the sound overpowered Luke. The uncertainty of direction for the next note, the next riff climbed to a pinnacle. When it hit it was like a sledge hammer. His name was Willy Black, his band, *Black Stoned Blues*.

Friday night in a club located just south of downtown St. Louis, Luke and his brothers sat at a table near the bar. Bottles of beer and whiskey chasers built their support for the music. Johnny often led the cheers, a guttural blast that pulled those closer to the stage to their feet and elicited a sneer, or a nod in his direction from Willy.

On Luke's Saturday evening drive to Elizabeth's house, he felt an uncomfortable throb at his temples. A mix of alcohol and music pounded there, but another, darker sense gathered near his heart, unrecognizable, except for one other time.

He remembered a feeling from the day of his father's death. It pierced his heart from the cold stare of his mother's eyes. An unconscious stirring from that day and the blues beat from this time stayed with him until he exhaled at Elizabeth's front door.

She met him there with a kiss and a long embrace, a welcome that soothed the throbbing. They ate at the kitchen table, salad first then cheese ravioli with a flavorful, red sauce.

Luke imagined he would add the sauce to a future shopping list, so he inquired about the brand. "The sauce tastes good. What kind is it?"

"Actually, Debbie and I brought home a jar from a restaurant, called Gipeto's. We like it a lot."

"It's very good."

They spent the rest of dinner talking about the restaurants that Elizabeth had discovered with Debbie and other friends from work, places she wanted them to try sometime.

"I don't know. If you keep cooking like this we may never need to go out again." He baited her.

She saw through it. "So, is that supposed to be a compliment?"

"Yes. No. Yes, I mean. I mean it really tastes good."

"It's ravioli from a package and sauce from a jar, but thanks, anyway."

He couldn't let it end that way. "Elizabeth, thanks for cooking dinner. It was delicious."

He relaxed when she kissed his cheek.

She simply replied. "You're welcome."

She offered him a beer as they cleared the dinner dishes to the sink.

He declined with an explanation. "I think I'll switch to a glass of water for now. My brothers and I went to a bar in the city. We hit the beers pretty hard, keeping up with the band."

Elizabeth smiled as she put the salad dressing in the refrigerator. "What bar was this, and what band?"

"I was afraid you would ask. Can't remember the name of the bar, but the band was called Black Stoned Blues. Willy Black is the band leader, a great blues guitar."

"Wow, sounds neat."

"It was pretty funky. Maybe we should put that place on the list for us to check out together too."

"All of a sudden it seems like we have a lot of possibilities." Elizabeth wiped her hands on a kitchen towel. "For now, let's just revert to the living room."

Luke swallowed deeply from the glass of water. He found comfort in Elizabeth's home.

"You have nice furniture."

"Thanks. You're full of compliments tonight."

"You've been to my place. It's pretty plain, and luckily you didn't have to eat any of my cooking. Believe me, I rely a lot more on packages than you do, pot pies and Rice-a-Roni, stuff like that."

"Oh, but it sounds so cosmopolitan."

"Ooh, you're so funny I can hardly stand it."

She lowered her voice two octaves. "I mean it. I really mean it."

Then she poked him in the ribs. When she tried again, he latched onto her arms and pulled her close.

"Now, I've got you." A sly smile punctuated his words.

"Oh, yeah. Maybe I've got you. This was part of my plan all along." A look of cunning accompanied her response.

He slumped into the sofa cushions. "I give up. I never really stood a chance, did I?"

"Me, either," she whispered.

In a wistful gaze, he caressed her and stroked her luscious, auburn hair. He kissed her with the taste of red sauce and a mix of unknown herbs and spices on his lips, and then he kissed her harder with a love that mashed together the mystery of all the places they had come to know, a concoction of their own pure love.

They whetted their appetites further on a feast of long kisses. All the tension left Luke's body, and Elizabeth sunk into his arms and surrendered there. From a source deep within her bosom, moisture found its way to her eyes, and they dampened at the corners. She held on with all her strength.

The love she felt now was the love that she had known before. Less than three months had streamed by since the last time they held one another in this way. Her mind drifted onto the next day, when he would leave and return to Boulder.

Like a continuous channel of rivers flowing one into the other, draining and filling their hearts, feelings and memories, wishes and dreams, made their way between her and him. Their love stretched time but could not hold back the present moment, and a river of tears burst her dam.

"Elizabeth, are you okay? What's the matter?" He held her hands gently pressed between his.

Her eyes were downcast. "It's just that...I need to tell you something...That I've done. That's about...you and me. But you'll have to leave tomorrow. And I don't know how to begin this time."

"This time...this time I could tell something was wrong. I can stay longer if you need me to. I...I could come back permanently if you want me to. I mean it. I really do. Tell me what you want me to do. Tell me about you and me. If something is wrong between you and me, I'll try to..."

He stopped when she looked straight ahead and past him somehow, through him. "I'm pregnant. I was...I was pregnant. When you and I had sex in Boulder, I got pregnant."

"God, Elizabeth, a baby, our baby! But you said 'was'. I don't understand. What does that mean? You said everything was okay. Remember? Back then, you were, we were okay, remember?"

"I used a diaphragm as birth control. My doctor prescribed it for me. I was having trouble with my birth control pills. It should've worked, but it didn't. Probably I made a mistake when I put it in."

"So you got pregnant?"

"I got pregnant."

"So what should I do?"

"You shouldn't do anything. You don't have to do anything. I did. I made a decision, a choice."

"What kind of choice? I still don't know what you mean. Are you, are we going to have a baby?"

"No, there's no baby! I had an abortion!" And a flood of tears washed over her cheeks.

"What? Elizabeth?" His voice quivered at the sound of her name, and he dropped her hand.

Sniffling and talking in spurts, Elizabeth latched onto his shirt sleeve. "I chose to end the pregnancy. I'm not pregnant anymore. That's all."

"But, I don't understand. I don't know much about...But I didn't think you could. I thought it was illegal. How could you?"

"I went to New York. We just got back. On Thursday night, the same night you arrived. Debbie and I went together, to a clinic. It's a medical clinic run by doctors and nurses. There are counselors that talk to you too. The nurses take good care of you and don't judge you. A doctor I know from the hospital told me about the clinic. He's from there. Anyway, I went, we went. And it's over. And now, I don't know what...now you're here, and then you'll go again. And then I don't know. I didn't know how to tell you, to explain to you."

He felt an anxious rush and streamed a sequence of conclusions and confusions. "And that's why you haven't written to me. I hadn't heard from you. I thought something was wrong between us. So I came back. And I guess it was. But I didn't think it was this. I didn't know for sure. I just felt..."

"I know, I know. You had no way of knowing. And I should've written to tell you, but I couldn't figure out how to say it. I just cried and cried, and I got sick in the morning. And I prayed, too, and then I decided. Once I decided, it was too complicated to even try to write about. I just made the choice and thought I'd tell you some way, some time."

"This is the time. This is the way." He choked and swallowed hard his own hurt. "It doesn't feel...right. But I..."

He hugged her tightly until a calm rhythm measured their breathing.

Then she whispered as though she were in a confessional. "I know that it's not right, but I did it. It's illegal in Missouri, but I think it's okay in Colorado. At least that's what I heard at the clinic. The counselor said it's okay in certain places, and someday it will be okay all over the country. But it's a sin against the Church, and I guess it will be forever. I'm guilty of that sin... forever."

Luke gripped both of her hands in his. "You're not guilty of anything. You're good. I'm the one who is...I'm the one who wasn't here when you needed me. That's what's not right. That's what I mean. I mean I'm sorry I wasn't here. I'm so sorry, Elizabeth. Elizabeth, I love you so. I wish I could make it right."

"The counselor said that this would be the hardest part, accepting it, accepting the idea that I had a choice about what to do. She said that each woman can decide for herself. It's her body. She doesn't even have to tell the man. And if you weren't here now, then I don't know, maybe I wouldn't have ever told you. I've just got to accept it. I've still got all these thoughts. They fill my insides. They're way down deep most of the time, but then I feel like I'm going to bust open sometimes. And then I do, and it's like my heart's going to crack open. And when it does, I just can't hold it in anymore." She lunged for him, her arms around his neck.

He spoke slowly and softly. "That's the way it should be. You shouldn't hold it inside."

She rested in his arms. His feelings rushed like water flashing white in Boulder Canyon. He squirmed to get comfortable, while she nestled in. The last wave of feelings flowed from her heart. She let them go, and he took them in. They tumbled inside of him, a wild mountain stream.

He transformed those feelings into thoughts. Claims and conditions churned inside his mind and did not reach his heart.

Still, he felt something and whispered, "This is the time and..."

Of the rest he could not be certain.

"What'd you say?"

"Nothing. You okay?"

"Yes, but I'm tired. Will you stay with me, sleep with me? I'd like you to."

"I want to. I want to be here. You sure you're okay though. No pain? I mean was it painful?"

"It hurt a little. I've had some cramps, some bleeding. I really didn't feel very good after our flight. I couldn't have seen you then. I'm sorry I had Debbie send you away. But it worked out okay. And I want you to stay with me tonight."

"Okay."

"Okay," she said, as she rose from the sofa. "I need to use the bathroom and change. If you need to call home, the phone's in the hallway. My room's the first one."

"Okay. I think I will make that call. I'm going to get another glass of water first."

At the kitchen sink, he splashed some water on his face and used his dinner napkin as a towel. He swallowed a glass of water. Darkness had fallen over the backyard, and the kitchen window acted as a mirror. His reflection held nothing familiar. He switched off the lights in the kitchen and the living room.

After he made the phone call, he entered Elizabeth's room. A lava lamp glowed from a table on the opposite side of the bed. Elizabeth lay with a sheet and blanket covering her. He undressed to his underwear, and she pulled the covers back as an invitation.

"You have enough room?" She cuddled near him.

"Yeah. I'm okay. Your bed is nice, better than mine, too."

"Actually it's new, a present to myself from myself."

"I guess it sleeps good."

"It did at first, but not so much lately."

"You sure you're feeling okay. There's nothing I can do for you."

"Actually, you could get me some water. Just use the pink cup in the bathroom."

"Right away."

When he returned, she took a drink and set it on table next to the lamp. She switched off the lamp and scooted next to him, lying on her side. He lay on his back, and she swung one leg over his legs. The touch of her bare skin against his caused him a few moments of tension. He lifted his head at the same time as she lifted hers. They kissed and settled back. One of her arms lay across his shoulder, her hand on the pillow beside his head.

Some time passed. Her breathing took on a regular pace while he lay awake. He imagined the loneliness Elizabeth must have experienced. Debbie knew, of course, and some doctor at the hospital, but she had to carry it. It was just her. She had said that it was her decision to make, her choice.

The words that Elizabeth had spoken rumbled through the channels of his mind. The force increased until a wall of water, the river of expectations, washed over him.

He heard Debbie come in and knew it must be the earliest hours of a new day. He was helpless, so Debbie had to take his place. This was no dream, and he was a fool. Did he truly believe he could lift this river, re-route the flood, and ease the weight of it?

Elizabeth rolled in her sleep toward the wall and moaned softly. Her back to him he rolled in her direction. He caressed her then and tucked the blanket near her chin. In that spoon, dreams covered them with the waters of the night.

Chapter 31

Boulder, early June 1972

"Hey, Luke, how've you been? Haven't seen much of you lately?" Julia stood on the porch with a plate in one hand. She caught Luke's attention before he could descend the stairs to his apartment.

He paused his foot suspended in mid-air. "Been working a lot, that's all. Getting caught up since my trip."

"Doesn't the store bring on some college kids for the summer vacation? I didn't think you regulars had to work that much."

"You're right. But we have to train them, and that's what takes some extra time. This afternoon's their first true test. Saturdays are usually busy days. Even my boss won't be there today. He said they can handle it on their own. I didn't argue with that."

"I would hope not. Besides, it's so nice outside. Anyway, Terry and I are going to have lunch at the picnic table in the backyard. We would love it if you would join us."

"Yeah, that would be neat." Terry came to her mother's side.

Terry held a thermos jug in one hand and plastic cups in the other. "I'll get another cup."

Fried chicken served on paper plates with potato chips and carrots cut into easy-to-handle sticks, finger food transformed into a tasty meal.

"Pretty fancy picnic." Luke licked his fingertips. "Well, it's also a celebration. Yesterday was Terry's last day of school, so we're on vacation." Julia poured a cup of Kool-Aid for Terry.

"Yeah, almost three months off." Terry was excited.

"On vacation! That is worth celebrating." Luke raised his cup in a mock toast. "The black cherry Kool-Aid is perfect!"

"It's my favorite," Terry proclaimed, "and we made cupcakes with chocolate icing too."

"Wow, what a day!" Luke snapped a carrot with a toothy grin. "Hey, what about Danny boy, doesn't he want to join us?"

"He's sleeping right now. We planned for lunch to be a little later than normal. Danny usually goes down around 1:00 or 1:30. I opened his window a little, see?" Julia pointed in the direction of the second floor.

Luke peered through the thick canopy of leaves at the top of the oak tree standing guard at the back of the house. "I guess he'll let us know if he wakes up."

"Oh, he'll let us know, all right. He's got quite a set of lungs. I'd be surprised if you don't hear him in your apartment sometimes."

"Well, as a matter of fact..."

"That's what I thought. I'm sorry if he's ruining your evenings."

"Don't worry about that. I'm not doing anything special, reading mostly, things like that. Been a challenge for you, I bet?"

"I have to admit that little Danny's been harder to deal with than I remember Terry being." Julia patted Terry's head.

Terry responded, "I'm goin' to get the cupcakes, okay?"

"Yeah, but be careful carrying them out here."

"I will."

Luke offered his assistance. "You think I should give her a hand?"

"She'll be fine. She's really been helping out these days. I think it was the training you gave her the day her little brother was born."

"I don't remember."

"She does. You told her about how you helped out when you were a boy and you had a baby sister. She's trying to live up to your example."

"That shouldn't be hard to do." Luke chuckled.

"Don't laugh. It's serious business for her."

"And those cupcakes, they look like serious business to me, seriously good that is." Luke took a hand-off of the plate of cupcakes and placed it in the middle of the table.

He consumed one of the cupcakes in three bites and finished his cup of Kool-Aid. "Do you think I could have another cupcake, or are we saving some for Danny's daddy?"

"No. I mean, no we're not saving them. You can have another."

"Thanks. Where is Mr. Williams anyway? He usually doesn't miss a celebration, and I have to say that I've noticed him coming around pretty regularly. That's got to be a help, too."

"When he's here, he's really more of a head coach than a member of the team. And this weekend, I gave him some time off. He went to the mountains with the boys, a cabin outside Estes Park."

"Ah, his school's out celebration."

"Something like that. I'm sure they're drinking beer, and probably whiskey, and playing cards. He's barking orders by now or complaining about the way somebody's dealing."

"Yeah, life can be a hard thing for some of us."

"Only if you make it that way."

"I know I prefer a picnic."

"More words of wisdom from Little Luke." Julia laughed.

Terry was surprised. "Mom, that's what Mr. Williams calls him. To us he's just Luke."

"You're right. My apologies, Luke, I got carried away."

"That's okay. It is a celebration after all." Luke laughed too. "Drinks all around." He poured Kool-Aid into each cup.

The festivities ended when Danny sounded the alarm, at least for Julia. After several minutes lapsed, Luke convinced Terry that they should double-team the trash and the leftovers.

Terry sighed as she balanced the stack of plates and cups. "That brother of mine, he can be a little stinker. That's what mom says sometimes."

"A party pooper this time." Luke repeated the cliché.

"Yeah, a party pooper, that's a good one." Terry giggled.

Later that afternoon, Luke settled atop Elephant Rocks for a reading session. A northeasterly wind blew a wide swath of clouds across the valley. He held the pages of his book, *The Sun Also Rises*, at the edges where the breeze ruffled them. A frown creased his face as the storm billowed overhead.

The first drops of rain hit the sidewalk just ahead of his footfall on the pavement at the bottom of the dirt path. Luke increased his pace, but the fierce wind drove the raindrops at a speed that he could not outrun. He stuffed the book under his shirt and sprinted the last block with one arm pinned to his side and the other extended for balance.

He ducked his head to better survive the pounding. Luckily, he had slowed to a jog as he approached the driveway. He avoided a collision with Terry when he came to a jump-stop, his basketball shoes squealing as though he were on a hardwood court. Terry held an umbrella thrust at arm's length to shield herself from the wind-driven rain. The umbrella also prevented her from seeing any hazards that she might encounter.

Luke dipped and came face-to-face with her. "What are you doing?"

"I saw you leave a little while ago, and when it started to rain, mom said I could take the umbrella and go get you."

"Thanks. But the rain got me before you did." Luke steadied the umbrella with his hand on top of hers.

"Yeah, you're soaked!"

When they reached the top of the stairway to Luke's apartment, he released his hand from the umbrella. "I'll just jump down here. You take the umbrella and head inside. See you later."

"Thanks," he called, as he took two steps in every bounce.

It didn't take long for Luke to shed his wet clothes and hang them over the shower rod. He splashed warm water on his face and towel dried it and his rain-washed hair. He chose sweat pants and a shirt to relax and ride out the storm, but a knock came at the door.

When he opened it, Terry and her umbrella stood in the entry. She tilted her head to see Luke, and as she did, the rain dripped off the edge of the umbrella.

Only her mouth was visible to him. "Mom wants to know if..."

Her words stopped when she was halted by the umbrella hooking on the door jamb.

"Here let me have the umbrella. Go all the way inside." Luke held the umbrella high, and Terry slid under his arm.

He released the latch of the umbrella, shook some of the water off of it, and swung it inside.

After closing the door he propped the umbrella in the corner. "Now what were you saying?"

"I was saying that mom wants to know if you can help us out."

"I guess. What's going on?"

"We want to go shopping, and we want you to take care of Danny."

"Oh, do you think I'm ready for that?"

"He's sleeping now, so I guess."

"Yeah, as long as he's sleeping, but what if he wakes up?"

"Mom'll show you what to do."

"Then we've got nothing to worry about. I'll just put on some different clothes."

Terry giggled as Julia demonstrated diaper changing for Luke on one of her dolls.

Terry reminded both of them. "Danny's bigger than my doll, and he might be crying."

"That's all right. The quicker you get the diaper changed the quicker he'll stop crying." Julia undid the diaper, and gestured for Luke to give it a try.

"I don't know how quick I'll be." Luke cautioned his instructor and the young observer. "This will be my first time changing a diaper. Unless you count the time when I was a boy and the neighbor girl insisted that I be the one to put a diaper on her doll."

Terry slapped Luke's hand as she laughed. "Boys don't play with dolls."

But Julia offered another opinion, as she muffled her own laughter. "I think it's likely that more and more dads will be changing diapers. The times are changing."

"Yeah, but Luke's not a dad." Terry spoke with the self assurance of a soon-to-be fourth grader.

"He might be someday." Julia undid Luke's initial effort.

"Yeah, he's got a girlfriend. Remember, we met her. She's nice, and if she had a baby, Luke would already know how to change his diaper."

"That's right, and Danny won't mind being the one that Luke practices on." Julia patted Luke's back as he completed his second effort at diaper changing.

"Pretty good for a rookie." Julia elbowed Luke. "Now, let's get you some training on Danny's bottles, and you'll be set."

Before Julia and Terry left, Luke acquired permission to use Julia's washer and dryer. Julia provided the necessary orientation.

On their way out the door, Julia repeated her expression of gratitude. "Thanks for this. With the rain and all, I didn't want to take Danny out today."

"Hey, don't worry. I've got my book and my laundry, and some great baby coaching. Danny and I will be fine."

"Mom, come on. Let's go. I can't hold this umbrella all day."

"She has been doing a lot of umbrella duty today." Luke held the door as Julia exited. She assumed responsibility for the umbrella.

Luke tiptoed upstairs and into Danny's room to make sure he still slept. After a stop at the washing machine, he slumped on the sofa. He relaxed and mentally rehearsed the diaper changing and bottle warming routines.

Since the morning he had awakened in the warmth of Elizabeth's bed, nearly three weeks had rushed by. His daily experience became a competition with himself. He raced away from Elizabeth and his feelings of helplessness. Guilt and self-judgment ran with him.

On his way to the bookstore each morning, he sprinted along the sidewalks and jogged the park pathways. He increased his workload at the store. Each evening he reversed the morning exercise routine. He bettered his physical condition. His body gained strength and stamina, but his outward appearance belied the weakness hidden below the surface.

When he thought of Elizabeth, he doubted himself, uncertain what he could have done, what he could do now. He resigned himself to Boulder, pushed ahead by a determined will to do better. Surely he could change a diaper, feed a baby his bottle. He insisted he could at least go faster. When Danny cried, he raced up the stairs, his fastest yet.

———

Luke played with Danny atop a blanket on the floor in the front room. Danny lay on his back, Luke beside him. Luke suspended a stuffed bear above Danny's head. When Luke jiggled it, the bell tied around the bear's neck jingled. Whether responding to that sound or to the soft brush of the bear's fur when Luke rubbed the bear against his cheek, Danny was visibly delighted. Luke found joy, too.

When Julia and Terry returned, Terry joined the fun. Terry reported on their successful shopping trip. They purchased new summer clothes for her and an item for Danny.

Luke made a commitment to assemble Danny's gift. It was a mobile that was designed to be attached to his crib. Powered by a battery, four tiny animals, a giraffe, a monkey, a zebra and a tiger, would rotate above Danny's head.

In consideration of Luke's help for the afternoon, Julia prepared dinner for everyone. Afterwards, she orchestrated baths for both of her children, while Luke installed the mobile. Raindrops splashed against the window in Danny's room, as the storm had gathered intensity since the sun had set.

Luke recalled the claims of many of the long-time locals who maintained that this spring had been unusually wet. He finished the installation just as Julia entered Danny's room. She propped Danny over one shoulder and held a bottle in her hand.

Julia requested that Luke give Danny his bedtime bottle so that she could spend time with Terry, helping to calm her daughter after a first day of summer vacation and the excitement of picnicking, shopping, new clothes, and rainstorms.

Near the glow of the night light, Luke rocked Danny in the chair that had once been in Terry's room. The feeding satisfied Danny, and Luke took pleasure in having successfully handled this task for the second time in the same day. When Luke laid Danny in his crib, Danny whimpered. Luke switched on the mobile, and the melody of *Danny Boy* played softly as the animals revolved.

Luke hummed, and half-sung, his own version of the classic song.

Oh Danny boy, the mountain mist is falling
It's time to sleep and let your dreams take flight.
Tomorrow the sun will once again be shining.
And you'll feel the warmth of love so soft, so bright.

The tune continued playing as Luke backed toward the door. When he bumped into Julia, she guided him into the hallway.

At the top of the back stairway, she touched his sleeve. "Were you singing to Danny?"

The shadows hid the blush of his cheeks as they descended the stairs. "Kind of. I don't know the actual lyrics, but I heard that song when I installed the mobile and was testing everything. I've been thinking of some words since then. It was supposed to be a secret thing between Danny and me."

"Sorry, I didn't mean to spoil it. It was very beautiful."

"I wouldn't go that far. It was just a few lines."

Julia stopped Luke at the refrigerator. She offered him a bottle of beer, and when she took one for herself, he accepted. They sat across from each other at the kitchen table.

Julia tipped her bottle toward Luke. "Thanks for everything today and tonight."

"Don't mention it. I got two good meals and finished my laundry. Plus, it was the most fun I've had in a while."

Julia swallowed a long drink of her beer. "Luke, you're a strange man."

"Now I guess I should be the one that says thank you." Luke chuckled and then drank from his bottle.

Julia tapped her bottle with a fingertip, a syncopated rhythm. "Sorry, that's not what I meant. I mean you're a young, good-looking guy. And yet, you're singing lullabies to my baby boy and having picnics with my daughter and me. That's the part that's strange. Don't you want to go out? Be with your friends, have some fun?"

"Maybe next Saturday." An awkward grin marked his face, and he stuttered. "No...listen...my brothers are coming out for the Fourth of July weekend. We'll be partying for sure. I'm kind of saving up for then."

Julia stared intently at him. "I'm serious. I worry about you, as a friend."

"Hey, really, I'm okay." Luke swallowed half his beer. Nervousness gurgled in his stomach. He wanted to belch but wouldn't. The silence increased Luke's butterflies. Julia's next words stopped the rumbling.

She blurted. "Luke, Elizabeth called me this morning."

Luke bumped the table when his leg jerked inadvertently. Both beer bottles teetered, but he caught them before they fell.

Julia recoiled but then relaxed. "Elizabeth said she hasn't heard from you since you left St. Louis. She asked me not to tell you. She just wanted to be sure you made it back okay and that you were all right. So, I told her that you were working a lot. I hadn't seen much of you, but I thought you were all right. You are, aren't you? All right, I mean."

Luke drank the rest of his beer. "Maybe I better call her. It's not too late."

"No, you can't. I mean, she'll know I told you. You're my friend, more than she is, but I promised her I wouldn't tell you about our conversation, so please don't call. I don't want her to know I chose you over her, that I betrayed her trust. Us girls, we need to stick together. Who knows, maybe we can pull off a surprise party again sometime. But you, you should write to her, like you used to."

"Did she tell you she was hurting? She's been hurting for a while now. I'm part of that. I don't know what to say in a letter, how to make it better. It's like you said. All I do is work at the store, come home, sit and read. I've written some poems."

"Then send her some of your poems. You just composed something to sing to my baby. I bet you write good poetry."

"They're hard, hard-hearted. That song tonight, that's the only sweet thing I've done in a while."

"I don't believe that for a minute."

"You should. It's the truth. I'm not much fun to be with right now. That's probably why I'm better off just being with you and your family. I'm okay here, but all the rest, I can't seem to get a handle on it lately."

"Forget about all the rest of it. It should just be about you and her. Her coming out here, the two of you together, I could tell. I could see. It was the sweetest thing."

"I know it was the sweetest. I wrote some poetry about that, too. But I should've been there for her. It was not so long ago, but now I think it's too late. She was really hurting."

"I don't understand. Was she sick? Is it serious? She's a nurse. I'm sure she's gone to a doctor."

"Yeah, the doctor took care of her."

"Then, she's okay. I'm sure she's okay. She said she's going to write you a letter. I'm sure she's going to tell you she's doing fine. You should stop worrying about her. Her main concern is you."

"But I shouldn't be. That's what I'm saying."

"Then write to her and tell her. Or call her. I guess it'd be okay. I don't care about the other stuff. What you two have, it's more important. You don't necessarily get that forever. I know. And I know you should try again."

"You sound certain. I...I'm not so sure."

"Well, then, take my word for it. As a woman, as your friend, it's better if you keep trying. Just say you're not sure, not certain. Christ, nobody knows it all. Nobody can. But you can try. Damn, now I'm cursing. Damn, she's a thousand miles away. You've got to close that gap. You've got to try. Hell, send her some of the hard-hearted and the sweet-hearted things you've written. It's better if she knows it all."

"I wished I had known all of it before." Luke clenched his empty bottle with both hands.

"You do now."

"That's the truth." He released his hands from the bottle.

"Then say what's true for you. You said before that you thought it was too late. It's not, not when you tell her the truth."

The truth came to Luke in the form of Elizabeth's letter. Julia or Terry had slid it under his door, as had been the routine procedure, and he found it at the end of the workday. He placed the letter inside his book and carried it that way to Elephant Rocks.

Rainstorms had passed through Boulder valley intermittently for four days. The wet weather became the mainstay of conversation at the book store. Most expressed disbelief and frustration, while a few focused on the benefits of greener lawns and blue skies washed clean.

On this day, the rain had finally stopped, and Luke squinted as the sunlight bounced off the pages of Elizabeth's letter. In the pure light of the rain-sweetened day, her words reflected her feelings, her once broken heart, now opened wide.

She related her decision to move to New York, the borough of Queens more specifically. She would become a nurse in the clinic that had performed her abortion. Her perspective as a one-time patient would lend a unique sensitivity to the care she administered.

The director of the clinic had made arrangements to provide her a place to live, a furnished apartment, an easy subway ride from the clinic. Elizabeth made a commitment to work through the summer months, a way to give back. She asked for wages enough to cover the cost of rent and food. It would be a mission, something she felt she had to do. She remembered how he had spoken similar words before he left for Boulder.

She would depart St. Louis on Monday of the following week. She acknowledged that her move would separate them by a wider distance, would take her in the opposite direction. She held steadfast to the certainty that she would return to St. Louis and wondered whether he would someday too. She closed with the words *I love you now, more than ever*.

The content of her letter shocked him, but he still trusted her. He blessed her with the light of the Colorado blue sky.

He replied with a letter of his own, a deluge of words flooding the page, his feelings, and his truth falling there too. He revealed that he had applied to CU. He speculated about the number of credits that would transfer from Oakwood and his prospects for financial aid.

He folded the pages precisely, including some of his recent poems, addressed and stamped the envelope. Early the next morning he ran to the post office, and before he entrusted the letter to the mail slot marked out-of-town, he raised his eyes to another blue sky.

Luke's letter reached Elizabeth on the morning that she was packing for her trip to New York. She tucked the letter inside one of her suitcases with a promise to read it after her arrival. She knew Luke's letters. She was certain of his feelings for her. Their hearts were bound together. Many times he said it, wrote it in letters, and expressed it in the imagery of a poem. She felt it, sensed it in her bones and knew it in her heart. She would carry those feelings with her. They would fly with her to another part of the country.

———— • ————

Elizabeth used more than half of the cash she brought with her for the two taxi fares that completed her travels, one from the airport to the clinic, and the other from the clinic to the apartment where she would be living. A hard rain fell during the ride from the clinic.

The taxi driver commented that the rain was unusually heavy, but he thought the storm would pass sometime during the night. He held an umbrella for Elizabeth as she carried her suitcases and descended the concrete stairs to the garden level apartment. A water puddle had formed on the landing at the bottom of the stairs.

Elizabeth tiptoed to the door and found the key on the top of the door frame, just as she had been told. Once she found a light switch and stepped inside, the driver followed her with the suitcases in hand. She gave him an extra tip for his assistance.

Before Elizabeth closed the door to her new place, a mature female voice shouted from the sidewalk above. Beneath the shelter of an umbrella, Mrs. Sanders, the building manager, welcomed her.

Her words poured down the stairway amidst the swelling rain. "Mary called and said you were on the way. Ms. Hoffman has covered the first month's rent. We can talk more after you get settled. I'm on the first floor, right above you."

Elizabeth shouted from her station just inside the door. "Yes, ma'am."

"Anytime in the next day or so, except not too late. You girls work such long hours. I don't know if they told you or not."

"No, ma'am. But I'm used to it."

"I hope so. Anyway welcome to the city. Don't know about this rain, it's kind of unusual. I think it'll blow over. Watch out for some water on that landing there."

"Thank you. Yes, the driver thought the drain might be clogged."

"Those taxi drivers, they tend to have opinions about a lot of things. My experience is that they're not necessarily valid ones."

"No, I suppose not, but he did think that this rain would end later tonight."

"Hope he's right about that at least. Anyway, tomorrow's another day."

"Yes, ma'am. Good night."

Elizabeth chose one of two stuffed chairs beside a circular table adorned with a white crocheted covering. Light from the table lamp was helped by the fuzzy glow from a street lamp that penetrated the small front window of the apartment. Together they illuminated the pages of Luke's letter, and she paused before she read to wonder what he would think of her newest place.

She pulled her bare feet under her and nestled into the chair. She read with only momentary distractions, as cars driving by crashed waves of rain water against the curb and onto the sidewalk. The sounds came at irregular intervals, but the words rushed onward in a steady rhythm. She absorbed it all, the letter, the poems, and the hard rain. She sensed the beating of his heart and an image of him walking the CU campus.

Finally, she stood arched her back to loosen her muscles. Rain smeared the window pane. A bubbling sound came through the glass, like water gurgling in a fountain. She followed the sound to the front door, and when she came within one stride of the entrance, the carpet squished under her feet. She dammed the water that oozed under the door with one bath towel and used another to absorb what water she could from the carpet.

She knelt in the same chair where she had been sitting. She held firmly to the back and stretched to relieve the tension that lingered in her body. She leaned close to the window pane.

Although the glass protected her, her eyes blinked rapidly at the onrushing raindrops. She remembered the rain that Luke had described in his letter and questioned the storm she witnessed. Was it the same rain that had fallen on Boulder, days before? Had it flown with her to the city?

Tears moistened her eye lashes. She smudged mascara with the back of her hand, but she could not restrain the feelings that emerged, the love that had certainly traveled with her. The New York City rain poured throughout that first night.

Chapter 32

New York City, July 1972

After four weeks in New York, Elizabeth's day assumed a city routine. She commuted to and from the clinic via the subway. Particularly in the mornings, crowded station platforms surged with waves of people. She was captivated by the many shades of skin color, the wide-range of clothing styles, the differences in mannerisms, and in speaking accents, even the languages themselves. She rarely interacted with her fellow commuters, but she engaged with their collective energy.

The mechanical aspect of traveling underground at high rates of speed overwhelmed the positive nature of her daily experience with the people. Especially during her earliest days in the city, she fought against an invisible threat. It hid in the darkest portions of the tunnels and shrieked to life when the subway horns blasted the stations as they flew past. She cowered at times, her eyes lowered, holding tight to the nearest handle.

She often rushed toward the daylight that welcomed her to the street level. She ignored the multi-directional jostling of arms and hips. In fact, it lifted her spirits as she hustled to keep pace with the throngs that inhabited the sidewalks.

She wore her purse like a bandolier, the long strap cutting across the front of her uniform. The pouch usually contained a sandwich, sealed within cellophane wrapping, potato chips stashed in the same manner, her wallet, sometimes a book, many times one or two of Luke's recent letters. She fingered the zipper to make sure it was secure.

Her hair bounced just above the tops of her shoulders. Her blue eyes steeled straight-ahead and clear, her disposition cheerful, she left the threats she had been feeling buried underground.

She successfully wove around the one corner that led to the clinic and half-expected to bump into someone whom she would recognize. She proceeded undeterred through the clinic door and found inspiration in the work that she had chosen. She lived as she had intended, even though she could not anticipate what each day would bring.

Ten hours per day, six days per week, and on-call every other Sunday, her new life was a work life. She accepted each case just as she had been accepted, without judgment, without reservation. She calmed and comforted the patients, remained objective while they made a decision. If they chose to proceed, she invested the best of her nursing skills to care for them. In a few special instances, she shared her personal story.

Sharon, a fellow nurse, and Mary, the clinic's receptionist, became Elizabeth's friends. Their relationships were defined by their interaction within the confines of the clinic. Sharon's and Mary's early twenties age and single status were characteristics similar to Elizabeth's, but they had little else in common. Sharon was a black woman from Hoboken, and Mary a woman of Italian heritage from Brooklyn. Outside of the clinic, their paths did not intersect.

Elizabeth made her way home each evening, weary, almost robotic. Her meals were unimaginative and unhurried. She tuned the radio to a station that blended rock 'n roll and jazz, songs like those played over the St. Louis airwaves and inside the walls of The Sweet Spot. Before she slept, she composed letters, most often addressed to Luke, but sometimes to her parents or to Debbie.

The lone window in her bedroom faced the alley. Two buildings, each several stories taller than hers, covered the skyline in that direction. She awoke to an alarm each day because the morning sunlight could not penetrate the narrow opening provided to her apartment.

———

The Sunday after the Fourth of July, Elizabeth encountered a fellow tenant of her apartment building at the corner market. Mrs. Sanders had introduced Marilyn to Elizabeth. Marilyn worked for a brokerage firm in Manhattan. Elizabeth amused Marilyn with a story of a young, homeless man who had approached her each day on her way to the clinic.

During the previous week, this young man had asked Elizabeth for directions on four consecutive mornings, even though she had admitted during their first meeting that she was new to the city. Elizabeth assumed he was a war veteran because he wore a military coat. Elizabeth called him *Army*, borrowing a nickname from a story Luke had related in one of his letters.

Marilyn invited Elizabeth to accompany her on an excursion into the heart of New York City the following Sunday. After she checked the schedule at the clinic, Elizabeth consented. Marilyn and she shared details of their backgrounds during the subway ride.

Marilyn was born and raised in New Haven, Connecticut. She attended Columbia University and graduated with a major in mathematics. She confessed that the position she landed with a stock brokerage resulted more from her family's connections with the vice-president of the firm than from her academic achievements.

After ten years in the business, though, she had proven her worth to the company. With a recent promotion and raise, she might even be able to afford an apartment in Manhattan. She postulated that she would then cheerfully give her third floor apartment to Elizabeth. Elizabeth assured Marilyn that she was happy to maintain her place in the garden level, since she would only be in New York for a limited time.

Marilyn cautioned Elizabeth regarding that commitment. "You haven't really experienced the city yet. Stay much longer and you might stay forever."

Elizabeth nudged Marilyn. "You mean I shouldn't consider *Army* the highlight of my time here?"

They shared a laugh that carried them out of Grand Central Station. Marilyn insisted on treating Elizabeth to a cab ride to Wall Street. She pointed to a row of windows on the twelfth floor of a twenty story building where her firm's offices were located. She admitted she had not yet earned a windowed office of her own.

Marilyn then guided Elizabeth to a park where they had a view of the Statue of Liberty. "We'll save the ferry ride and climb to the top of Lady Liberty for another day. I'm telling you there's a lot to see and do here."

Marilyn was a browned-eyed brunette who stood a few inches taller than Elizabeth. She wore a trendy, strapless dress and moved with confidence along the streets of the city. Her fashion sandals and pedicure provided stylish appointments.

Elizabeth had been comfortable when their outing began. The sun dress and loafers she had chosen to wear were the newest additions to her summer wardrobe. As she strolled next to Marilyn on Broadway, and then Times Square, she realized how Midwestern she looked. Her feelings of inadequacy eased when they stopped for lunch at a sidewalk café.

The self-deprecating way she elicited help from the waiter to make a selection from the menu contained a flirtatious element. The cute waiter responded with overly attentive service and directed his friendly smiles at Elizabeth, even though it was clear that Marilyn would be paying the bill.

Marilyn signaled for a taxi and spoke without looking at Elizabeth. "You better be careful not to act too familiar with these big-city men."

Elizabeth slid past Marilyn into the cab. "You're the second friend who's given me that advice."

"Apparently, you haven't been listening." Marilyn directed the driver to Central Park and a knowing grin toward Elizabeth.

Central Park dwarfed Forest Park. The lagoons and the fountains, all aspects of the park were connected by wide pathways. When the heat of the day caught them, they took a seat on a bench in the shade of several magnificent oaks. Elizabeth insisted on purchasing ice cream cones from one of the many cart vendors.

Hundreds of people occupied an open section of the park. They rallied around a stage where a speaker led them in chants protesting the Vietnam War. At the fringe of the crowd a band of guitar players and singers performed *Blowin' in the Wind.* A girl in patched jeans and a tie-died t-shirt distributed buttons that read *McGovern for President.*

As Marilyn and Elizabeth made their escape from the crowd, an older man, grungy, rumpled, and wild-eyed, pressed a piece of newsprint into Elizabeth's hand. Marilyn gave him her McGovern button.

He pointed to the paper and blurted out. "This proves that Nixon is a Tricky Dick."

After the long subway ride and the last few blocks that led to their apartment building, Elizabeth hugged Marilyn and offered to return her kindness with a tour of St. Louis if she ever traveled there.

"That's a possibility," Marilyn replied. "Our firm has made some big investments in McDonald Douglass."

Once inside her apartment, Elizabeth retreated to the bathtub. She soaked her body until the intensity of the sights and sounds of the day faded in the steam of the hot water. She soothed the heat of her sun burnt cheeks with Noxema cream.

She propped the pillows against the flimsy headboard of her bed and read the newspaper clipping the old man had given to her earlier. The brief article told the story of a burglary at a place called Watergate. She re-read it but did not find any mention of President Nixon.

She wrote the first paragraphs of her letter to Luke with questions about his knowledge of the burglary at Watergate and his attention to the war in Vietnam. She remembered that Julia's husband had died in the war. Did he know that over 50,000 others had lost their lives?

She blocked the sense of despair that dampened the joys of the day, just as the setting sun diminished the light at her window. She switched on a bedside lamp but struggled with the troubling notion that she had not given more than a few minutes of consideration to a war that had been raging for several years. Is it right that this war should dominate the actions and reactions of so many? What is fair about the injuries and deaths that had been the grotesque wages of the war?

———

When Elizabeth awoke on Monday morning ahead of her alarm, she used the extra time to finish her letter. She described the excitement of the previous day's excursion into the city. The expansive beauty of Central Park nearly overwhelmed her, and then made her feel most at-home. She related her friend's offer to lead future Sunday outings. She closed with the surety that there were not enough Sundays left in the summer to experience everything and the certainty of her desire to see him again.

In the first floor hallway of the apartment building, she dropped her letter in the outbound slot and found Luke's letter in her mail box. She reflected on the previous Saturday's difficult workload and realized she had forgotten to check for mail.

During her lunch break, Elizabeth relished reading Luke's letter. His recollections of the first 36 hours of his brothers' visit read like a tale from an outdoor adventure magazine.

His brothers, including his older brother Matt, had traveled from St. Louis through the night and reached Luke's apartment in the early morning. By mid-afternoon they were hiking beyond the waterfall that Luke had shown her. They camped in a cave and passed around a bottle of whiskey along with stories of college sports, rock 'n roll concerts and even some of Matt's Air Force experiences. All the while, a powerful rainstorm swept through the canyon.

Luke had made all the appropriate preparations for their one night backpacking trip. The food, water, other libations, fire starter, sleeping bags, supplies and equipment were assembled and divided among the four backpacks. Luke led the group on the trail and supervised the establishment of the campsite. What he had not anticipated was the intensity of the storm that still scoured the canyon when he and his brothers awoke the next morning.

The creek had overflowed its banks in places and flooded the trail. At one point the high water blocked their descent. Amidst the second-guessing and the name-calling, Luke struggled to maintain his calm. He chose a course that required them to blaze a new path through rain-drenched brush and soggy, knee-high grasses.

When he mandated that they scale a snow chute made of shale rock and loose boulders, knees were skinned and curses abounded. But, as a result of their struggle, they gained a vantage point where the trail's end and the canyon road were visible even in the lingering mist. The grumbling ceased, and they consumed a sleeve of Oreos and a canteen of water before wending their way back to the car and then into town.

Remembrances of the balance of his brothers' visit were clouded, not by a rainstorm, but by the ever-flowing rounds of beer and concoctions of various alcoholic distillations. Johnny insisted on the wildest drink available as a celebration of his inaugural mountain adventure.

Luke claimed every element of the experience: the tension, the excitement, the times of struggle, the festive times, the fearless connection between brothers, the peaceful nature of their good-bye. He attached a short verse on a separate page.

No one forgets
Stars born as truest light
Stars falling through the night
None shall compare

At the last, Elizabeth eyes moistened. She folded the pages and gently slid them into her purse. That night she re-read the letter and placed the verse under a candle on the bathroom vanity. The words, the candlelight, and steamy waters of her bath formed a vaporous alchemy that seeped into her forlorn spirit.

Chapter 33

Boulder, early August 1972

Terry quickly ate her dinner, anxious to re-convene with her neighborhood friends. As she exited, Julia reminded her to come home when the street lights came on. Luke served himself another slice of beef and a spoonful of potatoes.

Julia cleared the other dishes. "I couldn't help but notice that you've been getting mail pretty regularly the last few weeks."

"Yeah, Elizabeth's in New York now. She's probably feeling like I did last year here in Boulder. When you're in a new place and there's not a whole lot going on, you have lots of time to write. She's been to Central Park with a friend recently. That made an impression on her."

"I bet that would." Julia diverted to Danny's play pen.

She had placed it in the center of the kitchen, a spot where everyone could see Danny, but where he would not be in the line of traffic between the stove, the table and the sink. She wound the mobile toy that hung from the top rail and then wiped a drop of drool from her baby's chin.

"There were protest rallies against the war." Luke mumbled, still chewing his food.

"How's that?"

Luke swallowed the last bite. "There have been protests in the park, against the Vietnam War. She and her friend hung around for a while. A band played Bob Dylan's *Blowin' in the Wind* and some other songs. She got a McGovern button."

"Who's that?" Julia made another trip to the sink.

"You don't know?"

"No, should I?"

"He's a Democrat, trying to get the nomination. I might consider him. I get to vote this year for the first time. There's not much that Nixon is doing that I like."

"It doesn't matter," Julia said with certainty.

"What?" Luke stacked his plate on the counter atop the others.

Julia cranked the hot water faucet to its highest level. Bubbles of dish soap billowed, and she swished a dishcloth to disperse them.

She plopped a handful of flatware in the water. "Democrat or Republican, it doesn't matter."

She scrubbed the first plate vigorously, rinsed it and placed in the drainer. "Didn't the war start under Johnson or Kennedy? Nixon's just carrying it on. Seems that's all we know how to do is make war. We've got all these reasons why we need to be fighting, all these weapons and ways to kill people. And for what, what are we proving? How tough we are? How we get our way no matter what? Well, it's not my way. Not any more, not when they kill my husband, my daughter's father, my best friend, and his friends, other people we know, and all the people we'll never know."

Julia wrung the wet cloth, like she was strangling it. She mopped a pool of water from the counter. "Democrats and Republicans, they're all dying over there. And the President, and all his people and all the people that want to be President, they're not doing anything. So they can just get screwed!"

The clang of wet flatware against the bottom of the draining rack emphasized her point. Luke shuffled toward Danny's play pen, unsure of what position to take regarding Julia's statements.

"Who can get screwed? Honey, you usually don't talk that way." Clay swung the screen door open.

Frank and Sally were close behind.

Julia pivoted and her eyes swept the room, an angry glare for everyone. "It's the damn war and the goddamn politicians. They're a bunch of assholes. Four years ago, four years today, my Jim died in that damn war. And it's still going on! And for what? For the damn politicians, that's what. It's screwed up, totally screwed up."

On the strength of her words and the passion in her voice, Clay and his entourage froze in their tracks. Luke stared at Julia, incredulous. Julia's cheeks flushed, and Danny whimpered, the only audible response. Julia swept Danny into her arms and pressed his cheek to hers.

She gently whispered, "Don't worry, Mommy's going to hold onto you."

By then Clay had thawed and rushed to Julia's side.

Honest concern registered in his voice. "You all right?"

An instant later, Clay whirled toward Luke. "Damn, man, why're you gettin' her all riled up? Don't you know anything?"

"I didn't know. I had no idea. I...I'm sorry, Julia."

Luke ignored Clay's verbal assault, but he released the hand that had been gripping the top rail of the play pen. Instinctively he prepared to defend himself.

Clay's aggressive nature compelled him. "You're damn right, you're sorry. You're a sorry excuse for a...for a..."

Julia shifted Danny to her shoulder and bumped Clay. Clay shuffled away from her. The others recoiled too.

The power in Julia's voice hushed everyone, especially Clay. "You two stop it, just stop it! Clay, you don't know any more than he does."

Danny cried at the harshness of his mother's voice, and Julia used a circular massage on his back to comfort him. Danny stopped crying when she opened the refrigerator door. The coolness hit Danny's and Julia's cheeks.

She motioned to Luke and pointed into the refrigerator. "His bottles are on the top shelf. You can give him one now and another before you put him to bed."

She closed the refrigerator door. Frank, still speechless, pushed open the screen door. Sally moved along side of Frank, and Clay stepped in the direction of the exit as well.

Julia touched Luke's arm. "He'll probably stay up till after dark. Make sure to change him before you put him down. I left a little shirt for him, hanging over the rail of his crib. Just put that on him for tonight. You know how the TV works, and Terry can stay up for a while after she gets home, but no later than 10:00. She thinks she's a big girl, but she doesn't get her way at bed time."

"Okay, I understand."

"I know you do," she said as she passed Danny to him.

Danny buried his face in Luke's shoulder. Luke rested his cheek against Danny's peach-fuzz hair. Julia kissed her baby and exhaled any remaining anger.

She smiled when her eyes met Luke's. "It's okay. Thanks."

Luke blushed but deflected the attention, when he ushered her toward the door.

He chuckled as he employed a parental tone. "You kids be good tonight and don't stay out too late. Julia, don't worry, I've got this covered."

Frank finally spoke. "Luke, you never cease to amaze."

Luke didn't acknowledge Frank's comment but winked at Sally instead. "I like that new blouse of yours."

"Thanks, I figured there's no point in waiting on the Broker Restaurant. The Hideout may be the best I can do."

"They won't know what hit them!" Luke exclaimed and then turned to Frank. "I'm a little disappointed in you, man. I thought you knew how to treat a lady."

Frank hung his head and stammered. "I just couldn't get my act together. I didn't know. I wasn't too sure that..."

Clay couldn't stand the groveling. "Fat Man, you're pathetic."

Julia gripped Clay's arm and steered the foursome down the porch steps. "Clay, that's enough, or this night's over before it's begun."

"Okay, okay, let's go already."

By 10:15, Terry and Danny slept soundly. The only noise in the entire house emanated from the TV, a news report on Vietnam. Luke couldn't accept any more information about the war and made a deliberate move to silence the TV. Unconsciously, he turned the knob the wrong way, and the audio blared for an instant before he whipped the knob the opposite way to the off position. He listened warily for any indication that his error had stirred those above him. When no sign came, he retreated to the sofa.

He sat there with his eyes closed, reflecting on the day. It had evolved much like a normal Saturday, half day at the store and a long hike to decompress from the week's work, but late in the afternoon an unusual request came from Julia.

She asked that he babysit for Danny and Terry while she went out with Clay and friends. Her last-minute request had been necessitated because she had forgotten about their date until Clay's phone call to verify the agreed-upon timing.

She elaborated by describing Clay's repeated pleas for a night-out, and his insistence that Danny would be okay with a baby sitter. She made allusion to very personal reasons for having blocked the arrangements from her memory, especially for this particular day, but she did not provide any specifics.

Since she hadn't made any calls in advance, none of her regular baby sitters were available. She promised a dinner of pot roast, potatoes and carrots that she had originally planned for Sunday. That offer produced a positive response from Luke.

Julia had prepared a tasty meal, and Luke had been generous with his praise. The apron she wore did not detract from her stylish wardrobe, and he complimented her. Her hair appeared a shade more ashen, and when he mentioned that, she assigned it to her pregnancy. Luke joked that he would be on the look-out for other changes, but Julia didn't join his laughter. Throughout the time they spent together, Julia maintained an uneasy distance. She seemed distracted, and their usual, friendly interaction became his one-sided monologue.

Luke tiptoed upstairs to make sure Terry and Danny still slept. Peeking inside each room, the soft glow of the night lights illuminated their calm breathing. When he passed the door to Julia's room, a compelling sense of her earlier agitation hit him.

He re-lived the scene in the kitchen and her rant against the sanity of the Vietnam War, any war. Her instinctive urge to hold Danny close, a protective, nurturing embrace, stirred a feeling of failure in Luke. He doubted his capacity to do the same.

At his place on the sofa, he strived for vigilance but soon nodded to sleep. He dreamed that his body somehow shielded Elizabeth's. She lay under him in a field of long, mountain grasses, while raptors of prehistoric, dinosaur proportion circled overhead.

When the predator shadows disappeared, they separated. In the exuberant relief of the moment, they leapt in celebration and then tumbled in a ball to the foot of the hillside. When night fell and the stars exploded across the heavens, they paired in symmetry and formed a constellation commemorating their time, for all time.

She uttered his name, "Luke," and again, "Luke."

He replied as though she had questioned him. "I understand."

She spoke softly, "I know you do."

As she repeated his name, she gently patted his shoulder and spoke a reassuring command. "Luke, wake up. It's okay."

When Luke blinked, Julia stood in front of him.

"You were really dreaming." She smiled and gave him another friendly pat.

He rubbed his eyes, the palm of his hands covering much of his face, and he mumbled an apology.

Julia acknowledged his weariness. "Don't worry. Taking care of the kids will wear you out. Believe me, I understand."

He stood as he stated his intention. "I'll head downstairs."

Julia walked with him toward the kitchen door. "Good night."

"Oh, yeah, did you have a good night, a good time?"

"Yes, we had fun. Such a weird thing happened at the end though. The band played *Blowin' in the Wind*, and we all sang the refrain. Everybody but Clay, I think he was hoping for some more rock 'n roll. But I liked it. It was Jim's favorite Dylan, made me cry. Maybe that's why Clay didn't like it. He's such an oaf, just doesn't understand."

"I understand."

"I know you do. Good night."

Chapter 34

New York City, mid-August 1972

Near the curb of the crowded sidewalk, Mitch peeked around the base of a street lamp that provided him a partial hiding place. Elizabeth's head bobbed along at the surface of the fast-moving stream of humanity. Her hair may have been shorter or styled differently than Mitch remembered, but he recognized her instantly.

An aura of cheerfulness and the azure light that emanated from her eyes were a beacon of brightness within the somber surge of the multitudes heading to work on a Monday morning. The sun's rays had not yet cleared the tallest of the surrounding buildings, but the temperature had risen as though it were high noon.

Mitch tossed his half-full cup of coffee into a trash container and slipped into the throng of people behind Elizabeth. From there, he swooped in and grabbed her around the shoulders. She screamed at the surprise assault, and the mob parted for a moment. In the open space, he spun her as though they were performing a dance move.

Dizzy with confusion, fearful and surprised, she shouted. "Mitch!"

He lifted her in his arms and kissed her passionately. The crowds rushed by, as though such scenes played routinely on the sidewalks of New York.

"Come with me!" Mitch grasped Elizabeth's hand.

He guided her to the edges of the crowd and hunched over her at the side of a building. A stunned look clouded Elizabeth's face. The constant push of the crowd swarmed around them.

Mitch wiped perspiration from his forehead. "I couldn't stop thinking about you. It's been more than two months, so I just had to come and see you. Don't be mad."

He hugged her as though he could squeeze a response from her. When they separated, her smile graced Mitch like a cool breeze.

She kissed his cheek. "I'm not mad. Shocked, but not mad. What are you doing here?"

"I told you. I came to see you."

"Yes, but I have to go...to go to work."

"I have some things to do in the City today, so I'll come back when you get off."

"That's usually 6:00, but sometimes I have to stay later."

"I know. Debbie told me that you've been working hard. It's okay. I'll wait for however long it takes. We need to celebrate."

"Celebrate what?"

"I'll tell you later." Mitch kissed her and pointed her in the direction of the clinic.

He disappeared into the crowd. The momentum of the masses propelled Elizabeth forward. A few minutes later, she was immersed in the care of the first patient of the day.

———

At dinner that first night, Mitch told her how he had traveled from St. Louis to his family's home in New Jersey. He shared his decision to resign his position at the hospital in St. Louis. He had accepted an assignment to locate in Window Rock, Arizona, where he would be the only doctor in a clinic that provided health care to the community. He described the Navajo Indians as one of the poorest tribes in the country, and he viewed this opportunity as an initial step along a new path for his career as a doctor.

He wanted her to celebrate his choice, and she delighted in the pasta they had for dinner, the wine and the soft music. He stole kisses from her throughout the night, and finally at the steps leading to her apartment. She fell asleep as wistful visions of rocks shaped into windows floated toward a mysterious future.

On the second night, they consumed savory dishes in an Asian restaurant and sipped potent liqueurs with names she did not recognize. As exotic music played in the background, Mitch asked her to come with him to Window Rock. The idea of an adventure bewitched her, and as he spoke about it, a dream of traveling to faraway places stimulated them. Eventually, they fell in a feverous passion onto the bed in her apartment.

The third night rocked at an American style grill. The band played in a penthouse club, and the view of the city inspired them. They danced and imbibed sophisticated drinks made with high-priced vodkas and rums. When the band took a break, he pleaded with her to make the journey with him, help him to make his dream come true. After all, the clinic needed nurses too.

She did not answer him, only tugged him onto the dance floor, where a steady drumbeat signaled the beginning of the next set of songs. At the end of the midnight set, Mitch and Elizabeth left the penthouse for her garden level apartment. They succumbed to a joyous riot, and waves of longing threatened to drown them until sleep became their life boat.

Mitch drove her to the clinic the next morning. Unshaven and pensive, he passed her a note when he said good-bye. The note listed his family's phone number with the lines, *Call me when you know what you have decided. I want you to come with me. I love you.*

Elizabeth awakened, tired to the bone. The glow of light from her bedside alarm clock assured her of the early morning hour, although the absence of cool air contradicted it. Perspiration matted her hair at the temples, and an ache arched across her forehead.

She remembered Mitch's note. He had used a piece of her stationary paper to scrawl his words. That paper rested now, side by side with Luke's verse on the bathroom vanity. A candle had illuminated both while she bathed, but the candle light and the relaxing bath had revealed no answers for her.

After her bath, sleep had quickly enveloped her. She had expected to awaken refreshed. Instead a middle-of-the-night dream had tossed her on her side and stirred her to half consciousness. She rolled onto her back and massaged her head with the thumb and ring finger of her right hand.

With a grunt, she lifted herself from the bed. Her shoulder brushed the wall on her way to the kitchen. She sipped water from a glass and stabilized herself with one hand gripping the sink.

Seated in one of the chairs in the front room, a dusty film on the window filtered the light from the street lamps. The screen sifted a hint of breeze that cooled her. She hid in the shadows and struggled with the fatigue of guilt and doubt. Questions wrestled with her until she surrendered.

She dozed in the chair, and nearly fell to the floor, when the high whirr of a street sweeper awakened her. She had resolved nothing, except her headache had disappeared. Earlier than usual, she prepared to leave for work. Surprised to see Elizabeth, Marilyn greeted her with a cheery good morning while Elizabeth removed one envelope from her mail box.

Elizabeth encountered smaller crowds on her normal route to the clinic. She opened Luke's letter and read about how Julia had reacted to his comment about the war protests in Central Park. Like Julia, she did not see any way to stop the pain that had been inflicted on so many by the war in Vietnam, but throughout that day at the clinic, she resolved to help where she could.

That night in her apartment, Elizabeth ate her dinner while sitting in one of the chairs near the front window. On the table next to her was a stack of papers, Luke's letters and poems, and Mitch's note. The leftover Asian food had lost its flavor when she re-heated it in the oven, and she scraped most the contents of her plate into the trash.

The churning in her stomach increased when she gulped a glass of water. The unappetizing food sloshed amidst the hard choices that she had not fully digested. Luke and Mitch, New York and St. Louis, Debbie and her family, Boulder and Window Rock, the people and places tumbling inside of her.

She didn't know how to decide, but she wrote a letter to Luke anyway. Her words spilled onto the stationary and told of a doctor she had met and how this doctor had planned to open a clinic in Window Rock, Arizona, and that he had asked her to move there with him to serve as his assistant.

She alluded to the fact that the poor Indian tribes of that region were in desperate need of professional health care. She compared their situation to that of the patients she had been helping at the New York clinic. There was so much suffering in the world, and the only certainty that she expressed was her desire to help wherever she could. She wanted Luke to understand, but in the last sentence she admitted. *I don't know how all this will end.*

She telephoned Mitch from Marilyn's apartment and told him she would go with him, at least as far as St. Louis. She would give a week's notice to the clinic, and if he could wait until then to leave, she would travel with him. Just as she had related in her letter to Luke, she wanted Mitch to accept the fact that she was unsure where their travels would end.

Mitch eagerly agreed to those terms. The next day Elizabeth notified the clinic director of her decision. That night she informed Mrs. Sanders. She gave herself completely to her work during that final week at the clinic. She re-wrote her letter to Luke nearly every night, but each revision ended with a similar uncertain conclusion. On Friday morning she placed it in the outbound mail slot at the apartment building and reminded Mrs. Sanders to forward any mail to her St. Louis address.

That evening she hugged Sharon and Mary on the sidewalk outside the clinic. After their farewell, she rode the subway for the last time. Mitch waited at her apartment. On Saturday morning, she rode the New Jersey turnpike with Mitch in the driver's seat. Elizabeth shifted to glance through the back window. New York had disappeared from view, and her time there had ended.

<hr />

The sun set behind the rolling hills of Missouri as Mitch exited Highway 40. Within a few minutes, he was parking his van in the driveway of Elizabeth's Clayton home. Debbie ran to meet them. Elizabeth's call earlier that afternoon had surprised Debbie, especially the part about Mitch and a possible move to a place called Window Rock, but she welcomed her roommate home with a burst of enthusiasm.

Elizabeth commented favorably about the condition of the lawn and how the pots of geraniums flanking the porch added a colorful touch. She did not remember the screen door at the entrance, and Debbie confirmed that it was a new addition.

The long afternoon traveling west and fighting the glare of the sun through the van's windshield had reddened Elizabeth's eyes, but the familiar sight of home eased the strain. The slices of cheese, the crackers, and sliced apples arranged on two plates, along with a plastic pitcher of ice water and two glasses, all bespoke of a pleasant welcome.

Mitch placed Elizabeth's suitcases in her room, while she refreshed herself in the bathroom. Once she had finished, he used the conveniences too, and then found the two girls in the kitchen. Debbie plugged in a box fan and ushered everyone into the front room. She positioned the fan in the open, kitchen doorway.

As she switched the fan to its highest setting, she conveyed some information to Mitch. "I talked to Andy, and he's looking forward to getting together with you. He called not too long ago wondering if you had arrived yet. I'm sure you remember how to get to his house. You two probably have a lot to talk about. I know Elizabeth and I do."

Mitch held no preconceived idea of how the meeting with Debbie would unfold. He had overheard the strained tone of Elizabeth's end of the phone conversation, when she called Debbie from a crowded truck stop in Columbus, Ohio.

He accepted Debbie's plan but wanted Elizabeth's reassurance. "What do you say? Should I head over to Andy's and let you two talk?"

Elizabeth did not resist the idea. "That sounds good. I'll call you later."

She hugged Mitch and kissed his cheek. "Thanks for getting us home safely."

"Nice van," Debbie said as the screen door closed.

Elizabeth had already partaken of some crackers and cheese and poured herself a glass of water. After a long drink, she snatched a few apple slices and relaxed into the cushions of the sofa.

Elizabeth crunched an apple. "My New York apartment wasn't as comfortable."

"What'd you expect? It wasn't home."

"You're right about that."

"But you made some new friends, and went to some neat places."

"You're right about that too, but the work at the clinic was the best part. The girls, the women who came into the clinic, they needed our help. I know I did when we went. I think I helped some of them. I really do."

"I'm sure you did."

Elizabeth filled her glass and poured one for Debbie too. "I like the things you've done to the place."

"Our place," Debbie spoke quickly. "It's your home, too.

"Yes, but I'd still be in New York, except that Mitch came. And he...and things changed."

"I've been wondering about him, even before you called today. I heard he had left the hospital. Then, when Andy told me he was going home, I figured he would try to see you."

"He came to the clinic one Monday morning. That was only two weeks ago. Things have happened pretty fast."

"That's what I was thinking too. Don't you think we ought to slow things down a little?"

"I don't know. Maybe, but maybe I should just let them happen, whatever happens."

"That sounds scary to me."

"Not to me. You know, Mitch loves me."

"I'm sure he does. But I can't follow beyond that. How does that lead to you going off with him to some place called Window Rock? All of a sudden you're living with him. You're doing this permanently."

Debbie stacked a slice of cheese on a cracker and drank some water.

She raised the cracker to her mouth but didn't bite into it. "It's not just a short term thing like the clinic, like a mission almost. Even your parents understood that. I understood that. You wanted to give back, give something back. That I understood. This I don't. I don't even think you do. I don't think you really love Mitch that way, that much. It's more than scary. It's crazy!"

"I love him, I do. He came to New York to find me. And..."

"Elizabeth, he's from there, or near there. He's the one who found out about that clinic in the first place. But now he's found this other place. What does that have to do with you?"

"He wants to do something with his medical knowledge, more than just the surgery. He wants to help people, the poorer people. The Navajo tribe is one of the poorest in the country. I told you before that he wanted to go to Mexico or South America. Well, a friend told him about this place and what the people needed."

"I understand. But that's for him, that's his thing. Is it yours?"

"They need nurses too. Mitch thinks we'd be a great team."

"I thought we we're a team too." Debbie paused for a drink and a moment's consideration. "I'm glad, really glad that you're home. I've missed you, everybody's missed you. We should talk more about this. Have you talked to your parents yet? And Luke, what about Luke?"

"I wrote him a letter and told him about my plans. I was going to Window Rock, Arizona, to work at a clinic."

"What about Mitch?" Debbie saw a more important aspect that Elizabeth needed to cover with Luke.

"What do you mean?"

"What'd you say about Mitch?"

"Nothing, I just said I was going with a doctor, a doctor that I met."

"Now I know you're crazy. You can't just say that in a letter like that. What's he going to do?"

"I don't know. I tried to explain it as best I could. I told him everything that I knew for sure, but I said I wasn't totally sure how it would work out. I told him not to write to me because I wouldn't have a way to get mail for a while."

"Christ, Elizabeth. You might as well have told him to go jump off a mountain cliff."

"No, it's going to be okay."

"I don't think you really get the picture. He reads your letter, and he thinks that you're going to Arizona with some doctor to work in some clinic. You can't say anything more than that, but you tell him not to write to you for a while. He may be an understanding guy, but I don't see how he can understand this decision. You didn't tell him, before you had the..."

"The abortion. God, Debbie, you can say abortion out loud."

"I know. I know, but that wasn't that long ago, and you didn't tell him beforehand and now this. Hell, he's probably on his way here right now."

"Why would he come here? He doesn't know that I'm here. That would be crazy!"

"It's no crazier than what you're doing. You've got to tell him about this, all of it and about Mitch too."

"I don't think I can do that, not yet anyway, not now."

"Then, I don't think you should go with Mitch to this clinic in Arizona."

"Why, what do you mean?"

"It's too far, too far out there, going half way across the country with Mitch. Are you going to marry him?"

"No, God no. Debbie, I'm not getting married. I'm taking this one step at a time."

"Yes, but this is a big damn step. It's too damn scary, and you're scaring everybody."

"I'm not scared."

"Then you should be able to tell everybody, everything. Especially Luke. You should call him, like you should've called him before. Tell him everything."

"I don't know. I'm not ready."

"Then we should call Andy's house and you should tell Mitch the same thing. That you're not ready. Elizabeth, it's too much, too scary."

"Will you stop with that? I'm home, in St. Louis. How's that so scary?"

"It's not, but Luke doesn't know. He thinks you're going to Arizona. Your parents, they don't know any of this. You'll be a long way from home, a long way from everybody who loves you. You have to be a little afraid. I'm sorry. I mean there has to be some uncertainty."

"Maybe, I don't know."

"And remember when we first talked about you having an.... us going to New York for...?

"An abortion, Debbie, I had an abortion. I'm not afraid of that any more. I'm sure of that."

"Okay, I know. But remember before you made that decision, you said you really thought about it, even prayed about it. Have you done that this time?

"No, but...I'm just too tired. Right now, I'm too tired to think about anything, at least not tonight."

"You're right. I'm sorry. You must be exhausted. You stay here. I'll put your suitcases in the hall. I've got the day off tomorrow. We've got all day tomorrow to talk."

When Debbie returned, she explained. "I put your overnight case in the bathroom and turned down your bed. I wasn't sure about the sheets, so I changed them earlier this evening. Everything's just the way you left it."

Debbie intertwined her hand in Elizabeth's. At Elizabeth's bedroom door they hugged.

"Good night," Debbie whispered. "I love you too."

"I know," Elizabeth responded.

Elizabeth dried the tears welling in Debbie's eyes. "Don't worry. Everything's going to be all right. I'll see you in the morning."

"Maybe you can stay a few days at least." Debbie coaxed Elizabeth to her bed.

Elizabeth answered, "Yes, maybe."

Chapter 35

Boulder, end of the same week in August, 1972

No longer morning, in fact just a sliver of daylight, a slim purple hue cast by the last moments of the sunset merged now with the glow of the lava lamp across Luke's apartment. The light in the bathroom had burned as long as it could, then it burned out.

Luke's body splayed at a difficult angle, hunched and humbled. The left side of his face stuck to the floor, his eyes crusted at the corners. The linoleum flooring in the bathroom had served as his bed.

During the darkest hours of the new day he had staggered into the bathroom, lurching in the direction of the toilet. He had regurgitated, but his aim was more unsteady than he.

He sank, then, into a stupor, and vomit drained from the corner of his mouth, forming a gluey substance that held him low and tight to the floor. He remained unconscious through the high hours of daylight, and now on the downward slide into another night, the whining in his ears awakened him.

On hands and knees to the bathroom threshold, he used the door jamb to pull himself upright. He fingered the light switch and found that it was already in the on position. He flipped it twice with no resulting light.

He squinted into the gloom and brushed the wall with one hand as he stumbled toward the kitchen. The lamp on the kitchen counter guided him like a lighthouse through the storm that raged inside his skull.

At the sink, he ducked his head under the water that flowed from the faucet. He soaked the back of his head and captured the overflow in his hands and rubbed his face with a massaging motion. He kept his eyes closed and dug his fingertips into the sockets so the water would clear the crud.

While his head was still buried, he fumbled with the fixtures to turn off the water. He swung his head to the side and hit the edge of the sink with a thud. He punished the counter with a fisted blow, and then reached for the kitchen towel that was draped through the handle of the cabinet door.

Frustrated with his clumsiness and the self-inflicted pain, he moved too quickly and knocked a glass container off the counter onto the floor. The sound of breaking glass provided a harsh background to his muffled groans as he dried his face and hair with the towel.

He peered from the towel and blinked several times to bring the room into focus. The lava lamp provided enough light, and the broken glass proved to be a Jack Daniel's pint bottle now in several pieces at his feet. He still wore shoes. For that matter, he was fully clothed.

The water from his washing had given life to a few patches of vomit on the front of his shirt. The smell found its way to his nose, so he removed his shirt, bunched it into a ball and backhanded it onto the counter. He made an about-face and turned the water faucet on, this time cupping his hands and rinsing the cotton from his mouth.

He maneuvered past the broken glass to the doorway, switched on the overhead light and found the broom and dust pan. He was determined to remove the broken glass, but when he bent to place the dust pan to the side of the broken glass, vertigo stopped him. He dropped to one knee, and holding the broom just above the straw, he pushed the pieces of glass onto the dust pan.

The trash can was piled to overflowing, the bulk of the spillage consisting of empty beer cans. He placed the dust pan on the counter and retrieved several paper grocery bags. One by one, he loaded the cans and other garbage into the bags until three bags were aligned against the wall. He dumped the contents of the dust pan into the last bag and topped it off with his t-shirt.

He sidled through the kitchen, all the way to the front door, where he switched on the overhead light. He then did the same with the lamp beside his chair, but the bulb did not illuminate.

He checked near his chair and saw a drinking glass with just a splash of murky liquid at the bottom. He assumed the contents to be the remnants of melted ice cubes. An empty whiskey bottle leaned precariously against the glass, and this evidence told him that he had lapsed into unconsciousness sometime during the previous night. The bulbs in the lamp and the bathroom had burned out sometime after he did.

He retreated to the bedroom and hit the overhead light in that room too. An empty bottle, Jack Daniels pint, stared at him from its place on the nightstand next to the clock radio. He found his flashlight in the drawer under some of Elizabeth's letters and snatched up the bottle.

In the kitchen he placed the bottle in one of the trash bags and took a package of two light bulbs from one of the cabinets. After entering the bathroom, he used the beam from the flashlight to show a path around the mess he had made on the floor and to find the decorative nut on the front of the light fixture.

He unscrewed the nut and placed the fixture on top of the toilet tank. He changed the light bulb and blinked into the glare when the new bulb illuminated instantly. He turned 180 degrees to see that the switch was still in the on position.

At the lamp he repeated the bulb replacement process. After that, every light in his apartment shone brightly. He stood there and gathered from his memory the bits of broken glass and the crushed cans that comprised the last several nights he had spent in his apartment.

He remembered the stops at the liquor store on the way home from work and the clerk inquiring about the ongoing party. He pursued his party of one, insuring at least one light continuously shone, the light from his lava lamp, the lamp exactly like Elizabeth's lamp.

He rushed into the kitchen, where the lamp still glowed. Pinned under it, he saw Elizabeth's letter. The last lines curled upward, and he read them as he had many times before, *I still care for you deeply, but you may not hear from me for a while. I don't know how all this will end.*

The other content of her letter remained as murky as the liquid inside the lamp. Her trip would take her to Window Rock, Arizona, a place she had never seen, nor heard of before. Some of the specifics that she had written muddied the picture even more. She would travel with a doctor that she had come to know, and they would provide health care to the local people, a poor Navajo tribe. She related that he should not write to her because she would not be able to receive any mail.

The colored globes floated inside the lava lamp. The principles employed to design and manufacture these lamps were a mystery to Luke, just like the concept that there might be places where a person could not receive mail.

Except for one piece from the University, he had not received any mail for almost two weeks, until this single page from Elizabeth had arrived. The handwriting was clearly hers, but he didn't understand what she had written. He didn't know her destination until he referenced an atlas at the store. He wondered about all the places unknown to Elizabeth and all the places he did not know. Most of all, he wondered about this doctor he did not know.

He turned off the lamp then, and the colored globes dropped to the bottom. His shoulders slumped too. He wriggled his torso to relieve the stiffness, loosen his self, and free himself somehow. He pulled Elizabeth's letter from under the lamp, and it tore at the corner.

The letter from CU was revealed. It confirmed his registration and the classes that he had selected. He folded Elizabeth's single page in half. He carried it with his hand extended out in front of him like he was offering it to someone, asking someone to take it from him, explain it to him. In his bedroom he opened the drawer of the nightstand and placed it on top of the other letters.

The drawer remained open, as he sat on the edge of the bed. All the pages of the letters lay neatly, folded one atop the other, except the last. It bulged from wrinkles and puckered with smudges of ink and spots where unknown liquids had dried.

Luke searched again his memory of the past several days and nights. He had abused this single page, crumbled it and threw it away, retrieved it, and threw it away, a senseless cycle. He punished the page for its bewildering message.

Night after night, he sat in silence reading as long as he could. All the poetry of the 20th century spoke to him of disillusionment and alienation. He wallowed in it and re-read Elizabeth's single page to grind the feeling deeper. After the first three nights, each with the rhythm of a six pack, he decided to stick the letter under the lava lamp, and from that vantage point he read just the last few lines.

In protest, in spite, he sat at the kitchen table and scribbled furious tirades, *I'm writing you a fucking letter anyway, wherever you are. I don't get it, and you probably won't either!* He drank more and cursed himself for his anger and his sadness. He threw those pages at the trash can. Hit or miss, he left them.

He kept his head down at the store, inventoried the shelves in silence, packed and re-packed old merchandise. The owner had vacation scheduled that week. Luke would supervise the temporary staff, and he simply told them to help out the customers while he worked in the stock room. He didn't, couldn't help them.

At home he fell into helplessness too, carelessly throwing empty beer cans on top of the pile made of angry pages and more empty cans. Where they tumbled sporadically to the floor, they formed a long string of his own garbage, a path to a place he did not know. Finally he switched to whiskey, stopped pacing, stopped reading, and stopped trying. The empty pint bottles he had left sitting wherever he happened to be when he finished them.

He wiped his fingers across the top of the nightstand. An oblong ring of darkened wood marked one of the places he had stopped along the trail of his quiet self-pity. He closed the drawer and reached to unlace his shoes. He removed them and his socks.

With his elbows resting on his knees, he closed his eyes and bowed his head, his hands folded before him. All the lights continued to shine, and an image of Elizabeth formed before him. Some time passed, his and hers. He could not see the end, her destination, but he yearned to know.

He held his head in his hands then, still aching to know.

Chapter 36

St. Louis, end of the same week, August, 1972

Debbie had convinced Elizabeth to remain in St. Louis for a few days. Elizabeth lounged at the house and visited with her family and her friends from Children's Hospital. Through Francine's intervention, Elizabeth even secured two shifts at Children's. Inertia built by comfortable surroundings and familiar relationships strengthened as the end of the week approached.

On Saturday, Mitch couldn't wait any longer and journeyed west without Elizabeth. Her confidence in the decision to stay in St. Louis was reinforced when one of Luke's letters dropped through the mail slot in the front door. It had been forwarded by Mrs. Sanders.

The original postmark told Elizabeth that Luke had mailed his letter on the same day that she had mailed her most recent letter to him. He had no way of knowing that she had traveled to

St. Louis, or any of the plans she had related in her letter, but she opened his missive with trepidation anyway.

Luke's intuition was strong. She worried that Debbie's warning about Luke on the day she had arrived from New York was a valid harbinger. It was, indeed, possible that Luke could be making his way to St. Louis, unexpected, even as he had been a mere three months ago.

The envelope delivered a paper cut as her fingers tore it open, a hint of discomfort. Elizabeth fumbled the single page, but it was just a brief note and an untitled poem.

> The meadowlark and I, our wild song is released
> To welcome each summer morning
> High cliffs of rock, open doors on every block
> Bend with the trees and the grass just to hear us
>
> He in the fields, and I walking to my station
> Sing such a full-throated yearning
> It's as if the day aches, because my heart breaks
> And naught but her presence will ever cheer us
>
> Our melody is pure but is lost to the winds
> My soul, a new way is learning
> How a place within me is the place she can be
> And for now, there is where she lingers near us.

Elizabeth trotted to her room. She set a cardboard box atop her bed and lifted a handful of envelopes from it. She fanned the envelopes in front of her, like a casino dealer displaying a deck of cards on the blackjack table.

She picked one at random and read it, and then repeated the process over and over. At some she laughed, others brought tears, and the amalgamation of the pages became a mirror for her.

She lost track of time, but when she finally checked her bedroom alarm, she determined it wasn't too late, and besides it was Saturday night. Desperation drove her now, as she paged through her journal for Julia's phone number.

She stood in the hallway and made the call. "Hello, Julia? It's Elizabeth. You know, Luke's girl..."

"Oh, hi."

"I hope it's not too late. I know before...Well, I was hoping this time...I wanted to actually talk to Luke. Do you know if he's home tonight?"

Julia communicated that she hadn't seen Luke. In fact, it had been a hot, sunny day, and that usually meant that Luke would be outdoors somewhere.

"We almost always encounter Luke either coming or going from the house on a beautiful day like today. I'm kind of surprised we didn't, but I'll check downstairs."

With her back against the wall, Elizabeth slid to a seated position. She laid pages that she had carried with her on the floor. Tension mounted in her shoulders, and she wagged her head when it crept up the back of her neck. She could not shake a sense of foreboding, as though a shadowy figure had cloaked itself in the silence on the other end of the line.

Chapter 37

Boulder, the same Saturday night, August 1972

Luke jumped at the sound of the knock on his door. He was half way there when he realized that he wasn't wearing a shirt. A second, louder knock caused him to stub his toe on the bed frame, when he attempted to pull a t-shirt over his head and walk at the same time.

"Luke?" Julia scraped her hand on the rough concrete wall as she back-pedaled from the person who greeted her.

Luke's appearance shocked her. His hair was matted in wet clumps and tufted at obtuse angles. His eyes, reddened, glazed and cloudy stunned her. He was a frightening caricature of the Luke that she had expected to see.

"Are you okay?" Julia edged closer to the open door.

"Hey. Hi. Yeah, I'm just...okay. What's going on?"

"A phone call, it's Elizabeth for you. I told her I would check to see if you were home. Can you come now?" Julia's voice trembled with sincere concern.

Luke didn't respond. Instead, he lost his balance and nearly fell on his face when he bent to press a finger to his big toe. Blood oozed around the perimeter of his toenail.

Julia questioned Luke's capabilities. "Should I just tell her you'll call back?"

"No. Yeah. I mean. I definitely want to talk to her. You won't believe...I was just thinking about her. Tell her to hold on. I'll be right there." He left Julia standing in the doorway.

<hr>

An awkward few minutes lapsed in small talk between Julia and Elizabeth. Julia shared that she had taken Terry and Danny to the swimming pool. The sun and the water had tired even Terry, so they had both fallen asleep earlier than usual.

Julia reassured Elizabeth that Luke was home and anxious to talk with her. She fabricated an excuse for his delay, based on an injury to his big toe. Shortly after she heard the screen door close, Luke entered the room.

Julia spoke into the telephone. "Here he is. I'm sure he's dying to talk to you."

Luke wore a long sleeve shirt over his t-shirt. The untucked shirttails flopped unevenly because the buttons were misaligned. Still barefooted, but wearing a ball cap, strands of hair twisted above his ears and beads of perspiration saturated his forehead.

His mouth hung open like he was inhaling long breaths, and his grin appeared plastered to his face.

Julia held her hand over the receiver and mumbled. "Or he could just be dying."

She met Luke in the middle of the front room, the phone cord stretching behind her.

Luke squinted as though he was having difficulty seeing. "What'd you say?"

"Nothing. Here." Julia handed the phone to Luke.

When Luke placed his hand over the receiver and cleared his throat, a whiff of malodorous breath caused Julia to wrinkle her nose. Luke swayed like a sapling bending in the wind. Julia crossed the room to the TV and turned it off and then picked up a water glass from a low table in front of the sofa.

Luke cleared his throat again. "Hey, that's new, the thing with the TV."

Luke was unrecognizable, a bad joke personified.

Julia chuckled and jabbed a disgusted hand into her side. "The entertainment center, yes it is. So's this coffee table."

"They're..."

Luke froze when Julia charged directly at him. "Don't you think you should be talking to Elizabeth instead of me?"

Julia raced past Luke and had climbed most of stairs before she heard the tentative hello he spoke into the telephone.

Luke murmured an explanation to Elizabeth. "Sorry I took so long. It's been a weird day. I had to take care of something."

Luke's voice husky, almost hoarse, provided no relief for Elizabeth's nervous anticipation. She squirmed at the scratchy hollowness.

She second-guessed the wisdom of her decision to call. "You want me to call back. Julia said you injured your foot or your toe. Maybe tomorrow would be..."

"No, it's just...My toe, I just bruised it."

"But you don't sound like yourself."

"I know. It's weird. I think I caught a cold somehow, even though it's summer."

"You sound pretty bad."

"No, really. I'm fine. Things are good here." Luke rattled off a string of disconnected comments. "The bookstore's been busy. I start school in a few weeks. Maybe that's making me sick. You know me and college classes don't get along very well."

Luke chuckled and his voice echoed like a squeaky toy. Silence ensued, and Luke gulped the stale air. He swallowed all of the questions that he had been asking of himself for days, ones that were the true source of his sickness. He regurgitated them again.

His voice quivered as he asked, "Where are you? I mean, are you traveling? You said you were going to Arizona. I looked it up. It's a long ways. In your letter you said it might be the end. I didn't know what you meant. Where are you now?"

Luke heard a sniffle and he blurted out. "I wish I was there. Wherever you are, I wish I was with you. I'm sorry. Elizabeth, I'm sorry."

"I'm in St. Louis at my house," Elizabeth responded quietly. "I started on the trip, but decided not to go. It's kind of complicated, but I've been home for a week. I'm not going, not now anyway. I was going with a doctor that I know, but he's already left, so I'm not going with him anymore."

Luke formed a question about the doctor but didn't speak it, only a comment. "I kept thinking it's a real long way, a long way from New York and from St. Louis, a long way in a lot of ways."

"Debbie talked me into thinking about it more. You know, I wrote that letter late one night. I probably didn't make much sense. Debbie said it doesn't make sense to go to some place in Arizona that I don't know anything about. I guess she is right."

"But you're not so sure."

"Just tired, I guess. I worked the late shift last night."

Luke interjected a hopeful question. "At Children's, you got your job back?

"No, I'm just filling in when they need me."

"That's a start."

"At least I'm making some money."

"And getting back into the swing of things. It'll take a while."

"That's what Debbie said."

"But you're doing okay. You're home. That's good."

"I'm fine. You still don't sound too good though. Luke, I'm worried about you. You should get out more, not just be there by yourself so much. I know it was hard for me in New York, and that was just a couple of months."

"I'm fine, I'm fine. We're a little different in that way. Besides, you're the one I'm worried about." Luke's voice sounded sharper. "Don't go to Arizona. Don't go to New York again. Just stay where you are. That's where you belong."

"But I liked it in New York, and I might've liked it in Arizona. It's pretty there, you know. Anyway, I want to make my own choices."

"I know, and you should. I'm sorry. I shouldn't try to tell you what to do. Me especially, I'm the last person to be telling anyone what to do. But I care about you. I love you, Elizabeth. I want you to be happy."

"I am. It's good to be home."

"That's what I like to hear. You made a good choice."

"For now, but maybe not forever." Elizabeth stared straight ahead.

She shuffled the letters beside her, and an image formed in the space before her.

She described what she saw. "There's more. The doctor that I was going to Arizona with, you don't know him. I'm getting to know him. He's a good guy and wants to help the Navajo people. I want to help him and help them. I might still choose to be part of that too."

"But you said he's already left."

"Yes, but I might go sometime later. I don't know. I don't know how all this will end."

"I know. You said that before, in your letter."

"It's the way I feel."

"I know. We can't really know everything. But I like knowing where you are. I bet that right now, you're sitting in the hall, Indian-style. You're good at that. That would be one good thing if you were helping out the Indian tribes. I can't do that very well." Luke began to chuckle.

"You're just being silly now." Elizabeth laughed too.

"How's the saying go? I'm laughing so I can keep from crying."

"Luke, don't be sad. I've been reading some of your letters. I love your letters." Elizabeth lifted the pages into her lap.

It surprised her when a tear drop landed on one of them. She remained silent, and the silence permeated the eight hundred mile distance that separated them. Doubts lingered in that space, and illusive feelings of guilt bounced back and forth like the apologies that they kept repeating.

"Elizabeth?" Luke broke the spell.

"Luke, I should go. I'm getting tired."

"I understand."

"I know you do."

"I'm glad you're home and that you called. I've been thinking about, worrying about you."

"Please don't worry, not anymore, not about me." "I won't. I mean, since you called now I won't. I don't have to. And don't you see? It's a good thing I wasn't out carousing tonight. Otherwise we wouldn't have gotten to talk. But it is getting late, so I'll just say good night."

"I really should get to bed. Good night."

"Good night, Elizabeth. I...."

"Good-bye Luke."

A click and a monotone came through the phone, and Luke replaced the receiver on the telephone base, which sat atop a small table in the entry hall. He cracked his shin on the edge of the new coffee table, as he made his way to switch off the lamp.

On his way out, Luke turned off the other lights, including the light over the porch. Ambient glow from the street lamp shone on the steps until the glare of headlights stopped him. Clay's truck screeched to a halt.

Clay jumped off the running board. "Out kinda' late tonight, aren't ya' Luke?"

"Actually, I just finished a phone call. Elizabeth called me."

"Good thing she didn't just stop by. You look like somebody just kicked the shit out of you."

"It's been a tough couple of days."

"At the bookstore? You're kiddin' me?"

"I've just been hitting it hard. I might've caught a cold or something."

"Yeah, a cold shoulder maybe. Little lady's got you on the run, does she? I don't let that stuff bother me." Clay bumped Luke on his way by. "You're too much of a pansy, Little Luke."

"Screw you, Clay. What do you know anyway?"

"I know when I'm lookin' at a guy that's gotten fucked. And I don't mean in a good way. Besides, you'll be sleepin' on your own again tonight."

"That's the way I want it."

"There you go. That's what I mean. Nobody gets what you're talkin' about half the time. 'That's the way I want it.'" Clay made a hoarse croaking sound when he quoted Luke's words, and then smacked the door frame with his fist. "It's bullshit, man. You're just lonely, Little Luke."

A diabolical laugh reverberated when Clay slammed the kitchen door. Luke kicked his apartment door closed, and the blood broke through the crust that had formed on the top of his toe nail. He hopped to the bathroom and wrapped the toe in a wad of toilet paper. He punched the air, rapid fire fists hitting an ephemeral opponent.

A surge of energy straightened his posture. He set a fast pace, starting with the empty pint bottle and the glass near his chair. He took note of two damp spots in the carpet. He put the glass in the sink and threw the bottle in one of the bags of trash.

His feet stuck to the kitchen floor in spots, and interpreting that sign correctly, he first swept then mopped the entire space. With his discarded t-shirt turned inside out, he wiped the remaining vomit in the bathroom. He changed the water in his bucket and mopped the bathroom floor as well.

He cleaned the commode with a wash cloth and spray cleaner. After rinsing the cloth thoroughly, he used it to remove the spots on the carpet near his chair.

He switched off the lights in the front room and kitchen and decided to take a shower. He washed every part of his body twice and his hair three times. He treated his big toe with ointment and a band-aid. Several strands of hair tangled in his comb. He tossed the nest into the commode and flushed it away. He sprayed his under arms with deodorant, but a raunchy odor lingered around him.

He sourced the rancid smell to the grocery bags of trash and decided to finish the job, every last piece handled. He accomplished the task in careful steps, quietly, deliberately. Each bag deposited outside his door and one by one carried to the end of the driveway.

He then snatched all three into his arms simultaneously, hugging the bags to his chest. The stench stayed with him all the way to the park. There he stuffed the bags in one of the large park trash cans, firmly closing the lid.

He left the debris behind, waste he could no longer abide. By the time he arrived home, the stench had left his nostrils too. He eased into bed and rolled to his side. He clenched the end of his pillow in one hand and fell asleep, holding on with all his strength.

Chapter 38

St. Louis, August 1972

Elizabeth awakened first. Her conversation with Luke the previous night had sputtered along, stopped, and then raced ahead. Unsure of how it should end, and weary of the uncertainty, she had ended it with a terse good-bye. She longed for comfort, and she found it in Luke's letters.

She shuffled the stack of letters on her bedside table, squared the corners, and placed them in the box. From her knees, she slid the box under the bed and paused as if to pray. Luke had not been himself, definitely didn't sound like himself.

At one time, every one of his letters had made sense to her. Her thoughts of Luke tangled now with her feelings for him, and interwoven into the fabric was the vital nature of her feelings for Mitch. Her conclusion, *I don't know how all this will end*, was the only truth she could comprehend.

She felt a responsibility to Luke, how he felt and what he thought, but she refused any regrets for the unfolding of their individual lives. Her heart trusted the choices she had made. She bounced from the floor and into the new day, that Sunday.

She showered, washing every part of her body, some more than once. She allowed the conditioner extra time in her hair, but when she blew it dry, several tangles clumped in her brush. She combed them together and threw them in the bathroom waste basket.

Debbie entered the kitchen, as Elizabeth sipped from a glass of orange juice. "Can I get you something?"

A slice of bread popped out of the toaster.

Debbie replied. "I'm just going to get some coffee. Looks like you're all ready for the day. What's happening?"

"Nothing planned so far."

"Going to church maybe?" Debbie placed the coffee pot on the burner.

"Don't think so. Maybe the park, you want to go?" Elizabeth felt that the park might hold a blessing.

"I don't know. It's supposed to be hot."

The coffee percolated, splashing against the glass top of the pot. Elizabeth finished her toast and orange juice.

"Not if we go this morning. We'll miss most of the crowd, and then we can go somewhere nice for lunch."

Elizabeth envisioned a holy day without obligations, without the masses or the mess.

She would share it with her friend. "How does that sound?"

"Okay." Debbie tapped her finger on the counter impatient for her coffee.

"Okay? It'll be better than okay. Come on, start getting ready. I'll bring you your coffee."

They spent the morning at Forest Park, strolled past a few exhibits in the zoo even. The sea lions played, dipping and diving in their pool area. The birds sung, chirping and cawing. Their chatter encouraged Elizabeth, and she shared more details about her experiences in New York.

After leaving the zoo, Elizabeth led them casually to the hill overlooking the American Legion Fountain. A group of children splashed water and played near the fountain. Elizabeth described the vastness of Central Park in New York and the many grand fountains and exhibits located within its confines.

"You really liked it there, didn't you?" Debbie detected Elizabeth's enthusiasm.

"It's quite a place. The people were hard to get to know, though. I suppose that's the nature of a big city. It feels good to be here, be home."

"I'm glad, everybody's glad you're here. We all need a home. Feels like that to me, anyway."

"I think that's the way it should be too. All the girls at the clinic, the patients who came there, they needed our help. That's what they needed at the time, but eventually they needed a place to go, someone to be there for them. That's home."

"I like that, the way you said it. It sounds like the old you."

"What do you mean old?" Elizabeth nudged Debbie.

"Not old like that." Debbie bumped Elizabeth.

"I know. I know." Elizabeth said with a chuckle. "Let's make our way to the car."

Debbie tugged Elizabeth's hand. "Hey look. That little boy's waving to us."

A boy, now separated from the group by the fountain, waved vigorously. He took three running steps up the hill, and when strands of his light brown hair flopped into his eyes, he tripped over a fallen tree branch.

By the time the boy re-gained his feet, Elizabeth had pressed close to the wall. She waved to the boy, and he stood like a statue for a long moment. He waved again and then ran to join his friends.

Debbie marveled at the scene. "Wow, do you know him?"

"I'm sure I don't."

"Then, what was that all about?"

"I have no idea. I just felt I should respond somehow."

"Okay. But, now can we go?"

"Sure, I'm hungry."

During lunch, Elizabeth related the strange circumstances of her phone conversation with Luke.

"He kept repeating how he was worried about me. He thought I was already in Arizona."

"See I told you." Debbie pointed her fork at Elizabeth.

White sauce from her pasta dish dripped off the end of the fork onto the tablecloth.

"Hey, be careful. You're making a mess." Elizabeth used her napkin to clean the spot.

"Not as big as you almost made."

"That was never my intention."

"I know. But it's best the way things have worked out." Debbie swallowed some iced tea.

"You mean me staying here? Luke seemed to be happy about that." Elizabeth twirled a mouthful of pasta around her fork.

"He probably wants things to be like they were. That's what he knows."

"Yeah, but they're not. I'm not. He's not, either, I don't think."

"But we all just want to know that...that you're all right."

"I'm all right, all right?"

"Okay, okay." Debbie rose from her chair, crunching an ice cube.

Debbie took care of the payment, and Elizabeth covered the tip. They slipped past a group of patrons waiting to be escorted to a table. Two men nodded at Elizabeth. A steamy sun greeted them when they stepped onto the sidewalk in front of the restaurant.

Debbie unlocked the passenger door of her car for Elizabeth. "You really do look nice today."

"Thank you. I feel much better, like my old self."

With the box fan positioned strategically and blowing full blast, they napped during the heat of the day. Each of them curled at opposite ends of the sofa.

Neither of them had energy to eat, but shortly after sunset, Debbie served sliced apples, more of a snack than a meal. As they munched, the telephone rang. Debbie ran to answer it, Elizabeth on her heels.

Debbie spoke into the receiver. "Oh, hi. Just a minute."

She covered the receiver with her hand. "It's him."

"Luke?"

"No, Mitch."

Debbie handed the phone to Elizabeth. "Whatever he wants, just tell him no."

Debbie retired to the sofa. When the phone conversation ended a few minutes later, she insisted on a report from Elizabeth.

"He just wanted me to know that he's doing okay. He said the local people are almost all Indians."

"What'd he expect? He's on a reservation, for Christ's sake."

"Debbie, do you want to hear or don't you?"

"Yeah, but jeez, these men."

"Okay, okay, you made your point. Anyway, he said that the people are pretty reluctant to come to the clinic. They still rely on their own customs, their own ways of healing. He might as well be in a foreign country."

"I believe it. But at least he has a telephone."

"He called from a pay phone. He said it could be more than a month before he gets a phone. He's not sure where the phone company is. It's not part of the regular phone company. But, that's not important. He just wanted me to know that he missed me and..."

"Wait! Let me fill in the rest. He wishes you were there with him and that he really loves you. How's that?"

"You have the last part right. Actually, he said that he was glad I didn't come with him, that it's probably best. And that he might not stay that long, either, maybe just a few months."

"Damn, that man's more fickle than a junior high school girl. At least when Luke decides to do something he sticks with it. He may be a strange in other ways, but your doctor, Mitch, he's acting strange too."

"Mitch just wants to make a difference in someone's life."

"How about he starts with your life, and not by taking you off to some place in the desert?"

"Debbie!"

"Okay, I'll give him some credit. At least he admits it was good that you didn't go with him."

"And he said he was coming back to St. Louis sometime soon. That's good too."

"Maybe, maybe not, we'll see. For now, I need to go to bed and so should you. We're going to get you your old job back this week. It's time to get things totally back to normal."

During that week, the administration department called from the hospital, Barnes not Children's, and offered Elizabeth a position in the Emergency Room.

She remembered her rotation through ER during nursing school. At that time, she had been knocked off balance, even frightened by the intensity of that experience. However, from her recent work at the New York clinic and managing its fast-paced environment, she had emerged stronger, more confident. She felt at home, no feelings of fear.

Chapter 39

Boulder, Same Day August 1972

The sun blazed, high and hot, in the cloudless morning sky. Luke squinted to see the trail through the sweat that smeared across his eyes. He loped beyond Elephant Rocks and did not stop until he reached the place where the pathway leveled. There he caught his breath, his hands on his hips and his arms akimbo, a view to the eastern horizon.

Hardy oxygen coursed throughout his body and steadily replaced the toxicity of the alcohol he had imbibed in the early days of that week. He found some comfort in the previous night's conversation with Elizabeth, the knowledge that she was safe, at home, and would be working at the hospital soon too.

He wiped the perspiration on the inside of his T-shirt sleeves, but within seconds, the salty beads burst again from every pore. He leaned forward to place his hands on his knees. Droplets moistened the bits of rock and dust at his feet.

His memory raced in reverse. Although he recognized the mileposts, even as he hurtled past them, regrets blurred the meanings of many of those places.

He dashed away from that spot. Within minutes, he made the bend in the trail where it led around the natural curve of the hillside. He sprinted past the sign warning of the end and squeezed in between the two pine trees. He rested against one of the tree trunks.

Low hanging branches created shade, and he relaxed, while he studied the narrow path at his feet. It was made of smooth granite and linked the place where he stood to a hard rock ledge some fifteen yards away.

He ducked under the limbs and re-calibrated his breathing as he proceeded toward the ledge. Near the very edge, he widened his stance. The sweat evaporated from his forehead, as a peaceful breeze cooled his body and quieted his mind.

An ancient creek, now just a marshy stream, likely a snow chute in the winter, cut a ragged gulch between him and a twin foothill, a mirror image of the one he had come to know. As a bird could fly straight across to it, Luke guessed that fifty yards of clear air spanned the distance to that neighboring hill.

Below where he stood and extending toward the opposite hill, a flat, grassy spot formed a green circular pad several yards in diameter. He focused on that spot and estimated the drop at twenty-five feet and the lateral distance at nearly twenty feet.

He passed some time in prayerful contemplation, as though he attended a higher church on this Sunday morning. When he left, he maintained the reverent feeling. His pace quickened as he retreated, but his head remained bowed.

A low hanging branch of one of the pines halted him. Like a pointed lance, it pierced the crown of his head, slashing the scalp. He pressed one hand to the injury, and when he brought his hand into view, a stripe of his blood cut across the palm. In one motion, he stepped away and slapped the end of the branch with the back of his hand.

Anger raced from his feet through his body and reddened his face. Steaming hot, he whipped the branch again and again, a fast one-two, one-two rhythm. In the next instant, he pivoted and then bolted, head down, eyes fixed on the end of the ledge.

When he hit the take-off spot, his legs continued their sprinting motion. He batted the air, the buoyant, thin air, with his fists clenched, all of his extremities pumping in sequence like he would fly to the other side.

Everything stopped when he landed, his heart, his arms and legs. The race ended as quickly as it had begun, boiling blood frozen in time, a mind-sprint stopped in its tracks. His first breath was met by a sucking noise, stuck to his shoe tops in a wet, reddish muck where the grass found its roots.

With his second breath he let out a triumphant yell, "Ya... hooo! Yea...eah!"

The celebratory sounds startled two ravens, and they scurried into flight from a point above Luke. When he repeated his cheer, they soared even higher and carried his affirmation to the heavens.

Luke released himself by lifting one foot at a time. He lost his left shoe in the wet clay. After retrieving it, he plopped onto a large rock near the bank of the gulch. He took off his right shoe and both of his socks.

He scraped the mud from his shoes using the flat edges of shale rocks and rubbed his left sock on the top of a smooth stone in an effort to clean it. He draped both socks on top of his shoes, pulled his sweat pants to his knees and rested there.

The two ravens cast shadows in a repeating pattern as they circled overhead. The top branches of the pines that guarded the trail quivered in the breeze. From a place of humility, he took another measurement, of himself this time. He imagined himself more confident and resolute, solidly rooted in this earth.

He pulled on his socks, laced his shoes, and adjusted his sweat pants. After he scooted off the top of the rock, he took only a few paces before he stopped and turned to sear this place and time in his memory.

The murky depressions he had made were already disappearing. Above him on the ledge, one of the ravens sat, squawking its own impressions of the day. When it took flight, it swooped past Luke, a dark blur banking side to side. Luke bounded after it.

———

On Monday morning at the bookstore, the owner complimented Luke on the orderly condition of the stock room. Luke recapped the previous week's work, his own efforts and those of the crew's. He reminded him that the summer staff had handled everything without supervision on the previous Saturday. Classes would begin for him and most of those employees in about ten days, and work schedules would need to be adjusted accordingly.

Luke established a new after-work routine. He changed into his sweat pants, t-shirt, and sneakers. On the first few nights he tried to clean the reddish brown stains from his white shoes, but the Colorado clay had left a permanent mark on them. By mid-week, he accepted the imprint and laced them with a growing sense of pride.

He jogged up the street and onto the dirt path. He passed Elephant Rocks and took the steep incline to the top of the trail. He thought of Bake and training camp for football, the players had to run hills just like these as part of their conditioning. He remembered what it was like to be part of a team, but he worked alone now, the path he had chosen.

After his work-out, he showered and ate a light meal. Throughout that week, no knocks came to the door, no phone calls were taken, and no letters arrived.

The passage of time quickened. On Saturday evening, he wrote a letter to Elizabeth and described his recent routine. He related the story of his leap from the end of the trail. He tried his best to portray his feelings then and a new feeling of acceptance. He asked about her routine and admitted anxiety about starting classes. He closed with a statement of conviction, *I'll be here in Boulder. It feels like the right place for me.*

Chapter 40

Late on Sunday morning, Luke jogged to the post office to mail his letter. He took the most direct route there, south along Broadway to Walnut then east, but on his way home he jogged into the neighborhoods west of Broadway before turning north. When he reached the concrete path of the neighborhood park a few blocks from home, he steadily decreased his pace. He used the bottom front of his shirt like a towel to wipe the perspiration from his entire face.

Before anyone else noticed, Terry jumped to her feet and waved. "Luke, hi! Luke, we're over here."

At the edge of the picnic blanket, Luke rocked from one foot to the other. "Hello there. How's everybody today?"

"It's a picnic in the park. We're celebrating the last day of summer vacation."

"Ahh, yes, back to school, I bet Mom's sad about that."

Julia motioned to an open spot on the blanket as she countered Luke's suggestion. "That would be a bet you would lose. You want to join us?"

Clay scrutinized Luke. "You look like you put in a few miles and went through some mud or somethin' along the way. So, if you're joining us you better take off those shoes."

Luke planted his feet more firmly. "Actually, I picked up some of that good Colorado dirt about a week ago. Just got to live with it now. But I best decline your kind offer."

"You could probably clean that stuff if you wanted to." Clay pointed to Luke's shoes.

"Not sure I do." Luke responded.

"Well, there you have it. I always said you were weird." Clay wagged his finger at Luke's face.

"Maybe just a little crazy." Luke wiped his face on his shirt sleeves.

"That, too." Clay nodded.

"Crazy or not, you look better today, compared to the last time I saw you." Julia recognized a familiar clarity in Luke's eyes and the healthy color in his cheeks.

"That's true for me, too." Clay admitted.

"Thanks. I am feeling much better. It's nice of you to notice, especially you, Clay. I must be getting some of the meanness out of me."

Terry refuted Luke's point. "Luke, you're not mean. At least that's what I think."

"Well thank you, too. I better keep moving. Clay, ladies, have a nice day."

"Mom's a lady, not me." Terry stated.

"Oh, yes you are, in my book, at least." Luke motioned as though he was bowing. "Give Danny boy a hug for me too."

Luke trotted away.

Terry scooted next to Danny and kissed his cheek. "Luke sure is a funny guy, isn't he?"

Clay had his own spin on that theme. "Yeah, funny-weird, that's what I've been sayin'."

"It's just that he has his own way." Julia explained to Terry.

Clay insisted on his interpretation. "Yeah, and it's a weird way."

Julia ignored Clay's remarks. "No, it's just his way, his way of doing things."

"I kinda' like it." Terry stood and gestured to the swings as if she was asking permission.

"Me too. I want to swing." As Julia slipped on her sandals, she gave instructions to Clay. "You watch Danny. Maybe try giving him a hug if he wakes up. Where your baby is concerned, you could learn from Luke's way of doing things. He sings to him sometimes. That song called *Danny Boy*. I know you think it's weird but Danny doesn't. He really likes it."

A single cloud floated across the sun and shaded the family's picnic blanket, but where Julia and Terry played on the swings the light continued to shine. Soon they were both giggling, while Clay grumbled in the shadows.

Clay lay on his stomach, a cloud of annoyance billowing inside of him. He peered at Danny, innocently sleeping in his pumpkin seat. As Clay propped his head on his elbow, the cloud moved away. The burst of sunlight caused Danny's eyes to pop open. He greeted Clay with a baby grin and a bubble of excitement.

Clay held onto thoughts of weirdness though, and frustration applied a sharp edge to his words. "What are you lookin' at?"

A hard question his baby son could not answer. Danny began to cry. Clay pushed to his knees and swept Danny into his arms. The quickness of that movement frightened Danny. He sucked in the fear and seemed to hold his breath.

Clay stood and hugged Danny to his chest. Danny squirmed as if he would free himself, but Clay latched on even tighter. Danny screamed louder, and Danny's wail sounded throughout the park.

Julia jumped from the swing and ran to their picnic spot. Terry drug her feet to bring her swing to a stop. Another cloud chose a path across the sun, casting a wider swath of shadows. Sunlight disappeared from the entire section of the park. Clay tried to steady Danny's head, but Danny pressed against the coolness of Clay's hand. His infant voice resounded with fear.

By then, Julia came close enough to kick Clay's shin. "What are you doing?" She screamed as loud as her baby. "You're hurting him!"

Julia yanked Danny from Clay's arms.

Clay tilted his head and roared. "Aaarrrh! Aaarrrh!"

All the picnickers surrounding them reacted to the scene. Some gathered their belongings as though they had received a signal that it was time to leave. Others stared stupefied, their mouths gaping at odd angles.

Clay kicked the blanket and yelled at the top of his voice. "What are you looking at?"

As Clay stormed toward the street, Terry rushed to her mother's side. Danny's cries lost their terrible tone, but his body heaved with each breath. Tears flowed from Terry's eyes, and Julia dropped to one knee with Danny still caressed on her shoulder. Terry patted Danny's back.

Julia then moved Danny so that she cradled him in her arms. She dropped her other knee and leaned on her haunches. She rocked Danny, and his cry became a whimper.

"There, there now, Danny boy. Everything's going to be all right."

Danny succumbed to Julia's soothing tone and touch. Terry kissed her baby brother's cheek.

Julia whispered to Terry. "Our little guy's okay. Just take a tissue out of my purse and wipe his nose, will you, please?"

The clouds cast an increasing pall, and Julia instructed Terry to collect all their picnic supplies and leftovers and put them into the basket. Julia folded the blanket, while Terry held Danny.

A gentleman, one of the nearby picnickers, offered his assistance. He carried the blanket, basket and Danny's seat to the car. Julia took Danny from Terry and boosted him to her shoulder. Terry stayed near her mother's side. The man loaded everything into the trunk, except the pumpkin seat, which he placed on the back seat of the car.

Once Julia had settled Danny in his seat and Terry had hopped in beside him, she thanked the stranger.

He shrugged and glanced overhead. "Glad I could help out."

When the first drops of rain hit the roof of the car, Julia opened her door. "We better go."

"Yes, these afternoon showers, they'll get you every time." The stranger closed her door and waved.

The windshield wipers flapped a friendly rhythm. Julia drove carefully as the intensity of the rain increased.

Julia caught Terry's eyes in the rear view mirror. "Everything okay back there?"

Terry shook one of Danny's rattles in the air before him. "He's just lookin' at his rattle, the red one. I think he likes the color."

"I'm sure he does."

The mirror reflected the strain in Julia's smile. She felt rattled and hoped Terry didn't notice. They progressed slowly toward home, and Julia's hands shook as she feathered the steering wheel to make the final turn.

Clay's truck came barreling in reverse onto the street. His brakes screamed, then his engine roared, and the truck lunged in a rubber squealing race past Julia's car. Clay's face furrowed in a scowl and grimaced redder than Danny's toy.

Julia crept along the last block. The car moved so slowly that she barely applied pressure to the brakes as she stopped in front of the garage. The rain fell faster, harder.

"Let's wait here a minute." She turned her shoulders to get a better view of Terry and Danny.

Terry merely smiled at her mother, and that satisfied Julia. Julia turned off the car's engine but gripped the steering wheel again with both hands. She dropped her head atop her hands. Her tears fell like the rain of an afternoon shower.

Chapter 41

The rumble from the engine of Clay's truck lured Luke to the window. Droplets of rain sprayed from his tires as he sped away. The force of the storm intensified, and the raindrops splashed in the puddles that had formed on the driveway. The tires of Julia's Volvo rolled so slowly, they barely caused a ripple in the puddles.

Luke waited for Clay's or Julia's legs to appear in the frame of his window. When the rain fell in sheets like an opaque curtain across a theater stage, his patience gave way to an uneasy feeling. He draped his jacket over his head as he went through the door.

Julia didn't raise her head until Luke tapped on the car window. Terry waved and shouted hello.

He opened Julia's door a crack. "If the kitchen door isn't locked, I can grab an umbrella."

"Yes, that would be good." Julia agreed, but her words were muddled by something Terry was saying from the back seat.

Luke closed Julia's door and shifted to the rear. Terry's door bumped Luke's side.

He grasped it before it could swing open. "You two wait there. I'll be back in a jiff."

Luke first escorted Julia under the umbrella. She then held the umbrella high while Luke lifted Danny out of his seat and into his arms.

He commented to Danny as though a baby could appreciate the insight. "Your first summer on the planet sure has been a wet one. The summers are usually pretty dry around here. At least, that's what your momma says."

Julia exchanged the umbrella for her son. "His first picnic interrupted by the rain."

By then, Terry had squeezed into the middle, and they scrunched together. No one moved.

Luke formulated their dilemma. "Okay, so how do we all get from here to house without getting wet?"

Julia laughed aloud. "Let's just shuffle in unison. You know, with baby steps."

Luke felt some comic relief. "It'd be like a scene from The Three Stooges."

Rain spilled onto Julia's shoulder when their laughter jiggled the umbrella.

Luke provided another idea. "I tell you what. Terry, you take the umbrella. I'll make a run for it and hold the door for you guys."

"No, let me make a run for it," Terry shouted as she sprinted toward the house.

"Terry, wait!" Julia screamed too late.

The hard raindrops blurred Terry's vision, and she stumbled on the first step. Her subsequent stride slipped off of the next higher step, and she crashed hard and fast. Her shin split against the edge of the wooden step, and she cried in anguish.

Luke shoved the umbrella handle into Julia's hand and bounded to Terry.

He scooped her into his arms on the run and flew her into the kitchen. Luke knelt as Terry sat on a kitchen chair. He pressed a wet dish cloth against the wound. Terry's wail matched Danny's from earlier that afternoon.

Julia sprinted to lay Danny on the front room carpet and retraced her steps to the car. She carried Danny's pumpkin seat into the kitchen and situated it in the middle of the room.Once Julia had Danny tucked into his seat, she focused her attention on Terry.

She continuously rotated clean cloths soaked in cold water to Luke. Luke kept the pressure on Terry's shin. The force of Terry's cry had lessened to shallow sobs until Julia suggested that Luke apply an ice cube to the gash.

Terry tasted her salty tears when she cried out. "No Mom, I don't like that. I don't want ice on it!"

Terry's loud objection startled her baby brother, and his cry provided reinforcement to hers.

Julia hugged Terry and hushed her baby from afar. "Shhh...It's okay. No ice. Shhh..."

Julia repeated her words of comfort. "Shhh...It's okay."

Her voice softened, and her children quieted. Luke applied additional rotations of the cold compresses, and after several minutes passed, the bleeding no longer formed visible blooms of red on the outside of the cloths.

Julia communicated the progress to Terry. "Luke might have the bleeding stopped. Do you want to see?"

"No, you just tell me." Terry averted her eyes.

Luke spoke his assessment. "It looks pretty good."

Terry tilted her head and stared at the ceiling, determined to avoid making her own judgment. Julia peered over Luke's shoulder, and he peeled the cloth away from the wound.

Julia patted Terry's leg. "You're going to be just fine. Luke's a pretty good nurse, don't you think?"

Terry leveled her eyes at her mother. "Mom, Luke would be a doctor, not a nurse."

"You're right, but either way, he did a good job of taking care of you."

Luke thought that he should take it a step further. "Let's try one ice cube now. I'll just hold it on top of the cloth. We don't want the bump to get too big. The ice keeps it from swelling too much. What do you think?"

Terry only sighed this time. "Okay, but on top of the cloth, not right on it."

"Yes ma'am. That's the proper procedure anyway." Luke sounded official.

Soon, Luke was able to apply a gauze pad to the gash. A red dot oozed through the bandage as he secured the last edge with a strip of adhesive tape.

<hr>

Intermittent rain showers fell throughout the rest of the day. Julia insisted Luke stay for dinner. She teased him about his doctoring skills. Terry used her injured status as an influential factor in persuading Luke to engage in several board games with her. At sunset, Julia coaxed Terry to bed and carried Danny to the same destination. She felt certain the events of the day had tired them sufficiently.

When she entered the room, Luke sat straighter at his place on the sofa. "How did it go?"

She took a seat next to him. "I'm not sure about Danny, but Terry's asleep. We decided on the new pants and top instead of the new dress. She wants to wait a day or two to show off that gash on her leg."

"She hit it pretty hard. It'll probably turn black and blue."

"You think so, doc?" Julia chuckled.

"Hey, cool it with that stuff." Luke nudged her shoulder with his.

"I have some beers in the fridge, and I wouldn't mind opening a bottle of wine either. School starts tomorrow. For me, that's worth celebrating!"

"Okay, I can handle a glass of wine. I've been pretty good lately."

"You really are looking better, better than last weekend. I was worried about you. And Elizabeth, how's she doing?"

"She's back in St. Louis, working at the hospital again. She's had a pretty tough summer, but she's doing better now."

"You know we can work something out if you want to call her sometimes. Especially on the weekend, long distance costs less then."

"That's okay. I wrote her a letter, just mailed it earlier today. Things might go back to the way they used to be, me here and her there."

"That's okay for now, but that's not how you want things to end up is it?"

"I'm going to borrow something from one of Elizabeth's letters. I don't know how all this will end."

"Now that is a weird thing to say. Eventually you two will be together, don't you think?"

"Yes, I believe that. But I'm not going to worry about it, not anymore."

"Luke, you really are...your thinking is...Sometimes you talk a little crazy."

"Maybe, just a little, but later this week school starts for me too. So let's have some wine." Luke rose from his place. "I'll get it."

"Sounds like a perfectly sane idea to me. I'll take charge of the music."

Julia placed an album on the stereo, Judy Collins, *Wildflowers; side two,* while Luke served the wine. Two sips later, Judy Collins' voice hit the crescendo of *Both Sides Now.* Danny's cry mingled with her high notes.

Julia swallowed the entire contents of her glass. "That little stinker!"

Julia scooted to the edge of the sofa, but Luke's hand on her knee kept her in her seat. He set his wine glass on the coffee table atop a coaster.

Luke offered a critique of the song. "Maybe Danny's more of a rock 'n roll kind of guy? I'll go talk it over with him."

"Okay, I'll turn off the stereo, but I'm going to get more wine too."

Luke held Danny on his shoulder, alternately stroking his back and patting his bottom. After he laid Danny in his crib, he wound the mobile and recited, with only a vague attempt at the melody, his adaptation of the Irish ballad that resonated with Danny's name. The calm repetition of the verse produced a meditative spell, and Danny drifted into sleep.

Luke whispered a final wish. "Sleep tight, Danny boy."

Outside Danny's door, Luke waited in the hall for a few additional minutes. He checked Terry's room to make sure all was quiet there as well. He was so deliberate in his descent of the front stairway that a boom of thunder caught him in mid-stride.

It was Clay's voice that rolled through the house. "There she is. You're lookin' good tonight!"

Clay strutted into the room. From her place on the sofa, Julia took a warning from the slamming of the screen door, but Luke and those sleeping upstairs were caught unaware. Luke froze in the shadows and listened for a response from above.

All he heard was Julia's stern hush. "Shush! The kids are sleeping, you big ape."

"Ooopps." Clay came to a halt and hunched his shoulders while raising a hand to his mouth. "Sorry about that. But I can see you've started with a glass of wine. That's the right attitude. We should be celebrating 'cause tomorrow's the start of school."

Clay waited for a signal from Julia indicating she would accept his approach. Luke retreated to the second floor, and even though the volume had subsided, he overheard clearly the exchange of verbal blows on the first floor.

"Yes, and that means you'll need to get your butt up in the morning too." Julia's stern tone held Clay at bay.

"I know. I know. Me and Frank and some of the others have been down at Larry's cryin' in our beer about that part."

"That figures. You and your friends won't be worth a damn. You know some of the kids are looking forward to school starting again."

"Yeah, all the sissies and the book worms."

"Those are the kids that will be running things when they're adults, not you jocks. You guys better be prepared. At least get a good night's sleep and stop drinking so much."

"Oh, honey, it's just PE. And besides, when did you become the den mother looking after all the boy scouts?"

"Clay, you asshole, you don't know anything, do you? Do you even remember earlier today, remember leaving me with the kids at the park, throwing your tantrum?"

"You know I don't like it when Danny starts to cry like that. I don't know what to do."

"Well, one thing's for sure. You don't try to manhandle him. He's not one of your football players."

"I know. I know that much. I'm not stupid. I just need more practice."

"Then you should stick around, not run off every time he starts to fuss a little."

For Luke, some of his internal conflicts were being verbalized. Words like *stick around and don't run off* held some meaning. As he tiptoed down the back stairs, he heard another familiar refrain, *there's nothing to be afraid of.*

Clay edged closer to Julia. "I know. It's just...I know I was outta' line. So, I came to say I'm sorry. Anyway, it looks like everything worked out all right. I saw you comin' home, ya' know."

Clay hoped to salvage something from the day, perhaps even the night.

473

Julia stopped him again with the vehemence of her words. "No shit, really? You were going so fast, you probably couldn't see anything, anybody."

"Yeah, I was hot."

"That's what I mean. You're the one who's supposed to be the adult in the situation. The kids can get mad once in a while, get a little fussy. You're supposed to keep your cool."

"All right, already, I get your point!"

Luke entered the front room behind Clay. "What point is that?"

Clay made a quick about face. "What the hell? Who invited you? Why're you always hangin' around my...comin' around here?"

Clay's voice rose with each question, but Luke remained calm. "Take it easy, man. I just wanted to make sure everything was all right. I heard you guys talking so I figured it wasn't too late."

Clay was stuck on the questions. "Whatta ya' mean, is everything okay? Of course, everything's just peachy keen. Besides, what business is it of yours?"

"I just thought I'd check on Terry. How's her leg?"

Clay was baffled, and his head swiveled first to Julia then to Luke. "Now what're you talkin' about? The kids are sleepin'. They're both fine. Aren't they?"

Clay twisted toward Julia, and she hit him with a dose of sarcasm. "If you say so. You're the one who's calling the shots."

Julia took a drink of wine and then tilted the glass toward Clay. She repeated that gesture in Luke's direction and smiled at him. Luke's face beamed.

Clay took a sideways stance. Clearly, he was the only one not smiling. In fact, his frustration mounted and his cheeks caught fire. He had anticipated a celebration but found conflict instead. Either one suited him, he was certain of that much.

He wagged a finger in no particular direction. "Fuck you! Fuck both of you!"

He banged Luke's shoulder with his own as he passed him. "Stay out of my way, you little jerk. And wipe that fuckin' grin off your face, or I'll do it for you."

"Jeez man, take it easy! It's no big deal."

Clay raised his fist this time. Luke's smile flipped into a scowl. Julia leapt off the sofa, no longer smiling either.

Clay pressed forward. "I got your big deal right here, mother fucker!"

Luke made a physical move away but his voice confronted Clay. "Man, you're losing it!"

Julia stepped in between the two men. "Clay," she commanded, "stop being an ass. Just go! You hear me, just leave!"

She grasped Clay's fist in both of her hands as though she would pry his fingers apart. Clay opened his fist. He shrugged and made a half turn at the hip as if acquiescing to Julia's command.

"Yeah, yeah." His words signaled a surrender, but he simultaneously wheeled, and with an open hand, took a roundhouse swing at Julia.

In the same instant, Luke reacted. His arms flew forward, and he grabbed Julia's shoulders one in each hand. He jerked her backwards, and she fell awkwardly at Luke's feet as Clay's arm arced in the air just overhead.

Luke kept his hands on Julia, and the momentum of her fall bent him over at the waist. For a brief moment he felt himself hovering over her, a protective arch formed by his upper body.

Clay re-loaded and landed a fisted blow against the side of Luke's head. Luke fell on top of Julia, a stunned and heavy heap.

Julia squirmed out from under the weight. She kicked at Clay, rage pumping her legs like pistons.

She screamed. "Damn you, you son-of-a-bitch. Get out. Just get out!"

When she scrambled to her feet, Clay retreated.

"Yeah, yeah, I'm goin'." He shouted to drown out her curses. "This is none of his business. I told him before. Maybe now he got the message!"

Julia dropped to her knees and touched the side of Luke's face. It felt cold, but she boiled inside. Luke groaned, his movements imperceptible, his wits and his limbs scattered in various directions.

Julia hissed, steam releasing in her words. "You fool, you big fucking fool! Can't you see? He's not getting any message now, is he? Get the hell out of here, or I swear I'll...I'll!"

"You'll what?" Clay stopped his retreat.

Julia sprung to her feet and rushed him. She rammed her shoulder into his chest.

The ferocity of her words stunned him. "Clay, this is the last time! Get out, and don't come back!"

Her words knocked him off balance. Hot tears flooded her face, and they washed over him.

He tumbled now on a wave of confusion. "Whatta ya' mean? I don't know. I...I...Uh..."

"That's just it. You don't know!" She slammed Clay's chest with all her might, and their march of rage took them into the kitchen.

Behind them, Luke grunted and struggled to all fours. The sound caused Julia to pivot in that direction. Clay swung her around, forcing her to face him.

He challenged her, his nostrils flaring. "Is that what this is about?"

"What? You stupid!" She cried, the tears blinding her.

When she lunged at him again, he latched onto her wrists and flung her aside. She fell headlong to the floor.

"That little shit," he yelled at her while he pointed into the other room. "I'll take care of..."

Luke now stood unsteadily. Clay hurled himself on a line directly at Luke. Unaware of the forces focused on him, Luke staggered and took an extra-long stride toward the center of the room.

Clay barreled forward, his own head lowered, intent on demolishing his target. He made impact at the instant that Luke slid his legs together. The elongated side step that Luke accomplished had shifted him just enough that only Clay's extended arm struck Luke.

Even at that, the force of Clay's blow threw Luke to the floor. This time his head slammed to the carpet with a thud. Forward momentum hurled Clay onto the coffee table. When he hit the table, the smash rang throughout the house, and the wine glasses flew across the room.

Julia re-gained her feet. She heard Danny's unmistakable cry, and light footsteps then moved rapidly along the hallway above her. Terry had been awakened too. Julia's muscles tensed, and fear propelled her forward.

Clay rolled to the side of the flattened table. He stabilized himself on all fours, and with the swipe of one arm, he scattered the legs and other splintered pieces of the table. He cleared his head with a violent shake and found Luke.

On his hands and knees, Clay scurried toward Luke, raising one fist above his shoulders. Still dazed from his fall, Luke took the full force of a blow to the jaw. Luke groaned as his head flew to the side, and blood gushed from his mouth.

Clay collected more strength, his fist poised well above his head, ready to land another powerful punch. At that moment, his skull cracked. A violent vibration transfixed his body. A scream originated from somewhere nearby, then profound silence. Clay fell like a stone statue. His fury ceased to exist.

———

Terry's scream was an operatic wail of horror. Danny's cry added a pulse of orchestral dissonance. Terry froze, when her mother's windmill chop felled Mr. Williams. Her mom wielded a wooden object, like a short baseball bat. The resounding thwack stopped Terry cold. Luke lay next to Mr. Williams.

Her mother's glare felt cold, like the ice that Luke had pressed against her leg that afternoon. Her mother's jaw was set hard at the edges, a monstrous disfiguration. Terry knelt and a burst of tears betrayed her conflicted emotions, unsure whether the monster had been slain or had done the slaying.

Julia dropped the weapon, a leg of the coffee table. A metal bracket still attached to its end had become a hatchet's edge.

She took Terry in her arms. "Don't cry, baby. It's over now."

Danny's howl silenced as though he had heard his mother's words, but as soon as Julia released Terry, Danny's fearful weeping began again. Luke groaned and coughed.

Julia spoke sternly to Terry. "I need you to help me now. Be a big..."

Terry could not be distracted. "Mom look, it's blood! Mr. Williams is bleeding bad."

Julia cupped her hand around Terry's chin. "Terry, look at me. It's okay. I'm going to take care of Mr. Williams and Luke, too, but I need you to go upstairs and get Danny out of his crib. Just sit with him in the rocking chair. Hold him."

"I can sing to him like Luke does." Terry responded to her mother's request.

"That's it. Just help him to calm down. I'll take care of the guys. We have the wash cloths that Luke used on your leg. I'll stop the bleeding."

Luke heard his name through the ringing in his ears. The white ceiling that spanned his field of vision blurred to a milky substance when he blinked moisture into his eyes. A touch to the left side of his face produced a wave of pain. He clenched his teeth and slapped the carpet.

Julia knelt at Luke's side to give him instructions. "Don't move. I'll be right back."

Julia ran to the phone and dialed the police number.

At the top step, Terry turned as Julia completed dialing. "Mom, what are you doing?"

"Calling the police. Just go help Danny like I asked."

"But, Mom, I don't like that...the sirens. Just get the cold rags like Luke did and maybe some ice."

"I know. I will. But I need some more help."

"Mom, Danny will be scared too."

"Terry, it'll be okay. I'll come and help you as soon as I can. Just go get Danny now."

The next words Julia spoke she directed into the telephone, describing what had happened. The dispatcher promised that a patrol car would be there soon, and Julia rushed to help Luke and Clay.

She soaked two wash cloths in cold water, and pressed them into the wound she had inflicted to Clay's skull. She elevated his head on a platform that she assembled from various pieces of the table that were scattered nearby.

Inside another wash cloth, she bundled several ice cubes. Luke wrestled with her hand when she placed the ice pack against the swollen left side of his face. Spikes of pain knifed from his jaw to his temple.

Julia supplemented Luke's weakened limbs with the strength of the adrenaline that coursed through her body. She employed the proper leverage to get him to his feet and guided him through the field of debris to the sofa.

Luke grabbed Julia's wrist, when he heard the siren.

"Yes, I called the police." Julia broke Luke's grip. "Clay's wound is bad. I knew I would need help."

Julia sprinted to the kitchen. Her path marked by the spots of blood that fell to the carpet. Seconds later, she pressed a new pair of cloths into Clay's skull, transforming the clean white fabric to crimson.

She cradled Clay's head in her hands and leaned an ear to his mouth. Clay's breathing was faint, but steady. His blood pulsed through her fingers. She screamed when Luke touched her shoulder. He passed her the cloth with the ice cubes.

The police sirens increased in pitch and volume, and cries from the second floor commenced the very moment that the sirens stopped.

Luke murmured through gritted teeth. "Terry and Danny?"

"They're together upstairs." Julia motioned with the ice compress.

Panic glossed Julia's vision when the pounding at the door rattled the window. Luke didn't switch on the lights, just opened the door a crack. Two police officers rushed into the entry hall.

They forced Luke against the wall. "Sir, a lady called. An emergency!"

Julia yelled. "Here, not him! I need help here!"

Simultaneously, Terry stomped her feet at the top of the stairway. "Luke, Danny's crying again. This time I don't know..."

Pain stiffened the left side of Luke's face, stifling his speech and his reactions. Before he could move, one policeman darted up the stairs, and the other made a beeline to Julia.

From upstairs, the policeman carried Danny in his arms, but at a precarious distance from his body. The end of Danny's blanket swung near the policeman's feet, threatening to trip him as he descended. Danny howled at the top of his infant lungs.

Terry raced behind the policeman. "Luke, make him stop. Danny's too scared."

Luke confronted the policeman at the bottom of the stairs.

The policeman in the front room barked an order. "Ma'am, I've got this. Take care of your kids."

Julia hurried to the entry way but stopped abruptly when the policeman extended his arms. Danny still screamed, and Julia instinctively touched her baby. Her fingertips smeared blood on Danny's face, and Julia was repulsed.

"No, I can't. Luke, you take him." Fear darted from Julia's eyes.

The policeman froze, and so did Luke and Terry. Julia rushed into the bathroom.

Terry sounded the first order. "Give Danny to Luke. Give him now!"

Over the din of Terry's shouting and Danny's wailing, a second order came from the officer in the front room. "Officer Cook, hand the kid over. Get to the car and radio for an ambulance! We need more help here!"

Luke nested Danny more securely in his arms and wiped a streak of blood from Danny's cheek with the edge of his blanket. He took a seat on the stairs and gently rocked Danny. Danny's weeping became sobs, and Luke hushed him further with his voice.

"Shhh...Shhh..." Luke repeated the sound over and over, ever softer.

That sound had a soothing effect on Luke's pain too. He relaxed his face, his self, and Danny calmed as well. Terry settled beside him, her head resting on Luke's arm. Danny's face gradually transformed from red to pink. Luke counted one lucky happenstance from this night, the fact that he hadn't turned on any lights in the entry hall. Danny closed his eyes.

Julia traversed the hall, and Luke carefully passed Danny into her arms. Julia took Luke's spot on the stairs. He then placed one hand on her shoulder and one on Terry's. He bowed his head, and that moment unfolded like a blessing.

When a distant siren broke the silence, Luke spoke a soft instruction. "Take them up to your room and wait there. I'll take care of the rest."

Before he could turn away, Julia formed a silent thank you with her lips. Luke nodded and they exchanged the faintest of smiles.

Chapter 42

O n Wednesday afternoon, Luke hurried along Broadway. The previous evening Julia had reported Clay's condition to him, and she had secured his agreement to meet her at the hospital after his last class. Julia planned to have Clay stay at her house for a few nights after his doctor released him from the hospital. She felt a responsibility to make sure he fully recovered from his injury, and she needed Luke's assistance to get him home safely.

She related her reasoning and some of the details. "I'd get Frank, but he's in school until after 3:00. You said that all your classes were in the morning, so we can meet at 1:00. With Danny, it's too much to do by myself, and I want to get Clay settled before Terry comes home. You know I made her stay home the last two days, so tomorrow'll be her first day of school too. She'll have a lot to talk about, so I want to be ready for that."

Luke had expressed his concerns about her caring for Clay. "You know, my jaw's still hurting from the other night. The guy tried to hit you, hurt you too. You both keep saying I'm a little crazy, but this idea really is."

"Luke, I'm only teasing when I..."

"I know, but I don't think he is, and now it turns out, he's the one who's mad, the epitome of a hot head."

"I know. You're right, but in the end he's the one who got seriously hurt."

"That's not the way I see it. He got what he deserved. You saved me from a big time ass-kicking, maybe even saved my life."

"No, now that is nuts."

"Not from my perspective. On Sunday night you felt the same way too."

"Luke, I was scared."

"You're damn right you were. And I would've been too, except that I was too out-of-it to feel anything."

"You never did go to the hospital. Maybe you should have. Maybe you should now, just to be safe."

"That's not what...Julia, you're the one who's not going to be safe, and neither will your kids, not with him around. I just don't think you should do this. It's..."

"Luke, I've made up my mind. I've made my decision about this. All I'm asking is that you help me out."

"I know and I'm going to help, but damn it, it's..."

"Luke, it's not your decision. It's mine. There's nothing more to say."

"Okay, okay, I'll see you tomorrow."

When Clay demanded his second glass of water within the first twenty minutes of being home, Julia brought him a whole pitcher of ice water, placing it on the nightstand beside the bed. Luke excused himself as a way to relieve his frustration.

In the chair in his apartment, Luke read the first chapter of one of his textbooks. Terry arrived home in a flurry, just as Julia had predicted. She yelled for her mother's attention.

Julia used the afternoon to prepare chicken noodle soup, made it from scratch, and she listened to Terry describing her day, her classmates and her teacher. The aroma from the soup simmering on the stove penetrated Luke's apartment.

As an expression of gratitude for his help, the soup satisfied Luke. It seemed to satisfy Clay as well. Julia attended to him while Luke and Terry ate at the kitchen table. Even throughout Danny's feeding time and the completion of cleaning duties, no complaints were registered.

After dinner, Julia allowed Luke to borrow her car, and he used it for a trip to the University bookstore to purchase a composition book he had forgotten to obtain earlier. A few lights burned inside the house, as he parked in the driveway. Julia lay on the sofa, a bed pillow propped under her head and a sheet and blanket stacked on the floor next to her. She wore striped pajama pants and a US Army t-shirt, multiple sizes too big for her.

Luke waited at the end of the sofa. "Big day, huh? Everybody sleeping?"

"Yes, it's been quiet anyway."

"So, who turned out to be the biggest baby?"

"Clay, I guess."

"Oohh. Hate to have to say this, but I told you so."

She raised her feet and motioned for Luke to sit. As he did, she used the opportunity to poke him with one foot.

"Okay, you win that argument." Julia only wanted to rest.

Luke's stretched his legs. The stains on the carpet made him queasy. "What did the carpet cleaner say?"

"He wasn't very reassuring. I think I'm going to have to replace it."

"That's probably best anyway, new start and all. Well, I better head to my place. Still have reading to finish. Here're your keys. Thanks for the use of the car." Luke set the keys on the lamp table.

Julia lifted her legs. "You're welcome. How'd it go for you today?"

"Pretty good. I might just get the hang of this college thing after all."

"I expect that you're going to excel." Julia was still prone and tried to unfold the sheet from that position.

Luke took the sheet from her and spread it so that it covered her feet. "Looks like you're bunkin' here tonight."

"Clay's kind of sprawled out all over the bed."

"That doesn't surprise me. He seems like the sprawling type." Luke muffled a laugh with his hand, not really hiding his amusement.

"You have Clay all figured out, do you?"

"Well, I am in college, you know."

"Yes, and you better go get your homework done."

"And you better get some sleep. Looks like you have that houseful of babies after all." Luke released a bigger laugh.

On his way out, he waved without looking back. "Sweet dreams."

She smiled and blew him a kiss, but he missed them both.

Chapter 43

Luke flipped the cheese sandwich in the pan atop the stove, perfectly browned on the one side. Frank had agreed to give him time to go to his apartment, change his clothes, and eat dinner. They anticipated a standing-room-only crowd for the concert at Tulagi's and wanted to arrive early.

Luke had found Frank at Larry's, an easy assumption for the first Friday afternoon of the new school year. The poster taped to the door of the University Memorial Center promoted a welcome back concert. The featured band was Fire Fall, but the photo and information about the warm-up group provided the more significant attraction for Luke.

It clinched it for Frank, too, when Luke proposed it to him. "You won't believe who's performing first."

"Yeah, who?"

"A band from Wichita, Kansas, called Wild Prairie, with a lead vocalist by the name of Melinda Baxter."

"No shit!" Frank banged his beer on the bar.

"Isn't that far out?" Luke flashed back to Hays, Kansas.

"Yeah, man! Who said the beginning of school wasn't goin' to be any fun? We'll be partyin' tonight."

Frank ordered a beer for himself and Luke. "Hey, did you ever write to her like you said you would?"

"A couple of letters, but I may have freaked her out. I told her how I kept hearing that one song she did, *Guess He'd Rather Be in Colorado*. It was the truth, but she never wrote back, so I figured I better lay off."

"Luke, people keep sayin' you're a little strange. Try not to scare off all the good-lookin' ones, will ya'?" Frank slapped him on the back.

"Writing letters to someone is not strange." Luke insisted.

"So you say. Here, drink up."

Luke chugged his beer, and Frank checked his watch, allotting one hour for Luke to get ready.

———

Luke heard the first scream, *not that way,* as he crested the top step. Frank scurried by in the direction of the porch. A horror-filled screech stopped Frank in the kitchen, and Luke sprinted past him toward the back stairway.

Terry careened toward Luke, and he avoided the collision by sweeping her into his arms. Frightened and now surprised, she burst into tears.

"What is it?" Luke lifted Terry to his eye level.

"It's Danny and Mr. Will..."

"Where are they?"

"In Danny's room, he's not doin' it right. I told him and he yelled at me. That's when Mom came. She yelled at him, too, but he wouldn't stop."

Luke set her on her feet but held her shoulders. "Listen, you wait here. Frank and I will..."

Frank pushed past Luke and Terry.

Luke repeated himself. "Just stay here. We'll..."

Without completing his thought, Luke leapt the first steps, instantly on Frank's heels.

In Danny's room, Clay pinned Danny to the changing table with one hand, but his eyes were fixed on Julia. She challenged him with an angry tirade, while he spewed a torrent of curse words. Above it all, Danny howled.

Frank charged by Julia and smashed a forearm into Clay's chest. The blow staggered Clay, and Luke used the opening to snatch Danny. He knocked diapers and other supplies to the floor, when he wheeled and gave Danny to Julia.

With the scuffling and cursing at his back, Luke yelled to Julia. "Take him! Go! Terry's downstairs."

A big body thumped to the floor behind Luke, just as the door closed. Then, a two-handed shove to his shoulder blades launched Luke face first. When he hit the floor, he rolled to the side before springing to his feet.

Clay lurched toward him, his head wound stiffening his movements. He was a Frankenstein monster terrorizing the nursery. Luke shuffled toward Danny's crib and jerked it into a position that formed a barrier between himself and Clay. He held firmly to the railing on his side, leaning his upper body away from his adversary.

Clay clung to the opposite railing and yanked. Luke lunged toward Clay but kept his grip and his distance. They danced in jerking motions, and Clay panted. Perspiration dripped from Clay's forehead, and blood spotted his bandage.

"Clay, you have to settle down! Danny's okay. Julia, everybody's okay. You just need to cool it!"

"I don't need to do nothin'!" Clay bellowed and charged forward.

The force of the crib hurled Luke against the wall and trapped him there. Luke re-positioned his hands on the railing. He was determined to free himself but realized too late that he had lost track of Clay. Clay's punch stung the top of his head.

Luke reacted by throwing his hands high. He flinched at what appeared to be a second blow, but his forearms blocked a piece of wood instead. In the flurry that whirled around him, both Clay and he had missed Frank's rear assault.

Frank had re-gained his feet and chose the rocking chair as his weapon. He wheeled it in a semicircular arc, swinging it around his upper body and smashing it into Clay's side. The pieces flew in multiple directions, and Clay slumped to the floor. Police sirens signaled the end of the battle.

———

This time Clay spent the night in a cell at the city jail. The policemen stopped at the hospital emergency room, where a doctor changed the dressing on Clay's head wound and gave him a dose of pain killers. By the time he was processed and taken to the cell, he wanted to sleep.

First, he needed a drink of water to sooth his dry mouth and throat, but none of the comforts of Julia's home were offered to him. He didn't have strength enough to demand them, so he lay on the bunk-style bed that was too short to accommodate his over-sized body.

He wrestled with his blanket and pillow. The steady grind of activity in adjacent rooms, and whimpering noises from a near-by cell, agitated him. He curled his legs, rolled to his side, and placed the pillow over his head. He pressed the pillow tightly to his ear, blocking out everything, and fell asleep.

Luke awakened with a jerk. When he opened his eyes, only darkness opposed him. He realized that a subconscious replay of the night's events had startled him. He lay there for a moment trying to remember the details of his bad dream.

When he flipped on the bedside lamp, the hands on the clock radio approached 4:00 a.m. The glow of the lava lamp guided him into the kitchen, where he rinsed the stale taste in his mouth with a drink of water.

Choosing his reading chair instead of his bed, he covered himself with a blanket, pinning it to the floor with his feet. Light from his bedside lamp and the lava lamp soothed the edges of his field of vision.

He relaxed and his eyes closed. He had missed the Tulagi's concert, but one of the songs he had anticipated hearing, now played inside his head. He hadn't been able to hear Melinda Baxter in person, but her voice carried the tune of *Crazy*. The melody lulled him to sleep.

Chapter 44

St. Louis, early September 1972

Violence shot through Elizabeth's dreams, and she bolted upright. Usually she slept in the morning light and through to the early afternoon, but this day an unfamiliar fury jarred her awake.

She rubbed her eyes, and the clock read nearly 11:00 a.m. After washing her face in the bathroom, she dropped onto the sofa in the front room and slumped into the cushions. Sunlight streamed over her shoulders, and she relaxed.

She had worked in the emergency room, nine consecutive night shifts. The cases she had attended grew in intensity, and penetrated her psyche. They surfaced in her subconscious. Injuries that resulted from bar fights, car accidents, and domestic disputes, everything and everyone sped toward her. Delivered by ambulances, police vehicles, and even a family member or friend's car, the patients appeared frenetic, and oftentimes bloody.

She and her colleagues, the other nurses and doctors, raced too. They met many cases at the door, sometimes ran to meet them. Children were carried by their parents, so sick that they had awakened from a sound sleep. Adults themselves sought relief from their acute pain. They came through the door supported by a friend.

Elizabeth learned how to best meet the needs of her patients. Many of them survived their trauma. Her shifts ended in the darkest hours of the day, and she rode the bus home. The first few nights she went straight to bed, thinking that sleep would come easily after such physically demanding work. Instead, she found herself re-working many of the cases, all the while working against sleep.

Eventually, she developed a different routine and kept a journal. She made entries by lamp light sitting on the sofa, snuggled in a blanket. The soft gray light of pre-dawn showed her the way to bed, and she set the alarm to wake her at 2:00 p.m.

On this day, ferocious dreams had stirred her. In the full light of day, she realized this tenth day would be the first of two days without an emergency. At least, they would be two days that she was not scheduled to work.

In the kitchen, she quenched an unrealized thirst with a glass of water. A note addressed to her was propped against the window above the sink. Chattering from two squirrels distracted her for a moment. They chased one another through the tall grass in the backyard.

Debbie's note suggested a night-out and alerted Elizabeth to the letter to which she had taped her note. *If you find this note before I get home, start getting ready because I'm taking us out for happy hour and dinner. I found this letter in between the sofa cushions last night. Doesn't look like you ever opened it.*

Elizabeth lifted the half-page, and Luke's letter appeared. She left the letter on the counter, while she grabbed a pen from a kitchen drawer. She flipped the note over and on the opposite side she wrote *mow the lawn.*

She sat on the sofa in the sunlight again and sunk into its warmth. Amidst hazy memories of the past few nights, the letter appeared. In her haste to make an entry in her journal, she had set it down. It must have been buried in the aftermath of a difficult shift at the hospital.

She didn't have to go to work today, so it worked out for the best.She grew uneasy with the reading at first. Luke confessed to his poor physical and mental state the night that they had spoken on the phone and described a feeling of uncertainty, fear even.

She stiffened at the part when he jumped off the cliff. Even though she knew he had survived, she only relaxed when he emphasized how the experience had jolted his awareness. He was less afraid of what the future held, for him and for her.

He closed his letter with reassurances. *I think I figured some things out that day. I guess I was mad at you, and at myself, too. But not anymore! I'll be here in Boulder. I feel like it's the right place for me.*

Like a bookmark, she inserted the letter among the pages of her journal. She blended his caring message flying from an ancient mountainside with her anguished expressions anchored in the pain and suffering she had witnessed at the hospital. She cherished his revelations, and in fullness of the day felt forgiveness. A blessing somehow had been revealed.

Chapter 45

Boulder, late September 1972

The scent of new carpeting wafted in the air. Short shag woven in patterns of soft brown and orange covered the room wall to wall. Luke's footsteps fell in silence until he reached the hardwood of the entryway.

Although he knew the answer from having seen Julia's car in the driveway, he called from the bottom of the stairs. "Anybody home?"

"Up here," Julia's voice replied.

Julia knelt in Danny's room near the closet. She stuffed newspaper around the perimeter of a small box, and Luke offered his assistance.

Danny made a gurgling sound from his pumpkin seat, and Julia shook her head. "I left these things on the shelf in the closet, and we forgot them on the day of the move."

She closed the lid on the ceramic night lamp and the music box. "What brings you to the old homestead?"

Luke lifted the paper bag he was carrying. "Left a few things behind myself. When do the new owners move in?"

"This weekend." Julia's eyes glistened from the sting implicit in her words.

"And how's everybody doing at the new house?"

"Okay. Sally and I finally have the kitchen organized."

"No more eating out. Bet Terry's missing that."

"She'd gladly have missed everything. She keeps reminding me that she's not the one who wanted to move. She said it again on the way to school this morning, 'Mom, why can't things be the way they used to be?'"

"It's hasn't been that long. She'll get used to it. I'm sure it helps that you were able to keep her in her old school."

"It's a drag having to drive her every day, but I really didn't want to turn everything upside down for her all at once. She'll have the whole school year with the kids and teachers she knows. Then next year we'll make the transition to Table Mesa." When Julia slid the box near Danny's seat, he fussed until she lifted him in her arms.

"Well, you've got a nice place, and the views are fantastic. Plus, you don't have the nuisance of a renter always hanging around." Luke chuckled.

Julia's laugh caused Danny to squeak.

Julia switched Danny from one shoulder to the other. "That's the other part that Terry complains about. She's worried that you don't have a nice place to live anymore. And she doesn't think I did a very good job of finding a new house, because there wasn't a place for you."

"You just tell her that my new apartment is fine. In fact, maybe I'll have her come over to see for herself real soon."

"I'm sure she'd like that."

Danny wiggled, and Julia bent to put him in his seat.

Luke intercepted her. "Here, let's trade, my sack of papers for him."

Luke lifted Danny over his head and held him there for a brief time. Danny seemed to like that view.

Julia attached another reason to Danny's smile. "He probably misses you too."

When Luke lowered Danny into his arms, he shifted Danny so that he faced forward and could see his mother. Danny whimpered as though this position was not to his liking.

Luke assessed Danny's attitude. "Maybe it's this room. He had one really tough night here, and it was just a few weeks ago."

"He didn't sleep very well in this room after that night. Terry and I were a wreck, too. It all just happened so fast, that first night in the living room, then up here, my decision to move, and selling the house. Maybe I didn't do the right thing."

"Actually, you did real well considering. When it all comes together like it did, it means that it was meant to be. At least, that's my opinion."

"Thanks, doc." Julia smiled at Luke and tickled Danny.

Luke bounced Danny. "You just won't leave that alone, will you?"

"Don't begrudge me a little fun." Julia picked up the box and tossed it in the air as though she was playing with a ball. Danny smiled at his mother's actions. She put the box under one arm and spun in a slow circle.

She lowered the shade on the window that overlooked the backyard. "I'll miss this big, old tree and a lot of things about this house."

"It was your home. But you're the one who made it that way, and you'll do it again at your new house."

"Think so?" Julia wasn't sure.

"I believe it's so. You can take the doctor's word for it."

"Okay, then I suppose we should go." Julia placed the bag and the box in Danny's seat.

In the hallway Luke asked, "Do we need to double check the other rooms?"

"Already did." Julia confirmed.

Luke held Danny, while Julia arranged Danny's seat on the passenger side of the car. She stowed the box on the floor next to a backpack-type baby carrier that Clay had sometimes used when they took Danny on a walk.

Luke tapped Julia's shoulder. "Hey, I see Danny's carrier there. Let's hike to Elephant Rocks. It's a pretty day, and it might be a good thing. One last time, for old time's sake."

Julia wasn't convinced. "Well, maybe."

"Oh, come on. If I recall correctly, neither one of you have had the benefit of my perspective from that vantage point."

"Okay, but since you're sounding so scholarly, now can I call you doctor?"

"If you must." Luke handed Danny to Julia and strapped on the carrier.

"The aspens are colorful this year." Luke surveyed the landscape.

"They're beautiful, and it's nice here today. Thanks for suggesting this."

"My pleasure. Looks like Danny's enjoying it, too." Luke propped Danny in a seated position, one of his long legs straddling each side, and his hands supporting Danny's back. "Your family really likes this spot."

"I think I told you. Jim used to bring Terry here. She was just a baby like Danny. Anyway, we had most of the summer after he graduated from CU. The three of us came here together too. By this time of year he had already left for basic training. After that...I can't remember, but this might be my first time up here since then."

"It's probably not changed that much."

"Guess not, the places anyway, but everything else..." Her voice trailed into a soft breeze.

When she spoke again, she addressed Luke, but the vista held her gaze. "You're probably regretting getting mixed up in all this stuff with me and my family. Looking forward to being on your own again, being back in school. And Elizabeth, how's she doing, anyway?"

"I actually haven't heard from her in a while."

"Oh, my god, Luke!" Julia grabbed Luke's arm. "I'm so sorry. The letter's in my car, in my purse. It's from her. It was forwarded to my new house. The post office must have made the mistake, unless you didn't do a change-of-address card."

Luke lifted Danny into his arms. "What are you talking about?"

"You need to notify the post office of your change of address."

"I did, but only a few days ago. I didn't think it was worthwhile doing one for Frank's address because that was just a temporary situation."

"You're right. But I apologize. I've been carrying that letter around, and with everything else that's been happening, I just forgot all about it."

"Don't worry. I'll get it today. It's going to be okay."

"Yes, but let's go now, so I'll be sure to give it to you."

On the walk to the house, Luke asked about the disposition of matters with Clay. Julia had hired an attorney and taken formal action against Clay through the court system. She wanted to make sure that her children and she would never again be hurt or compromised by one of Clay's outbursts or assaults. She described Clay's reaction as passive, almost submissive, like he was a boy being punished by his parents.

She only saw him in court during the two proceedings that had occurred since the night in the nursery. The judge had ordered him not to try to contact her or see her. He described it as a cooling off period, and Clay did not argue with that.

As they came along side of the car, Julia concluded. "Unless someone else told him, I don't even think he knows that I sold the house and moved to the other end of town. I'll let him see Danny. We'll make that work out somehow, maybe one afternoon at his house. He's really just a big baby himself."

"Yeah, but he has some problems, big problems."

"I'm sorry you got messed up in all our problems. Hey, how is it that you happened to be here today, anyway? Shouldn't you be in class or at work?"

Luke laughed as he replied. "You'll probably say I'm crazy, but what I'm going to tell you is the truth. I was on my way to the administration building to tell them my new address and wasn't paying attention. I tripped over a paper bag. It was just trash that someone had left on the edge of the sidewalk, but when I stuffed it in a nearby trash can, I suddenly had this vision. I remembered this bag of stuff."

Luke opened the passenger door of the car and lifted the bag from the floor. "I ran to the store and told my boss I needed some extra time. I was nervous that I might not be able to get into my apartment, but it worked out and the bag was right where I had left it."

Luke reached into his pocket and pulled out the key to his apartment. "I won't need this anymore, but I'm glad I held onto it."

Julia placed Danny in his seat, and when she turned to Luke, she exchanged his letter for the key. Danny squealed.

Julia put a rattle in Danny's hand. She demonstrated how to shake it and the noise quieted Danny. Luke escorted her to the driver's side.He held her door, and she paused much too close to him.

He couldn't complete a thought. "I...Thanks...It's good..."

She struggled with her words as well. "Luke, you've been so...I don't know how..."

When the words failed, she kissed his cheek and ducked into the car. A teardrop released from the corner of her eye, and she turned toward Danny. He whimpered, and she tucked a blanket around his seat.

Luke bent inside the car. "It's okay, Danny boy. You're mom's taking good care of you."

Luke closed the door. Julia started the car, but when Luke backed away, she opened her window.

She wiped tears with the back of one hand. "I didn't really want to leave, but it was my only choice."

Luke stepped forward and gently touched her cheek. "It's the best for everybody."

Julia took the steering wheel in both hands, but didn't put the car in gear. "Maybe you could come over this Friday night?"

"I'd like that. Need to test out some of that new furniture of yours."

"They're supposed to deliver it tomorrow."

"Then it's settled. See you Friday. You can tell Terry it's a party."

"Think she'll go for it?"

"Probably not, but I'll back your play." He smiled then, and she did too.

———

Luke set the paper bag on the picnic bench next to him and opened the envelope containing Elizabeth's letter. He had stashed all her other letters in the bag and stored it in his bedroom closet. The day he had packed his belongings, he kept thinking he would put that bag on top of all the rest. Instead, he had forgotten about it. Good fortune allowed him the opportunity to retrieve it.

Elizabeth's letter related her reactions to his most recent missive, her fear about his leap from a mountainside and her happiness about the fact that he wasn't angry anymore.She related her struggles with sleep, the effects of working in the ER.

She described the night that she and Debbie went to a Soulard night club. She believed the band they had heard was the same one he had heard when he was last in St. Louis. She determined that the *blues* didn't appeal to her.

She wanted him to know about other feelings emerging from within her, a sense of forgiveness, and a hope for inner peace. She ended her letter as she had their last phone conversation with a simple *good-bye*.

After folding her letter and sliding it into the back pocket of his jeans, Luke found the nearest trash can. He rummaged through the top contents of the large container and stuffed the bag of old letters into the hollow that he had created. He covered the bag with the other trash and secured the lid.

On the path, dappled shade formed markings on the concrete like footprints intended to guide Luke on his way. In the bright sunlight on the other side of the park, a boy and a girl played near a young Aspen tree. They kicked at the golden leaves already strewn around the trunk of the tree.

The boy shook the sapling and caused more leaves to break free. The girl swirled amidst the falling leaves. The yellow ribbon in her hair was more pastel than the golden leaves fluttering around her.

As Luke approached her, she giggled. "The leaves are pretty when they let go."

Luke smiled and said, "I know."

BRUCE EHLENBECK was born and raised in
suburban St. Louis. He attended William Jewell College,
and after moving to Boulder, Colorado, graduated from
the University of Colorado with a degree in English.
During his professional career, he worked in wholesale
book distribution for several years before succeeding in
various sales and marketing management positions in
the newspaper and Yellow Pages publishing industries.
He and his wife currently reside near Durango,
Colorado. Some Time Till Knowing is his first novel.

Email comments or questions to:
writtenbybruce@gmail.com

14341987R00296

Made in the USA
Charleston, SC
06 September 2012